Raves for
Season of the Witch

"This is compelling and original storytelling: a mesmerizing blend of alchemy and sexuality. Prepare to be seduced by it."
—Mo Hayder, author of *The Devil of Nanking*

"[A] spellbinding tale of magic and seduction . . . a feverish tale that's goth SF at its finest."   —*Publishers Weekly* (starred review)

"Black cats, snakes, spiders, mystical signs and symbols, and dangerous sex are skillfully stirred together in this brain-squeezing thriller. . . . Mostert manages it all quite impressively, concocting an intellectual puzzler that will keep the reader hooked, and guessing, until the final page."   —*Kirkus Reviews* (starred review)

"Filled with sexy romance and chilling twists . . . [a] seductive thriller."   —*Harper's Bazaar*

"A glamorous web of . . . lovely, dangerous women who play with magic, alchemy, African masks, tarantulas, potions, and above all, the lost art of memory."   —*MORE* magazine

"Mostert creates a taut, sexy thriller from disparate sci-fi and fantasy elements."   —*Entertainment Weekly*

"Intriguing gothic thriller . . . suspense, an atmosphere fraught with eroticism, and compelling characters. Fans of Anne Rice and Joyce Carol Oates should appreciate Mostert's take on mysticism, magic, and the ancient art of memory."   —*Booklist*

"Saturated in beauty, with wonderful observations, insights, and eroticism . . . a bewitching book." —Ian Watson, author of *The Jonah Kit*

"*Eyes Wide Shut* meets film noir murder mystery. . . . Love!"

—*Marie Claire*

"Intelligently conceived, well-crafted, intricately plotted . . . the mystery of the two alluring sisters is compelling . . . mind-bending."

—*The Charlotte Observer*

"Dazzlingly clever and original. . . . One can only marvel at the author's own witchlike power to enchant her audience."

—*Daily Mail* (UK)

"This heady fiction doesn't so much push at the edges of the genre as ride roughshod over them."

—*The Observer* (UK)

"Mostert has taken a blend of alchemy, the art of memory, mysticism, and high magic and created a page-turner."

—*Time Out* (UK)

"Fair witch project with a touch of beguiling feminine charm."

—*Daily Express* (UK)

"Part thriller, fantasy, love story, and mystery . . . balances all of these elements with a sensual and brilliant voice."

—Blogcritics

"By far the best novel I have read this season . . . an incredible, unique book."

—BookLoons

"Mostert is an amazing writer with the ability to lead you into her characters' minds and give the plot enough twists and turns to keep up the anticipation and tension throughout."

—Romance Junkies

"Vividly and evocatively written . . . enthralled me right to the end."

—*The Times* (UK)

Season of the Witch

Natasha Mostert

NEW AMERICAN LIBRARY

New American Library
Published by New American Library, a division of
Penguin Group (USA) Inc., 375 Hudson Street, New York, New York 10014, USA
Penguin Group (Canada), 90 Eglinton Avenue East, Suite 700, Toronto,
Ontario M4P 2Y3, Canada (a division of Pearson Penguin Canada Inc.)
Penguin Books Ltd., 80 Strand, London WC2R 0RL, England
Penguin Ireland, 25 St. Stephen's Green, Dublin 2, Ireland (a division of Penguin Books Ltd.)
Penguin Group (Australia), 250 Camberwell Road, Camberwell, Victoria 3124,
Australia (a division of Pearson Australia Group Pty. Ltd.)
Penguin Books India Pvt. Ltd., 11 Community Centre, Panchsheel Park,
New Delhi - 110 017, India
Penguin Group (NZ), 67 Apollo Drive, Rosedale, North Shore 0632,
New Zealand (a division of Pearson New Zealand Ltd.)
Penguin Books (South Africa) (Pty.) Ltd., 24 Sturdee Avenue,
Rosebank, Johannesburg 2196, South Africa

Penguin Books Ltd., Registered Offices:
80 Strand, London WC2R 0RL, England

Published by New American Library, a division of Penguin Group (USA) Inc.
Previously published in a Dutton edition.

First New American Library Printing, March 2008
10 9 8 7 6 5 4 3 2 1

LIBRARY OF CONGRESS CATALOGING-IN-PUBLICATION DATA HAS BEEN APPLIED FOR.

Set in Granjon
Designed by Carla Bolte & Spring Hoteling

Printed in the United States of America

— FOR CARL —

pint-sized warrior

PROLOGUE

He was at peace: his brain no longer blooming like a crimson flower.

Slowly he opened his eyes. Above him, a black sky shimmering with stars. A pregnant moon entangled in the spreading branches of a tree.

Vaguely he realized he was on his back, floating on water. A swimming pool. Every now and then he would move his legs and hands to stay afloat. But the movements were instinctive and he was hardly aware of them.

A violin was singing, the sound drifting into the night air. It came from the house, which stood tall and dark to the right of him. The windows were blank and no light shone through the tiny leaded panes. The steep walls leaned forward; the peaked roof was angled crazily.

His thoughts were disoriented and his skull was soft from the pain, which had exploded inside his brain like a vicious sun. But as he looked at the house, he could still remember what was hidden behind those thick walls.

And how could he not? For months on end he had explored that house with all the passion of a man exploring the body of a long-lost lover. He had walked down the winding corridors, climbed the spiral staircases, entered the enchanted rooms and halls. It was all there—locked away inside his damaged brain—every minute detail.

The green room with its phosphorescent lilies. The ballroom of the dancing butterflies. The room of masks where the light from an invisible sun turned a spider's web to gold. Wonderful rooms. Rooms filled with loveliness.

But inside that house were also rooms smelling of decay and malaise. Tiny rooms where the walls were damp and diseased, where, if he stretched out his hand, he could touch the unblinking eyes growing from the ceiling; eyes whose clouded gaze followed his antlike procession through a tilting labyrinth of images and thoughts.

He knew their order. *The order of places, the order of things.* He had followed the rules perfectly. Why then, his mind a spent bulb, his body so heavy, was he finding it increasingly difficult to stay afloat?

A wind had sprung up. He felt its dusty breath against the wetness of his skin and he wondered if the fat moon might topple from the tree.

He was becoming tired. His neck muscles were straining. He should try to swim for the side of the pool, but the one half of his body felt paralyzed. It was all he could do to move his arms and legs slightly to keep from sinking. Below him was a watery blackness. And he realized he was no longer at peace but horribly afraid.

But then the darkness was split by a warm beam of light. Someone had switched on a lamp inside the house. He wanted to cry out but the muscles in his throat refused to work. The light was coming from behind the French doors with their inserts of stained glass carefully fitted together in the shape of an emblem. *Monas Hieroglyphica.* See, he still remembered . . .

A shadow appeared behind the glowing lozenges of red, green and purple glass. For a moment it hovered, motionless.

The shadow moved. The doors opened.

She stepped out into the garden and her footfall made no sound. As she walked toward him, he thought he could smell her perfume.

His heart lifted joyously. She had known he was out here all along. Of course, she did. And now she had come to save him. No longer any need to be afraid. But hurry, he thought. Please hurry.

She was still wearing the mask. It covered her eyes. Her hair was concealed by the hood of her cape. On her shoulder perched the crow. Black as coal. Even in the uncertain light he was able to see the sheen on the bird's wings.

Sinking down to her knees at the very edge of the pool, she leaned over and looked squarely into his face. A wash of yellow light fell across her shoulder. Around her neck she was wearing a thin chain, and from it dangled a charm in the shape of the letter *M*. It gleamed against the white of her skin.

From inside the house, the sound of the violin was much clearer now and he recognized the music. "Andante Cantabile." Tchaikovsky's String Quartet no. 1, opus 11. The ecstatic notes struck a fugitive chord of memory. The last time he had listened to this piece of music there was a fire burning in the hearth, a bowl of drooping apricot roses on the dark wooden table and next to it three glasses with red wine waiting on a silver tray.

He was sinking. His feet pale finless fish paddling sluggishly. He couldn't keep this up much longer. But she would help him. She would pull him to safety. With difficulty he moved his arm and stretched out his hand beseechingly.

Her forehead creased with concern but the eyes behind the mask were enigmatic. She placed her hand on his face and pushed it softly into the water. The crow left her shoulder with a startled shriek.

His mouth opened in protest and he almost drowned right then and there. He turned his head violently to one side, sneezing and coughing. Panic-stricken, he tried to swim away from her but his limbs were so heavy.

Again she leaned forward and pushed him down. And again. Each time he broke the surface, he gasped for breath, aware only of her white arms and the chain with the initial *M* hanging from her neck. Her movements were gentle, but laced with steel. As his head bobbed in and out of the water, he knew he was about to die.

Exhaustion. His lungs on fire. He made one last enormous effort to free himself but she was too strong.

She had relaxed her grip now, but he could no longer find the strength to push himself upward. As he started to sink, he kept his eyes open, and through the layer of water he saw her get to her feet. She looked down at him and lifted her hand: a gesture of regret.

Air was leaving his mouth, rippling the water, dissolving her figure, her masked face. And as he slowly spiraled downward, he wondered with a strange sense of detachment if he might not still be on a journey, still searching for the path that does not wander . . .

HOUSE OF A
MILLION DOORS

I always wanted to know what was knowable in the world.

—Johannes Trithemius, *Steganographia* (Secret Writing), 1499

CHAPTER ONE

Was there anything as cool as rush hour traffic on a hot day?

The light turned red. Gabriel Blackstone brought his bicycle to a stop at a crowded intersection. Balancing himself with one foot on the pavement, the other still resting on the pedal, he half-turned and looked around him. He was surrounded by cars and he could sense the expectation—the barely tamed aggression—lurking in the hearts of the motorists sweating gently behind the wheels of their vehicles. They seemed relaxed; elbows pushed through open windows, heads casually cradled against the headrests of their seats. But he was not fooled. When the light turned to green, he would have to move quickly. In this part of the City of London, cyclists were barely tolerated. That was part of the fun, of course: moving in and out of tight spaces, taking chances. Still, the possibility of getting squished was rather high. In front of him he could see a cabdriver's eyes—puckered and creased with lines—watching him in the taxi's rearview mirror. Behind him a TV van was already inching closer with unnerving stealth.

It was hellishly hot. He wiped the back of his hand across his forehead. Summer had come early. The tarmac underneath his foot felt soft. The air tasted like paraffin. But he liked the city this way: sticky, unkempt, the pedestrians moving languidly. People's emotions were closer to the surface, not muffled by scarves and thick coats or hidden by hats turned down against a freezing rain.

A flash of red caught his attention: a girl walking on the sidewalk next to him, swinging a fringed bag and wearing a crimson skirt and blouse. Her navel was bare and he could see the tattoo of a butterfly on her flat stomach. She walked with such devil-may-care insouciance that he smiled with pleasure. Life was good. Four o'clock in the afternoon in the Square Mile . . . and the City was his.

The light turned to green. The traffic bulleted forward. A rapturous roar of sound ricocheted off the steep walls of the buildings, making the ground tremble. He pedaled furiously across the intersection, dodging a green Mercedes whose driver seemed more intent on shouting into the cell phone in his hand than keeping his car on the road.

It was on days like these that he was also acutely aware of that other—secret—dimension to the City. Mingling with the car fumes, the layers of noise and the haze of heat was something even more ephemeral. Digital stardust. As he pedaled past the looming facades of London's banks, insurance companies and businesses, he imagined himself moving through an invisible but glimmering cloud.

Humming quietly behind the walls of the City's skyscrapers were machines filled with dreams. Dreams of money and power. Dreams broken down into binary code. Data. The most valued currency of all in this city where the foreign exchange turnover equaled 4637 billion dollars every day. Hidden in the brains of the computers were files, memos, research documents. A treasure trove of information protected by locked doors, computer firewalls and killer passwords.

But nothing was impossible, was it? He smiled into the wind and curved his back as he made a sharp turn into a narrow side street, leaving the worst of the traffic behind him. Doors can be knocked down; walls can be scaled and the magic of encrypted incantations dissolved. Secrets were meant to be broken. You only needed focus and determination—and wasn't it fortunate that he was gifted with both.

Today he was on a scouting expedition. His client was Bubbleboy, a toy company specializing in toys for the six- to ten-year-old age group. His target was Pittypats, Bubbleboy's biggest competitor. In this bunny-eat-bunny world, the way to gain the edge was to know your rival's secrets. Companies can glean a great deal of information about the competition by studying reports by the city's financial analysts and by trawling through newspapers and trade journals. This modus operandi is boring, unadventurous but—to be fair—not ineffective.

Public documents, however, will only allow you a partial reading of the tea leaves. Ultimately, a more innovative approach is necessary. And that was where Gabriel came in. His scouting expedition today would be only the first step in an elaborate operation designed to give Bubbleboy deep access into its main rival's secrets.

Pittypats's City offices, he was interested to see, were located in two modest, if charming late-eighteenth-century houses complete with Venetian windows and scalloped arches. Very unassuming for a company with an impressive global reach. The offices sat quietly at the end of a narrow street, dwarfed by a sixties concrete tower that was unashamedly ugly. A steel railing ran the length of the building. He chained his bike to the railing, and as he straightened, he caught a glimpse of his reflection in the plate glass window. Ankle boots, jeans, grubby T-shirt with the words "City Couriers" emblazoned on the front. Leather satchel slung across his back. Clipboard clenched underneath one armpit. Good. He looked the part.

Security at Pittypats's front door was basic: the ubiquitous security camera and a buzzer and voice intercom unit. He placed his thumb on the button and almost immediately the door clicked open.

Inside it was a different matter. Against the ceiling were motion detectors, and the door leading from the tiny reception room to the rest of the building was equipped with a magnetic key card reader. No cameras in this room. Although no guarantee there weren't any somewhere deeper inside the building.

A girl, sitting behind a green-and-gold leather-inset desk, looked up as he walked in. Her hair was coiled primly behind her head, but her lips looked as though they belonged to one of the replicants in *Blade Runner*. The gloss was stupendous and her mouth seemed to *glitter*. Quite stunning, actually. But also somehow forbidding. You had the feeling that if you kissed those lips you might lose some skin.

"Can I help you?" She was looking at him coolly, one eyebrow lifted to form an impressive arc.

He smiled at her and swung the leather bag from his shoulder. "Package to deliver."

She waited while he opened the bag, her fingers clutching a pencil and tapping it softly on the old-fashioned blotter in front of her.

"Here you are." He extracted a small package wrapped in brown paper, placing it along with the clipboard on top of the desk. "Package for Mr. Peake. And it needs signing for."

"Peake?" She frowned. "No. There's no one here by that name."

He knew there wasn't. He had made sure of it beforehand, but now he spoke with exaggerated patience. "Yes. Peake. See. It says so right here." He stabbed a finger at the clipboard. "Mr. Donald Peake."

"No." She pushed it back at him, irritated. "There must be a mistake."

"This is Pittypats?"

"Yes, it is. But—"

He peered at the address on the package. "Mr. Donald Peake. Human Resources."

"Oh." Her face cleared. "Our human resources department is out in Croydon. You've got the wrong office."

No, sweetheart, I haven't, he thought silently but continued, "Would it be possible to leave the package here—for you to send it on to Mr. Peake, like?"

She looked uncertain. He watched as she worried her lower lip between her teeth. Surprisingly, the lipstick showed no sign of smudging, staying preternaturally glistening and smooth. Amazing.

"Maybe you could just ask?" he prompted. "Please, love. Help me out."

For another moment she hesitated. Then she opened the drawer of the desk and took out a small square of plastic. "Wait here."

She turned and swiped the key through the electronic scanner. The tiny red eye at the top of the scanner turned green and she pushed the door open. He caught a brief glimpse of a well-lit but completely bland hallway. There was no indication whatsoever as to what went on inside the building.

As the door swung shut behind her, he dropped to his knees and opened the bag wider. Inside was his iPAQ. Small, discreet, it was still his favorite tool for this kind of work. It was already powered up, and as there were no cameras around, he would be able to sneak a quick peek.

The screen blinked, and what it showed him made him smile with delight. Oh, great. The path forward would be relatively easy. This commission was not going to require any athletics, thank God. With his last job he had had no choice but to break-and-enter and he had found himself crawling around false ceilings, fighting his way through phone lines, air-conditioning equipment and fire sprinklers, all so he could bypass some truly maddening security controls and gain access to a restricted research area. This time around, he would be able to pluck the information from the air, so to speak.

The door opened. It was the girl. He got to his feet and closed the leather bag without fuss.

"Yes." The girl nodded. "You can leave the package here. We'll take care of it."

"Actually," he shook his head regretfully and hitched the bag onto his shoulders, "looks like it has to be Croydon, after all. Just spoke to my boss." He gestured at the cell phone clipped to his belt. "He says Mr. Peake has to sign for it personally. Sorry for the trouble."

She sighed with exasperation, but he could tell that she had already lost interest in him. "Just shut the door on your way out, please."

He opened the door and looked back. It had been a brief visit. No more than ten minutes had passed since he first walked in here. But the trip had been a definite success. Apart from everything else, it surely would have been worth it just to see those lips. He was going to have fun describing them to Isidore.

Outside on the street, he unclipped the cell phone and speed-dialed Isidore's number. Isidore didn't answer his phone, but that did not mean he wasn't at home.

The answering machine kicked in, and for the next few moments he was forced to listen to Isidore's newest outgoing message. Isidore's idea of humor was to record Bible verses of the muscular kind—painful penance and eternal damnation—before inviting his caller to leave a message. Gabriel waited impatiently for the beep.

"Isidore, pick up. Now."

A click. "Gabriel, my man. Where you hanging?"

Gabriel sighed. Isidore had been to Eton and Cambridge but was hopelessly in love with black street rap, and every so often he would sprinkle his conversation with a highly personalized version of American street slang. As his accent remained stubbornly upper-crust, the effect was startling to say the least.

"I'm still in the City. Guess what? Bluetooth."

Isidore chuckled. "You don't say. Well, we be good boys. We due a break. See you soon?"

"I'm on my way."

He closed the cell phone and found himself smiling. This job was going to be a breeze.

His iPAQ had told him Pittypats was making use of wireless technology. Very cool. Wireless technology certainly made for lovely uncluttered work environments, with computers talking to one another without being connected by a rat's nest of hardwired cables. But there was one problem. Wireless electronic emissions can be picked up if you have the right equipment. And he and Isidore most certainly did have the right equipment.

He unchained his bicycle and took off his black-framed glasses, substituting them with a pair of Ray-Bans. The sting of the sun was easing slightly, but the glare was still considerable. He glanced at his watch: 4:30 P.M. Another twenty minutes at least before he'd get to Isidore's place.

Isidore lived close to Smithfield meat market and he liked it there, something Gabriel did not understand. The sight of bloody rib cages was too reminiscent of a horror painting à la Francis Bacon. Meat had been sold at Smithfield for eight hundred years, and for close to four centuries it had also been the site where witches, heretics and traitors were burned or boiled alive as so many pieces of meat themselves. Probably another reason why Gabriel was immune to the stunning architecture of the marketplace with its ornate ironwork and imposing arches and pillars.

Isidore lived in a narrow up-and-down duplex, squeezed in between two abandoned houses with boarded-up windows. Just as well he didn't have any neighbors: Isidore preferred his music loud. As Gabriel walked up the shallow steps leading to the front door, he could hear music pulsing through the double-glazed windows. It was a good thing he had a key to the house: there was no way Isidore would be able to hear the doorbell over this racket. He turned the key in the lock and braced himself for the onslaught of sound.

It was even worse than he had expected. Rap was Isidore's poison, but it seemed his friend was in a nostalgic mood. Vintage Guns N' Roses was the choice du jour. *Welcome to the jungle!* screamed Axl Rose with enviable lack of inhibition.

With his hands over his ears, Gabriel mounted the steps two by two and walked rapidly through the wide-open door at the top of the flight of stairs. Without pausing, he continued over to the wall unit and pressed his thumb hard on the power button of the CD player. The sudden silence was a shock.

He turned around. In the swivel chair in front of him, blond hair falling untidily across his forehead and eyebrows raised in pained surprise, was Francis James Cavendish, aka Isidore. Isidore was a nom de guerre, chosen in homage to Jack Isidore, the dysfunctional hero of Philip K. Dick's *Confessions of a Crap Artist*. The fictional Isidore believed the earth to be hollow and sunlight to have weight. The real-life Isidore was able to come up with theories easily more off-the-wall than that.

He now threw his hands in the air in mock surrender, the long fingers calloused from hours of slamming the keyboard. "Hey, bro. What's your problem?"

"I don't want to go deaf, that's my problem. Shit—" Gabriel paused and looked around him. Every available surface that wasn't taken up by computers, screens, keyboards, tech manuals, wires and other computer detritus was cluttered with empty pizza boxes, chocolate wrappers, soda cans and greasy chip packages. "It stinks in here. You're turning into a cliché, you know that? This is the stereotypical hacker hell. Why not try for a little originality for God's sake."

Isidore managed to look hurt. "Like you? Driving a Jaguar and listening to Chopin. Oh, yeah. That's original. I'm waiting for the day you start smoking cigars. Besides which, five years from now you'll still be paying off the mortgage on that fancy flat of yours and I'll be rocking in the sun sipping mai tais."

Gabriel knew that Isidore's plan was to retire within five years to Hawaii and spend his days surfing the waves off Banzai Beach. Which would be a good plan, except that he had never surfboarded in his life. And the idea that he would actually be able to break his addiction to the computer screen and leave the keyboard for the great outdoors was even more ridiculous. But *Point Break* was Isidore's favorite movie and the Patrick Swayze character his hero.

Gabriel sighed. Isidore was an ass but he was also a genius. No one could hack together code more robust and elegant.

"OK." Gabriel sat down on the edge of a pumpkin-colored velour chair, pushing two empty beer bottles out of the way. "Here goes. I wasn't able to see inside the offices themselves, but there's no doubt Pittypats are using wireless technology. I think it could be because they're situated in a protected building. Regulations probably prevented them from installing cables and disturbing the structure."

Isidore nodded. "Don't you just love planning permissions. What about WEP?"

"Yes. It looks as though their CTO is doing his job on that front."

Isidore grunted but, as Gabriel expected, didn't look in any way concerned. WEP was a cinch: it could be cracked by anyone with half a brain using freely available software. Isidore had more than his share of gray matter to begin with and seldom used anything but his own custom-designed software anyway.

It was amazing, Gabriel thought, how cavalier companies were when it came to computer security. High-tech companies and the biotech industry were more cautious, but in general very few companies scanned their network regularly or even ran an integrity checker to see if their system files had been altered in any way. And very often with wireless networks, WEP encryption wasn't even enabled.

The bottom line was that the only way Pittypats could protect itself from electronic penetration would be to install layers of steel inside its offices. And one thing was for sure: that house didn't have any steel walls. So it was only a matter of fishing within the pond of electronic emissions and hooking a password, the name of a file, or a project handle and he and Isidore would be home free.

Gabriel yawned suddenly. For the first time today he was feeling tired. He glanced at his watch. "I have to get home. I wanted us to work out the surveillance schedule today but let's wait until next time."

"Heavy date tonight?" Isidore was watching him sardonically. "Is it still . . . what's her name . . . Bethany?"

"Briony. And no, it's not."

"She dumped you, huh."

"You could say that. I'm pretty cut up about it."

"Oh, give me a break. You dated her only so you could get close to her friend, the blonde with the cute lisp."

Gabriel frowned. "Not true. Well," he amended, "maybe at first, but that's all changed. Briony broke my heart."

"Heart? Man, you have no heart."

"So maybe hearts are overrated."

"Essential equipment for most of us, bro."

"Not me. I get by on sex appeal alone."

Isidore scowled. "Get out of here, you smug bastard. I have to get ready for a date myself."

"Don't tell me." Gabriel grinned. "Some digital babe in the kingdom of *Dreadshine*." He was referring to one of Isidore's regular haunts on the Internet: a multi-user domain of the more surreal kind. Here, in a cyberworld entirely built up of words, Isidore regularly turned himself into a medieval knight slaying gremlins and demons with ruthless gusto. Isidore and a host of other *Dreadshine* residents—all equally dazzled by the products of their own imagination—had a grand old time amazing one another with their cleverness and virtual feats of daring. But never any face-to-face contact. Romance and adventure via keyboard. It was all a little sad.

Gabriel gave Isidore an abbreviated salute. "So have fun."

"Always." Isidore grinned wolfishly.

As Gabriel walked down the stairs, the music started up again. Belinda Carlisle, this time. Good grief.

Contrary to what Isidore thought, Gabriel did not have a date tonight. He was looking forward to a glass of twenty-year-old Scotch, some spicy stir-fry and a long soak in his cedar-paneled and very expensive bathtub.

As he walked into the loft, the light was blinking on his answering machine but he ignored it. After hanging the bike on the wall, he walked across the huge room with its beautiful jarrah wood floor and pulled open the sliding door that gave access to a narrow balcony. His apartment was the biggest in this converted warehouse, and the balcony ran the entire length of the loft space. It was close to Tower Bridge, and the view onto the Thames never failed to make Gabriel feel deeply content.

He loved the river. He loved it in winter with the fog hanging still and white, shrouding the gold-tipped bridge with its high walkway so that it looked like a ghost. He loved it in summer, when the river became a lazy brown snake and the smell of wet earth hovered in the air.

The loft apartment with its radiant views was not merely a pleasant place to live. It was much, much more. It represented to him everything he had hungered for as a child. The Bristol neighborhood in which he grew up had been dreary and joyless. His father had been a long-distance trucker, while his mother added to the family income by making beds and cleaning bathrooms in a hotel. The family wasn't poverty-stricken, but their lives had very little grace. Seared into his memory was the house in which he had spent the first seventeen years of his life: the paper-thin walls, the cramped rooms and low ceilings. The television forever tuned to some or other Australian soap; the house smelling of macaroni and cheese and his brothers' dirty woolen socks. His mother's panty hose and bras dripping from the shower railing. The dreadful feeling of claustrophobia, of never having enough air to breathe.

His parents barely tolerated each other, their relationship worn thin through the repetitive strain of their daily routines. Some of his earliest memories were of the toneless bickering they kept up with mindless, dogged intensity: a despairing white noise. They were not cruel parents—no abuse or intentional neglect—but they did not seem to like their offspring very much and had very little interest or energy to invest in them.

By the age of twelve, he was running with a group of boys whose behavior hovered perilously between obnoxiousness and outright hooliganism. He might have found himself in serious trouble if it hadn't been for a teacher who had managed to find him a scholarship to a school where the emphasis was on hard work and high standards. The school ironed out his accent and gave him an excellent academic grounding, and he'd been offered a place at Oxford. Then, six months shy of graduation, he dropped out. His friends were aghast, but he never sought to explain his reasons to anyone. He simply packed up and left for London. And became a thief.

He had no illusions about his chosen field of endeavor. He had turned an aptitude for computers into a lucrative but criminal enterprise. Isidore, he knew, subscribed to the romanticized version of what it is to be a hacker, seeing himself as a caped crusader in cyberspace where corporations were fat-cat exploiters of the little man and fair game.

Much as Gabriel loved Isidore, he had no patience with this kind of bumper-sticker libertarianism. Theft was theft: whether in cyberspace or in the real world. Just because the medium was different didn't mean the principle was. If you download a piece of copyrighted music from the Internet without paying, you have just walked into Tower Records and pocketed a CD on the sly. If you hack into the research data of a company and peddle it to the competition, you're affecting the research and development budget of that company, stealing from them years and years of effort and monetary commitment. And although the bigger corporations might be able to survive the loss of trade secrets, smaller companies could be devastated.

So he never fooled himself. For ten years now he had been making a living—and a very good one at that—illegally leeching off the creative endeavors of others.

He stretched his arms wide—he had a knot in his back from the hours of cycling—and placed his hands on the railing of the balcony. As he stood there, suspended between sky and water, he experienced a profound sense of well-being. Dusk was his favorite time of day. He loved the feeling of the city letting go, kicking back. The glitter of lights on the other side of the river. The softer glow of the streetlamps reflected in the dark water slapping gently against the muddy bank.

It was as he turned away from the water, walking back into the apartment, that he spotted it again: the flickering light on his answering machine. For a moment he debated with himself whether to leave it until the next day—it was Friday evening after all—but then he walked over and pushed the play button.

The voice on the tape was unfamiliar. It was a male voice; rather thin, the words uttered with measured precision. The message was innocuous: a request for a breakfast meeting the following Monday to discuss a business proposition "that could be to our mutual benefit." The caller did not give his last name, identifying himself merely as William and specifying that he would be sitting in the booth farthest from the entrance.

The caller's reticence at identifying himself was not unusual. Prospective clients usually acted coy, at least initially, and it was quite understandable considering the kind of services they were hoping to procure. So the message seemed perfectly normal. Nothing out of the ordinary here, certainly nothing that could have set off an alarm bell inside his mind.

But months afterward he would think back on this moment

when he had stood inside his beautiful apartment, his finger still on the button of the machine, the light fading outside the window, the sound of voices and laughter drifting upward along with the smells from the kebab house on the corner. He would look back on that moment as though it were frozen in time and search for some sign that might have indicated that his life was about to change completely. On that warm summer evening, when he had felt in absolute control of his destiny, was there not something that had served as a warning? Surely he should have sensed something. Surely there must have been an omen.

He lifted his finger from the button, unconcerned, merely making a mental note to himself to rise earlier than usual on Monday in order to get to Piccadilly in time for the meeting with his new, and as yet unknown, client.

But as he walked toward the kitchen, whistling tunelessly under his breath, a cool wind suddenly lifted one of the silk hangings on the wall. And in the wine red sky a fat moon was rising slowly.

Entry Date: 20 May

Follow the path that does not wander.

M is building a new door. The key will be large—as long as a woman's arm—and fashioned from silver. She is working with such feverish haste, I am getting concerned. But it is true that the door is looking splendid.

On the other side will be a window. The sky outside this window will always be dark and the windowpanes smeared with frost.

Who will live in this place between door and window? A mummer with a heavy heart and blind eyes turning, turning.

I must meditate upon my name.

CHAPTER TWO

He looked wealthy. You couldn't put your finger on what it was exactly, but the aura of money was unmistakable. He was dressed conservatively in a dark blue suit with a crisp white shirt and a pale blue tie with tiny yellow flowers. His shoes were black brogues. But it wasn't really the clothes—even though the cut of the suit was impeccable—that gave you the idea that this was a man of material substance. It was something else altogether. Blue blood and money. A potent combination, as distinctive as a smell.

The well-born, truly rich are used to having their own way. They are seldom opposed or contradicted, usually protected against their own bad manners or errors in judgment. And everyone laughs at their jokes. This happy state of affairs—happy for the beneficiaries, not for their flunkies, of course—imparts an indefinable quality that can best be described as oblivious self-confidence. The man sitting in the booth farthest away from the entrance to the coffee shop had that quality.

He also had faded blue eyes, which were rather piercing.

"William?" Gabriel held out his hand.

The blue eyes surveyed him for a long moment, their expression slightly calculating, as though the man was trying to make up his mind about something. Then, unhurriedly, he held out his own hand. His grip was firm but not crushing.

"Gabriel. Thank you for coming. Please sit down."

Gabriel slid into his seat, and a waitress with a mournful smile approached the booth. "Coffee?"

"Yes, please. And poached eggs on toast. Three eggs. Runny."

The man opposite Gabriel made a negative gesture with his hand. "Nothing for me, thank you." Up close he was quite a bit older than he had appeared from outside. His movements were effortless, but the skin around his mouth was dry and raddled with tiny grooves. He was very thin.

Gabriel looked him full in the face and smiled. "Before we start, a few ground rules. I take it you have an information-gathering problem and you think I might be able to supply a solution. I probably can. But first I need to know your full name. I like to know who I'm dealing with. And then we can take it from there." He finished with another smile calculated to diminish the sting of his little speech. It was always best to get straight down to business. Sometimes prospective clients entered into a long courtship dance, too embarrassed to come straight out with what it was they had in mind. This could be very tiring.

"By all means," the man said courteously. "My name is William Whittington."

He had been right about the money. William Whittington. Well, well. Philanthropist and investment banker who had managed to add substantially to an already vast fortune inherited from his grandfather. A brilliant strategist. And a bit of a recluse. This could be interesting.

It was also puzzling. Why would Whittington meet with him in person? Gabriel did not usually deal with players at this level. In the normal swing of things he did not get to meet with CEOs, board directors or other members of top management. He was usually approached by someone much lower down the food chain. William Whittington was taking a big risk.

Whittington smiled faintly. "You're right, of course. I do have a problem and I do have need of your special talents. Except, maybe not quite in the way you expect."

For a moment he had the uncomfortable feeling that Whittington was enjoying a private joke at his expense. Before he could respond, the waitress appeared at the booth and plonked a chipped white plate down in front of him.

"Three eggs, runny. Right?"

"Right." He looked at Whittington. "Are you sure you won't join me?"

Whittington shook his head. He was looking at the plate with a mixture of amusement, horror and respect. "I couldn't possibly. But please go ahead."

The eggs were exactly as he liked them. After taking a bite, he said, "You were saying?"

"Do you have children, Gabriel?"

This was a new one. "No, I don't."

"I have a son." Whittington's face was suddenly set, no hint of amusement left in his eyes. "His name is Robert. Robert Whittington. He is twenty-one years old." A pause. "He is missing."

"Missing?"

"He disappeared nine months ago. I want you to find him."

Gabriel lowered his fork to his plate. "I think you may have been misinformed about what it is I do. I'm an information broker. I'm not a private investigator. I don't look for missing people."

"But you used to." A long pause. "At Eyestorm."

For a moment Gabriel felt as though the oxygen had been sucked from the room. He tried to keep his face expressionless, to wipe away the shock he knew must be reflected on his face. He found himself focusing intently on a black fly, which was walking delicately along the very edge of the Formica-topped table. It was the warm weather: the city was crawling with them.

"Gabriel?" The man opposite him was watching him speculatively.

"I can't help you." He took a deep breath and carefully wiped his mouth with his paper napkin. "You and I have no business. I am sorry about your son, but you should be talking to the police, not to me." He was trying to keep his voice calm.

"Don't you want to know how I know about Eyestorm?"

"Not particularly." The fly had taken flight. It settled on the rim of the sugar bowl on the table in the next booth.

"Cecily told me."

He had started to edge out of his seat, but at this he stopped. "Cecily. Cecily Franck?"

"Yes."

"Frankie is in the United States."

Whittington shook his head. "Not anymore. For the past two years she's been living in London."

"You're mistaken again. She would never come back here."

"She is back." Whittington smiled, rather sadly. "I know this, for a fact. You see, we were married two years ago. She's my wife."

CHAPTER THREE

"Call me Frankie," she had said the first time they were introduced. "Everyone does. Cecily was my grandmother's name. And to tell you the truth, I was never fond of the old lady. She was a mean broad."

She smiled widely—a delightful smile—and Gabriel found himself smiling back. Not exactly pretty, Cecily Franck was nevertheless immensely attractive. Narrow face. Light brown hair springing from her forehead in a widow's peak. A sweet mouth and surprisingly shrewd eyes. Flawless skin. Her voice was low but carrying, the American accent pronounced in that room filled with the hum of British voices.

He looked around him. There must have been close to forty guests in the large old-fashioned living room of Alexander Mullins's Oxford house. The room had a tired feel to it, with its dusty moss green carpet, fringed lamps and porcelain knickknacks. The guests, all of them sipping lukewarm wine and nibbling on pieces of rubbery cheese, were an odd-looking bunch. Judging from the information displayed on their name tags, they seemed to come from different walks of life and from different parts of the UK. Frankie was obviously American but her name tag stated simply that she was a student. As did his own, which was probably why they had instinctively sought each other out. The only common denominator linking all the guests was that each person present was there because he or she had responded to the same advertisement in one of the national newspapers.

"What do you think of him?" Frankie's eyes followed his gaze to where a tall, thin man with an impressively aquiline nose was talking to a woman with an eager expression.

"Mullins?" Gabriel shrugged. "Too soon to tell."

"He doesn't look anything like I thought he would." Frankie's voice was dubious.

"What did you expect—someone clutching a crystal ball?"

She smiled ruefully. "Someone more colorful, at least. You know what I mean."

"Well, the man's a scientist. They're not usually known for their flamboyance." But Gabriel knew what she meant. Considering the reason for tonight's meeting, she could be forgiven for expecting someone a little more theatrical. Not that Mullins was the kind of man you could ignore. His eyes behind the incongruous cat's-eye spectacles were cold but laser sharp. And his reputation was impressive.

Alexander Mullins was an eminent neuropsychologist with a thirty-year research background in statistical methods and cognitive processes. But his true passion lay in the field of psychic phenomena. *Eyestorm*. The reason this motley collection of people had gathered here tonight.

"Can I ask you something?"

"Of course." Gabriel glanced at her inquiringly.

"Do you . . ." Frankie hesitated, colored. "Do you feel a little silly being here? You know, don't you feel like this is all just too woo woo?"

He smiled but before he could answer, Alexander Mullins was tapping a knife to the stem of his wineglass.

The hum of voices ceased and all eyes turned toward the host.

"Welcome. I am very pleased you have decided to attend tonight's meeting." Despite his words, Mullins's voice lacked warmth. "The fact that you have responded to my advertisement means that all of you believe you may be in possession of a latent talent—a rare gift. Tonight will be the first step in determining if this is the case."

A wintry smile. "Not all of you will be successful. But if you make the grade, you will receive an invitation to join a great adventure . . ."

But in the end, of the forty-seven original participants, only three made the grade. After six months, only Gabriel, Frankie and a middle-aged plumber by the name of Norman were invited to join an existing group of psychics known collectively as Eyestorm.

Eyestorm was the British equivalent of the American STAR-GATE project. First launched in the U.S. by the Department of Defense, STARGATE was designed to study real-life applications of telepathy and clairvoyance or, as it subsequently became known, *remote viewing*.

The term "remote viewing" was chosen on purpose. It was considered an acceptable, neutral term and was adopted by two physicists at the Stanford Research Institute, Dr. Harold Puthoff and Russell Targ, who were involved in some of the earliest work. As Mullins explained that first night, "Unfortunately, terms such as 'clairvoyance' and 'telepathy,' which could have been useful, have been hijacked by charlatans. We needed something fresh in their place. 'Remote viewing' is a term not yet tarnished by the exploits of fake psi practitioners."

Gabriel lifted his hand. "There are those who would argue that psi practitioners are per definition fake."

Mullins's cold eyes glittered from behind his spectacles. "Mr. . . . Blackstone, is it? If you're not a believer in psi, why are you here tonight?" Without giving Gabriel a chance to answer, he continued, "Please accept my assurance that STARGATE's exploration into inner consciousness was based on very strict methods. And this is the way we work at Eyestorm as well."

He looked away from Gabriel and allowed his eyes to travel over the faces of his audience. "Let me be very clear indeed," he said forcefully. "The protocols used at Eyestorm are exceptionally rigorous. This is *not* a forum for Loch Ness searches or UFO sightings."

Even though Eyestorm was largely following the model and ideals of STARGATE, there was one big difference, Mullins continued. Unlike its American cousin, which received federal funding before it was closed down in the nineties, Eyestorm did not benefit from direct government sponsorship. The group had to rely on fees paid by private clients and, as Mullins explained with a self-deprecating smile, on the considerable inherited wealth of its founder member.

The approach of the two groups was very similar, however. Both

Eyestorm and STARGATE were firmly oriented toward results in the outside world. The two units were not merely think tanks; their research was applied to real blood-and-guts problems.

One of the bigger successes of the American unit was in tracking down smugglers of illegal narcotics. Working with the U.S. Coast Guard, STARGATE's remote viewers had used their clairvoyant skills to identify suspect ships and in several instances had been able to sketch the exact location of hidden drug caches. Another notable achievement was helping the American Air Force search team track down a downed Soviet airplane in Africa. A remote viewer managed to pinpoint a site to within three miles of the downed craft.

In contrast, Eyestorm's clients were not government-affiliated but people who turned to it after exhausting the more conventional routes of police and private investigators. Many of Eyestorm's cases involved tracking down stolen artworks or lost heirlooms. And then there were the search-and-rescue missions. Using their remote view-ing skills, Eyestorm members would assist in finding missing rela-tives and hostages.

This was what attracted Frankie: the human factor. "Just think how awful it must be, Gabriel, not to know if a loved one is truly lost. Isn't it wonderful that we can bring peace of mind to these people?"

He nodded in agreement, but in his heart of hearts Gabriel knew that for him, the attraction lay elsewhere. Remote viewing was power. He reveled in the opportunity to exercise this talent that was hardwired into his brain. For him it was a rush. For Frankie it was a calling.

Ah, Frankie. Frankie of the soft mouth and bright mind. Frankie who slept with the night-light on because she was afraid of the dark, but who did not hesitate to confront a street thug menacing an elderly shopper. Frankie who was laughter and comfort and serenity. When they met in Mullins's living room, they had liked each other on sight. The connection was strong, immediate and blessedly uncomplicated. And liking soon turned to love.

The transition had been free of the extreme mood swings and

passionate excesses usually associated with a first romance. This wasn't thunderclap stuff. It was an exceptional friendship gradually elevated to a more intimate level. Around them on campus, fellow students were involved in brief, passionate flings; testing their boundaries, experimenting at love. He and Frankie did it differently. It was a remarkably mature relationship considering it started when they were both only eighteen years old.

Still, it probably was their youth that finally let them down. If they had been older, they might have weathered Eyestorm a whole lot better. Instead of being blown apart, they might have been able to emerge from that whirlwind without the anger—or worse, the terrible sense of disappointment they had ended up feeling in each other.

Eyestorm tore them apart. But Eyestorm also forged a bond between them that was unbreakable. And it created an environment where they could give free rein to an exceptional and mysterious talent shared by them both.

Remote viewing. Second sight. The Gift. The Shining. In the end, though, they all came down to the same thing. And ever since he was a little boy Gabriel had been aware of it: a tiny bump in his unconscious. At the time he had no way to explain what it was, either to himself or to others.

Only after joining Eyestorm was he taught the concept of "psi-space," that nebulous field of information that encapsulates the accumulated knowledge of different minds. It was explained to him that as a psi-sensitive he already had a highly developed neurophysiological network in place, which made it possible for him to enter the psi environment and merge his thoughts with information generated by the minds of others. With practice, he would be able to pick up on the resonance of those thoughts with increasing ease.

As a small boy, of course, he had been unable to articulate what was happening to him. All he knew was that he had an uncanny ability to track down missing things—to "see" where they were.

He did not test this ability, and he certainly did not receive encouragement from his family to develop his talent. His mother reacted suspiciously the few times he found objects that had been lost or misplaced by members of the family, accusing him of hiding them himself in an attempt to get attention. After Jack, his older brother, stomped on him because he had inadvertently betrayed his brother's secret hiding place, he decided firmly that this was not a talent worth exploring. No one else seemed to share his gift, and it made him feel "different." And who the hell, at that age, wanted to feel different?

Maybe, he thought, if he ignored this weird skill it would go away. By his late teens, however, he realized it wasn't going to be that easy. Wishing it away was not going to work. He was stuck with it.

The realization brought him to Eyestorm and Alexander Mullins.

Alexander Benedict Mullins. The name sounded intimidating. The man certainly was. For three years Mullins was his mentor and surrogate father. Not that there was anything even remotely paternal in the way Mullins treated him. Mullins was not given to extravagant praise or, for that matter, any kind of feel-good interaction with his students. But the loyalty and admiration he inspired among his remote viewers was undeniable. Gabriel, although he would never admit to it, vied fiercely with the other RVs at Eyestorm to gain Mullins's approval.

Gabriel knew the older man thought him arrogant. "Remember," Mullins would preach. "Never, ever fall in love with your gift. Never allow yourself to become blinded by its light. It is merely an ability—like someone who is blessed with perfect pitch, or wide-angled vision. Psi sensitivity is widespread in the general populace. A policeman's hunch, a woman's intuition—these are all everyday examples of latent psi ability. Yes, only a small number of people are truly psi-talented. People like you. But the talent for remote viewing is not something you've earned: you can't take credit for it. It is merely something you were born with."

But even though there was friction between student and teacher, they needed each other. Gabriel required the older man's help to impose some kind of discipline on a gift that was wildly unpredictable. And if Mullins nursed misgivings about his pupil, he was nevertheless tremendously excited by the systematically high level of hits scored by Gabriel during that first year of training. In all his years of research, Mullins had never come across a subject who performed as consistently.

What interested Mullins in particular was Gabriel's versatility. Most remote viewers had a particular cognitive style, which they favored and followed almost exclusively. Some RVs were more successful in accessing targets while awake; others were incapable of psi activity unless they made use of dreams—lucid or otherwise; yet another group relied on a deep meditative state to do their work. Some scored better at accessing and describing landmarks, objects and geometric shapes; others preferred to home in on personal aspects such as feelings and thoughts. Gabriel, though, showed no preference for any specific cognitive style, and was able to describe visual configurations as well as emotional impressions with equal ease.

After twelve months of "staring" experiments, "double-blind" tests, "dreamwork," "filtering" and more, Gabriel was outperforming the rest of the class by a wide margin. By this time he was champing at the bit. He wanted to get into the field and work on actual problems, and he did not appreciate his mentor's caution.

"What the hell is he waiting for?" he would complain to Frankie. "You're already working on cases, and I don't want to sound conceited, sweetie, but I'm better at this than you."

"Oh, thanks."

"Come on, Frankie. I love you too much to BS you. You know it's true."

Frankie sighed. "OK. Why don't I see if I can't get Alexander to rope you in."

"Yes," Gabriel agreed eagerly. "The old man has a real soft spot for you. Give him that killer smile and bat some eyelashes, why don't you?"

"Sometimes, Gabriel," Frankie said strongly, "you're a total asshole."

But she did actually manage to get Mullins to allow Gabriel to assist on some relatively minor cases. There was the recovery of a stolen T'ang horse from the Qing period. The tracking down of a lost manuscript. Another time he and Frankie were paired with a veteran RV to pursue the whereabouts of the perpetrators of an Internet scam.

They were not always successful, of course. Remote viewing was free energy. Harnessing that energy was like threading a needle in a hurricane. Specific data such as exact street addresses could not be accessed as easily as opening a telephone book.

Furthermore, remote viewing was often a less than comfortable business. Remote viewers referred to the "seeing" process as *slamming the ride* and the ride often took you into someone else's mental space. This was not always a warm and cozy place to be.

Not that Gabriel subscribed to the clichéd image of the tortured psychic forever at the mercy of his dark gift. He was no victim; he was a warrior. And the thrill of success was addictive. He became hooked on that massive surge of self-satisfaction that accompanied every ride.

To a certain extent he was leading a schizophrenic life. On the one hand was Oxford, his school friends and his studies; all-nighters in the library, papers, tutors, study groups, "boat races" in the pub. On the other was Eyestorm. The only link between the two worlds was Cecily Franck. Inevitably, the fact that they were both living a kind of double existence deepened the bond between them. It was an exciting time.

And then the Cartwright case came along.

Six weeks later he quit Eyestorm, left Oxford and headed for London and a different life.

Entry date: 28 May

I was dreaming of R last night. He was smiling at me and his hands reached for mine. The idea that I will never see that lovely angel smile of his again is so painful I sometimes feel my mind shutting down.

M is losing patience with me. She thinks I'm stuck in the past—"wallowing" as she puts it. And she wants us to look for someone new to play with. Maybe she's right: the work is so important. It needs to continue. But I am heartsick. Where will we find someone like my sweet boy again? Someone who is looking for new challenges not new comfort zones. A searcher. An initiate. A man apart.

For what it's worth, we built another room last week. In this room will live a man with the head of a baboon. Thoth. God of magic and writing. Of alchemy and arithmetic and astrology.

I must meditate upon my name.

CHAPTER FOUR

Gabriel knew who was on the other side of the door even before he opened it. Although he had expected her to turn up on his doorstep ever since his meeting with William Whittington three days ago, he was suddenly feeling completely unprepared. Thirteen years. A long time by anyone's standards.

She rang the bell again.

As he opened the door he got an immediate whiff of her perfume. Jasmine, cinnamon and the hint of a more exotic bloom. Her tastes had changed. She used to prefer lighter, more woody scents. But her eyes were still the same. Clear gray eyes set underneath delicately feathered eyebrows, which looked like the wings of a bird in flight. Cecily Franck. No, not Franck. Whittington. Mrs. William Whittington III to be exact.

"Gabriel." She smiled at him, a tentative smile. For a moment he thought she was going to hold out her hand, but then she leaned over and her lips brushed his cheek.

"Aren't you going to invite me in?" She smiled again, and the smile was slightly bolder this time, though the expression in her eyes was still wary.

He stepped back and held the door wider. She walked past him into the room.

"Oh." Her voice was surprised. She looked around her, her gaze taking in the satisfying proportions of the loft, the glow of lights filling the skyline outside the windows. "This is lovely."

"Thank you. Let me have your jacket."

She turned around and allowed the jacket to slide down her arms. The rustle of the fabric sounded expensive. The drape of the deceptively simple dress she was wearing suggested that someone had taken a great deal of care in both cut and design.

He gestured at the sofa. "Please."

She sat down on the very edge of the seat, but then, probably realizing how tense she looked, settled deeper into the cushions.

"Can I offer you a drink?"

"Sherry. If you have it."

He walked to the drinks cabinet and took out a glass and a bottle of bone-dry amontillado. Another change here. She never used to drink. Well, no doubt all the fancy cocktail parties and glamorous socializing of her new lifestyle necessitated her moving on to something a little more sophisticated than OJ.

She took the glass from him. He noticed she wore no rings. The light of the floor lamp gave a golden sheen to her brown hair. He sat down in the deep leather armchair, which stood in the shadow, outside the circle of light.

She was staring down at the amber liquid in the glass, frowning slightly. As he watched her he was surprised at how detached he felt. After all, he had loved this woman. Not only that, she had been his first love. And what with the first cut being the deepest and all that, surely he should feel some emotion; a little quickening of the pulse, at least. Instead, here he was, his mind Zen calm, his heartbeat even. Pretty amazing.

"You look good, Gabriel. You've hardly changed."

"Thanks."

"You're supposed to respond in kind, you know." She smiled faintly. "It's only polite."

"Oh, sorry. You look great." Which was actually true. Her face had matured and she had lost the baby fat she had still carried around at age twenty. She looked elegant, groomed, and she had the air of a woman who was sure of herself and her abilities.

She had become a stranger.

"You've done well for yourself." She glanced around her.

"So have you."

She flushed at the irony in his voice.

"You've met William. He's a remarkable man."

"Indeed. How old is he?"

The flush deepened. "Sixty-three."

He lifted his eyebrows. "Well. He looks good for his age."

"Doesn't he." There was something in her voice now that he didn't understand. Not that he was all that interested. Time to cut to the chase and end this.

"Why are you here, Frankie?"

She placed the glass on the side table flanking the sofa and looked at him steadily. "You know why I'm here."

"Your husband sent you."

"No." She shrugged her shoulders. "This is me coming to you. But yes, I'm here on his behalf."

"Why didn't you approach me yourself in the first place?"

"We thought you might be more interested if you thought it a purely financial arrangement. If you had given him a chance, William would have explained how he can make it very much worth your while." She paused. "I hope I'm not offending you."

"Money never offends me."

There was a tiny mole at the side of her cheek, just above her jaw-bone. He remembered it well. She saw him looking at it and touched her fingers involuntarily to her face. And in that movement, slightly awkward, he suddenly saw the old Frankie. The shy but determined girl whose smile had been enough to make him dizzy. She used to have such faith in him; it made him feel ten feet tall. Until the day her face went blank with disappointment. Disappointment in him . . . the man she was supposed to love no matter what.

He took a deep breath, looked away. "You should go to the police. They deal with missing persons."

"The police have given up. Oh, they don't say that, of course. But it's obvious. And I also think they believe Robbie's not so much missing as wanting to be missing."

"Why?"

"Robbie and William have a rather . . . problematic . . . relationship. Robbie took off once before—William finally tracked him down to a commune in California. Sort of a New Age hideout where they start the day with a group hug and grow hemp and weave baskets. You know the kind of place I'm talking about. That was three years ago."

"So what makes you think he's not there now?"

"He's not."

Below in the street someone was pressing the horn of a car impatiently. The sound was strident, irritating.

He leaned forward and smiled at her. "So Daddy and his little boy don't get along."

"You could say that." There was hostility in her eyes now. She clearly didn't like where this was going.

"Let me guess. The heir doesn't measure up. Footsteps too big to fill. Parental expectations too high?"

She didn't answer but he sensed he had hit the bull's-eye.

When she spoke again, he could hear her trying to keep her voice level. "I wouldn't have come to you if there was any other choice, Gabriel. I'm asking you to help me . . . for old times' sake."

Old times' sake? God, what a cliché. What a crock. And suddenly he was angry. Gone was his calm. His breathing came fast and he knew his face was flushed.

"You'll be a rich widow one day. With no son around, things will be a whole lot less complicated when it comes to the will. Have you thought of that?"

"Jesus." Her face contorted. "What the hell's happened to you?"

He stood up, his movement so violently abrupt that she flinched. "OK. Enough of this. I can't help your husband. Not in the way you want. You of all people should understand that."

"He's dying."

"What?"

"William. He's dying."

He stared down at her, his mind refusing to compute what she said. "What do you mean, dying?"

"Just that. Another year, eighteen months at the most." Her face was eerily serene. Her hands were clutched together so tightly, the veins stood out at the wrists. "William wants to reconcile with his son. As you can imagine, it's become a matter of urgency to him. I don't think that will be possible. I think Robbie is dead. In fact, I'm almost sure of it."

He sat down heavily. His remark about the rich widow suddenly seemed unbelievably crass. "If he's dead, Frankie, then what do you expect of me?"

"I want to find out what happened to him. I want William to know why his only child disappeared. I can't give him that certainty. I wish I could. You can. You have the gift."

"You have the gift as well."

"No, I have an aptitude, that's all. You have the fire, I don't."

He didn't deny it. What she said was true. Her RV skills had been of a high enough level to get her into Eyestorm. And she had worked hard at sharpening a natural talent. But practice, craft and discipline can pump up the muscle of the mind only so far. Despite Alexander Mullins's insistence that remote viewing was merely a latent sense that could be refined and developed by hard work and application— like honing a reflex action or developing a nose for wine—every RV knew that there came a point where remote viewing moved not only beyond science but also beyond art. Capricious energy. Flashes of fantasized lightning illuminating the dark side of the brain. Some were better at slamming the ride than others.

"I take it you've tried to locate him yourself."

"Of course." She nodded emphatically. "And that's why I don't think he's alive anymore."

"You sensed nothing."

"Total strikeout. No ride. And I knew him well, Gabriel. Before he moved into his own place, we had lived in the same house for almost a year."

Gabriel knew that Frankie's cognitive style relied heavily on personal rapport. She needed to establish some kind of emotional connection with her subject in order to generate any psi-data. The more she knew of her subject's feelings and emotions, the more likely she was to get a reading when she exercised her remote viewing skills. Therefore, if she had actually lived in the same house as her missing stepson, the personal framework she needed to "switch on" would already be in place. If Frankie couldn't sense Robert Whittington at all, that was bad news. Sadly, it would mean she was probably right. He was in all likelihood dead.

She reached down to her ankles and picked up her handbag. Opening the bag, she extracted from it a buff-colored envelope and from the envelope a snapshot.

"That's him. Robbie."

The face in the picture was young and handsome. A thick thatch of hair sprang from a high forehead in a riot of short glossy curls. Gabriel was able to detect a hint of William Whittington's hawkishness in the set of the younger Whittington's eyes and nose, but that was where the similarity between father and son ended. Robert's mouth was soft and his chin rounded. And the eyes. God, the expression in the eyes was shockingly vulnerable. Such innocence. Gabriel couldn't recall the last time he had seen such trust and acceptance in the gaze of anyone over the age of three.

"Will you do it . . . ?" She didn't add the words "for me" but they hung in the air as surely as though she had spoken them out loud.

He didn't answer. Carefully he placed the snapshot on the arm of the chair, nudging it away from him.

The corners of her mouth sagged and she closed her eyes briefly. Then, with a swift, graceful motion she got to her feet. Her voice was formal. "May I have my jacket, please?"

In silence he helped her slip back into the jacket.

He opened the door. "Good-bye, Frankie."

She stood half-turned, her body facing the door, her head twisted to one side.

"Damn you." Her voice held no passion.

"Frankie, come on . . ."

"I love my husband. I would do anything to restore some peace to his world. I'm begging you, Gabriel. For once, just once, think of someone besides yourself. You've never used the ride for anything but selfish purposes."

He was starting to get angry. "You can say that—"

"I can say that because it's true. Alexander was right. The lives you saved, the good you did was incidental. It was all about you and the ride. And because of one bad ride you've decided to discard it like some worn-out shoe, which no longer fits."

She turned around and faced him directly. "Do you know how jealous I was of you at Eyestorm? That shocks you? Sweet little Frankie jealous of the man she loved? Well, guess what. There were times my envy was eating me up. There you were, slamming the ride so sweetly, with such ease, and treating it with such utter disrespect."

He was stung. "I never disrespected it."

"You were arrogant. And as for the rest of us . . . in your heart of hearts you had contempt for us all. We were just a bunch of dogged second-raters as far as you were concerned."

He stared at her, speechless. The ferocity in her eyes pushed against him with almost physical force.

"Why did you decide to quit, Gabriel?" She leaned forward, standing on tiptoe so that her face was almost level with his. "Did you really quit because of Melissa Cartwright or was it simply because your pride was hurt so badly that you couldn't face the possibility of failure again?"

"Get out." He looked down at his hands. They were actually trembling. He could feel the blood draining from his face. "Get out."

Her eyes suddenly stricken. "Gabriel, I'm sorry—"

"Just leave . . . please."

She lifted her hand as though to place it on his arm. "If you change your mind . . . ," her voice trailed off uncertainly, "my telephone number is on the back of the photograph."

He didn't answer. After a brief moment she let her hand fall to her side and turned away from him. Her footsteps were heavy. At the bend in the hallway she paused and he thought she was going to look back at him. But then she continued walking and disappeared from sight.

He was suddenly deathly tired. He tried to make his mind a blank, to shut out the scene he had just lived through; the emotions, which had sapped his energy and his mental calm. Melissa Cartwright. Ash blond hair and violet eyes. Very pretty. In life that was.

No. Stop this. It would lead to nothing. What he needed was rest. Sleep. And tomorrow he would wake up and life would continue as before. He liked his life the way it was. He had worked hard at it. There was no room in it for old ghosts.

Just as he was about to turn off the light, his eye fell on the snapshot of Robert Whittington where it perched on the arm of the chair. For a moment he hesitated. But then he flipped the switch sharply, leaving the young face with the absurdly vulnerable eyes to stare gently into the darkness.

Entry Date: 3 June

It is time to stop grieving. R is gone.

Time to take life by the scruff of the neck again. To go to work.

What gives meaning to life? What is passion? These were the questions R was trying to answer.

R was a seeker. We were helping him on his journey. We allowed him to play the game. A sublime game: a divine experiment that would have helped him find the answers he was looking for. But in the end, the light was too strong for him. He could not go the distance.

He left.

M is right: we shouldn't feel guilty. Man is designed to experiment. And if the experiment is a glorious failure, well—rather a glorious failure than a life that ends up being nothing but a dismal accident.

I feel strong again. And if not happy—at least happier. Yes, I miss R. I miss the man who held me by the hand as we watched oceans melt. Rocks burn. But there are bright poppies with glowing eyes growing in my heart again. Even though he did not find what he was looking for, I believe R may be traveling still, his feet still searching for the path that does not wander.

I must meditate upon my name.

CHAPTER FIVE

"Watch out!"

Gabriel slammed on the brakes. A pedestrian—an overweight man carrying a package clutched to his stomach—had stepped out right in front of the car. Gabriel leaned on the horn. Opening the window, he shouted at the man, deriving some satisfaction from the pale, startled face and O-shaped mouth.

"Idiot." He closed the window and put his foot down. The car jerked in a way that was very bad for his temper. The next moment it stalled.

"Shit." He felt like punching something.

From the corner of his eye he could see Isidore watching him.

"What's up, bro?"

Gabriel shrugged. But he knew his irritability threshold these past few days had been low. And there was no way Isidore would not have noticed. Especially as he had been the target of Gabriel's ire more than once.

"I know what it is." Isidore nodded wisely. "You're still thinking about the lady."

Gabriel grimaced. A week before he had told Isidore about Frankie's visit during a sudden and unexpected urge to share. Brought on, it had to be said, by three excellent bottles of Rupert and Rothschild Baroness Nadine. It had all come pouring out. Frankie. Eyestorm. The missing heir. He had become quite maudlin if he remembered correctly—although the haze of alcohol that hung over the events of that evening made his recollections of their conversation not as sharp as they could have been. At the time the emotional purging had felt cathartic, but now he was sorry for it.

He could feel Isidore's curiosity plucking at him, but he didn't want to talk or think about that part of his life again. He didn't need old memories turning his mind soft. And he hadn't told Isidore about the Cartwright case. Not even a dozen bottles of wine could make him talk about that.

Melissa Cartwright. For years he had practiced not to think about her. But she had never gone away, had she? She was always around: an ethereal presence walking through his subliminal self.

Isidore's voice was casual. "I think your problem is that part of you really wants to do it."

"Do what, for God's sake?" Gabriel turned the key in the ignition. The car turned over lazily, finally caught.

"Help her. Help her and her old man find the son."

"You're wrong. I don't have the faintest inclination to get involved. Besides which, I told you. I don't slam the ride anymore. Remote viewing is something I no longer do."

"If that's what the man say." The tone of Isidore's voice made Gabriel glance over at him. Isidore was pursing his lips together in a very irritating fashion.

"What the hell do you mean by that?"

Isidore abandoned the street slang. "Oh come on, Gabriel. Be honest. Do you really want to make me believe that your hacking skills aren't sometimes just a wee bit amplified by this second sight thing of yours? In fact, it now explains a lot I've always wondered about."

"You're way off track." Gabriel jerked the steering wheel savagely to the side, and the Jag cleared a demented motorcyclist with an Evel Knievel complex by a few inches. "And let's switch topics, shall we."

But Isidore continued unperturbed. "I surfed the Internet the other night after our talk. Did you know that a group of remote viewers in the United States foresaw 9/11 four years before it happened? They even posted their scribbles of an airplane crashing into one of a pair of skyscrapers on the Net and wrote an open letter to the FBI warning them that something like that was going to happen. No one paid any attention. This is hot shit, man."

Gabriel didn't answer. As a matter of fact, he did know about this incident, and he was aware that many remote viewing companies in the U.S. were now vying with one another to try and pinpoint al-Qaeda operatives. There was even talk that the CIA was consulting with some of these companies on a regular basis. But he had doubts about the effectiveness of many of this new breed of commercial RVs. Too often they were making the kind of far-fetched claims he had been taught to dismiss at Eyestorm. True, Eyestorm had also been a company for hire, but it had stuck religiously to the protocols developed by the American military during the seventies and eighties. And those protocols were exceptionally strict.

Isidore was talking again. "One thing I don't understand, though. This Robert Whittington. Let's say the dude really is dead, how can you zoom in on him or track him or whatever the term is? I mean . . . he's dead, right?"

"His thoughts at the time of his death may still resonate in the psi-space."

"Resonate in the psi-space. Wicked. I don't know what that means. But it sure sounds cool."

"I'm pleased you're thrilled."

"So how does it work? Will you be able to see through the guy's eyes? You know, right at that moment when someone cut his throat or clubbed him to death or whatever?"

"Bloody hell, Isidore. I never took you for a ghoul."

"OK, sorry. But you know what I mean? Will you be able to read his very last thoughts before he died?"

"If I happen to access those thoughts, yes."

"So you'll be able to see who the perpetrator is."

"Oh, for goodness' sake. The kid may not even be dead. He's probably hanging out in Goa smoking hashish and learning how to be a swami."

"That's not what you said the other night. You said if Frankie wasn't able to sense him anymore then the poor kid had probably copped it. Isn't that what you said?"

Gabriel didn't answer. He brought the Jag to an abrupt standstill. "There's the tube. I'm dropping you off here. Get working on that antenna for Pittypats and we'll talk again tomorrow, OK?"

"OK," Isidore said, unabashed by Gabriel's frown or the curtness of his tone. Opening the door on his side, he hopped out and gave a cheery wave. In his rearview mirror Gabriel watched his lanky figure move away from the car and disappear down the stairs to the Underground. With a sigh, he let out the clutch. Isidore was probably the only person he truly considered a friend. Not that it precluded him from sometimes feeling as though he wanted to strangle him.

It took Gabriel another fifteen minutes to get home. After parking the Jag in the underground garage, he took the elevator up to the penthouse. Usually, he would take the stairs but today he simply could not summon the energy. Actually, everything these past few days seemed to exact an inordinate amount of effort. As if to confirm his fears, he sneezed wetly and at the back of his throat he felt a suspicious itch. Oh, hell. This was just what he needed. A cold.

He opened the front door and threw the keys into the hand-carved Ghanaian fruit bowl he had purchased at a Sotheby's auction only a month before. An impulse buy, that. And he had probably overpaid for it. Moodily he picked up the stack of unopened letters waiting for him on the table. He hadn't looked at his mail for over a week.

He came upon it as he was checking through the envelopes—the photograph of Robert Whittington. He couldn't remember placing it with the mail, but here it was, pushed in between a bill from his dental hygienist and a reminder that his subscription money for *Gourmet* magazine was due.

Slowly he sat down in the armchair facing the window, the photograph still in his hand. The kid really did have the most defenseless face, as though he was open to whatever came his way. And the expression in his eyes: no hint of self-importance or pretension. He remembered the cool self-assurance of the father, the slightly ironic detachment with which Whittington senior seemed to survey the world. Oh yes, he could well imagine that friction existed between these two.

He yawned and let his hand fall to his lap, the snapshot held loosely between his fingers. He was suddenly sleepy. The sun pouring through the window was warm. He wondered what color Robert Whittington's eyes were; in the photograph it was difficult to tell. Either a dark gray or maybe blue . . .

The linen curtains flanking the window lifted and billowed. A breeze had sprung up. He was aware of it only vaguely. He was not awake, but not yet asleep.

His mind shifted. The gate to his inner eye opened.

On one level his conscious mind knew he had stepped into a ride, that only his mind was traveling and not his body, but as always when he slammed into a ride with this much precision, he was rapidly losing contact with the man who at this moment was sitting in an armchair, his legs stretched out to catch the sun. One instant he was still aware of being in the chair, head tipped back slightly, limbs completely relaxed, staring at the ceiling with unseeing eyes. The next moment he found himself standing in a small room facing a closed door.

As he placed his hand against the massive frame of the door, he noticed that the hand was narrow and the fingers long and pointed. It was a male hand but it was not his own. He was looking through someone else's eyes.

He had stepped into someone else's mind.

At that moment the last tenuous connection between his own mind and the host mind severed and he crossed over—completely submerging himself in the host mind's thoughts.

The door in front of him was made of heavy timber. The wood was dark with age.

Mounted on the door was a coat of arms. A circle on top of a cross. The design was strangely modern: it almost looked like the sign for female sexuality. Cross and circle were embraced within the petals of an open rose.

The sign was familiar to him. He remembered it well. He had studied this symbol in detail. The *Monas*. He could feel the excitement rising within him.

No doorknob was visible, but as he leaned against the door, it swung open on silent hinges. He stepped over the raised threshold into a narrow room. The ceiling seemed dizzyingly high. The walls were covered with shelves stacked to the rafters with books. The smell inside that confined space was of old mildewed paper and leather bindings rotting at the spine.

And somehow he knew the exact dimensions of this room. Thirty-eight of his footsteps by sixteen. Strange, how he knew that.

A slight sound made him tilt his head. High above him, perched delicately on top of one of the immensely tall bookcases, was a crow. The bird was big and its feathers shimmered with green-black phosphorescence. For a moment they stared at each other. The crow shifted on its perch, lifting one wing. Behind it, on the wall, its shadow self moved like a restless ghost.

He looked away from the bird and started walking again. He had no time to waste here. Two doors faced him. He knew without even having to think about it that he should exit the room through the door on the right. As he walked toward it he was aware of the crow following him, staying at his shoulder.

A corridor. And even more doors. An entire row of them. He needed to make a choice, but which one was it again? Seven doors down or six?

Think. This was important. *Remember*. Oh, yes. Seven doors down on the right. His foot fitted perfectly in the hollow of the single stone step leading to the door. The door clicked open.

He was standing inside a ballroom and it was filled with butterflies. Millions and millions of monarch butterflies, their trembling wings dazzling his eyes.

But he was not allowed to stay for long in this place of beauty. He had to continue. He had hundreds of doors to open still. Thousands. *Millions.*

Remember, *The order of places, the order of things*. And there was the next door that would allow him to continue his journey. And without looking, he knew the crow was above and behind him, gliding silently in his wake.

He moved forward cautiously, picking his way carefully through the cloud of amber wings. Without hesitation he opened the middle door facing him.

As he continued to move from room to room, the excitement tightened inside his chest. He was on target. His memory today was flawless, allowing him to pick the correct door every single time. The order of places, the order of things. He knew the formula by heart and his journey was faultless. He looked over his shoulder, searching for the crow, his companion, and there it was staring at him with jet-black eyes. A wordless communion passed between them.

With trembling fingers he opened door after door, traveling from one fantastical space to the next, feeling more and more empowered as each door he picked turned out to be the correct one. This time he would succeed, he had no doubt of it. He was infallible, *invincible*. An immense feeling of exhilaration gripped him, an excitement so intense, his blood seemed to fizz.

Of course, not every door opened onto a room filled with beautiful butterflies. Some of the rooms held objects and figures, which even after all this time, he still found disturbing. There were tiny rooms with lashless eyes growing from the ceiling. Big echoing spaces filled with giant glass marbles, the sound deafening as the glass spheres rolled from corner to corner. A room filled with hundreds of clocks ticking at random, each producing its own agitated, irregular beat. Behind one door an eyeless monk incessantly polished his empty eye sockets with a piece of bloodied sandpaper. The sight made him queasy and he hurried past, face averted. One room housed a flock of softly cawing fantailed doves. In the dim light they looked like spun sugar, but he waited tensely, anticipating the sound of the shot that was to follow. And there it was—a sharp crack—and the next instant the sugar birds dripped scarlet.

And still his journey continued. He found himself walking down labyrinthine corridors and up staircases delicate as spiders' webs. The corridors stretched into the remotest distance and the staircases seemed endless. A journey without end: a journey filled with millions upon millions of doors waiting for him to access them *in exactly the right order* . . .

For a moment he closed his eyes: his mind suddenly shrinking from the magnificence of it all. How was it possible for him to even be here? He wasn't worthy of this place. This vast edifice, with its chambers and galleries, its winding, enigmatic passageways and endless steps, was sacred space. Hidden in its divine depths were the answers to all the problems of the universe, the answers to all the questions of the past and of the future. It held prophecies and spells. The content of every book ever written. The content of every book still waiting to be written. The value of every unimaginable number. The notes of music yet to be composed. Even the story of his own birth and the minute details of the life he could have lived but hadn't . . .

Something brushed against his arm and he opened his eyes, startled. It was the crow, swooping past him, winging its way to the other side of the room. His eyes followed the bird's passage. The light was dim and the shadows dark in this room, and at times the crow seemed to disappear in the gloom. But then it stopped flying. It settled itself delicately on the shoulder of a woman who was watching him from one of the many sheltering doorways.

His breath caught. What was she doing here? This was supposed to be his own journey. He was meant to fly solo today.

As always she was wearing a cape and her eyes were masked. The cape was deep green in color, the velvet folds richly draped and the hood covering her hair completely. Her fingers were long and white. They were calling him.

Come.

He hesitated. That was not the correct door. He knew he should be exiting through the third door on his immediate left. The order of places, the order of things dictated that.

Again she lifted her hand. The finger beckoning: *Follow me* . . .

Hesitantly he walked toward her, and she nodded her head in satisfaction. He opened his mouth to speak but she brought her finger to her lips: an imperative for silence. Turning her back on him, she edged the door behind her open and slipped into the blackness beyond.

He followed quickly even though his heart was beating nervously. This was not right. This was breaking every rule. He should still be on his journey, opening the familiar doors, encountering the familiar places. He had no idea where he was now. He had never been this way before.

But then he chided himself. What was he so concerned about? As long as he stayed with her, he would be safe. Who better to guide him on his journey? But apprehension stirred like swaying seaweed underneath the surface of his calm.

She moved quickly, always staying a few steps ahead of him. He could smell her perfume, a tenuous thread of fragrance. Her cloak swirled around her ankles as she hastened down long, winding corridors opening up this way and that. A labyrinth, but one she was traversing unerringly.

On and on they sped, past darkened rooms with uncurtained windows, past closed doors, past signposts cracked and peeled, the lettering illegible, the arms pointing the way to who knows where. Alien. Unfamiliar. He had lost all reference points; he had lost the order of places, the order of things. He could feel the terror rising inside him. To be lost, to be lost forever . . .

He tried to clamp down on the panic and kept his eyes desperately on the slim figure hurrying ahead of him. She seemed wraithlike, scarcely more substantial than the flitting shadow following in her footsteps.

Suddenly she stopped and placed her palm against an uneven stone set into a smooth wall. When she pulled her hand back, he saw that the stone she had touched was carved into the symbol of the *Monas*.

For a moment nothing happened but then—ponderously—the wall started to move, revealing a dimly lit space on the other side. The ground beneath his feet was vibrating and there was a hum in the air.

He found himself in a massive circular room with a high domelike ceiling. It was empty. The dome was filled with blinding light but the room itself was only faintly illuminated. Still, the gauzy light was strong enough for him to see that the walls of the room were not solid. They were constructed of wheels: concentric stone wheels densely covered with symbols. Moons, crosses, candles, pentagrams—symbols as familiar as everyday objects. But there were also other symbols— esoteric and mysterious.

His heartbeat quickened. Could this be? Could this truly be? He suddenly knew what this place was she had brought him. *The portal*. She had described it to him, and on the basis of this description he had even attempted a drawing, but he had never thought he'd live to see it himself. Exhilarated, his heart bursting with love and gratitude, he turned to find her.

She had disappeared.

His eyes probed the shadows around him but she was gone, as though she had been merely a ghost. Only the crow was still there. It sat on the floor a few paces away from him, squat and unmoving, beady eyes glowing red within its head.

For a moment he felt as alone as he had ever felt in his entire life. But then he took a deep breath. He would make her proud of him.

Slowly he turned on his heel and looked about him. Set within the wall were doors. Thirty to be exact.

Thirty doors. Behind one of them the prize. But which door was the one he was meant to open?

He hesitated. Why couldn't he remember? He had never visited the portal before but he should know the answer. Which door?

The doors stared back at him, relentless in their similarity.

Which door must he choose? Remember . . . but the certain knowledge, which had guided him throughout the earlier part of his journey, had deserted him. And he knew he would never be able to retrace his steps.

He was lost.

Terror-stricken, he spun around. Which door? Which door? He tried to control the panic, which was taking possession of his mind. No! Stay calm.

But which door? Which door?

He tried to empty his mind of all emotion. To breathe with discipline. To *decide*. And, like the answer to a prayer, one of the doors opened a crack . . .

The relief was overwhelming. Stepping forward, he placed his hand on the door, pushing it wide open.

He screamed as a cacophony of sound and movement slammed into his brain with the force of a freight train. The onslaught was so intense, he was unable to process the information, unable to make sense of the images hurtling toward him like a giant fist. It was as though someone was pouring information into his brain at lightning speed, an avalanche of images and emotions filling up his head, only his mind wasn't big enough—not nearly big enough—to contain it all. He stared; unable to blink, eyeballs dry, lips stretched painfully over his teeth in a grotesque smile, feeling his mind collapsing under the stupendous weight of the information dumped into his brain all at once. It was as though he could suddenly see underneath the skin of his body and watch as every individual organ inside him pulsed and labored against the massive attack. He was going insane. And the horror of it was that he knew it.

His mind popped like an overripe fruit. Bright globules of blood ran down the inside of his eyes.

Quiet.

Peace. Like moonlight on water.

Water. He was floating on his back in a swimming pool. His mind was blessedly still.

He heard music. A violin. And looking up at the sky, there was the moon: heavy and swollen, caught in the arms of a tree.

But he was becoming tired. His body felt paralyzed on one side. The water pulled at him. He turned his head to where the house loomed black against a charcoal sky. The only light came from behind the French doors. A woman's figure was silhouetted against the buttered glow.

She stepped into the garden. Thank God. He knew she would never abandon him. His eyes filled with tears of gratitude.

Her face was still masked. Her breasts were ice cream against the green velvet of her dress. A pendant was swinging from her throat: a thin silver chain from which dangled a charm in the shape of the letter *M*. On her shoulder was perched the crow.

Help me. Rescue me.

Her pale white fingers reached out to him.

And pushed his head under the water.

The crow shrieked. With a wild flap of its wings it swooped to the side, alighting on the overhanging branch of the tree.

Her grasp was soft but her fingers were steel. His nose and mouth filled with water. He was drowning. His chest on fire. She had one hand on his shoulder, the other on his head. He tried to twist away from her, to loosen the hand holding him in a gentle death grip.

She pushed his head down again. Oh God, no. Why? He had followed the rules perfectly . . . perfectly . . .

He couldn't fight her. He didn't have the strength. And his body so sluggish, so heavy. He was starting to sink.

She lifted her hand: a gesture of regret. The water was blurring her figure, but as he continued to spiral downward, their eyes locked.

Why? His mouth opened and closed fishlike, the water drowning his words. *Why? Why?*

CHAPTER SIX

Sunlight. Splinter-sharp in his eyes. His body no longer chilled by water but bathed in sweat. Around him the comforting familiar environment of his loft apartment. For a few moments Gabriel sat without moving. One part of his brain knew that the ride was over, that he was safely inside his home, but another part of him was still reeling from the experience he had just been through.

His mouth was stretched wide, and he had to make a conscious effort to relax his face. He was sitting in his armchair next to the window, the picture of Robert Whittington on his knee. It was quiet in the apartment but the air seemed alive, as though he had just screamed and the sound of his distress was still lingering in the room.

Clumsily he got to his feet, the photograph clutched between his fingers. Frankie. He needed to talk to her. Rather urgently.

As he dialed, he squinted at the numbers she had written on the back of the picture. He seemed to have problems focusing. He dropped the picture on the tabletop and saw that his fingers had left damp smudges on the photograph's glossy surface.

The sound of the ringing reverberated inside his head. A click. A crisp "Whittington residence." The slightly officious voice of a well-trained manservant.

"I'd like to speak to Cecily Franck, please." He found to his surprise that he had trouble speaking.

"I beg your pardon?" The voice sounded pained.

"Cecily Franck. I mean, Whittington. I'd like to speak with her." His tongue was unbelievably sluggish. No wonder the asshole on the other side of the phone sounded so disapproving. He probably thought there was a drunk on the line.

"Tell her it's Gabriel. And that it's urgent."

A doubtful pause. Then, "Please wait. I'll see if Madam is available."

You do that, you twit, he thought. Placing his hand against his forehead, he found it dripping with sweat. In fact, his entire body was drenched. And his brain . . . his brain felt like mashed potato.

It seemed that Madam was indeed available.

"Hello? Gabriel?"

"Frankie."

"Gabriel? What's up? You sound strange."

"Maybe you should come over."

"Why? What's wrong?"

He started to laugh weakly. "A ride. I've slammed a ride." For some reason it suddenly seemed funny.

An even longer silence this time. When she did speak, her voice sounded tight as though she was trying to rein in her excitement. "Wait for me. Don't go anywhere. Wait for me."

"Believe me. The way I feel now I'm not going anywhere."

Just before she hung up she asked, breathless, "Gabriel . . . is he alive?"

"I don't know." He remembered the feeling of drowning: the heavy legs, fire in his chest, and then the blessed feeling of letting go as he spiraled downward. It had certainly felt like the end of something. "I'm not sure."

"Well, was it at least a good ride?"

"Good?" He thought of the nightmarish journey, the insane images that had battered his mind. "Again, I don't know. Just get here, OK? We'll talk when you get here."

He replaced the receiver in its cradle, his mind still on the question she had asked him. A good ride?

Well, that depended now, didn't it? If with "good" she meant "detailed," then yes, it had been a spectacular ride. The best ever. But if with "good" she wanted to know if the ride made good sense, then no, afraid not. Of course, remote viewing was not exactly like baking

a cake. Images and emotions accessed during a ride were often am-
biguous.

But this was beyond weird. He had never slammed a ride this
nightmarishly surreal in his entire life. That journey through the
house—if such a vast space could be called a house—had been
bizarre in the extreme. And was that a murder he had lived through?
A death? The scene had a curiously stylized feel about it—a woman
with, of all things, a crow on her shoulder and the moon hanging in
the sky like something from a Chinese woodblock print. But the
physical agony he had endured had certainly felt real enough.

And why had the ride happened at all?

He most definitely had not planned on slamming this one. His
subconscious mind must be more engaged with Robert Whittington's disappearance than he had thought.

Shit, he had a screaming headache and his brain felt very, very
stupid. Did he always feel this disoriented afterward? Surely he
used to snap back a lot faster? He couldn't recall this tremendous
bone-draining exhaustion, which now gripped every limb. And
lurking at the edges of his consciousness was still the horror he had
experienced during the ride, the fear.

He got to his feet, only to find that he was actually incapable of
walking in a straight line. With difficulty he steered his way into the
kitchen. Opening the fridge, he removed a jug of ice water and,
without reaching for a glass, started drinking from the jug's mouth.
At least this was something he remembered: this raging thirst, which
always followed a ride. The water splashed down his chin as he
drank greedily and clumsily.

By the time she arrived he was feeling better. Not good, but better.
Her first words, however, were not encouraging.

"My God, you look terrible. Are you all right?"

"Actually, no. I feel like crap. Sit down."

Frankie balanced herself on the very edge of the couch, her eyes
never leaving his face. "So, what happened?"

"I . . ." He stopped.

She leaned forward in anticipation, but for a moment he felt at a loss. Where to begin?

"Well?" She was impatient now.

At the door, he supposed. That's where he should start. He would begin at the door with the strange-looking coat of arms . . .

She hardly blinked throughout the entire time he talked, and she did not interrupt. But now she spoke, her voice tired.

"So he was killed. Someone drowned him. This woman."

"Probably. The feeling of drowning was very real."

"What I don't understand is how she managed to overpower him. Robbie was slender but he was no weakling. Physically, he should have been more than a match for her. And he was strong swimmer. It was his exercise of choice—he used to swim laps at the Queen Mother Sport Centre at least twice a week. He always said water was where he felt most at home. Why didn't he put up more of a fight?"

"His brain was damaged, remember. When I was in the pool one side of my body was heavy—like a stroke victim's. I think Robbie's brain suffered a trauma of some kind and that it affected his motor coordination as well."

"Well, at least you saw a house. That's always promising. That's a firm reference point."

"A house, may I remind you, which has, among other things, rooms housing fields of butterflies and blind monks. And something called a portal."

She frowned. "Could be symbolism."

"Could be insanity." He paused. How to explain to her the incredible sensory overload he had experienced? "That one moment when I opened the door inside the portal, was like nothing I had ever experienced in my entire life. I felt insane. It felt like my brain was on TCP; as though it was frying inside my skull."

"Well, maybe that's what it was. Maybe Robbie tried some kind of hallucinatory drug and he overdosed."

He shook his head. "I thought of that but I don't think so. The weird thing is that during this ride, I was conscious of great discipline. I was walking from room to room in strict order. There was a set sequence, which required enormous mental focus. I didn't just open doors at will. There was a definite pattern. Some doors I left closed . . . on purpose. And I must have opened hundreds of doors. Thousands."

"*Thousands?*"

"Hundreds of thousands, maybe. I know: it's madness. And there was this one phrase, which kept going through my mind like a mantra: *the order of places, the order of things.* As though this was some kind of guiding principle or prime directive, or something. Despite the chaos, there was an incredibly tight discipline to the journey—not like being spaced out at all. At the beginning of the ride I was in control and it felt good, I tell you. It was as though I was being tested, and the fact that I was able to choose the correct door every time was immensely empowering. Except that toward the end of the ride—when I followed this woman—I lost it. And shortly afterward I found my brain going into meltdown and then I woke up inside a swimming pool. Oh, hell." He sighed. "This is crazy stuff. Maybe you're right. Maybe this was some kind of acid trip. It was certainly a rush."

"It sounds like a fantastic ride." There was a hint of wistfulness in Frankie's voice. It reminded him of the surprise confession she had made the last time he saw her. *There were times my envy was eating me up.* All those years ago when they were together—happily he had thought—she had been resentful of his RV skills. He still couldn't equate such an emotion with the young, unassuming Cecily Franck he had loved. He rather wished she hadn't told him.

She spoke again. "What about the woman?"

He thought for a moment. "She was real," he said slowly. "She was real. I could sense her as a person. Yes, definitely. Which makes it even less likely that we're talking drugs here."

"I don't suppose you made any ideograms?"

He shook his head. She was referring to a method followed by many remote viewers, who, while viewing would allow their hand to engage in a kind of automatic doodling, which captured the images accessed during the ride. He rarely worked this way. Still, drawings were sometimes useful.

He got to his feet and walked over to his work desk. Opening a drawer, he removed a pad of paper and a pencil and started to sketch. A circle on top of a cross, the circle intersected by a smaller half circle. The whole thing set against the background of a rose in bloom. He was not great at drawing, and his rose looked more like a battered daisy, but it would do. After a few seconds he returned to where Frankie was waiting.

"Remember I told you about the coat of arms I saw? On the door and on the wall leading to the portal? Well, this is it. At least that's what I remember from the ride. Maybe it will remind you of something about Robert." Without much hope, he held the pad of paper out at her. "Does it ring a bell?"

"My God." She stared at the drawing.

"What?" His voice sharpened. "You know what it is?"

"Robbie had this tattooed on the inside of his right arm—above the wrist."

"Why? Was he straight? It looks to me like the symbol for female sexuality."

Frankie smiled. "This symbol has nothing to do with sex. It's a combination of several astrological symbols into one. He called it the *Monad* or the *Monas,* something like that. *Monas,* if I remember correctly. But exactly which symbols and what they mean, I don't know. But, Gabriel, that's not important. What *is* important is that this symbol is based on the coat of arms at Monk House."

"Monk House?"

"The Monk sisters." She looked up at him, excitement in her eyes. "Morrighan and Minnaloushe Monk. Robbie was friends with them. They live in this big old rambling redbrick house in Chelsea. I've only been inside a couple of times but I remember the coat of arms.

It's everywhere. I asked Robbie about it, and he told me that it dates back to the sixteenth century, and was something to do with the Monk family."

Gabriel looked at the drawing again. Sixteenth century. The design looked remarkably modern for the 1500s. "It still doesn't make sense."

"Believe me, very little of what Robbie did made sense. But the letter on the chain around the woman's neck in your ride was an *M,* which means it could belong to Minnaloushe or Morrighan. And the *Monas* coat of arms points to Monk House."

"Surely the house doesn't have a swimming pool?"

Frankie's eyes were stricken. "As a matter of fact, it does. One of the very few outdoor pools in Chelsea. It's not big, but it's deep. We had a pool party there last summer. That was the first time I met the sisters."

For a moment there was silence between them as they considered the possible implications.

"The house itself is quite fascinating, really, in a rather gloomy way." Frankie grimaced slightly. "There's a very impressive library, but I certainly don't recall seeing butterflies or fantailed doves flying around. And I rather doubt there were self-mutilating monks hiding behind the doors."

"And no pet crow, I take it."

"Sorry."

"You said they were friends with Robbie."

"Actually, for the last year he was constantly in their company. And after he met them, he moved out of our house into an apartment of his own. I always thought they had something to do with that decision."

"Daddy probably didn't like it, did he?"

"Quite the opposite. William approved of the friendship. About the only thing he did approve of where Robbie was concerned. He thought the sisters had a stabilizing influence on Robbie."

"Did they?"

She shrugged. "I guess so. Robbie seemed content for the first time I knew him."

Something in her voice was not right.

Gabriel leaned forward. "Why don't you like them?"

"I never said I didn't like them." Her tone was defensive. She was actually scowling. Gabriel suppressed a smile. Women. Time to change tack.

"Morrighan and Minnaloushe Monk. It sounds like something from a riddle. Their parents liked unusual. Why not Mary and Mabel, I wonder."

Frankie lifted her eyebrows. "Believe me, these two women don't look like a Mary and a Mabel. They're rather . . . exotic creatures. Robbie was smitten with them. Especially one."

"Which one?"

"You know what, I really don't know. Somehow I always think of them as a pair. And to tell the truth, I didn't pay that much attention. Robbie had these on-off crushes all the time." She smiled a little sadly. "He even had a little crush on me once."

"Well, I can't blame him for that."

"Well, thank you."

"No, really, I mean it." And he did. He glanced at her appraisingly. You would not call her beautiful, but Frankie's face was immensely appealing. She was sitting in profile, and his gaze took in the sweep of her cheekbone, the nose just slightly turned up at the end and the curve of the upper lip, which always made it seem as though she was just about to smile. Today she was wearing a flowery dress and looked young and fresh. He hadn't noticed how pretty she looked until now, which was very unlike him. Still, when she first arrived he had felt so rough he wouldn't have reacted if Monica Bellucci had walked through the door. Frankie's dress had a wide scoop neck, and he could see the delicate sprinkle of tiny coppery freckles on her collarbone. Sun kisses, he used to call them way back, when they were still together. Not very original, in hindsight. But what he remembered was how he had liked to try to count them. Usually after they had made love. A small private ritual.

She turned her head and caught him looking. He saw in her eyes that she had sensed what he was thinking. A faint blush stained her cheekbones and she brought her hand involuntarily to her neck.

So Mrs. Whittington wasn't quite as impervious as she liked to pretend. He smiled and touched her hand, allowing his fingers to linger. "I like this dress on you."

"Thanks. It's William's favorite as well. He bought it for me in Milan."

Right. That was pointed enough. He should have remembered that despite an innate sweetness, Frankie was no pushover. And she had always been able to put him in his place. He removed his hand.

"I take it the police interviewed the sisters?" He kept his voice cool.

"In depth." He could see she was relieved by his businesslike tone. "They found nothing suspicious at all."

"You said he had a crush on one of the women. Was it reciprocated?"

"Oh, no." Frankie's voice was emphatic. "They're quite a few years older than Robbie. And there is absolutely no way either one of them would be interested in him as a partner. I think they saw him as a little puppy dog following them around and were rather amused by his devotion."

She paused, tapped her finger against her lips. "I could get you inside that house. Pay them a visit and take you along."

He shook his head, wincing as he did so. The headache was still there. "What I need is unrestricted access. If you take me along as a guest, we'll be served tea in the parlor and that would be that. I need to be able to snoop around undisturbed. Also, I want to see the house first before meeting the owners. It would be easier to get a clean impression that way."

Frankie looked at him suspiciously. "You're not thinking of breaking and entering, are you?"

"With your help, yes."

"Gabriel . . . wait a minute. This is taking it too far."

"Well, it's up to you. I can walk away at any time."

Which wasn't quite true. The discovery that he still had the ability to view so clearly had come as something of a surprise. Whether this was going to turn out to be a pleasant surprise was the question. But he was hooked.

And her next words showed he hadn't fooled her. "You're lying. The ride got to you. I can see it in your eyes. Was this your first ride since . . ." She paused delicately, then must have read the answer on his face. "Wow. You must be pumped then."

He shrugged. He was exhausted but excited. And still amazed that it had happened at all. Admittedly, the circumstances had been favorable. Remote viewing ideally required the viewer to manage brain waves, which have a frequency range of four to seven cycles per second. These theta waves were present during deep meditation and created the optimal mental state for crossing over. When he had slotted into the ride, his body had been completely relaxed. And this was when it usually happened for him: when he was drifting, but not out.

"So let's make a plan."

"What did you have in mind exactly?" Her voice was wary.

"I need you to invite them to your house for dinner one night so that I can be sure the house is empty."

She chewed her lip, her face uncertain.

"Come on, Frankie. Take a walk on the wild side."

"Well, your repertoire has certainly changed. I can't recall burglary as being one of your talents."

"It's not burglary. It's looking without touching."

She frowned, but he could see she was starting to make peace with the idea.

"All right," she said. "All right. But I'm not saying anything to William yet. He admires those two women a lot."

Maybe a little bit too much, Gabriel thought, and maybe Mrs. Whittington doesn't like it?

Frankie glanced at her watch, picked up her handbag. "I should go. I have a lunch appointment. But I'll call the sisters when I get home. Set a date."

"OK."

At the door she stopped and looked at him. "You said that in your ride you were able to sense this woman as a person. What was it you sensed? Malevolence?"

"No. Not malevolence. Greed."

"*Greed?*"

"It's hard to explain. Not greed as in money lust but greed as in wanting to know. Curiosity, is the word I'm looking for, I suppose. Except that it's not strong enough. I'm talking intense curiosity. Curiosity to the square, you might say."

"Curiosity about what?"

He shrugged. "Beats me."

But as he closed the door behind Frankie, he realized that his description hadn't been quite accurate. Yes, he had picked up overwhelming curiosity from the masked figure who had looked into his eyes so searchingly. But there had been another emotion radiating from her as well. Something much more basic and unambiguous. This was a woman whose expectations had not been met. The overriding emotion he had sensed from her could be summed up in one word.

Disappointment.

Entry Date: 11 June

Disappointment is the saddest of all emotions. M agrees, but she says regret is the one that will eat away at your soul.

We finished the chamber of Toth last night. I am satisfied with it but I also feel emptiness. Like M, I long to find someone new to play with. And I have no doubt that there will be someone new. It is just a matter of time.

I wonder who he'll be. R was a seeker and an innocent. But maybe M is right. Maybe we need a man who carries more fire in his veins.

Someone who is not only a dreamer but also a warrior.

I wonder where he is now—our future playmate. What is he thinking of right this minute?

CHAPTER SEVEN

Monk House was the only Victorian house on an entire street of elegant Georgian facades. It sat bulkily on the corner; square, brooding and defiant in its otherness. The brickwork was deep orange and there was more than a hint of Gothic in the pointed gable and the oriel bulging from the house's flank. It was late afternoon, and the sun glinted redly off the tiny leaded panes, creating an impression that inside a fire was burning.

The front of the house was flush with its neighbor, and the front door was overlooked by houses on the opposite side of the street. The door had two locks and Gabriel had already ascertained that one of them was a Bramah. This would not be his point of access. It would be far easier to negotiate the back garden and enter through the French doors leading to the living room. He had Frankie to thank for this piece of information, as the back of the house was hidden from view. A wall that was all of sixty feet long and at least twelve feet in height ensured not only complete privacy but also good security. It would be difficult to scale.

But there was an alley round the back, and set into the wall was an access door. Gabriel suspected that this was used when the garbage cans were put out for collection. He had already traversed the alley earlier this week, checking out the small timber door. As he expected, the lock was a standard one. He did not foresee any problems.

He tapped his fingers impatiently against the steering wheel of the Jaguar. He wanted out of the car. Even though the sun was losing much of its sting, it was still hellishly hot. His shirt was sticking to his back where it pressed against the leather upholstery. He was parked about half a block away and had a good side view of the house. Nothing stirred.

He glanced at his watch. They were cutting it close. It was already ten minutes to the hour, and Frankie had told him the sisters had agreed to drinks at seven followed by dinner after. That should give him more than enough time to look around. He was also carrying his mobile phone. Frankie promised to call him as soon as the sisters had finished dinner and were leaving for home. He didn't want to be caught in the act—although he expected to be finished long before then.

A black taxicab came to a halt in front of the house. Gabriel watched as the cabdriver walked up the front steps and rang the doorbell. After a few seconds, the cabbie turned his head and spoke into the intercom unit set into the wall. He listened for a moment or two before walking back to the cab and settling himself behind the steering wheel. He kept the car idling.

Gabriel waited. The front door remained shut.

Earlier today he had stopped off at Robert Whittington's flat. Frankie had given him the key. He spent almost an hour opening cupboards, rifling through drawers and boxes. A sad little exercise. Not only did the flat have the forlorn feel of an unoccupied place, but Gabriel had the feeling that everything in that apartment belonged to someone who was searching.

Books on self-improvement rubbed shoulders with tomes on Buddhism, astrology and tarot card reading. Against the wall were two framed posters: an *X-Files* poster with its slogan "I want to believe" and the iconic features of Che Guevara, improbably handsome and debonair. Candles, crystals and a number of different Buddhas—some of them jolly and potbellied, others intimidatingly ascetic—lined the shelves.

Above the bed hung a wooden mask. It looked to be African in origin, thick eyelids surrounding hollow eye sockets and the mouth pulled back into a stylized grimace. The furniture was modest, the apartment small. It was difficult to believe the heir to a vast fortune had lived there.

On the bedside table was a framed picture. It showed Robert

Whittington as a teenager, all outsized nose and feet, with his arm around the waist of a thickset blond woman. There was a definite family resemblance—the mother, at a guess. Frankie had told him she had died in a skiing accident when the boy was only fourteen. The first Mrs. Whittington was no beauty, but she had soft eyes. As he looked at the two faces, Gabriel felt a sudden pang of sympathy. The loss of his mother must have been a tremendous blow, especially if relations with the father had been strained since childhood.

The only thing of real interest in the apartment was a pencil sketch pinned to a discolored bulletin board. The sketch was extraordinarily well executed and almost architectural in detail. It showed a circular space with a domed ceiling and walls composed of wheels densely covered with symbols. Some were easy to identify: a star, a candle, a book. Others were more obscure: squiggles and doodlelike icons impossible to interpret. At the bottom of the sketch, written in a slanted hand, was *Portal*, and underneath it a simple signature: *Robert*, followed by a date. Robert Whittington, it seemed, had a real talent for drawing.

But it wasn't the skill of the artist that made him pause and that caused his heart to beat faster. It was the fact that the penciled lines on the paper replicated a place he had visited only a few days before. A fantastical space he had entered shortly before being sucked into a nightmarish whirlwind of images and sounds that had sent his mind crashing into insanity. This vast chamber with its turning, symbol-clad wheels had been the gateway to madness and death. Just thinking back on it gave him a chill.

Portal.

As he looked at the drawing so finely rendered, he found himself shivering. Thought given substance. Proof that he had indeed managed to cross the slippery borders of Robert Whittington's mind.

The door to Monk House opened. Gabriel blinked, brought back to the present. The occupants of the house were finally about to leave. A woman with red hair reaching to her shoulders stepped out.

She turned sideways, and he was able to see the tip of a delicate nose and chin behind a gleaming veil of hair. She was obviously talking to someone who was still inside the house.

Red hair. So this will be Minnaloushe. Frankie had told him Morrighan was the brunette. Someone, another woman who was not yet in his line of vision, was pointing toward the taxi: a slim bare arm was reaching out from behind the front door. The redhead nodded and walked down the steps, adjusting a long, floaty scarf around her neck. Before he had time to have a proper look at her face, she had ducked into the interior of the cab.

A second woman walked through the front door, pulling it shut behind her. He saw a flash of keys. She was slightly taller than the redhead. Her hair was black as coal and pulled back in a sophisticated chignon. After locking the door, she looked up and down the street. For a moment he had a full view of her face: heart-shaped with cheekbones that could cut glass. V-e-e-ry nice indeed. Then she too stepped inside the cab. The taxi pulled away and accelerated down the street.

He waited for a few minutes after the taxi had disappeared around the corner. No harm in making sure they were really gone. Then he got out of the Jaguar and headed for the alley, taking care to walk briskly and confidently. The alley was overlooked by the back windows of a number of storied houses, but he wasn't too fussed. If one walked with enough assurance, people usually didn't pay attention. Furtive skulking, on the other hand, would get you noticed every time. The only glitch might be the lock on the garden door. He would have to work quickly.

He didn't have to worry. He was just about to take out his tools when his shoulder pushed against the door and it clicked open under his weight. It had been left unlocked. Quickly he stepped inside and closed the door behind him.

He was standing at the foot-end of a long, narrow garden, which had a wonderful feel of manicured wildness to it. A cascade of mauves, purples and pinks—lavender, lilac, love-in-a-mist—grew among the silken tassels and feathery plumes of softly swaying grasses. Rambling roses with pale petals covered the walls of the garden. But even though the overall feel of the garden was one of delightful randomness, if one looked closely, it was obvious that some real thought had gone into the planning of all this luxurious herbage. This might be botanical anarchy, but it was a controlled disorder. The mind that had created this floral fantasy was a meticulous one.

To his right was the swimming pool, shaded by a humpbacked tree with bright red flowers. He walked over and knelt down on the brick apron, trailing his hand through the sun-warm water. As Frankie had said, the pool wasn't big, but it seemed quite deep. The surface of the water was flecked with stray petals. He could see the delicate bodies of dead insects bobbing near the edges of the filter.

He wiped his mind clean of emotion and waited. Concentrated. He kept his hand submerged in the water.

Nothing. If Robert Whittington had died here, the echo of his passing had already disappeared. Gabriel could sense nothing at all.

He got to his feet and wiped his hand against his shirtfront. Maybe he'd have better luck inside the house.

The windows on the ground floor were shut, as was a pair of tall French doors. But as he started to walk toward the doors, he experienced a flash of recognition. The stained-glass panels set into the doors showed the coat of arms he had seen during his ride. The *Monas*. Astrological symbols, according to Frankie.

They didn't look like any astrology symbols he'd ever seen, but to be fair, he wasn't exactly au fait with the wonderful world of the zodiac. Isidore, on the other hand, was meticulous about checking his horoscope every day, and a negative forecast could make him fall into depression faster than you could say "Saturn in retrograde." Come to think of it, it might not be a bad idea to have Isidore check out the *Monas*. It had to be important if Robert Whittington had the design tattooed onto his arm.

He stopped and tried the doors. They were locked, but the lock itself was basic. There was also no indication of an alarm. Except for the higher than normal garden wall, the sisters did not seem to worry unduly about security. Which might mean they had nothing to hide.

Or not. It could also be a sign of arrogance.

If he had been a real burglar, he would have tapped out one of the glass insets in the door and simply put his hand through and let himself in that way. As it was, he did not want to leave behind traces of his visit, so a little more effort was required. From the inside pocket of his jacket he extracted the chamois pouch with his picks and removed one of the pronged instruments. As he started to work on the lock, he smiled. This was going to be easy. And indeed, after only a few seconds, he felt the lock give. He eased himself in and closed the door behind him.

For a few moments he stood without moving, giving his eyes a chance to become accustomed to the inside gloom. The windows were shuttered, allowing only filtered shafts of sunlight to shine through the slats. The air was heavy, the shutters not so much screening the house from the heat as trapping it and keeping it prisoner. A ceiling fan whirled lazily above his head. It hardly stirred the air, and the whisper of the slowly turning blades only accentuated the quietness of the room.

Every house has its own peculiar smell. Whenever he visited a house, this was always the first thing he noticed. Not the decor, the smell. It may vary from day to day. Cooking, cleaning, working—all these activities left their olfactory imprint, but the underlying essence of a house stayed the same. The scent of this house was powerfully feminine. And surprisingly old-fashioned. Talcum. Roses of the old, fragrant variety. Spices such as cinnamon and cloves. Tangerines? Also something else. Something he couldn't quite place but which bit into his palate, slightly bitter and acrid. And then, of course, the olfactory ingredient, which made the smell of any house as unique as a fingerprint. The occupants. The sisters themselves. He could smell them as well.

The room itself had a plantation-like feel to it. The cream-colored walls, dark oiled floorboards and shutters, rattan furniture and ghostly ceiling fan were reminiscent of an interior more likely to be found in some colonial outpost than a house in central London.

A peacock chair with a very deep seat was flanked by a rickety-looking wicker screen. One wall held a large number of carved African masks. They reminded him of the mask he had seen in Robert Whittington's apartment. It wouldn't surprise him if it had originated from this room.

Two dark green wingback chairs, the leather split and creased, faced each other on either side of a zebra skin going bald. A rattan coffee table and several rattan chests covered with magazines flanked an enormous sofa covered in velvet. On the far side of the room were two metal workbenches covered with a variety of objects.

There were roses everywhere. On top of the chest, on side tables, on the windowsills. Silky bloodred roses, deep apricot-hued ones and waxy, pink-veined blooms drooping over the rims of alabaster bowls. But no photographs, which was interesting. In his experience women living alone always surrounded themselves with images of their own likeness and those of loved ones. But except for a crucifixion print of Salvador Dalí's—a beautiful long-limbed Christ hanging eerily suspended in space—there were no other pictures in the room.

It was an exceptionally large room and obviously used not only as a living room but also as a library and workroom. One wall was completely covered in shelves filled to capacity with books, the shelves dipping dangerously in the middle from the weight of so many volumes. There were even books stacked up higgledy-piggledy behind the books in the front rows.

He turned his head sideways to read some of the titles: *De Imaginum, De umbris idearum, Ars notoria, De occulta philosophia, Book of Dzyan, The Hermetic Secret.* Not exactly the kind of reading material with which to relax in the bathtub, you might say. Not that all the books were arcana. There were also many volumes bearing the imprimatur of university presses, written by luminaries in the more austere halls of academia. Stephen Jay Gould. David Gelernter. Daniel Dennet. Freeman Dyson. Roger Penrose. Eclectic didn't even begin to describe this collection.

But the sisters had obviously kept pace with the electronic age. The bottom two shelves were taken up by stacks of DVDs. He made a quick calculation: ten DVDs to a stack, twenty stacks—there were more than two hundred DVDs all told. He pulled out one of the disks. The sticker on the front held a neat inscription: *Human Genome Project*. The second disk said *Encyclopaedia Britannica*. 1.2 gigs.

He lifted his eyebrows in surprise. If all these DVDs were full, then they contained a massive amount of information. It looked as though the sisters had the contents of the entire British Library stored in their living room.

He turned away from the shelves. He wanted to take a closer look at those two metal workbenches. They were home to some delightfully weird and wonderful things. There were gleaming brass compasses. An astrolabe. The skeletons of birds bleached white, startlingly ethereal, as if the slightest touch would cause the bones to crumble to dust. Bell jars. Dried herbs. Sheets of handmade marbled paper. Real ink pots and fussy nibbed pens.

What a strange collection. In another house some of these items might have been displayed as whimsical objets d'art— –that astrolabe must be worth a pretty penny, for one, and the beads on the abacus appeared to be real ivory—but in this room they looked startlingly utilitarian, as though they were in constant use.

There were also computers. An IBM and a Macintosh lined up next to each other. Both were booted up and running. Both shared the same screen saver: a woman with long flowing hair and a swirling cloak holding in her hands a brightly glowing sun, which would grow bigger and bigger before slowly shrinking again, the pulsing red mass becoming ever smaller until only a pinpoint of light was left between her palms. The effect of two suns waxing and waning in tandem was oddly mesmerizing.

He sat down on an old-fashioned typist's chair and tapped a key on the keyboard of the IBM. No password necessary. Actually, the computer was already open on an Internet Web page.

Great. He'd be able to get into the sisters' e-mail. Maybe access some old correspondence with Robert Whittington. There had been no computer at Whittington's apartment, but according to Frankie, he used to be the owner of a pretty decent machine until he had decided, shortly before his disappearance, to donate the thing to charity. To Gabriel this was a completely off-the-wall thing to do, but Frankie didn't seem to find the idea of her stepson giving away a six-thousand-dollar notebook all that unusual. "Robbie did all kinds of inexplicable things when the spirit moved him." She shrugged. "So today he's all excited about being a Luddite. Tomorrow it's something else again."

The machine was used by both sisters, but when he checked the e-mail in their in- and out-boxes and personal filing cabinets, he was disappointed. The messages were innocuous—friends, business colleagues—and as far as he could determine not one message sent to, or received from, Robert Whittington.

Perhaps there might be something of more value among their documents. He started accessing files at random. The contents seemed fairly mundane. A file named *Accounts* was just that, a neat synopsis of household expenses, although the figure at the bottom made him purse his lips in a soundless whistle. Frugality was not an issue in this house.

He continued scrolling down the list of entries and paused. *Diary*. Jackpot.

He centered the mouse on the file name and clicked. But here the easy part ended. The screen cleared and he was asked for a password. Gate barred.

Passwords, of course, were not necessarily foolproof. If you knew the person you were snooping on, it was sometimes not that difficult to guess a password. Most home users used words related to their everyday life and interests. But he did not know Minnaloushe and Morrighan Monk and had no idea what they were into. So after tapping in the names of the sisters—although how the heck does one spell "Minnaloushe"—and receiving no joy, he accepted defeat.

He leaned back in the chair, his hands cradled behind his head. So that was that. He was stymied. At least for the moment. But the mere fact that this was the only password-protected file in the list must be significant. He would have to consult with Isidore and make a plan. They would probably be able to gain access through a Trojan horse virus sent via an e-mail message. Not that this course of action would be plain sailing. Embedded in the taskbar of the machine in front of him was the icon for Kaspersky Anti-Virus software. KAV was the best there was: its ability to sniff out viruses and Trojans was excellent. Isidore was going to have to get creative.

He swiveled the chair around and faced the Mac. Maybe he'd have better luck with this machine. He tapped the enter key and the screen saver dissolved.

He paused. This was odd. First, the computer was not connected to the Internet. Second, the computer seemed to be dedicated to the maintenance of one document only. The document was named *The Promethean Key*.

This sounded interesting. At Oxford he had done a course in Classical Culture and History, and there was a time he had fancied himself a bit of a classics buff. Prometheus, if memory served him, stole a spark of fire from the gods to give to mankind to open their minds to knowledge. He was punished by Zeus and spent his days chained to a rock with a giant eagle feeding on his liver. Pretty tough stuff. Those Greek gods did not mess around.

He clicked on the file without much hope. As he expected, this file was password-protected as well.

Two password-protected files. They would certainly warrant a closer look somewhere along the way. Except that where the Mac was concerned, he was faced with a significant added complication. Since the computer was not connected to the Internet, he and Isidore would not be able to access the machine from outside via a convenient broadband connection. In order to crack this thing, he was going to have to return in person. Not exactly a prospect he was looking forward to. He very much preferred surveillance from a distance.

But for the present there was no use wasting any more time on the computers. Glancing at his watch, he was surprised to see that he had already spent a full forty minutes inside the house.

But as he got up from his seat, he froze. On the shelf right in front of him, at eye level, was a glass box. Inside the box were stone pebbles, sand, and pieces of rock illuminated by a weak violet light. An eerie little desert landscape. Hovering ghostlike on one of the rocks, its hairy legs delicately poised, was one of the biggest spiders he had ever seen.

He blinked. The creature seemed not quite real—a phantasm, a monster from a dream. He realized that his body was flooded with adrenaline—the sight of the spider had bypassed the analytical side of his brain, had elicited an impulse that came straight from the amygdalae.

Hesitantly, he brought his head up close to the box. The lavender light made the color of the spider difficult to fathom and contributed to the thing looking like something from a particularly bad acid trip. The spider's body alone must have been all of four inches long. The legs seemed to be floating. Massive fangs. He was no expert, but he was almost certain he was looking at a tarantula. Which should have reassured him. Tarantulas were harmless to humans— that much he knew. He had read somewhere that people even kept them as pets.

Pets? He stared at the spider in its glass box. It was moving its front legs almost imperceptibly. Feeling slightly queasy, Gabriel recognized the dark splodge lying to one side of the box. A half-eaten cricket.

Oh, man. This was too much. He had to force himself to step back. He couldn't spend all his time on this freakish thing. But what the hell else was waiting for him inside this house?

The next room was the dining room, dark with mahogany, followed by a guest bathroom designed for pygmies and a rather workmanlike kitchen. He opened the fridge and peeked inside. A bottle of Krug champagne shared shelf space with several delectable-looking cartons and trays sporting Harrods Food Halls stickers. He lifted the corner on one of the white boxes. Duck confit. Their taste in literature and decor, not to mention pets, might be odd, but the ladies showed real class when it came to food.

On the one wall on the far side of the room were some rather interesting-looking prints. They were not exactly the still-life pictures you'd expect to find in a kitchen: no jolly tomatoes or ears of corn. The prints were watercolors and pretty damn weird to say the least. Lots of naked hermaphroditic figures in rural settings, dancing next to roaring furnaces. A creepy proliferation of snakes, suns and moons.

Pushed against the wall was a rustic pine table at least ten feet long. It held an array of copper bowls and, more intriguingly, big-bottomed flasks of the kind you'd find in a chemistry lab. Rounded Florence flasks were clamped to chrome support stands, and long-necked filtering flasks shared the space with Bunsen burners and stand-alone hot plates. Neatly lined up on the shallow shelves against the wall was a large variety of brown paper bags labeled in a flowing hand: *juniperus virginiana, dwarf sumac (stem), trifolium protense, viscum album, rosa canina* . . .

The shelf below was filled with small plastic tubs. He picked one up and lifted the lid. It was labeled *alkaline ash* and he had expected the tub to be filled with dust. Instead it was brimful with a white gooey substance. He took a sniff. Not a bad smell exactly, but he now knew the origin of that acrid scent he had picked up on first entering the house.

Fascinating as all of this was, though, it did not provide any clues as to what might have happened to Robert Whittington. And so far during his exploration of the house, he hadn't recognized any of the rooms. They hadn't figured in his ride. The only thing he recognized was the *Monas*. The coat of arms was everywhere; it even sat on top of the kitchen door. The sisters must like it a lot. He made another mental note to ask Isidore to check it out.

The kitchen opened directly into the front hallway, which sported high walls and skirting boards at least a foot tall. The hall was packed with plants in pots: ferns, velvety African violets, a large number of milky orchids sitting ghostlike next to one another on a low windowsill. And even more roses. These women had a thing for roses. He liked plants himself, but this was like hacking your way through a freaking jungle.

Against the wall, hanging from highly polished hooks, were a number of light raincoats and jackets. As he walked past them, he noticed a silky fuchsia scarf, which had escaped the grasp of one of the hooks and was lying on the dark timber floor like a pool of melted jewelry. He stooped to pick it up. The scarf was fragrant with perfume. He could smell it even as he carefully draped the oblong of silk over the shoulders of a glittery evening jacket. It stirred a memory inside of him. The masked woman in his ride, hadn't she been wearing the same perfume? For a moment he concentrated hard, but then he gave up. The problem was that although smell was evocative, it made for a very tenuous memory byte. He couldn't be sure.

He placed his foot on the first step of the staircase, looking upward to where it unfurled itself in a graceful elliptical spiral. The lacy wrought iron banisters were quite beautiful. But as he started to climb, he grimaced. They were wooden steps and they creaked. Loudly. A real problem should he have to visit the house again when the occupants were present.

The first floor didn't yield anything much: a blandly decorated room in blue and white, which had guest room written all over it, and an adjoining bathroom. The only other room on that floor had been converted into an extremely generous-sized walk-in closet, which was obviously used by both sisters. The differing shoe sizes alone made that clear.

The walls were lined with rails from which hung dresses draped over padded hangers and shelves holding hatboxes, printed blouses and piles of sweaters. The sisters did not lack for clothes. And they certainly did not buy at H&M. He looked at the label stitched into the neck of a taupe dress suit: Gucci. The shoes to match were Christian Louboutin. He wondered where they got the money from. Frankie had been vague. She hadn't known what the sisters did for a living. It was probably a case of old money, he thought, running his hand down a silky backless evening dress with diamond trim. Some people were born under a lucky star. The rest had to make their own luck.

Under normal circumstances he would have been delighted to find himself surrounded by fragrant silk and lace, but at that moment, as he looked at all those shelves of female lingerie and other accoutrements, he couldn't help feeling like some sleazy Peeping Tom. Actually, to be honest, the house was getting to him. On the one hand he was fascinated by the place—it was certainly not your usual chintz palace—but there was just something about it that made him feel uncomfortable. He would have been hard put to articulate his unease except to say that it felt as though the house was holding its breath, causing him to hold his breath as well. Which sounded pretty damn ridiculous, he had to admit.

Anyway, he doubted he was going to find any traces of Robert Whittington here among the Jimmy Choos and Birkin Bags. Maybe he'd have better luck upstairs. He turned to the staircase once again.

When he reached the top landing, he stopped, slightly out of breath. To his right was an arch-shaped window. The landing itself was dominated by a high and very beautiful walnut tallboy. On either side of the chest was a closed door. They would probably lead to the bedrooms.

As he stretched out his hand to turn the knob of the door on his left, something made him pause. Why did he have this feeling of being watched, all of a sudden?

He turned and looked over his shoulder. The staircase stretched down empty behind him. The sun was setting in earnest now and the arch-shaped window framed a burnt orange sky hazy with pollution. The window ensured that there was still light up here, but when he stepped away from the closed door to look over the edge of the banister, the hallway down below was almost completely dark. The spidery ferns on the console table and the coats hanging from the hooks threw hardly any shadows.

Slowly, he straightened. He was being ridiculous. There was no one here. He approached the door once more and turned the knob.

A streak of black exploded past his ear with a vicious snarl. Something had jumped off the top of the tallboy behind him and was now disappearing through the half-open door. It was so unexpected, he found himself staring at the door stupefied. His mind told him it was only a cat, but his pulse was racing off the charts and the hairs on his neck were standing up.

Cautiously he pushed the door wider. It creaked on its hinges, setting his teeth on edge. A foot away a coal black cat was watching him malevolently, tail swishing, one paw lifted expectantly. The cat spat at him and made a harrowing noise at the back of its throat. It sounded like a baby being tortured.

"Here, kitty, kitty . . ." He held out his hand placatingly. Anything to stop that unearthly sound.

The cat moved at lightning speed, and the next moment he was looking at four deep scratch marks on his wrist. The amount of blood welling up from the gouges was quite extraordinary.

Holy shit. He felt suddenly queasy and a little light-headed, which was stupid—it wasn't as though he was mortally wounded. Taking a handkerchief out of his pocket, he tied it into a clumsy bandage around his hand. If he wasn't careful, he'd be dripping blood all over the place.

He flipped the light switch at the door to help him see better: no use giving this spawn from hell an added advantage. The cat's pupils narrowed. It was still screaming, and the noise was excruciating. He moved threateningly toward the animal, which must have sensed what he had in mind, because it scrambled up the side of the curtain and onto the top of a wardrobe where it crouched into a tense ball of fur, staring down at him with an evil expression. But at least it had stopped its caterwauling.

OK. Time to regroup. He took a deep breath. When he got home, he would disinfect the wounds. But for now, ignore the cat. Focus on the task at hand. He just needed to remember to kick the damn thing out of here before he left. The door had probably been closed on purpose especially to keep the dratted animal out of the room.

And a charming room it was too. Now that his heart had stopped racing, he could give it his full attention. The color scheme was peach and pink, but whereas such a color palette could easily be cloying, this room was anything but twee. The giant whale skull sitting on top of a dresser, one eye socket stuffed with daisies, was already a sign that the person who slept in this room had a taste for whimsy. Not to mention humor. The bed lamp was purple and plastic and in the shape of Michelangelo's David. David minus his head, that is.

On the bed was an open box of chocolates, and a tissue with an imprint of bright red lipstick. He couldn't help smiling. It was all delightfully feminine. A book with a fraying spine was lying open but facedown on the counterpane next to the box of chocolates. He glanced at the title: *Mind to Hermes*. Obviously a page-turner.

As he picked it up, he took care to keep it open at the original page. The book looked as though it had been read and reread from cover to cover several times. The coated paper was soft from use; the print was smudged. A passage, heavily underlined in pencil, drew his attention: "*If you embrace in thought all things at once, time, place, substance . . . you will comprehend God.*" In the margin someone had written in a cramped, but looping feminine hand: *The divine has been banished from the universe we live in. We are creating the ultimate mind machine but we have lost the alchemical impulse and the desire to transform ourselves into divine man. Instead of allowing us to embrace the riches of the universe, the mind machine has left our brains empty as a paper cup, a thing of no value, a lump of tissue only able to reflect the knowledge of the universe, not absorb it!!!*

He grimaced. Mind machine . . . a computer? And what alchemical impulse? The words themselves were pretty obscure, but the passionate conviction behind the words was hard to miss. The liberal use of exclamation marks was proof enough.

Well, whatever rubs your Buddha, as Isidore would say. Transforming himself into divine man was not exactly high on his own list of priorities. He subscribed to the motto: "Living well is the best revenge."

He was just about to replace the book, when the cell phone clipped to his belt went off. The sudden noise made him jerk.

"Hello?"

"Gabriel." One word only, but Frankie sounded tired.

"Frankie, hi. What's up?" He glanced at his watch as he spoke. He had been inside the house for sixty minutes. Over at Casa Whittington they probably hadn't started on the caviar appetizer yet.

"They're on their way back. Actually they left just over a quarter of an hour ago."

"What? Why didn't you call me?" Fifteen minutes. Hell. They were probably about to walk through the front door.

"I'm sorry. But William took ill. That's why the party broke up." A deep breath. Her voice tight. "As you can imagine, calling you was not exactly my first priority."

"OK. I must get out of here." A thought occurred to him. "Your husband. How is he?"

"He'll be fine. This happens quite often these days. But thank you for asking. Now go!"

He clipped the phone onto his belt again. Time to split. He turned to look at the cat, which was still giving him the evil eye from the top of the wardrobe. He was going to have to forget about shooing the animal out of the room and just hope the sisters would think they had neglected to close the door themselves. The book was back on the bed where he had found it, so that was taken care of. What else? The light. He should switch off the light.

As he walked out onto the landing, his eye fell on the door on the other side of the tallboy, which was still closed. Maybe he had time for a quick peek? Cautiously he opened the door and poked his head inside. Another bedroom, this one in shades of lilac and yellow. He was able to see without trouble because a lamp had been left on. Shell pink opera gloves were draped over a tilted mirror, which reflected a four-poster bed with a swath of gauze netting. But what drew his attention was the wall on the far side of the room. He had been looking for photographs and here they were, a veritable gallery. Snapshots, studio photographs, black-and-white, color. Dozens of pictures: many tacked up casually against a bulletin board, the edges overlapping; others elegantly framed.

Frankie had told him the sisters were attractive, and the glimpse he'd had of them when they left the house earlier this evening had seemed to confirm her judgment. But as he looked at these faces, encapsulated in silence, he realized "attractive" was far too anemic a word. These women were not merely conventionally pretty. They were startlingly—throat-catchingly—beautiful.

Minnaloushe—the redhead—was the softer of the two. Her cheekbones were as high as her sister's, but the planes of her face were more rounded, less sharp. Her mouth was full and blurred, her eyes pale green, their expression unfocused as though she had just tumbled out of bed and was looking at the world with dreamy eyes. Her figure bordered on the voluptuous: tiny waist, but quite heavy breasts.

Morrighan, in contrast, had the muscle definition of an athlete. Her arms were slim and corded; her long legs elegant but strong. She had blue eyes, the color so intense it looked almost fake. In one picture she was riding a horse, looking Andalusian in a severe black riding jacket and Spanish hat, at her throat a swirl of lace. It was an arresting picture, taken in profile. You could see the head of the horse, the black arch of its neck and one mad staring eye. The gloved hands of the rider held the reins in a steely grip. The overriding impression was of strength, concentration, grace.

There was very little family likeness between the two women, he thought, except that both had heart-shaped faces. As children, however, they had looked almost like twins. There were several pictures of them as little girls—gaps in their teeth, hair scraped back into tight little pigtails—and their mother had preferred to dress them in identical clothes, all sashed dresses, frilly socks and round-toed baby doll shoes. Rather old-fashioned, actually. No pictures of them in jeans and sneakers and baseball caps. As he looked at the photographs, he was reminded of a line by John Galsworthy: "One's eyes are what one is, one's mouth what one becomes." The faces of the little girls bore scant resemblance to their grown-up selves, but even at that early age, there was a surprisingly mature humor and intelligence in their gaze.

As his eyes continued to travel over the pictures on the wall in front of him, his heart skipped a beat. He had been searching for Robert Whittington tonight and suddenly, without warning, he had found him. There he was: thin, ascetic face, vulnerable eyes, a smile brimming over with delight. He was standing side by side with the sisters, and the picture had been taken against the backdrop of what looked like a public park. Hampstead Heath? In the background was green grass, flower beds and a number of colorful kites flying against a washed-out sky.

Whittington looked happy. He was staring straight at the camera. On his right side was Minnaloushe, one hand trying to keep her hair from blowing in the wind. Standing to his left and slightly behind him was Morrighan. Her slender fingers rested on his shoulder; her gaze was focused on a spot somewhere behind the photographer.

There were other pictures as well. In most of them Whittington was alone. In one he was in the garden, lying in a hammock, one long leg dangling over the side. In another he was sitting with his back propped against a tree trunk. It was the tree that grew next to the swimming pool—no mistaking those flame red flowers. There was a photograph of him pulling a funny face, eyes crossed comically, wearing a T-shirt stamped with the words *Hugs not Drugs*. Gabriel recognized the room. It was the living room at Monk House: those African masks on the wall were unmistakable. And peeping from behind Whittington's shoulder, the distinct design of the *Monas*.

There was also a framed eight-by-ten black-and-white photograph that for some reason he found disturbing. It showed Robert Whittington and the two sisters at what looked like the opening of an exhibition in some trendy art gallery. Whittington was peering earnestly at an oil painting. In the background were the sisters, each with a champagne flute in her hand. They were not looking at the painting, but at Whittington. And it was the expression on their faces that made him pause. Alert, eager, curious. There it was again: curiosity. Just like the woman at the swimming pool. They were watching Robert Whittington with a curiosity bordering on greediness. They seemed excited, fascinated, *turned on*. As though all their senses were quivering. Why?

He would have liked to take the picture with him, but it was framed and might be missed. He hesitated. Then he reached out and removed the snapshot of Robert and the two women on Hampstead Heath. There were so many pictures jostling for space here, it was probably safe to take this one.

Time to go. Time to go. Slipping the picture into the inner pocket of his jacket, he left the room, closing the door behind him. Quickly he descended the staircase, now black with shadows. As he reached the bottom stair, a sound made him pause. It was the sound of a key in a lock and it came from the front door—a door which, even as he glanced over at it, was already starting to open.

He made a beeline for the living room door, but the entrance hall with its army of potted plants was a bloody minefield. For one heart-stopping moment he almost kicked over a drooping aspidistra. But then he was in the living room and there, on the other side of the room, were the French doors. His route to escape.

Behind him in the entrance hall a light was switched on, the yellow stain stretching all the way from the hall to the living room door and spilling onto his feet. The sound of a woman's voice, the words indistinct, but the voice itself low-pitched and pleasant. Another female voice, this one light and breathy, saying, "You have to admit, though, he's pretty cute!"

Swiftly he traversed the room, making sure to give the wobbly wicker screen a wide berth. The French door opened under his hand, and he was in the garden. The sultry air and the sound of traffic was a shock after the hermetically sealed atmosphere of the house. He pushed the door softly shut and ran down the length of the darkened garden. When he reached the back door, which would give him access to the alley, he stopped to look back.

The French doors were brightly lit, the stained-glass insets glowing with color, and as he watched, someone pulled the shutters away from one of the windows and opened it wide. He could hear music playing. The garden was redolent with the scent of roses, the night air soaked with perfume.

Two figures were silhouetted against the bright light within. They were facing each other, their heads close together. There was something surreptitious in their posture, secretive even. Gabriel shivered though the night air was blood warm. The scent of roses seemed sickly all of a sudden, making him feel drugged and passive.

As he watched the two women, he felt as though the moment were frozen. A house with two figures in furtive conversation, an intruder looking in from the darkness, a garden awash in fragrance—this was an enchanted world with its own rules, remote from the city of London, which stretched around them in all directions like a pulsing organism. Time in here had stopped—even as it still flowed evenly outside the perimeters of these garden walls.

A car honked loudly, shaking him out of his stupor. What was he still doing here? He felt tired and his hand throbbed where the cat had scratched him. He suddenly had one overriding desire—to get away from this house. He looked back at the lighted window. The figures were gone.

He sighed, relieved now, eager to be on his way. But as he turned to leave, he thought he heard—faintly—the sound of a woman's laughter.

Entry date: 23 June

We still haven't found someone to play with. M thought she had a candidate but what a disappointment he turned out to be. He has no curiosity. No sense of adventure. He is definitely not a candidate for the game.

So M will now use him as a lover only. But I rather doubt he'll satisfy her. Very handsome but he knows it and no woman wants to feel that the man she's with thinks he's prettier than she is. He won't be around for long.

Thinking of which: the ideal lover, who would he be?

A man who is passionate. A man with a militant mind. A man with skilled fingers, who knows how to touch. He will seduce me with gentleness and know me in roughness.

Subtlety. Mastery. Danger.

Where to find such a man? What will be his name?

CHAPTER EIGHT

"So who did you say he was, exactly?" Frankie turned her head toward him and squinted against the sun. She had insisted on an outside table even though Gabriel hated sitting outside. In the country, dining al fresco had a certain bucolic charm, but in the city you were far too close to pedestrians spitting and sneezing all over your food. Not to mention the belching exhaust fumes.

"Isidore? He's an associate of mine. A computer specialist and very good at tracking things down. I asked him to look into Minnaloushe and Morrighan Monk and see if he can come up with anything interesting." Gabriel glanced at his watch. "Punctuality is not his strong suit, I'm afraid. But he'll be here." He lifted his arm and beckoned to the waitress. "More coffee?"

Frankie crumbled the croissant on her plate. "No, thanks. I had enough coffee last night to last me a lifetime."

"How's William doing?"

"Better," she said briefly.

He nodded. She obviously did not feel like talking. And she looked tired. The red dress she was wearing merely accentuated her fatigue, the joyous color at odds with the pallor of her skin, the dryness of her lips. There was a great sadness in her eyes.

So she really did care for the guy. He felt a sudden—and unwelcome—pang of jealousy. Frankie belonged to the past. Why did he care about the relationship she had with her husband?

"You really love him, don't you?"

"There's no need to sound quite so surprised."

"But I mean, honest now, Frankie. When you first met him . . . are we talking head-over-heels?"

She leaned forward. "We're talking butterflies in the stomach, clammy hands, and midnight fantasizing. I have never been more in love with any other man."

"Oh."

She smiled sardonically. "You think that after having you in my life, no other man would measure up, don't you?"

"Of course, not." But come on, he thought silently, what did Whittington have that he didn't? Only a few hundred million dollars.

She shook her head, gave a short laugh. "You're amazing. You've always thought you were 'the cutest thing in shoe leather.' That obviously hasn't changed."

He looked at her coldly.

"Oh, Gabriel. Stop sulking. Tell me about your visit to Monk House. You said apart from the photographs, there were no other signs of Robert?"

He sighed. "No. And I couldn't sense his presence in the house. No imprint."

"What about the woman in your ride, the masked one with the crow? Were you able to pick up an imprint from her?"

"Afraid not."

"Nothing at all?"

He shrugged. "Nothing definite, although I still think we're on the right track. The question is, of course, who was the woman in my ride? Minnaloushe or Morrighan? I've now seen pictures of both of them, but as the woman was masked and her hair covered with a hood, I still don't know which one it was."

She frowned. "Those two are very close. Who's to say it wasn't both of them?"

He shook his head. "I sensed only one woman in my ride. Not two. If a murder had taken place, only one woman was responsible. Only one woman physically placed her hands on Robert Whittington's head and pushed him down into the water. The other sister may be aware of what happened and she may even be an accessory after the fact, but only one of them actually committed the deed."

"The deed. God." She shivered. "It sounds so cold. You do realize you'll have to slam another ride? Try to go back; see if you can make more sense of it this time?"

"Yes, I know. I've been thinking about it."

"So when?"

"Soon." But he was starting to feel ambivalent about the whole thing. On the one hand, he was deeply intrigued—how could he not be—by what he had accessed during his ride. It had been a killer surge. So the urge to explore, which had always fueled his RV adventures, was very much present.

On the other hand, he had not exactly enjoyed the experience of going insane. And if he could give the drowning bit a miss as well, that would be fine with him too. Even more to the point: after this particular ride, when he finally got back to reality, his brain had continued to feel mauled—like a rugby ball after a hard season. This had never happened to him before and it was scary. He couldn't help feeling that if he slammed the ride again, he would be like a mad scientist injecting himself with his own untested and possibly lethal formula in order to see if it works.

"By the way, I've been meaning to ask you." Frankie was gesturing at his bandaged wrist. "What happened there?"

"I had a run-in with a rabid cat, last night. At Monk House."

"Oh, I remember that cat. Black, was it?"

"Nice pet. It almost took my hand off."

She smiled. "I'm sure you must have teased it."

"Teased it?"

"Well, when I visited the house it was purring and rubbing itself against my legs. A real sweetie."

He opened his mouth to reply but at that moment a shadow fell across the table. He felt a hand on his shoulder. "Sorry I'm late." Isidore, dressed in a pink tank top, his hairy, thin, white legs sticking out from a pair of lavishly printed swimming trunks, was grinning down at him. In his hand he held a sleek tan-colored briefcase. Briefcase and swimming trunks made for a rather interesting sartorial statement.

"You're very late."

"Traffic was a bitch, what can I say? And I used the Pringle can at Pittypats before I came. Guess what; the idiots are still using their WEP default settings." Isidore winked at him.

"Pringle can?" Frankie looked mystified.

Gabriel shook his head in warning at Isidore. Of course he knew that Frankie was aware what his chosen field of profession was these days, but no need to remind her of its more nefarious aspects. "Pringle can" was their code name for the very sophisticated directional antenna they used for targeting wireless systems.

Isidore flopped into the chair opposite. Holding out his hand, he said, "Mrs. Whittington. A real pleasure."

Frankie, looking a little startled, took the hand. "Thanks. But please call me Frankie."

"Frankie. That's a cool name."

She smiled, clearly charmed. "Thank you for helping me."

"No problem." He reached for the briefcase and threw a glance at Gabriel. "I managed to get quite a lot of stuff about the Monk sisters from the Internet. I'm not sure how helpful it will be, but for what it's worth, here it is." From the briefcase he extracted an orange folder. Placing it on the table in front of him, he opened it and blinked owlishly at the contents.

"Anything on that coat of arms, the *Monas*?"

"Not a coat of arms. A sigil."

"A what?"

"A sigil: a seal, or a device that supposedly has occult power in astrology or magic." Isidore spoke in the deliberately patient voice of someone having to explain something to a not-so-bright student.

"You don't say. So what are we talking about here, witchcraft?"

Isidore pursed his lips. "Well, witchcraft is such an emotive word, don't you think?"

"Oh for goodness' sake, Isidore. Get on with it. What the hell is it?"

"OK, OK." Isidore made a placating gesture with his hand. "First of all, the full name of this sigil is the *Monas Hieroglyphica*: the hieroglyphic monad. In 1564 it was used by one Dr. John Dee as the frontispiece for a book he wrote on mysticism, which includes all kinds of obscure references to numerology, the Kabala, astrology, cosmology and mathematics. Heavy stuff. By all accounts it is a work of mind-boggling complexity and Dee managed to write it in a mad frenzy over a period of only twelve days. This guy was a Jedi, I tell you."

"But what does it represent?"

"The *Monas* is several astrological symbols all bundled into one. Dee believed it to represent the unity of the cosmos."

"I still don't get what it is."

"Well, this is not just a symbol, understand. It is a seal infused with actual astral power. It not only talks the talk, it walks the walk. So not only does it *reflect* the unity of the universe, it is an actual tool with which to unify the psyche itself. And it's a symbol of initiation. Anyone who carries this mark on him is signaling that he is transformed."

"Alchemy." Frankie's voice was quiet. "That's what this is about, isn't it? Personal transformation."

Isidore looked at her, his gaze keen. "Yes. You know about this stuff, then."

"Alchemy was one of Robbie's great passions. He read tons of literature about it. I've always wondered why he had that thing tattooed on him."

Gabriel looked from Isidore to Frankie and back again. He felt left behind, as though they were speaking some foreign language, deliberately keeping him in the dark. "But alchemy is turning lead into gold, isn't it?"

Isidore shook his head. "That's only part of it. Alchemists were really involved in transforming the soul. Even the body. There are reports of alchemists becoming immensely old. Those who didn't get poisoned by the chemicals they were handling, that is."

"So who was John Dee?"

"Ah, now this is where it gets interesting. John Dee was your poster boy Renaissance man. He was a mathematical genius—his work anticipated Newton's by almost a hundred years—and without his mapmaking skills the most important naval explorations of the Elizabethan age could not have taken place. Furthermore, he was an adviser and a secret agent to Queen Elizabeth I. His spy name was 007. Neat, huh?" Isidore grinned, enjoying himself.

"Fascinating. So what?"

"Patience, my son. All will be revealed." Isidore nodded sagely and Gabriel bit his tongue.

"Among his many interests," Isidore continued serenely, "Dee had a deep and abiding fascination with the occult, which, in those days, was pretty risky, believe me. It could get you burnt at the stake before you could say abracadabra. Dee sailed very close to the wind indeed. The *Monas Hieroglyphica* is really a book on magic. Furthermore, Dee was an information freak, an absolute addict. He was not a wealthy man, but at one stage he had gathered in his house the most impressive library in the whole of Britain. Knowledge was his potion . . . or his poison, depending on how you look at it. He may have overdosed a bit. Turned gaga. He ended up thinking he could communicate with angels and became a laughingstock among his peers. Very sad, because he was seriously brilliant."

"All of this still does not explain why the Monk sisters have the *Monas* plastered up all over their house. You can hardly turn around without tripping over that emblem."

"Sigil."

"All right, then. Sigil."

"I think what we may have here is an example of ancestral pride."

"You mean . . . ?" Frankie leaned forward, eyebrows raised.

Isidore nodded with the smugness of a magician pulling an especially plump rabbit out of his hat. "Minnaloushe and Morrighan Monk are direct descendants of Dr. John Dee, the greatest mind of the Elizabethan era."

Frankie leaned back slowly. "Impressive."

"I'll say. I wouldn't mind an ancestor like Dee myself. That kind of genius in the gene pool is robust enough to survive the ages."

"No, I mean it's impressive that you managed to dig all of this up."

Isidore tried his best to look modest. "I have a small talent for—"

"Snooping," Gabriel interrupted. "Being nosy."

"No, it's healthy curiosity. Being aware. I'm sort of a Renaissance man myself."

Gabriel looked at Frankie. "Modesty is one of Isidore's more endearing qualities. You do realize that when he enters a room he has to walk sideways?" Frankie frowned in incomprehension. "Otherwise his swollen head will get stuck between the posts." Looking back at Isidore, he said, "OK, you. Good work. So the *Monas* is a magical seal created by a sixteenth-century madman."

"Inspired madman."

"OK. Inspired madman. Now what about his great-great-great-great-granddaughters?"

"I think you missed a few 'greats' there. But let's see. Well, to begin with, the sisters practice alchemy themselves. But of the less esoteric kind. They make perfumes, beverages and bath products based on spagyric principles."

"Spa—whatsisname?"

"Spagyric. To separate and reassemble. Breaking down the raw plant material into its active components and then remixing it along with the mineral residue—the alkaline ash—to become a whole balanced entity again."

Gabriel remembered the table with the chemistry equipment in the Monk House kitchen. "I think I saw their laboratory. So they sell this stuff?"

"Yes, on the Internet."

Gabriel grimaced. "This sounds very kooky. Did you happen to stumble onto any personal information about the sisters?"

"Of course. And fascinating it is too. The sisters Monk. Minnaloushe Monk is thirty-six years of age. Morrighan is a year older. Their mother passed away when they were in their teens—"

"Just like Robbie," Frankie interrupted.

"I suppose so." Isidore shrugged. "Anyway, Gabriel was right in thinking there's money in that family. By all accounts they do not want for anything and like the lilies of the field they need not toil or weave. Their commercial enterprises on the Internet are just pocket money for them."

"So let me guess," Gabriel said. "They also keep themselves occupied with charity. And they do the season. Glyndebourne, Wimbledon, Henley, the Cartier Polo Day? Late-night dinners at Gordon Ramsay's or Sketch? The south of France for summer, Aspen for winter?"

"Actually, no. Charity is high on their list but they also follow pursuits that are not exactly common among the ladies-who-lunch crowd. In Minnaloushe's case Great-Grandpapa Dee's genes are hard at work. She holds a doctorate from Imperial College and did her thesis on the topic of memory."

"She's a neurologist?"

"No, she's an academic. Her fields are mathematics and philosophy. She seems to be a perpetual student, though. No record of her ever teaching anywhere. But she has published several papers. I've downloaded a few and printed them out for you." Isidore slid a slim folder over to Gabriel. "Here you go. Bedtime reading for the brave."

Gabriel touched the folder listlessly. "Thanks. I can't wait."

"As far as I can make out, the response to her theories has been mixed. There are some who think she's the next Einstein, but most of her peers think she's a total flake. Part of the problem is that she seems to link religion—or at least spirituality—to what most scientists regard as simple brain function."

"Echoes of Papa Dee again."

"As you say. Anyway, she hasn't published anything for five years."

"So what does she do with herself these days?"

"Well, apart from mixing bubble bath, she also runs another business from home selling African masks."

Gabriel remembered the wall lined with masks in the living

room at Monk House. At the time he had wondered why anyone would want to live under the glare of all those empty eye sockets.

"The business is small but extremely lucrative," Isidore continued. "I've accessed her auction site, and some of those masks sell for several thousands of dollars. Not that she needs the money. This is just extra icing for the lady."

"And Morrighan? What gets her out of bed?"

"Well, she's an environmentalist. Very passionate about the welfare of mother earth."

Gabriel groaned. "Just what I need: another tree hugger. Remember Danielle?" For a period of six months he had dated a woman who, among other things, had persuaded him to tie himself to a tree trunk for five days in deepest midwinter to protest the building of an overpass. Very embarrassing and not his style at all. He had a vivid recollection of feeling wet and miserable and messing up one knee that still hurt in cold weather. And he also remembered that her friends were dauntingly well meaning and quite without any sense of humor. Thinking back, it was amazing he managed to stick it out with Danielle for so long. The sex must have been really good.

Isidore cocked an eye at him. "Of course I remember Danielle. But I don't think you get my drift here. You're thinking of the foot-fungus-and-Birkenstock brigade. Morrighan is on another level altogether. She's a genuine eco warrior. She'll eat Danielle for breakfast. Morrighan belongs to an all-female group that is very militant indeed. These women run with the wolves, man. They take no prisoners. She also has a record. She has been arrested three times and the last time she broke the jaw of a police officer. It landed her in a ton of trouble." Out of the folder Isidore slid a page with a grainy color picture on it. "I printed this from the Internet. The one with the red cap is Morrighan."

"Good grief." Gabriel stared at the image. It showed two women in combat gear rappelling down the side of a multistoried glass skyscraper like a pair of kamikaze trapeze artists. They were unfurling a monstrously big banner between them. The banner was still limp and Gabriel was only able to make out the first word of the slogan: "BOYCOTT."

"Boycott what?"

"Borgesse. They own and finance enterprises directly involved in genetically engineered food products."

Gabriel looked back at the picture again. "So the lady has a taste for danger. And violence. Interesting."

"I thought you'd like her. For the past two years, however, she's been quiet. I don't know what she's been up to during this time. Nothing which made headlines, that's all I can tell you."

Frankie touched the printout with one finger. "Does Minnaloushe share her sister's activism?"

"Well, actually . . ." Isidore paused and started to smile. "Minnaloushe isn't quite as physically oriented as Morrighan, you might say. Although, no—her interests are very physical indeed." The smile was now a grin.

"What are you talking about?"

"I think you should find out for yourself. Seeing is believing. You'll find her at this address in, oh . . ." Isidore peered at his watch. "An hour from now."

Gabriel glanced at the piece of paper. "The Wine of Life Society?"

"Yes. I've already made a reservation for you to sit in."

"Sit in on what?"

"Never mind. You just make sure you get there in time. Sorry, Frankie," Isidore said apologetically. "The reservation is only for one."

"That's all right. I need to get back home to William." Frankie stood up. "By the way," she said, as she gathered up her handbag, "what about partners? Do the sisters have significant others?"

"They certainly have 'others' but I doubt you can call them significant. These two girls believe in playing the field. From what I can gather from the society pages, there seems to be a steady stream of men in their lives. But their boredom threshold must be very low. All the guys they get involved with seem to have a very short shelf life."

"I'm on my way." Frankie held out her hand to Isidore, but then changed her mind and leaned over to give him a swift kiss on the cheek. "Thanks for going to all this trouble for me. I can't tell you how much I appreciate it."

Isidore ducked his head. "No problem. Happy to be of service."

She turned to Gabriel. "Call me?"

"Sure."

Another smile for Isidore and she was off, heels clicking, back straight. There was something gallant about Frankie, Gabriel thought. He had forgotten that quality of quiet courage, which had so attracted him when they were together at Oxford.

"Nice girl." Isidore touched his cheek. "Really nice. Why didn't the two of you make it? If it were me, I would have held on for dear life. She's the kind you want to get old with, man. How come you let her get away?"

Good question. Why did he let her get away? Because he hadn't been able to look her in the eyes any longer. Because a woman called Melissa Cartwright had crashed into their lives with the impact of a meteorite.

He shook his head. "Ancient history." Looking down again at the piece of paper in his hand, he said, "Three Lisson Street. This place is in Chelsea?"

"Yup. Only a few blocks away from Monk House itself."

"The Wine of Life Society. Why don't you just tell me what that is?"

"Oh, no." Isidore shook his head. "I wouldn't dream of ruining the surprise." He grinned widely. "But prepare to be wowed!"

CHAPTER NINE

*"Although art is indeed not the bread but **the wine of life**."* Jean Paul Richter *1763–1825*. The words were painted in flowing script high up against one wall. And below it: *"Art isn't something you marry, it is something you rape." Edgar Degas 1834–1917.*

Not exactly politically correct, Gabriel thought, but then Degas lived in an age when sensibilities were less easily bruised. His eyes traveled around the occupants of the room. Not that this lot would be easily offended. They were all men, and there was a decided air of bonhomie and a sort of faded rakishness about the group. Half-filled wine bottles—each tagged with the owner's name—shared space with easels, desks stacked with huge sheets of paper, pencils, paint-brushes, rags and boxes filled with stubby bits of chalk. It had already been explained to him that once you became a member, you were not only encouraged to bring along your own booze but were also allowed to leave it at the club for the next time—hence the identifying name tags. The air smelled pungently of turpentine, which surely must have deadened any palate to the more subtle nuances of a wine's bouquet, but he had the distinct impression it wouldn't trouble this crowd. And judging from what he could see, it would be no problem for most of the men present to polish off a bottle or two in one sitting. He glanced at his watch. It was only eleven o'clock in the morning but the cork was out of most of the bottles already.

A slightly built man with white hair and a straggly beard walked up to him. "Poetry or Life?"

"Pardon?" For a moment he thought the guy was trying to engage him in a philosophical discussion.

The man tapped the clipboard he was holding in his arm. "Are you signed up for the two-hour class on Chaucer or for the one-hour life class?"

Good question. After a moment's hesitation Gabriel said, "Life." Even Isidore wouldn't make him sit through a hundred and twenty minutes of *The Canterbury Tales*. Shit, he hoped not. With Isidore you never knew.

"Name?"

"Gabriel Blackstone."

The man studied the clipboard, one finger—green with pastel dust—traveling down a short list of names. "Blackstone. Yes." He jerked a thumb over his shoulder. "Easel three back there has been reserved for you. Make yourself at home. We'll start in another five minutes."

This was worse than Chaucer. He couldn't draw on the left side or the right side of his brain. Isidore was going to burn in hell for this. Approaching easel three with trepidation, he noticed a small leaflet tacked up against the crossbar.

A haven for professional and semiprofessional visual artists, writers and poets, the Wine of Life Society was first established in 1843 and has survived two world wars, a depression and several attempts to have it change its strict policy of gentlemen only. The club does, however, open its doors to ladies on the first Saturday of every month. Guest visits to gentlemen interested in joining the club can be arranged for a nominal fee.

No ladies. And this was not the first Saturday of the month. Isidore had told him Minnaloushe Monk would be present. If no women were allowed, what the hell was he doing here?

The door on the far side of the room opened. A woman, swaddled in a white toweling robe, walked toward the raised dais in the middle of the room. She was barefoot and had long hair reaching to her shoulders. Long red hair.

He stared. He could actually feel his jaw dropping. She turned around, her back to the class, and let the robe fall to the floor. She was naked. Quite wide shoulders, a lovely long back and, at the base of her spine, a delicate tattoo. It was with a sense of inevitability that he recognized the design. What looked like the sign for female sexuality superimposed on a rose. The *Monas*. Of course, what else?

Facing the class once more, she gracefully lowered herself and settled among the clutch of pillows piled up on the dais, her long limbs sprawling. There was no attempt at modesty. One leg was slightly raised, the other in a flat triangle, the foot resting on the inner thigh. The pose left absolutely nothing to the imagination.

Heavy breasts with dusky pink aureoles. Rounded hips and arms. She was far from being overweight, but there was a softness, a lusciousness, about her that was almost old-fashioned in this age in which a more angular kind of beauty was prized. She had long, deeply elegant legs and thin ankles. What struck him was how relaxed she was. There wasn't a hint of tension in her body. Her face was serene, and she had that unfocused look in her eyes he recognized from the photographs he had studied in Monk House. As though she was just waking up from a particularly potent dream. And to think that behind those limpid eyes lay a Ph.D. mind.

But her mind was not exactly what he was most interested in right this minute. *Prepare to be wowed*, Isidore had said. Well, he was certainly wowed all right. He could hardly swallow; his mouth was that dry.

But he couldn't just sit here stunned. Clutching the charcoal in one sweaty fist, he hesitantly drew a few whisper-thin lines. But how to reproduce glorious flesh and blood on the flat emptiness of an unforgiving piece of paper, that was the question. More to the point, how to ignore such glorious flesh and blood and concentrate solely on technique. He sneaked a surreptitious look around him. The other men in the class didn't seem to have a problem shoving their baser instincts back into the cave. There was no leering or lip smacking, that's for sure. They were sketching with vigor and, he couldn't help but notice, surprising skill. At the easel to the left of him was a man who was a dead ringer for Vin Diesel—checked shirt, bulging biceps, shaved skull. He was holding the stick of charcoal with great delicacy, drawing with enviable confidence. And what at first had looked like random strokes were starting to take on the form of something beautiful. And recognizable. Gabriel's own attempt—if not quite in the stick figure category—looked like a rather pathetic attempt at primitive art.

All those eyes on her but she seemed hardly aware of their presence. She was looking at a spot somewhere in middle distance, but there was nothing studied about her detached attitude. Every now and then she would blink—almost in slow motion—and her eyes would make a leisurely sweep of the room. They met his twice. The sensation was strange. The first eye contact lasted only a second, but he felt a tiny shock run through him. The second time her eyes lingered on him for longer, and the touch of her gaze stayed with him even after she had looked away.

He was surprised when she stood up and slid the robe back on. He looked at his watch. Difficult to believe, but a full hour had passed since she had walked into the room. Around him the men were stretching and packing up their equipment. The atmosphere of studious calm that had prevailed was disappearing. Someone said something under his breath, and it was met with a few loud guffaws.

He was bent over, rummaging inside his backpack for the keys to his car, when he became aware of two bare feet standing next to him. The toes were small with the nails painted a soft pink. He had just been staring at them for an hour. They really were quite lovely.

"So my bum looks that big?"

He straightened. Minnaloushe Monk was smiling quizzically, amused.

"Uh . . ." He stared at the canvas and his miserable attempt at artistry. This was truly embarrassing. Thank goodness she had a sense of humor.

He turned back to her, ruefully. "Please don't be offended. It is the skill of the artist, not the beauty of the sitter, which is at fault."

She smiled again. Her eyes were pale green with fugitive yellow flecks, and they tilted just slightly at the corners, conveying an impression of quite delicious catlike femininity. "Very gallant." Her voice was just the tiniest bit breathy. She lifted an eyebrow. "I may be wrong, but I get the impression that you are . . . new to drawing?"

"I think it's a question of enthusiasm outstripping talent. But let me introduce myself. Gabriel Blackstone, artist manqué."

"Hmm." After a few moments she held out her hand. "I'm Minnaloushe Monk." Her grip was soft but far from flaccid.

"So what is it you do, Gabriel Blackstone? When you're not in pursuit of the muse, that is."

She was still smiling, but he had the impression that her attention was not quite with him any longer, that for some reason she was losing interest in the conversation. She had turned slightly sideways, as though about to move away.

He took a deep breath. "I'm a thief."

"A jewel thief, no doubt." She was playing along, but she was humoring him. She probably thought this was a rather lame pickup line.

"Oh, no. Nothing as romantic as that. I steal information."

For the first time she looked at him fully. Her pupils swelled. He got the feeling that only now was she truly focusing on him, seeing him as a person.

"Information?"

"Data."

"How?"

"Mostly off the computers of big companies."

If she was shocked she certainly did not show it. She was staring at him avidly and her voice was tinged with excitement. "It must be an amazing sensation: having all that information at your fingertips."

He grinned. "You could say that."

"Do you make the information your own?"

He paused. He wasn't sure what she meant. "I sell it. Like thieves do."

"Of course." She continued staring at him. Her gaze had changed from soft focus to laser-sharp intensity. He was starting to feel uncomfortable.

"And you? Is this a well-paid gig? Modeling?"

She laughed. "Hardly. This is just something I do on the side. I sell masks. Mostly African. Some Polynesian."

"It sounds fascinating. I'd love to see your shop."

"I work from home." She was still staring at him. "If you're interested, why don't you come with me and take a look? Maybe you'll see something that strikes your fancy."

"You mean now?"

"No time like the present. I just need a minute to get dressed." She looked at the keys in his hand. "You have your car here? Good. I live close by but you can give me a lift."

He couldn't believe it was going to be as easy as this. He had meant to pique her interest by confessing to being a thief, but he had somehow managed to say the magic word and the door to Monk House was to be opened to him. If only he knew what the magic word was. Maybe she was simply turned on by the fact that he was breaking the law. Bored little rich girl looking for a vicarious thrill.

When she reappeared, she was wearing a long summery dress with thin spaghetti straps. She looked younger, less sophisticated. But what made him feel suddenly short of breath was the thin silver chain around her neck. A chain from which dangled a charm in the shape of the letter *M*.

"Are you OK?" She was looking at him inquiringly.

"Sure." He dragged his eyes away from her neck. If he kept staring at her throat, he was sure to creep her out. Furthermore, it was not yet the time to jump to any conclusions, pendant or no pendant. But it was difficult to keep his excitement in check. There was no doubt in his mind. The chain around her neck was the same as the one worn by the woman at the pool.

They had stopped next to the Jag. As he unlocked the door for her, he moved closer. If he could get a whiff of her perfume, and if it matched the scent worn by the masked woman . . . But in this he was disappointed. She smelled of soap and shampoo. Clean, fresh.

He closed the door and got in on the driver's side. As he turned the key in the ignition, she ran her forefinger along the dashboard. "Walnut?"

"Yes. Nonstandard, though. I was lucky to get it."

"The XK150 is my favorite model. It has the best bones. And great torque."

He took his eyes off the road for a second and glanced over at her. "You're into cars?"

"I like cars. But the petrol head is my sister. She could get a job as a mechanic. So where did you find this lady?" She patted the dashboard again.

"I found her on the Internet, actually. I was smitten and bought her before I even saw her in the flesh. Admittedly she wasn't in good shape when I finally got my hands on her. It took a lot of work and she's high-maintenance. But then, one has to remember she's all of forty-seven years old."

"A man who can appreciate a mature woman is rare. And anything worthwhile is high-maintenance, anyway."

"Amen to that." He suddenly realized he was involuntarily pointing the car in the direction of Monk House. As he wasn't supposed to know where she lived, it was a rather dumb move.

"Where to?" he asked quickly. "Am I going the right way?"

"Hmm? Oh. Yes, actually. Just another two blocks. Then turn right. It's the house on the corner."

There was a nonresidential parking space right in front of the house. While she was busy unlocking the front door, Gabriel fed some pound coins into the meter. Sixty minutes. He doubted he would be asked to stay that long, but you never knew.

As he stepped into the entrance hall, he again registered the strange potpourri of fragrances he had noticed the night before. An unusual combination of scents. That acrid, bitter smell of alkaline ash overlaid by the sweeter smell of roses and tangerines. But no one could ever doubt that there were women living in this house.

"Morrighan?" Minnaloushe stood at the bottom of the staircase, looking up. "Are you here?"

There was no answer. After a moment or two, she turned away. "I was hoping my sister was in. I'd like you to meet her."

Flattering. And baffling. He was not an unduly modest guy, but he still couldn't figure out why this woman had not only brought him to her house, but now wanted to introduce him to the relatives as well. He doubted it was because she was bowled over by his sex appeal. She was watching him with that speculative look he had noticed earlier. As though she were an entomologist and he was some kind of interesting lepidopteran. It made him feel slightly embarrassed. She, on the other hand, was completely relaxed. It still amazed him that it didn't bother her in the slightest to be in the presence of a man she didn't know who had been staring at her in the altogether for a good part of the morning.

He looked around him. "This is a lovely staircase."

"Isn't it?" She nodded emphatically, the red hair swinging silkily against one bare shoulder. "It's my favorite thing in the house. I love staircases. I won't be able to live in a place without one. I believe they're essential to anyone wanting to live an interesting life. There are so many wonderful stories of houses with staircases: *Gone with the Wind, War and Peace* . . ."

"*Bluebeard?*"

"Of course. I had forgotten that one." She smiled. "Through here." She gestured to the door leading to the living room.

The room looked even larger than it had the night before. He noticed that the computers were switched off, the screen savers of the woman holding an exploding sun replaced by blackness. It reminded him of another problem. The diary. And the other password-protected file: *The Promethean Key*. How to access those files?

The tarantula was still inside its glass box. Hairy, mean-looking, at least in daylight it seemed real and less like something from an insane hallucination.

Minnaloushe saw him looking at it and smiled. "Why do I get the impression you don't really care for spiders?"

"I can't say that I do."

"This one is from South America. He's quite harmless, you know."

"He's still ugly."

"Beauty is in the eye of the beholder." Without warning, she pushed the lid off the glass case and reached inside. When she extracted her hand, the spider was sitting on the inside of her hand, the hairy body almost filling her palm, the long legs balanced on her splayed fingers.

He took an involuntary step backward. "What makes you keep it? Is it a pet?"

"Let's just say I'm fascinated by it. As I am by all things magical."

"Magical?"

"Well, think of it this way. Goliath here moves so delicately, he leaves no prints. Can you imagine that? A creature leaving no trace of its passing. Like a ghost. As my sister always says, if that's not magical, what is?"

She brought her other hand close to the first. He noticed that the insides of her palms were pale pink and the lines ran deep and true. With a lifeline like that she was going to live to be a hundred. After a moment's hesitation, the tarantula stepped gingerly from one hand to the other.

"But you're not interested in Goliath." She inserted her hand back inside the glass box and deposited the spider gently onto the granite pebbles. "You want to look at my masks. Let me show you." Turning toward him, she touched his arm lightly and pointed at the wall. "Here they are. You like?"

Not really, he thought. They were rather sinister-looking.

"Where do you find them?"

"I have a number of scouts I buy from. And once a year I travel to Africa myself."

He let his eyes travel over the rows of stylized faces. Enigmatic. Brooding. *Unknowable.*

"How did you become interested in masks?"

"I'm interested in identity. And transformation."

Transformation. OK, this rang a bell. Isidore saying, *Alchemists were really involved in transforming the soul.* And there was that passage in the book in the bedroom. He wasn't able to remember the exact words but something about transforming yourself into divine man, or something equally kooky.

She spoke again. "Most African masking has to do with representing spirits, especially ancestral spirits. In some cultures—for example, the Mende of Sierra Leone—a mask is a tool for moving onto a higher plane. By donning the mask the masker actually *becomes* the spirit. So the process is not representation but transformation."

"I've always thought masks had to do with concealment."

"Concealment is a vital part, of course. Hiding your identity. Or adopting a false one." She looked at him quizzically. "You should understand that."

His heart missed a beat. "What do you mean?"

"Well, you live in cyberspace. And in cyberspace one can so easily adopt an alias. That's when pinpointing someone's true identity becomes the real prize, don't you think? One's true name is the ultimate secret."

"I suppose so." His heart was still racing. In order to hide his confusion, he pointed to a sloe-eyed mask with a wide nose and fastidious sneer. It also had teeth.

"I rather like this one."

"You have a good eye. That is a very rare mask indeed. It is from Central Africa—one of the *Makishi* masks. They are used during the male circumcision ceremony. Usually, after the ceremony, the masks are burned. So I'm very lucky that this one got rescued before it was destroyed."

He reached out his hand, but before he could touch the mask, she said: "I wouldn't do that, if I were you."

He stopped, hand arrested in midair. "Why not?"

"It is believed that *Makishi* masks like this one are so powerful and potent that uninitiates touching the mask will become diseased."

"Diseased?"

"The body may contract a horrible illness. Or the mind could break down."

He slowly lowered his arm. "Nice. Do you believe in this stuff?"

She lifted an eyebrow. "If you play safe, you don't get hurt."

"If you play safe, you don't have fun."

"How true." She gave him that appraising look once again, the green eyes considering. As though she were weighing him up, he thought. Wondering if he would make the grade.

"This may be more your style." She lifted a roughly hewn, heart-shaped mask from the wall. "From the Kwele tribe, Gabon."

He took it from her rather gingerly. "What is its purpose?"

"To fight witchcraft."

He glanced over at her, surprised. She was smiling gently, the expression in her eyes hard to read.

He looked back at the face in his hands. The features were quite delicate, unlike the *Makishi* mask with its aggressive teeth.

"Well, that could come in handy, I suppose. How much for this one?"

"Why don't you live with it first? See if you like it? I encourage all my clients to try out their masks first. Find out if they can share a room with it."

"That's very generous of you. Thanks." And it would give him a pretext to come back. A reason to contact her again.

"Are you thirsty?" she asked suddenly. "Would you like some tea? I usually make a pot of my own home-brewed ginkgo and alfalfa leaf tea at this time."

Alfalfa leaf tea didn't sound appetizing but he nodded. "Thank you, yes."

"Let's go through to the kitchen."

As they entered the kitchen, he stiffened. On top of one of the chairs was his nemesis of the night before. The devil cat. And the animosity was still mutual. He had hardly spotted the cat, when it got to its feet, tail swishing, eyes fixed on him with unwavering intensity.

"Hey, Bruno." Minnaloushe stooped and picked it up. "What's wrong?"

Gabriel eyed the cat with trepidation. It was tense as a coil and seemed ready to jump out of her arms and launch itself at him.

"I don't think it likes me."

She looked down at the cat and scratched it behind the ears. "That's strange. Bruno is very affectionate normally. Ah, well." She smiled. "He's male. You're male. This is his turf so maybe it's just a question of protecting his territory."

Great, Gabriel thought. A pissing contest. With a cat. Bruno's eyes gleamed. He opened his mouth and closed it again without making a sound. The effect was weird.

Gabriel cleared his throat. "Bruno. I've always thought that to be quite a macho name. You know, the kind given to stevedores. Or bouncers. Or opera singers."

"Or martyrs." She kneeled and allowed the cat to jump out of her arms. It immediately moved away, back slightly arched, tail straight, and again it opened its mouth in that unnerving silent grimace. "Bruno is named after Giordano Bruno."

Her tone of voice made it clear that he was supposed to know who that was. He made a kind of noncommittal sound.

Her lips curved. "He was an Italian magician who was tortured in the chambers of the Inquisition. And then burned at the stake."

How charming. He was trying to think of a suitable response, when he heard the front door banging shut and the unmistakable sound of a bag dropped to the floor.

"That will be my sister." Minnaloushe glanced at him. "Excuse me, will you? I'll be right back."

"Sure." He watched as she left the room, leaving him and Bruno alone to stare warily at each other.

He waited. The ticking of the old-fashioned kitchen clock sounded inordinately loud. He could just hear the murmur of voices coming from the hall, the tones low and hushed. He recognized Minnaloushe's breathy voice. Morrighan's was lower. Although he couldn't make out the words, he knew as certain as though he was standing right next to them that he was the subject of the conversation.

And then they were suddenly both in the kitchen. They stopped inside the door, blocking it, and for one brief moment he had the extraordinary feeling of being boxed in and taken prisoner. But then Minnaloushe moved forward, smiling. "Gabriel, this is Morrighan. My big sister."

The first thing he noticed about Morrighan Monk was her eyes. It would be the first thing anyone noticed. The photographs he had looked at the night before had given him an indication of how startling they were, but actually seeing her face-to-face was something else altogether. Her eyes were amazing. The iris was the bluest blue he had ever seen and her eyeballs were white as snow. But the effect was quite chilly. It wasn't that her eyes were expressionless, far from it. It was more a case of the brilliance and depth of eye color making their expression difficult to gauge. Minnaloushe's eyes made one think of the ocean. Morrighan's eyes made one think of space.

The second thing he noticed was the pendant around her neck. A thin silver chain with the letter *M* dangling from it. Oh, hell. Just when he thought he had it all figured out. So he still didn't know which of the two sisters was the woman he saw in his ride.

Morrighan was dressed in shorts, a light blue T-shirt and sneakers. She had, he couldn't help but notice, fabulous legs. Her long black hair was scraped back in a ponytail and fell down her back like a gleaming snake. She smelled faintly of sunbaked sweat. There was a sheen on her cheekbones and where the hair sprang from her forehead.

"So how was the jump?" Minnaloushe had put the kettle to boil and was now arranging some cups and saucers.

"Great. I'm going back on Saturday." Morrighan glanced at Gabriel. "Bungee jumping," she explained. "It's a passion of mine."

Bungee jumping. To Gabriel it evoked uncomfortable images of canyons and bridges and deep ravines. He wondered where one would go to bungee jump in London.

"Chelsea Bridge," she said as though he had asked aloud. "There's a crane there, which is just perfect. By the way," she turned her head toward Minnaloushe, "the locksmith will be coming by later this afternoon."

"Good." Minnaloushe pushed a cup toward him. It was filled with a rather oily-looking green liquid. She looked at Gabriel briefly. "We're having the locks replaced. We think we may have had an intruder on the premises last night."

He tried to keep his voice normal. "A burglar? Was anything stolen?"

"Not exactly. And no breaking upon entering."

"Oh?"

"But we noticed a number of small things that were not quite right, you know." Morrighan pulled out a chair at the kitchen table and sat down. "For example, my scarf had been lying on the floor when we went out last night and when we got back someone had picked it up. Also, Bruno was in a room where he shouldn't have been."

"Yes," Minnaloushe added. "And someone also went through the food in our fridge. Rather disgusting that. We just threw out everything we had in there."

What the hell was this? He had hardly touched the stuff in the fridge. He thought back. If he remembered correctly he had lifted the corner on a carton filled with duck confit. And he had turned the champagne bottle around to see the label. And the scarf on the floor? How could they have noticed? In the dictionary the names of these women should be next to the entry for "anal-retentive."

"And the bastard was in the bedrooms as well. He took something. Not anything valuable. But something of sentimental value to both of us."

So they knew about the photograph. A small chill touched the back of his neck.

"That must be distressing for you." He took a sip of the green liquid. The tea was quite vile but it gave him a second or two to collect himself. "Maybe you should let the police know."

Morrighan smiled a faintly contemptuous smile. "It's not worth the hassle. We'll deal with it ourselves." She stretched, lithe as a cat. "I need a hot shower." She stretched again. "It was a good jump. Nothing like pushing the edge to make you feel alive, don't you think?"

He made another noncommittal sound.

"From the expression on your face, I take it you don't agree?"

"Fortune cookie philosophy is not my thing."

"Meaning?" A slight frown.

"The whole idea that pushing the edge of the envelope will make you feel more alive . . . it seems pointless, to me. And a bit of a cliché, quite frankly."

He had gone too far. Her eyes were steel.

"What are you doing on Saturday morning?"

"Saturday?"

"Yes. Why don't you join me for a jump? Try out my fortune cookie philosophy for yourself."

For a moment he stared at her, his brain on pause. He had hoped to engage her in a little playful sparring. He certainly hadn't bargained on the possibility that she would challenge him to a duel. He didn't have the slightest wish to go tumbling through space with a rope fixed to his ankle. Surely even Frankie would agree that this would be going above and beyond the call of duty.

The women were watching him steadily. Under the unblinking gaze of the two pairs of eyes—one green, one blue—he felt like an insect pinned to a board. Something told him the correct answer to her question would be crucial if he wanted a return invitation.

He took a deep breath. "Sounds like a plan."

"Good." Morrighan looked at Minnaloushe, and for a moment he fancied that something passed between the two women. A kind of mental nod.

"OK. That's settled then." Morrighan got to her feet. "I'll meet you at the Chelsea Bridge on Saturday morning at 9:00 A.M. Yes?"

He nodded. "Fine."

At the doorway she paused and looked back at him over her

shoulder. "And don't worry," she said, eyes crinkling. "I'll take good care of you."

That evening he made himself bangers and mash for dinner. Comfort food. Rather than try and pair this fare with a suitable wine, he settled for lager even though it was not his favorite drink. While eating, he paged through Minnaloushe Monk's research papers, which Isidore had given him that morning. They were dauntingly esoteric. The language was often so dense and the math so incomprehensible, that he shook his head in disgust.

But her central hypothesis, as far as he could make out, was curiously simple and unscientific. Memory, she maintained, was what set man apart from his animal relatives. Man's soul is inextricably bound to his power of recollection.

And along with this hypothesis came a warning:

Our brains have become lazy. We are losing the skill of remembrance. Our long-term memories are eroding. Instead of exercising our natural ability to remember, the way our ancestors had to do, we rely on modern technology—the Internet, TV, photocopiers—to prop up our weakening ability to recollect facts and events. We are experts at skimming. We are failures at remembering

We walk along this path at our peril. Without a highly robust memory, we lack the ability to get a handle on the turbulent universe we live in. Without a flexible memory, we cannot draw connections between widely differing concepts.

More than that: we are in danger of losing our very souls. Memory is divine. It is what gives man his celestial spark.

No wonder she had picked up flak from her colleagues, Gabriel thought as he closed the folder. Any hypothesis involving souls and psyches—not to mention celestial sparks—would sit ill in the halls of institutional science. She was treading on some powerful taboos.

But enough of this. There was a kind of quirky charm to her theories, but they were hardly likely to have anything to do with Robert Whittington and his unfortunate demise. He pushed the folder away from him.

After stacking the dishwasher, he made himself a cappuccino and carried the cup over to his work desk. From here he was still able to see the lights on the other side of the river.

It was time he started making notes, organizing his thoughts. He sat down in his swivel chair and opened his laptop.

Robert Whittington had been an accomplished artist. Earlier today Gabriel had tried to check with the Wine of Life Society to find out if Whittington had been a member, but the club was nothing if not discreet about its membership and would not confirm whether this was the case. That hadn't stopped him, of course. It had been child's play to hack into the club's database and confirm his suspicions. Robert Whittington had indeed been a member these past three years.

He placed his fingers on the keyboard of his computer and typed:

Wine of Life Club. Robert meets Minnaloushe?
Minnaloushe=Mathematician and philosopher. Sells masks. Nude model.
Morrighan=environmentalist. Thrill seeker.
Both sisters=alchemists.
Descendants of John Dee. Elizabethan alchemist and creator of the Monas Hieroglyphica. Primary goal of Dee's studies: personal transformation. Robbie also fascinated by alchemy and personal transformation. Another link between Robbie and sisters?

He paused. He was now almost sure that the woman in his ride was one of the Monk sisters. But which one?

Woman wore a pendant with the initial M. Minnaloushe or Morrighan?
Woman wore a mask. Mask=Minnaloushe?

What else? The woman in his ride had carried a black crow on her shoulder. The same crow that had followed him as he had walked through the house of many doors. Not that this detail made any sense. But for what it was worth he added another entry.

Crow.

As he typed, the bandage on his wrist hampered the movement of his hand at the keyboard. He wished he could get rid of it, but those scratches made by Bruno were still raw and inflamed-looking, and instead of itching, which would signal healing, they were burning like the dickens. Thinking of Bruno, he frowned.

Cat. Named after Giordano Bruno. Scientist and martyr. Died at the stake.
Two computer files. Password protected.
IBM computer=Diary.
Mac=The Promethean Key.
Work out access plan for both computers.

He sat back in his chair and read through what he had written. Hardly impressive. He wasn't any nearer to knowing how and why Robert Whittington was murdered or to answering the one question that mattered most.

Murderess=Minnaloushe or Morrighan?

He held the question mark key down for a few moments too long and a row of question marks followed like an insistent call to arms.

Murderess=Minnaloushe or Morrighan?????

For a few seconds he stared at the screen absentmindedly. At some level his mind took in the noise of a faraway car alarm, the sudden burst of laughter coming from the pavement down below, the presence of eyes focused upon him.

Eyes.

He whipped around in his chair—heart pounding—and looked straight into the round eyes of the mask given to him by Minnaloushe.

Shit. He touched his forehead. He had hung that mask himself only a few hours ago. He had been quite pleased with it, actually. It went well with the Shoowa wall hanging he had bought during a holiday in Kenya.

After a moment's hesitation he got up from his chair and walked toward the wall. As masks go, this one really wasn't too grim-looking. The only thing that bothered him slightly was the slitted mouth. It was pulled back in the semblance of a thin smile, making it appear as though the mask were having a small joke at his expense.

Well, nix to you too, he thought and cuffed the wooden face lightly with his knuckles.

Now that his heart had stopped tripping, he was suddenly tired. Enough of this for one night. But tomorrow he should talk to Isidore on the progress he'd made on the Pittypats case. It wouldn't do to neglect the bread and butter in favor of playing Sherlock.

At the door he stopped and switched off the light. The room turned dark. The screen of his computer was a bright oblong of light in the gloom, the words dark against the white background.

Murderess=Minnaloushe or Morrighan?????

Entry Date: 29 June

Success! We may have found someone new to play with. He is the complete opposite of R. But M is right. R wasn't strong enough. He was not up to the challenge. One thing's for sure: G will be a different proposition altogether. We'll be playing with a sophisticate this time, not an innocent.

He is undeniably hot. He has the look of an adventurer—a modern-day buccaneer. I can quite imagine him standing on the bow of a tall ship with a knife between his teeth, ready to plunder and burn!

There is undoubtedly a strong streak of narcissism there. And with G it is more than just personal vanity; it is also a vanity of the mind. A deep belief in his own ability. A conviction that he can take on anyone, on any terms.

Let's hope a pedestrian mind doesn't hide behind that too handsome face.

But the indications are good. He is a risk taker and a thief. And not just any thief: an information thief. As M said, we could hardly ask for a more tailor-made description of the perfect playmate. A man who immerses himself in data every day but for whom knowledge is just currency.

We can change this. M and I can take him on a journey all the way to the stars.

Will he be up to it? Will he be strong enough? Maybe we'll have a better idea by Saturday.

CHAPTER TEN

Saturday. A beautiful morning. Blue skies, light breeze. When Gabriel stopped for his take-out coffee at Starbucks, everyone in the shop was slurping lattes and nibbling pastries. Not a frown in sight. Only shiny, happy people.

Except for him. He felt sluggish and his disposition was sour. He was also pretty much freaked out of his mind. Today was D-day. The day he was scheduled to experience the joy of the bungee jump. He wondered where the word "bungee" came from. It sounded so benign—like Tumbler Tots—some or other mildly strenuous activity meant for children. Except that in another thirty minutes or so, he would be shouting "Geronimo" and diving headfirst from a great height toward the Thames.

As he turned the Jaguar in the direction of Chelsea Bridge, he decided he must have been delirious when he agreed to partake in this insanity. He was going to die today, Morrighan Monk's promise to "take good care" of him notwithstanding. Besides which, it had just occurred to him that the woman who was going to supervise his attempt at playing Icarus might also be the person who had killed poor Robert Whittington. A great thought, that. Why didn't he think of it before?

The lady was waiting for him dressed in tight-fitting Lycra and a snow white T-shirt with a low scoop neck. On one breast was a small tattoo, a replica of the one on her sister's lower back. Very sexy, even though this preoccupation with the *Monas* was getting on his nerves a bit. Her black hair was once more pulled back in a ponytail and her eyes were even bluer than he remembered.

"Hi." She nodded at him. "So you came."

"Of course. Didn't I say I would?"

"So you did." She shrugged, smiled slightly. "Great car, by the way."

"Thanks." He looked past her and up into the sky to where a light blue crane reached upward to what seemed an obscene altitude.

She followed his gaze. "Pretty high. Three hundred feet. You'll be able to dine out on this for a long time."

"Uh-huh." He tried to think of something witty to say but his powers of repartee seemed to have deserted him.

"OK, well. Let's get this show on the road. I need to talk to Wayne to find out when we're scheduled." She pointed to where a short line of people were waiting with expressions that ranged from the extremely apprehensive to the "Look-at-me-I'm-such-a-tough-mother" smugness. At the front of the line was a painfully skinny man wearing a very tiny red swimsuit. He was talking to a man with blond hair who was dressed in overalls with the word "JUMPMASTER" emblazoned on the back.

Gabriel looked at Morrighan as a fresh wave of apprehension hit him. "Why is that guy wearing a swimsuit? Am I actually going to hit the water?"

"No, no." Her voice was soothing but there was a gleam in her eyes. "This is not a dunk jump. You won't get wet, don't worry. I don't know why that guy feels the need to show off his Speedo. People come here dressed in all kinds of weird outfits. I've been here when someone took the jump dressed in a bridal gown. Another guy arrived wrapped in a straitjacket."

"Well, he may have had the right idea."

"Oh, come on." The gleam in her eye was more pronounced now. "You're going to have fun, you'll see."

The man with the jumpmaster overalls came up to them and smiled winsomely. His accent was Australian and his intonation was decidedly odd. It sounded as though every sentence ended on an exclamation mark. "Morrighan! I'm going to let you guys go up first! Is this the lucky victim?!" A crushing handshake and another dazzling, minty fresh smile. "Cool! You're in for a treat! Sweetheart! There's no one up there right now! Can I leave it to you to get the ropes on this guy?!" It made Gabriel tired just listening to him.

"Of course." Morrighan gave the jumpmaster a smile that was pretty dazzling in itself. "I'll take care of it." She turned toward Gabriel. "Wayne and I are old friends. We used to go BASE jumping Down Under."

BASE jumping. She said it so matter-of-factly. No wonder bungee jumping wouldn't faze her. Gabriel had a friend who used to BASE jump as well. Not anymore. His friend's parachute had failed and he had gone into the wall of the dam from which he had thrown himself. With BASE jumping there was no reaching for a reserve chute in case of a crisis. There was no time. His friend had died within seconds of the moment his parachute malfunctioned. If this woman did BASE, she was looking for a kinky way to commit suicide.

He took a deep breath, trying to put thoughts of smashed bodies hurtling through space from his mind.

"So, what's next?"

Morrighan lifted an eyebrow. "Last chance to go to the loo."

He swallowed, trying to hold on to his dignity. "I'm fine."

"Good. What do you weigh?"

"What?"

"Your weight," she said impatiently. "How much do you weigh? We need to know so that we can get the right ropes on you."

"Oh. Eighty-six kilos." Which she might think was just a tad on the heavy side for his frame, but he was not going to give in to vanity and lie when his continued well-being depended on being given a rope that could handle his bulk.

"Right. Green for you. Orange for me." She caught his look. "Different-colored ropes relate to different weights."

"You're doing a jump as well?"

"Well, actually," she smiled slowly, "I thought it might be fun if we jumped in tandem. You know, this being your first time. It might be best if I held your hand, so to speak."

Jumping in tandem. How exactly did that work, Gabriel wondered. Somehow he had created a picture in his mind of plunging to earth with arms stretched out wide like a bird in flight. Slipping the surly bonds of earth and all that. The image of himself with arms clamped for dear life around his female companion was not quite as heroic.

The cage was really a basket, which, it turned out, was to be their mode of transportation up the crane. He stepped inside gingerly. It did not feel particularly secure, although probably nothing except terra firma would have felt secure to him right now.

As the cage started its ascent, Morrighan spoke briskly. "OK. I know you're probably feeling quite concerned, but bungee jumping is far from lethal. This is what you can expect. The first part of the jump is the most intense. You'll be falling from zero to fifty miles per hour in only a couple of seconds. After that your speed decreases until you reach the full extent of the jump, after which you slowly accelerate again. A few more oscillations and the crane will deposit you back on land."

"That's the part that sounds pretty good to me, right now."

"Truly, there's nothing to worry about. They do numerous safety checks. And I'll be right at your side." That tiny smile again. "It'll be a blast, I promise. For the last guy I took up with me, it was a life-changing experience."

"In what way?"

"It changed his entire outlook on the way he wanted to live his life. He realized that if you don't take risks, you may never know your limit. And if you don't know your limit, you don't know who you are as a human being. As the poet said: one should never be a butterfly collector. Rather be the butterfly itself."

"Very profound. So is this guy still jumping?"

Something flickered behind her eyes. "No."

"Who was he?"

"Robbie? Just a friend." She turned away abruptly.

It was just as well she had her back to him because he knew he would not have been able to keep his face expressionless. Robbie. Robert Whittington. It was a shock hearing his name on Morrighan Monk's lips. When he had studied those photographs of the boy in the bedroom in Monk House, he had the feeling that he was looking at a memorial. A shrine. Of course, all photographs are preserved in the aspic of past memories, but when he was looking at those pictures, there had been no doubt in his mind that Robert Whittington was dead. Now, hearing his name spoken by Morrighan Monk, it sounded fresh, immediate. As though he might turn around to find the kid standing behind him, looking at him with that ready smile, those vulnerable eyes.

The cage juddered to a halt. He glanced at his watch: 9:02 A.M. Morrighan stepped out nimbly onto the open platform. After a moment's hesitation, he followed.

It was windy up here. That was his first impression. The second was that it was a clear day and he could see forever. The view would not end. Rooftops. Spires. Green oases. Even where sky and earth met, the horizon seemed transparent.

Right underneath and to the side of him was Chelsea Bridge. The cars inching down the two lanes of traffic were toylike. The bridge itself so small, he could pick it up between forefinger and thumb. And flowing silently underneath the bridge was the Thames, the water crinkled and gray like the hide of an elephant.

"Isn't it gorgeous?" Morrighan was on her knees, once more checking the green ropes around his ankles. She glanced up at him.

"Yes." He was feeling light-headed. His heart was hammering. He looked at his watch: 9:11 A.M. Where had the time gone? In a daze he saw Morrighan stepping forward, coming so close her breath was warm on his cheek. She had a tiny scar at the corner of one eyebrow—he had only just noticed it.

"I have to bind us together," she said. "And then we hug. And we keep hugging all the way down, OK?"

He managed to nod. His throat was dry. His palms were dripping sweat. Her body was now touching his in a disconcertingly intimate way, but she seemed oblivious. Her eyes unreadable and dark as space.

She placed her lips close to his ear. "Time to be a butterfly."

Stepping into a void. The act that most goes against every instinct of self-preservation.

Falling. Falling. The speed of it ecstatic: propelling his mind and his body into a belly-clenching, delirious place. The sky a fierce rush of blue against his cheek. The wind in his ears like a hurricane.

Morrighan's body was pressed against his: legs and stomachs touching, hips close. Her face blotted out the sky directly in front of him. He saw on her face a look almost of pain: forehead creased, eyes half-closed, lavender veins appearing ghostlike through the delicate skin underneath the black lashes of her lower lids. Her jaw clenched. With a light shock he realized that what he saw reflected in her face was, in fact, the image of his own. He touched his tongue to his lips and so did she. He blinked and opened his eyes to their widest extent, and immediately she stared back at him with eyes rimmed with white. When she opened her mouth slightly as though in protest, he knew his own jaw had slackened. It was as though she was experiencing the sensation of the jump not through her own emotions, but vicariously through his. Even tumbling through the air at fifty miles per hour, the feeling that she was feeding off his sensations was disconcerting.

They were slowing down. The noise of the rope as they reached the full extent of the jump sounded like the ricochet crack of the sail on a tall ship. And now they were accelerating again, up, up and suddenly they were hanging suspended: weightless in space. No up or down. The feeling of disorientation absolute.

His chest was tight. He was holding his breath. As he gulped for air, the oxygen hit his blood like an additional shot of adrenaline. They plunged down again and he heard a shout explode from his chest: a cry of victory, a howl of defiance.

He saw her smile widely, her teeth a white slash in her face. She opened her arms wide, letting go of him and leaned back so that her throat formed an arc, the ponytail a rope of black swinging clear of her shoulders. All tension gone. And then they were both yelling and whooping, shouting their heads off; drunk with elation.

He went up a second time. Solo, this time Morrighan seemed content to wait for him, waving him on when he apologized for keeping her.

"Are you sure you don't mind?" he asked her when he fell in line behind the jumpmaster once again. A new line of jumpers had formed, but none of the other souls who had jumped that morning, he was interested to see, had followed his suit. He was the only repeat customer.

He looked back at Morrighan. "Please don't feel you have to stick around to keep an eye on me. I'll be fine." He was smiling, the same stupid smile of idiotic delight that had been plastered on his face ever since they finished the first jump together. All his senses were still on high alert.

She shook her head. "I like hanging around here. So go ahead."

"Well, after this one, I'll call it a day."

"Good. And then I'll buy you lunch. You'll be surprised to find how hungry you are."

She was right there. After he finished the second jump—the experience just as intense as the first—he was not just on a high, he was ravenous. The restaurant she had picked was a small, unpretentious place with very good food.

When he finally sat back, sated, she put her head to one side. "Are you sure I can't get you anything else?" she asked solicitously. "Another crème brûlée, perhaps?"

"Sorry." He colored slightly. "I've made a pig of myself. But you're right. This morning gave me a heck of an appetite."

"Flirting with danger tends to have that effect."

"Well, you should know. You seem to have a real predilection for it. BASE, bungee, what else? Is it fun being an adrenaline junkie?"

"Dopamine junkie. Like craving chocolate."

"Strong chocolate."

She pulled a face. "Don't try to fool me. You felt it yourself, this morning: the rush. The mere fact that you went back for another go is proof. Most people when they do the jump, don't do it again, you know. Only about fifteen percent of people repeat."

The approving tone of her voice made him pause. As though he had passed some test he wasn't even aware of taking.

He frowned, and moved his shoulders as if to push the idea away from him.

"So your quest in life is to find the ultimate thrill?"

"I suppose so." She looked pensive for a moment. "Of course, the chance that you'll ever find the ultimate thrill is slim. Surfers know the best waves remain unsurfed. They're breaking on unpeopled shores, traveling across uncharted oceans."

"Seriously, Morrighan. Why do you do it? Don't just give me that line about feeling more alive. It goes deeper than that."

For a moment she hesitated. "Don't you sometimes wonder how strong, how fast, how brave you are?"

"Sorry to disappoint you, but no. I can't say I do."

"Well, I suppose it's about taking yourself to a new level. And I'm not just talking about jumping off a tower. It could be a mental thing as well. Whether it's a challenge to the body or the mind, it doesn't matter. The common denominator is turning your back on safety and embracing the void."

Like slamming a ride, he suddenly thought. Like leaving the relatively secure environment of your own emotions for the alien landscape of someone else's thoughts. That feeling of losing yourself, of not being able to turn back. It was every remote viewer's fear. Of getting hopelessly, irrevocably lost in the labyrinth of someone else's mind.

"Gabriel?"

"Sorry. I was just thinking about what you said. About embracing the void. Some people may call it a latent death wish." He smiled, mockingly. "Freud probably had something to say about it."

"Oh, he did. Apparently thrill seeking has to do with repressed feelings of guilt."

He looked at her from the corner of his eye, wondering if he should chance it. "Guilt, huh? So, anything you feel guilty about?"

"Guilt? Let's say a few regrets, maybe. And some disappointments." She turned those amazing eyes on him. "What about you, Gabriel Blackstone? What keeps you awake at night?"

He stared at her, suddenly at a loss for words. In his mind, unbidden, came the image of a woman with a perfectly oval face and long blond hair. Although when they had found her in that outhouse, her blond hair had been black with sweat and dirt. Melissa Cartwright. He had heard later that she had won a beauty pageant in her youth while growing up in the United States.

He looked up. Morrighan Monk was watching him with unwavering intensity.

"I sleep like a log. And guilt is a wasted emotion." He tried for flippant but he knew his voice sounded harsh.

For a moment it was quiet between them. Tense. Then she smiled and raised a quizzical eyebrow. Leaning forward in her chair, she placed both her arms on the table. "Look. You had a very special experience this morning. For a brief moment you took to the sky and flew. But let's not get too serious. You know what G. K. Chesterton said about angels and flying."

"What?"

She smiled again and it lit her entire face. " 'They fly because they take themselves lightly . . . ' "

The afterglow of his experience stayed with him throughout the day. Even now, several hours later, he was still pumped.

He was back in his apartment, sitting in a deck chair on his balcony, a book on his lap, a cup of coffee cooling in his hand, watching the city being swallowed by the night. The smell of the river was strong. Seemingly floating in the gloom, Tower Bridge was a fairy-tale structure of inspired light. Closer by, on the street below, the lit sign above an optician's shop was sputtering, the giant pair of green neon spectacles flashing intermittently.

For the umpteenth time he found himself reliving the jump. The fear. The ecstatic sense of liberation. It might not have been a life-changing experience for him, but it had certainly been a mind-bending one. Thanks to the enigmatic Ms. Morrighan Monk. She was a fascinating woman. She and her sister both.

He was surprised, and a little amused, by how much he was look-ing forward to seeing them again. And he couldn't fool himself, it was because of his interest in the weird ride he had slammed, or be-cause of his promise to Frankie. He was intrigued by the two women themselves.

Minnaloushe was the more openly sensual of the two. Morrighan was a tad icier. But both women exhibited a self-awareness that was undeniably erotic even if—or maybe because—it was eroticism tinged with danger. When Minnaloushe looked at you, you sensed a powerful undertow hiding behind those soft-focus green eyes. Touch her and you might drown. Morrighan was diamond sharp. Touch her and you might bleed.

Before they went their separate ways earlier today, Morrighan had invited him to dinner at Monk House over the weekend. He still couldn't understand why the sisters were interested in him. He had a healthy self-image—Isidore would use the word "conceited" no doubt—and he knew he could pull, but he was smart enough not to flatter himself into believing it was his charm they found irresistible.

Well, no use worrying over it. They might have an agenda, but he had one too. Not only would he have the opportunity to spend time in the company of two highly attractive, intelligent women, but with a little bit of luck he might discover what had happened to poor Robert Whittington.

Thinking of the boy made Gabriel frown and look down at the open book on his lap. He had selected it from among the numerous volumes in Robert's apartment. It was old and the pages had a parchmentlike feel to them. Titled *The Alchemical Student*, it was a history of alchemy and its principles. He was finding it tough going, although there was some information in the book that was good entertainment value:

> *The German philosopher Agrippa, author of the alchemical treatise* De occulta philosophia, *was said to have paid his creditors with gold coins that shone with remarkable brilliance, but which invariably turned into slate or stone within 24 hours.*

Hah! He knew it was too good to be true. All that stuff about lead magically turning into gold. These alchemists were just a bunch of tricksters. And it seemed to him as though they pretty much made a point of writing as unintelligibly as they possibly could. If no one was able to understand what they said, no one could expose them for the fraudsters they were.

Gabriel took a sip of his coffee and replaced the mug on the small side table next to the chair. Leaning his head against the back of the chair, he yawned. His eye fell on the mask Minnaloushe had given him, hanging on his living room wall. On the other side of the glass door, which separated them, the wooden face smiled at him patiently. He gazed into the hollow eye sockets . . .

His mind shifted. The gate to his inner eye opened.

In a way he had been expecting it. He had known that in order to determine what had happened to Robert Whittington, he would have to slam the ride again. He could have forced it before now, and the idea had entered his mind more than once. He was still attracted to the thought of giving it another go—it had been a monster RV ride; detailed, immensely intriguing. But drowning in that pool had been a bloody awful experience. Whoever said drowning was a peaceful way to die had it flat-out wrong. He would very much prefer not to have to go through the whole chest-burning, eye-popping horror again.

But greater than his aversion to choking to death in cold water was his fear of having to relive that awful jaw-clenching moment when he had stepped into the portal and a torrent of visual information had rushed at him with unimaginable force. He still hadn't the faintest clue as to what it was he had encountered. All he knew was he had quite literally gone insane.

At Eyestorm he had slammed rides far more gruesome in the traditional sense of the word. He had even been inside the mind of a killer and a rapist. But those rides, disturbing though they were, did not measure up to the peculiar horror he had experienced during his ride through Robert Whittington's thoughts. It had felt as though the structure of his mind were disintegrating a strand at a time, as though the grooves of his nervous system were melting together like overheated wires before the final spectacular blowout.

Therefore, when he felt himself easing into the ride once more, losing contact with his immediate environment—his apartment, the balcony, the red striped deck chair on which he was sitting, Minnaloushe's mask smiling on the other side of the glass door—his conscious mind hesitated for one split second. At this point of the ride he would still be able to clamp down on the impulse.

But then he let go, sliding into Robert Whittington's mind as easily, as effortlessly, as walking through an open door. A door made of dark heavy timber, the sigil of the *Monas* mounted on the outside . . .

He was retracing his steps: walking through the library with its mildewed books, the hall with butterflies, the endless rooms with their enigmatic occupants and mysterious objects.

The monk was still there, still sandpapering his eyes. The clocks were still ticking with restless asynchronicity. The fantailed doves still died in a bloodied frenzy. *The order of places, the order of things.* The ride was a carbon copy of the first one. Identical. He was walking through the house of a million doors, opening and closing the doors with great discipline. And above and behind him the crow, gliding on silent wings.

Staircases, corridors, dizzying perspectives. He started to navigate a narrow suspension bridge, placing one foot gingerly in front of the other. He remembered this vertiginous walk from the previous ride as well. On the other side of the bridge was the hall in which he had first encountered the masked woman. He wondered if she was there already, waiting for him . . .

He traversed the bridge carefully, felt it sway. Careful, he told himself. Keep your balance—

And then it happened.

The bridge underneath his feet fell away soundlessly. Black space rushing up to meet him.

Even as adrenaline flooded his body, his mind registered with absolute clarity that he was no longer inside the house of a million doors. He did not know where he was, except that he was somewhere outside—free-floating like an eye in the sky.

The transition was totally unexpected. The ride had changed completely. The entire feel of it was different. It took him no more than a second to register why.

He was no longer looking through Robert Whittington's eyes.

He had entered a different mind.

Even as his own mind registered this fact with surprise, he was already experiencing his environment through the template of another consciousness.

Where was he? Whose eyes had become his own?

He was obviously close to the river; he could smell its dankness. Lights floating on the embankment. Tower Bridge. A giant pair of neon glasses flickering on and off, the neon a sputtering green against the black sky.

He was looking down on a figure who was sitting in a deck chair on a balcony. The deck chair had red stripes. The balcony was in shadow but there was light spilling through the sliding glass door. On the wall inside hung a wooden mask.

The figure in the deck chair had the boneless look of someone asleep, but his eyes were open. On his lap was a book, the breeze riffling the pages. The book seemed old, the pages had a yellowy, parchment-like look to them. He was curious to know what the book was about. If he moved in closer, he might be able to read the type on the page.

Ever closer he came, ever closer to the figure in the chair. And now he was looking directly into the face of the man in front of him. He was staring deeply, searchingly into his own wide-open eyes.

He screamed. The scream unraveled shrilly inside his head: wave upon wave of terrified echoes. With an almost physical jolt, he closed his inner eye, terminating the ride. Cutting the link between virtual and physical reality was painful; it felt as though his head were tearing to pieces. He shuddered with nausea.

Leaning forward, he gripped his knees, willing the sickness away.

OK. Calm down. You're safe. You're in your apartment. The ride is finished. You're safe. Now get a grip. You're safe. But his skin was clammy, cold with sweat. He was spooked out of his skull. He shuddered again.

What had happened? One moment he was still slamming the ride, looking through the eyes of the boy. The next moment the perspective had shifted and all of a sudden he was looking through a different pair of eyes. Whose?

What was more, the ride had jumped from past to immediate present. Robert Whittington was dead. During the first part of the ride, he had relived an experience that had already taken place in the past. The person whose eyes he had appropriated toward the end of the ride was very much alive. And what shocked him was the fact that the new pair of eyes had been focused on *him*: Gabriel Black-stone. Someone was trying to spy on him. The shock of the realization made his blood run cold.

With whose mind had he interfaced?

But he knew the answer to that question, didn't he? No mistaking the arrogance, the cold calculation, the all-consuming curiosity. He had sensed those qualities once before, when he was drowning in a pool, looking into the eyes of a woman with murder in her heart.

So how had he ended up inside her mind tonight?

Only one answer to this particular question.

And it scared the crap out of him.

Bloody hell, he thought. Bloody hell.

CHAPTER ELEVEN

Frankie was looking harassed. An open suitcase was on the bed in front of her and the bed was covered with clothes. Blouses, jackets, underwear. She kept glancing at the clock on the bedside table. When Gabriel called her at the crack of dawn, she had at first told him that she wouldn't be able to see him.

"I'm sorry but I'm running late," she said, sounding frazzled. "Why can't you just tell me on the phone?"

"No, I'd like to discuss it with you face-to-face. Dammit, Frankie. I slammed another ride last night. Aren't you at least curious?"

"Of course I am. But I'm meeting William in Switzerland and I still have to pack . . ." He heard her sigh. "OK. Why don't you come over now. But, Gabriel, keep in mind I have to be at the airport by ten."

"Where are you flying from? Heathrow?"

"Stansted. Private plane," she explained briefly.

Private plane. Of course. He wondered what it must be like to travel the world in your own private jet.

"So get them to hold it for you. I thought that was one of the perks."

"I can't. I have to be in Bern at noon. The thing is . . . ," he could hear cautious excitement in her voice, "the reason I'm going is because William is seeing this specialist at a medical clinic who might be able to help. Apparently, the man is a genius. He's going to suggest a new course of treatments. I want to be there for the consultation and I can't be late. So get here quick, all right?"

He had arrived at her Holland Park house—all white-and-cream stucco pillars and black lace fencing—in record time, but he was beginning to think he shouldn't have bothered. It was impossible to get her to concentrate on what he was saying. They kept being interrupted by phone calls and the sour-faced butler, who was clearly unhappy about a strange man joining the lady of the house in her bedroom. Especially, Gabriel supposed, as the lady wasn't dressed yet and was only wearing a nightgown. A very becoming nightgown, it had to be said. Blue had always been Frankie's color.

"Hand me that belt over there, will you?" She pointed at a tan belt with an intricately shaped buckle. "Thanks. Dammit, what did I do with my loafers? I had them right here. Do you remember? I had them in my hand just a moment ago, didn't I?"

He sighed. "Frankie, I need you to focus. Just listen, OK?"

"I've been listening." She opened the drawer to her dressing table and started gathering up lipsticks, powder brushes, toiletries. The dressing table's mirrors were enormous, reflecting the opulent splendor of the room more than adequately. It was a far cry from the dusty little apartment they had shared in Oxford, he thought.

Frankie picked up an eyebrow pencil and dropped it into her toiletry bag. "I have been listening," she repeated. "You're saying that last night you managed to jump from Robbie's thoughts to his killer's. That's great. That's progress. What's the problem? You've managed to switch from victim to perpetrator before. Remember the Rushkoff case?"

Of course he remembered the Rushkoff case. It had been one of his earliest successes at Eyestorm. He had managed to scan not only the thoughts of Oliver Rushkoff—a wealthy stockbroker—but also the mind of his kidnapper. For days he had been frustrated in his search. All he got from Rushkoff when he scanned him was darkness and a feeling of claustrophobia: the man had been blindfolded throughout his captivity, which meant there were no visual clues for him to access. But he had managed to make the jump from Rushkoff's thoughts to his kidnapper's and that had cracked the case wide open.

"Frankie, you don't understand. It's not that I switched perspectives."

She shook her head with annoyance, the shiny hair bobbing. "But you just said—"

"No. Stop. Listen."

Something in his voice got through to her. She stopped, then turned to face him.

"OK. I'm listening."

"Don't you get it? It wasn't merely a case of switching perspectives. *I* was not the one scanning the killer. The killer was the one scanning *me.*"

She made a startled movement with her hand. "That's not possible."

"I tell you that's what happened."

"You're saying Robbie's killer is a remote viewer."

"That's exactly what I'm saying."

"One of those women can slam a ride."

"Yes."

For a long, long moment it was quiet between them. He saw in her face the shock he had felt the night before.

"Why was she scanning you?"

"Well, that is the million-dollar question, isn't it?"

Frankie sat down heavily on the dressing table stool. "She must know you've been trying to find out what happened to Robbie."

He shook his head slowly. "It's possible, I suppose, but somehow I don't think so. She probably doesn't know that she accessed me while I was in the process of slamming a ride myself. When she started to scan me, I dropped out of Robbie's psi-space immediately. She was never in that house with me. No, I don't think her scanning of me has anything to do with the boy. I'm the one she's interested in. I don't know how to explain this to you without sounding incredibly conceited, but both those women find me fascinating."

Frankie lifted an eyebrow.

"I know, I know. But you should have seen the way Minnaloushe zoomed in on me when I met her at the drawing class. And Morrighan invited me back to the house again. As a matter of fact, I'm having dinner there tomorrow evening. The sisters aim to get to know me better, I tell you. Much better. Don't ask me why."

Frankie smiled suddenly. "Well, you're pretty cute."

"Not that cute."

"I agree. And quite frankly, those sisters can have any guy they want." She frowned and ran her fingers through her short hair, making it stand up like a halo around her face. It made her look like a bewildered pixie and it was a mannerism he remembered well. When they were still together, he would always reach over and smooth her hair back into order. But it probably wouldn't go down well if he tried it now.

Frankie was still looking shocked. "I can't get over the fact that one of them is an RV. What are the chances?"

"I know. It's bloody surreal."

"Oh." She put her hand to her mouth. "You know what this means. She probably now realizes that you're an RV as well. Just the fact that you managed to block her scan would have told her that."

"I know. But remember, she thinks she's incognito. She'll simply assume I sensed a scan and blocked it instinctively."

"Strictly speaking you *don't* know who it was. Minnaloushe or Morrighan?"

"Well, at least I know it was one of them. What I did sense was curiosity. And . . . arrogance."

"Meeting of minds, then."

"What do you mean?" Gabriel frowned.

"Well, let's face it: you're not the most modest guy on the block. You always assumed that no one can beat you at the game. You were Mr. Super Remote Viewer, who considered himself too good to be part of the team. I don't know if you were even aware of it, but some of the other members at Eyestorm did not take kindly to that kind of swaggering."

"Then I'm sure they were cheered considerably when I crashed and burned."

The silence between them this time was tense.

Frankie made a dismissive gesture. "All right, let's not go there. It serves no purpose." Her eye fell on the ormolu clock once more. "Oh, damn. I need to shower and get out of here. I'm sorry."

He stood up. "How long are you going to be away for?"

"Four days. William and I are going on to Paris after his appointment. Business. I could come home but I don't want to leave him right now, you'll understand."

"Of course."

"But keep in touch, you hear? You have my mobile number. Let me know what happens at that dinner tomorrow night."

"I will."

She turned to walk away but he placed his hand on her arm, holding her back. "Have you told your husband that I've decided to try and solve Robbie's disappearance after all?"

She hesitated. "Not yet."

"Why not? That's what he wanted."

"I know. But I didn't want to tell him you've agreed to investigate until I was sure you were committed. No use getting his hopes up just to disappoint him again. You weren't that keen at first, and I was worried that after a bit you might decide to walk away from it all."

"You think I'm that unreliable?" Gabriel couldn't keep the bitterness out of his voice.

She sighed. "I'll tell him today."

"Good. You do that."

"And you? What are you going to do now?"

"I'm off to see Isidore. I think the key to what happened to the boy might be locked up inside those two computers in their house. Remember the two password-protected files I told you about?"

She nodded. "The diary and *The Promethean Key.*"

"Right. We need to find out what's inside them. The fact that they're the only protected files must be significant. Isidore has been writing a virus to get into their system. We'll set it loose today."

"Good luck."

"Yes, you too."

She smiled, but it was such a sad smile, he felt it tug at his heart. What must it be like to live with someone who is dying, he wondered. Not to be able to plan for a future? Frankie was handling it with grace. But then, he wouldn't have expected anything else of her.

She spoke wearily. "Even if this new doctor comes through, it won't mean William will be cured. He'll just have more time."

"More time is good." He placed his arm around her. "Hang in there, Frankie."

For a moment she relaxed against him. The feeling of her head against his shoulder was startlingly familiar. He used to hold her exactly like this. They had always been a good fit. She was short enough that her head only came up to his chin.

His arm tightened around her waist, and for just a second he thought he could feel her respond, pressing closer against him.

She stepped back abruptly. "Thanks. I'm OK."

"Frankie . . ."

"You have to go now." Her face was rigid. A pulse was beating visibly in the hollow of her throat.

He felt suddenly depressed. What the hell was he thinking? Was he actually trying to hit on the wife of a dying man? Very classy, Blackstone. But he couldn't help it. She had felt so warm and soft in his arm. And over the past few days he had caught himself thinking about her far more than he wanted to. He had even found himself doodling on a piece of paper, not really concentrating, but when he finally focused on the page, he discovered he had covered it with hearts and arrows and intertwined initials. Pathetic.

"Gabriel . . ."

He looked at her warily. But her next words surprised him.

"Be careful. Please promise me you'll be careful."

She was worried about him? He grinned, suddenly immensely cheered. "I'll be fine. Remember I'm Mr. Super Remote Viewer."

"And don't get too complacent. And please don't get seduced by the sisters. They're dangerous. Be on your guard. Promise?"

He blew her a kiss. "Promise."

Isidore was watching a back episode of *CSI: Crime Scene Investigation* when Gabriel turned up at his house.

"Man, that Catherine Willows is hot." Isidore bobbed his head at the television set. "I love a strong, sexy, mature woman."

"I'm sure strong, sexy, mature women everywhere are rejoicing."

Isidore threw up his hands in dismay. "Oh no—we're feeling frisky today."

"Not to worry. I'll be back to my dour self in no time." Gabriel looked around him. Several empty Chinese food cartons had joined the anarchy of Isidore's desk since his last visit, the greasy little boxes stained red and orange. A dog-eared copy of Philip K. Dick's slim-volumed *Tractates Cryptica Scriptura* served as a coaster for a mug half-filled with cold black coffee and a stale swirl of yellow cream. How Isidore managed to function in an environment like this defied understanding. Gabriel looked at the man himself, who was still staring at the TV screen with an infatuated expression.

"I hope you've been doing more than watching reruns. I'm not paying you to wallow in sexual fantasies. I need to get into those computers at Monk House. Pronto."

Isidore sighed gustily and hit the off button on the remote control. Swinging his long legs down from where he had them propped up on the coffee table, he swept Gabriel a mock bow. "Fear not, oh great one. Your trusty servant has delivered. Lookee here. I think this might do it."

Isidore started tapping away at the keyboard, and as always Gabriel was captivated for a moment by the speed and skill with which Isidore engaged with the machine in front of him. Truly great hackers were like magicians. They could penetrate so deeply into the brain of a computer, they seemed to will it to respond to their thoughts, turning the relationship between man and machine into something telepathic—not mechanical.

Isidore leaned back in his chair. "OK. I banged together a nifty Trojan virus. But you told me the sisters have Kaspersky Anti-Virus on their machine, which is a real pain. KAV is a good product, man. It'll sniff out most Trojan viruses without even trying."

"Tell me this has a happy ending."

"Of course it does. My genius goes unbowed in the face of challenge. I have devised one son-of-a-bitch KAV buster. It'll knock it out completely. I'm calling it DAVID."

"As in David versus Goliath? How original."

Isidore smiled pityingly. "You're just jealous."

"Well, what are we going to do if they discover their KAV is no longer running? They'll be immediately suspicious. I don't want them to even suspect we're in there."

"Ah. Again you underestimate me. I have added a brilliant feature to DAVID. As soon as it kills the KAV, it will add a fake icon to the task bar to give the illusion that the KAV is still alive and breathing fire. Now, how cool is that?"

Pretty cool, Gabriel had to admit.

"So," Isidore continued, "I've done my part. Now it's up to you. How were you planning on sending it? If these women are sophisticated enough to have KAV on their machine, methinks they're not naively going to open an attachment from someone they don't know."

"Well, maybe they can be tempted. I've drawn up a fake letter pretending to be someone looking to sell a very rare Congolese *Makishi* mask and asking Minnaloushe if she's interested. Along with the message, she'll have to download a photograph of the mask. She'll bite, believe me."

"And then? When she wants to buy and finds out there's no mask?"

"Simple. We'll just send her a message saying she's too late and someone else has already bought it. That must happen all the time. Why would she be suspicious?"

"Where did you get a photograph of the mask?" Isidore asked curiously.

Gabriel grinned. "Lifted it from an old V&A catalog."

"Devious." Isidore nodded solemnly. "I'm proud of you. Well, that takes care of the diary. You'll be reading those pages in no time. The other one is of course the real problem."

"*The Promethean Key.*"

"Yip. As the host computer in this instance is not connected to the Internet, you're personally going to have to install a hardware keylogger to get inside, old son. Sorry."

Gabriel sighed. Hardware keyloggers were a nuisance. The only way to install them was to have physical access to the computer itself. Which meant that tomorrow, when he had dinner with the women at Monk House, he was just going to have to hope that they left him alone in the room long enough to install the damn thing.

"Don't despair," Isidore said brightly. "At least you won't have to struggle with a clunky inline logger. I've managed to find you a smashing little custom-made keyboard spy. Cutting edge, man. You won't be able to buy this baby off the shelf. I got lucky: the guy I borrowed this from is a fellow wizard at *Dreadshine* and he owes me a favor." He handed Gabriel a small rectangular box. "Here you go. Take good care of it. Unless you want my friend Aaron to pay you a visit."

"Thanks." Gabriel slipped the little box carefully into the pocket of his jacket. "I'll put it to good use tomorrow night."

"So what's happened so far?" Isidore asked eagerly. "Any leads on our boy?"

Gabriel looked at Isidore's enthusiastic face. Should he tell him about the ride he had slammed the day before? Usually he was pretty reluctant to discuss the topic of remote viewing with anyone who was not an RV himself—the incredulity, the ignorance was wearying. But Isidore, despite the flakiness, was no idiot.

As Gabriel described the ride, Isidore listened with commendable solemnity. But when he stopped talking, Isidore let out a massive whoop. "Man, oh man. This is . . ." He searched for an appropriate word, finally gave up. "You know, I still can't get over the fact that you've been scanning the thoughts of a dead man. How creepy is that?"

"They're not the thoughts of a dead man, Isidore. Robert Whittington experienced these thoughts just before he died—he was still very much alive at the time. And as these thoughts are still part of the psi-space—the consciousness field—I can slam the ride."

Isidore nodded knowingly. "I know all about psi-space now. Did I tell you I hacked into some military files at a site in College Park, Maryland? Those guys wrote a lot about psi-space during the time the U.S. government sponsored the STARGATE project. Really wicked stuff."

Gabriel looked at him warningly. "You're playing with fire. If they catch you, they're going to bury you with the U.S. Patriot Act."

"Oh, please. Catch me? I'm a ghost. They'll never catch me. Besides, what's so dangerous about knowing about psi-space? The way I understand it, it's like an information storage medium. Like mind data stored in some quantum consciousness computer, which RVs can access because they have knowledge of the password."

Gabriel couldn't help but smile. Trust Isidore to come up with an information-based analogy.

"What I do want to know, though, is whether you ever blank out on the password. I mean, do you always manage to interface?"

Gabriel thought of Frankie. *Mr. Super Remote Viewer.* But even Mr. Super Remote Viewer struck out at times. And the results could be devastating.

He looked up to find Isidore watching him curiously. He shrugged. "With varying degrees of success. It's not what you would call an exact science. The impressions I get are more often than not very vague. Sometimes they're so scattered, they're unusable."

"But when you slammed the ride through Robbie's mind the details weren't vague at all, right?"

"No, but it was nuts. What this kid saw just before he drowned is simply not possible. I mean, he was walking through a house with millions of doors? How likely is that? Usually in a ride, you see things partially. You know, bits and pieces—blurred impressions. This ride is as detailed as a film reel. But it makes no bloody sense whatsoever."

"Maybe Whittington was doing drugs."

"Frankie suggested that as well. I still don't think so."

"OK, what about the second ride? When you climbed into the

mind of the lady with the crow? Or rather she climbed into yours."
Isidore smiled. "Lady with the crow. This is straight from Dungeons and Dragons, man. I can't get over how cool all of this is."

Gabriel hunched his shoulders in irritation. "I don't find it cool that Robert's killer is also a remote viewer herself."

"Yeah. Sort of takes away your advantage, doesn't it?" Isidore struck a gladiatorial pose. "The battle of the RVs. Mind versus Mind!"

"This is not a computer game." Gabriel looked at Isidore with exasperation. So much for an inspired exchange of ideas. He should have remembered that in Isidore's life the boundaries between reality and virtual reality were pretty iffy. What happened inside the virtual space of *Dreadshine* was just as relevant to Isidore as the events he encountered daily in the brick-and-mortar world. More so, probably.

"Anyway, I can't sit around here all day." Gabriel got to his feet. "I'll e-mail you the letter and photograph for Minnaloushe later today. Get DAVID in there and send her the message. Let me know as soon as she opens the attachment, OK? I'm very curious to know what's inside that diary."

"Sure thing. I can't wait for a peek myself. A diary written by one of those two women is sure to be hot stuff. Not," Isidore added virtuously, "that I'm motivated by anything else than a desire to find out what really happened to poor Robert."

But as he let Gabriel out the front door, Isidore suddenly turned solemn. "Will you watch your back, man?"

Gabriel glanced at him, amused. "You too? Frankie got all mushy as well. But I wouldn't have expected this of you. You're actually worried for me? How touching."

"Seriously, Gabe. The woman is a killer. And she'll want to get inside your head again. You'd better be prepared. Will you be able to pick up when she tries to scan you?"

"Definitely. I'll recognize her immediately." Gabriel smiled a little grimly.

When he was still at Eyestorm he had received more than sufficient training in this regard because Alexander Mullins had insisted that the RVs at Eyestorm scan one another as a matter of course. It was fair to say that he had always disliked that part of the training intensely. To allow someone to walk through your inner eye was a hard thing to do. As soon as another RV entered his mind, his skin would crawl and the sweat would break out hot on his skin. The impulse to clamp down was always irresistible.

But the one thing the scanning exercises had taught him was that every RV had a different "signature." He could always tell who was trying to probe his mind. The imprint an RV left on the host mind was unique: formless, colorless, but unmistakable. Oddly enough, he had always associated it with smell. Frankie's fragrance, he remembered, was like pine needles. Like a breeze. Whenever she entered his mind, it felt fresh. The woman who had entered his mind the night before had a different signature altogether. Musk, frangipani. Very powerful.

He looked into Isidore's anxious eyes. "Don't worry. If she tries to scan me again, I'll recognize her and I'll block her."

"You're sure you'll be able to do that?"

Gabriel nodded emphatically. "Absolutely." He snapped his fingers. "No sweat."

Entry Date: 8 July

Great excitement!

G is a remote viewer. M and I have hardly talked about anything else since we made the discovery.

On the one hand, it was like opening a package and finding a fer-de-lance inside. On the other, the challenge ahead stirs me like an erotic dream. A snake can be charmed. It is only a question of choosing the right music . . .

Admittedly, the shock was overwhelming at first. But now that we've had a chance to think it through, we realize this is the sign we've been waiting for.

G is a viewer. I wonder if he knows how amazing he is. He represents the next step in evolution. Multi-sensory man.

Think of the possibilities.

Think of speed. Lightning. Ekstasis.

And danger. This could be dangerous.

Which is why we must allow some time to pass before attempting another scan. G will be on his guard now. We need to get him to relax. Lower his defenses. And the next time, the scan will be as delicate as Goliath moving on silk. No imprint. A phantom ghosting through his thoughts.

G is coming to the house tomorrow night. We both can't wait to see him again. The three of us are about to embark on a wonderful journey, our true names forever linked.

CHAPTER TWELVE

Gabriel climbed the steps to the front door of Monk House and placed his finger on the bell. The bell pealed long and melodiously.

As he waited, he shifted from one foot to the other. The bunch of flowers in his hands felt awkward. He was sweating gently—as much from the heat as from nerves.

He suddenly wondered if he was dressed correctly. He had decided on jeans, a white shirt and a jacket. The jacket was Armani but maybe he should have dressed more formally? For all he knew this was a dinner party and the other guests would be all dolled up in their glad rags.

Why was he so nervous? Timidity was not exactly a quality he associated with himself, but where these women were concerned, he felt as clumsy as a teenager. It probably didn't help that he was also overly conscious of the keyboard spy in the inside pocket of his jacket. Every time he moved, he could feel the little tin box where it rested on top of his heart.

Nothing stirred inside the house. The porch light was not on and the front windows were dark. The house seemed deserted. For a moment he wondered if he had got the day wrong.

But then the fanlight above the door lit up and light steps approached the front door. The next moment it swung open and Minnaloushe Monk, dressed in a frothy black skirt and a gossamer-thin blouse, smiled at him. She looked gorgeous: all peaches and cream and wanton hair.

"Gabriel." She leaned forward and kissed him on the cheek. Her lips were soft. "For us? Thank you, they're lovely." She brought the flowers up to her nose. "I love freesias."

Despite her professed delight, it suddenly occurred to him that another gift might have been more appropriate. Wine, maybe. Or chocolate. Bringing flowers to this house was like bringing ice to Antarctica. Following her into the entrance hall with its tightly packed potted plants, he was reminded that there was already more than enough foliage to go around. And he had forgotten about the roses. He stepped into the living room and the scent of roses was everywhere. It came from the alabaster bowls with their overblown blooms and also drifted in—thick and sultry—through the French doors that were open to the garden. The fragrance hovered in the air; settled on the furniture like an invisible shawl.

Morrighan got up from the large peacock wicker chair where she had been sitting. She was wearing a simple white linen shift. Bare feet. Her black hair for once not in the long ponytail to which he had become accustomed but falling freely onto her shoulders. She looked younger and more approachable. Still beautiful. This family had some bang-up genes.

"Welcome." And from her too, a kiss—lips barely brushing his cheek. "Make yourself comfortable." She gestured at one of the wingbacked chairs. "What can I get you to drink?"

"Gin and tonic, if you have it."

"Of course." She moved over to a heavy oak chest and opened the doors. Inside were glasses and an array of liquor bottles.

"Red wine for me," Minnaloushe said. She looked at Gabriel. "Excuse me for a minute. I just want to put your flowers in water."

"And check on the lamb, will you?" Morrighan glanced over her shoulder. "Turn it down a little." Handing Gabriel his glass, she said, "It's just the three of us tonight, but Minnaloushe and I felt like pulling out the stops. So we're having lamb with pesto sauce for our main. Lobster ravioli for starters. I hope you brought along an appetite."

"It sounds wonderful."

Morrighan nodded. "Setting modesty aside: we're pretty good cooks." She walked back to the deep-seated chair and sat down again, slender feet tucked in underneath her. "Anyway, cheers."

"Cheers." He took a sip of his drink. Perfect. Not too heavy on the gin. Just the way he liked it.

He looked around him. The room tonight looked inviting. It was lit by a large number of candles, the tiny flickering flames winking from shelves, side tables, even the floor. The objects in the room seemed to shimmer. The compasses and the astrolabe were burnished brass. The bell jars gleamed. In that dimly lit room, the pale bird skeletons seemed no longer startling, but had acquired a fragile beauty. Even the masks on the wall had lost their aura of menace and appeared whimsical rather than weird. The only discordant note was still Goliath, still looking decidedly unfriendly inside his glass box.

Minnaloushe came back into the room. She flopped onto the velvet sofa and reached for her wineglass. "Things are under control in the kitchen. We'll be able to eat in another half an hour or so." Turning to Gabriel, she smiled. "We should really have champagne tonight to celebrate your jump the other day. Morrighan tells me you took to it like a fish to water."

She had a way of looking at one with such attentiveness. It could lead you to believe she truly was enthralled by your presence, Gabriel thought. An impression intensified by that breathy, whispery voice. He wondered how many guys had fallen for it. No doubt, they enjoyed the fall.

"It was fun." He turned to Morrighan. "But I had a good coach."

"Thank you, kind sir." Morrighan smiled and lifted her glass in an abbreviated salute.

He returned their smiles, wondering all the while who had visited him earlier that week. He had shared a very intimate experience with one of these two women only two nights before. One of them had entered his mind. You couldn't get any closer than that.

But if he had hoped to pick up an echo from one of them, he was disappointed. The conversation flitted aimlessly and harmlessly from one topic to another. Books, movies, the situation in the Middle East. The kind of conversation you could find at any dinner party. The women were charming, stunningly well read, wittily opinionated and nicely appreciative of his company. And for once he didn't get that creepy sense that they had some kind of hidden agenda.

They were even remarkably forthcoming about themselves, talking easily about their childhood.

"When we were girls, we hated each other," Minnaloushe said cheerfully. "Everything was a contest between us. Boys, school, everything. Morrighan was a brat. Impossible to live with. Quite a violent little girl, actually. I can show you the mark where she threw her hairbrush at me once. It left a scar."

"Oh, yes?" Morrighan elevated an eyebrow. "And you? Spoilt little princess. You were Daddy's girl. Mummy's too. And so manipulative. What Minnaloushe wanted, Minnaloushe got."

Gabriel looked at them with astonishment. "This is unexpected. Somehow I pictured you as almost twins. Best friends since birth. Inventing a secret childhood language just for the two of you. That kind of thing."

Minnaloushe laughed. "Not at all. Things got so bad between us that my parents decided to send us to different boarding schools. Throughout most of our childhood we only spent holidays together. And those were pretty tempestuous, believe me."

"So what changed?"

"Difficult to say. Things started changing in our late teens."

"Do you keep secrets from each other?" Like seducing an impressionable boy, he thought silently. Like murder?

"Of course. Sisters always keep secrets from each other, no matter how close they are. Sisters are genetically predisposed that way." Minnaloushe wrinkled her nose. "We still have wildly divergent interests and ideas, you know. And we still like nothing better than to argue with each other. But we now tend to look on each other's idiosyncrasies with tolerance and"—she threw a laughing glance at her sister—"pity. But seriously: we're watching out for each other now. We worry for each other. I certainly worry for Morrighan when she's out on one of her environmental crusades."

Gabriel turned to Morrighan. "What was the toughest assignment you've ever had?"

She put her head to one side, considering. "Probably the time I spent two months in a tent on Egg Island in the Arctic. The weather was atrocious and it was just me and one other girl and our laptop and digital camera."

"What were you doing out there?"

"Recording violations by companies drilling for oil."

"Were you successful?"

"Absolutely. Based on the evidence we gathered, one of the companies was fined very substantially. But it was a tough gig."

"It was a foolish gig." Minnaloushe's voice was low. "Morrighan almost died. She was rigging something on a platform and fell and broke her spine. She was paralyzed for weeks. It took months of physio work before she was back on her feet again. She practically lived in the swimming pool."

Gabriel glanced out the window, his eyes drifting to the far end of the garden. The light streaming from inside the house was strong enough to illuminate the brick apron of the pool and the black water. Next to it the humpbacked tree, its fiery flowers colorless against the night sky.

He felt a chill touch his heart. The water seemed murky in the near darkness. For a fleeting moment he thought back on the ride and remembered how cold the water had felt against his skin. How exhausted and sluggish his limbs. And then his head being pushed under the surface and his lungs exploding in pain . . .

He looked back at Morrighan. "The therapy obviously worked."

"I was lucky."

Minnaloushe said fondly, "It was more than luck. It was willpower. Morrighan is nothing if not tenacious. She never gives up."

He could believe that, Gabriel thought. Morrighan's femininity was unmistakable but there was steel underneath the loveliness. For a moment he remembered the jump they had made together. The feel of her body against his. That look of almost pained ecstasy on her face. The utter fearlessness with which she had tumbled out into space.

He looked up and straight into those remarkable blue eyes. Their impact was like a small electric current running through his body. *Can she tell what I'm thinking?*

Morrighan blinked. Turning her head deliberately in the direction of her sister, she said, "Don't be fooled by Minnaloushe, Gabriel. She's far tougher than I am. Her way of approaching things is different from mine, of course. I tend to go straight for the jugular whereas Minnaloushe is more circumspect. But she can be relentless, believe me."

Gabriel glanced at Minnaloushe, who was listening with a quizzical expression.

"Oh?"

"Definitely. And she has more courage than I have. Just think about her modeling at the Wine of Life club. If that's not heroic I don't know what is."

Minnaloushe's lips twitched. "The men are very professional. The leering is kept to a minimum."

Gabriel looked at her directly. "Why do it? Not for the money, you said."

"And not because I'm a narcissist either, if that's what you're thinking." She twisted a strand of silky red hair around one finger. "It's an exercise in concentration. If I manage to keep my concentration with all those eyes on me, it strengthens my mind. Toughens the brain. To regain inner stillness when you find yourself in such a vulnerable position, requires discipline, believe me."

He did believe her, although it still sounded to him like a damned weird way to sharpen up one's concentration skills. Hadn't she heard of chess? Crossword puzzles? Buddhist *Zazen?*

"So what do you think of when you're sitting there? Do you make grocery lists in your head? Count sheep?"

She smiled again. And for the first time that evening there was something in her smile he didn't understand. Something secretive. "No. I can safely say I'm not counting sheep."

She glanced at her watch and her voice became practical. "That lamb should be just about ready."

"OK, let's get started." Morrighan got to her feet. "Gabriel, why don't you come through to the dining room? We'll join you in a minute."

She looked at him expectantly, waiting to usher him through. He followed reluctantly. He had hoped they would leave him alone in the living room while they dished up. It might have given him just enough time to install the keylogger inside the keyboard of the Mac.

The idea that one of the sisters could be a killer was beginning to seem more far-fetched by the minute, though. Sure, they were not predictable women. And they led rather unconventional lives. But these could hardly be considered indications of a murderous mind. Did one of them really kill Robert Whittington? Drown him? He could almost convince himself it was all a mistake. That he had misinterpreted that first ride. That it was not a death he had lived through. Almost . . . He glanced out the window once more at the pool of water gleaming darkly in the far corner of the garden.

Entering the dining room, he sat down on one of the high-backed chairs. The last time he had visited, he had thought the dining room gloomy and stolid with its heavy pieces of mahogany, but tonight the room was transformed. The crisp white linen on the refectory table, the gleaming cutlery and the graceful candelabra were formal but festive.

And Morrighan had not been exaggerating when she said they were good cooks. The food was excellent. Against his better judgment he was starting to relax. He was enjoying himself. This was turning out to be a very pleasant evening indeed. And it was as though time had slowed down inside that room, making everything seem dreamlike. Or maybe it was just that he was drinking a little too much. Morrighan kept refilling his wineglass, and the atmosphere was so convivial he had difficulty refusing.

"How long have you lived in this house?" he asked her as she set down his dessert plate in front of him: lemon tart with what looked like pistachio ice cream.

"It's been in our family for many years. We grew up here. I was even born in this house. Of course, in many ways a modern flat would be much more practical." She sighed. "The upkeep of this place is horrendous. The plumbing is vintage. When it rains, the roof always leaks when the wind blows south. Still, I wouldn't want to live anywhere else."

"Nor me." Minnaloushe nodded her head emphatically. "This is home." She brushed a stray tendril back from her face and for a moment Gabriel was distracted. What amazing hair. In certain light it looked like gold, then she'd move her head and the color changed to rose madder.

Morrighan placed her elbow on the table and looked at Gabriel chin in hand. "What about you, Gabriel? Where's home for you?"

"I grew up in Bristol, if that's what you mean. But I haven't been back in many years. So, I suppose the answer to your question is London." He took a bite of his lemon tart.

"And London is probably better stomping ground for a thief, I would think."

He looked up quickly. But there was no disapproval in her voice.

"Tell us about it." She fixed her extraordinary eyes on him. "What's it like to be a thief?"

He hesitated.

"We won't judge." She held up one slender hand as if taking an oath. "So don't be shy."

He decided to be flippant. "Let's just say stealing beats working."

"Why information?" Minnaloushe's voice was equally light.

"Information is what makes the world go round."

"I thought it was love."

"Sadly, no." He shrugged. "Bits and bytes and data is where it's at."

"How romantic."

"For some people it can be. Not to mention addictive. Information is the cocaine of the twenty-first century. More seductive than money, more addictive than sex."

"Are you? Addicted?"

"Probably. But I'm never sentimental about information. Not like my friend Isidore who thinks information should be like oxygen. Free—out there—belonging to no one and everyone. Uncorrupted by issues such as profit and ownership."

"Your friend sounds interesting. I think I'd like to meet him." This was Morrighan.

Gabriel grinned inwardly. Isidore had trouble keeping his cool around women. Gabriel had been surprised by how much at ease his friend was when he was introduced to Frankie for the first time, but then Frankie had that effect on people. They always felt as though they had known her for years, and would open up to her in the most amazing fashion. It had stood her in good stead during her time at Eyestorm. These two, on the other hand, would have poor Isidore reduced to tongue-tied incoherence in the time it took to say "Linux."

"Well . . ." For just a second Minnaloushe's eyes met Morrighan's, and that wordless communication he had noticed the last time he had seen the sisters together passed between them. But it was over so quickly, he might have imagined it. She looked back at him. "Time for coffee, I think. And what about a brandy, Gabriel?"

"A brandy would be great, thanks."

"Good. Let's go back to the drawing room. Sis, will you take care of the coffee?"

"Of course."

Gabriel pushed his chair back. "Let me help you clear the table."

"Absolutely not." Morrighan was firm. "But thanks for offering. Maybe next time."

So there was to be a next time. Way to go, Blackstone.

But as he followed Minnaloushe into the living room, his eyes fell on the two computers and he experienced a light shock. He had almost forgotten what he came here for. He still needed to install the keylogger. But how?

Unexpectedly, he was given the opportunity. Minnaloushe was just handing him his brandy when the phone rang in the hallway.

"Excuse me." She glanced over her shoulder. "I need to get that."

He waited until she had disappeared into the hallway and then moved quickly over to the computers. He ignored the IBM, which was connected to a modem. Isidore's virus would take care of that one. He turned his attention to the Macintosh, which was not connected to the Internet. It was switched off, the screen black. But that did not concern him. He was interested in the keyboard only. He glanced at his watch. Three minutes to eleven o'clock.

Turning the keyboard over, he examined the three tiny screws that held it together. As he would not be able to simply plug the logger into a porthole, he would have to open up the keyboard in order to slip in his little spy. Some keyboards were held together by plastic plugs that could be popped out, but from his first visit to the house, he knew this one was not so accommodating. He had come prepared. Before setting out for Monk House, he had slipped a small power screwdriver into his jacket pocket. And he had practiced this afternoon as well, opening and closing keyboards and timing himself.

He started work on the first screw, forcing himself to keep his eyes on his hands, even though the compulsive urge to glance at the door leading to the hallway and the one giving access to the dining room was strong. But he could hear Minnaloushe's voice as she talked on the phone, and from the direction of the kitchen came the clatter of crockery.

The first screw was out. He placed it carefully to one side and inserted the point of the screwdriver into the head of the second tiny screw. His hands were sweaty and the screwdriver slipped slightly in his palm, causing his heart to miss a beat.

Calm down. Concentrate. In the hallway, Minnaloushe was laughing.

He cursed the candles. They made for great atmosphere but lousy light to work by. He deliberately slowed his movements. If one of these screws fell to the ground, it would be impossible to find it in the shadows. The image of himself on hands and knees, wildly searching for a screw only millimeters big crossed his mind and he swallowed hard.

Before coming here tonight, he had considered simply substituting the old keyboard with a completely new one: the keylogger gadgetry already installed. It would have saved him having to mess around with fiddly little screws and it was a trick he had used before. He had a variety of used, deliberately dirtied keyboards of all different makes and sizes at home, and usually the targets never even noticed that their keyboard had been replaced by another. But he had decided against it. The sisters were too observant. The feel of the keyboard—the resistance of the keys and their texture—might be just slightly different. They would pick up on it.

Two down. One to go. It was quiet in the hallway. He glanced nervously at the door. Was she on her way? But then the wispy voice started talking again.

A breeze stirred gently in the garden, lifting the curtain at the window. The third screw was already slightly loose and he was able to remove it at speed. Great. He carefully separated the two leaves of the keyboard before taking out the small oblong tin from his inside pocket. He opened it.

The logger looked like a shiny steel button. As he placed it inside his palm, it flashed silver in the gloom. A tiny spy with an electronic heart. This keylogger was the most sophisticated he had ever worked with. No files to install. No giveaway signs of log files or processes running at operating-system level. Undetectable by software. And no clumsy cables either. It would be totally invisible. In a few days' time, he'd come back to retrieve it, and the keystrokes it recorded should allow him to crack the password of *The Promethean Key*.

As he expected, installing the logger was the quickest part of the operation. And replacing the screws was easier than removing them. He sneaked a look at his watch: 11:00 exactly. It had taken him three minutes flat. So far, so good.

But as he was tightening the third screw, he thought he detected from the corner of his eye movement in the near corner of the room.

He turned his head and squinted. Nothing. Only the shadowy flicker of the candles against the wall.

He turned away, but there it was again and this time he caught it. It was his old nemesis: Bruno, the demon cat. As if in sympathetic reaction, the scratch on his wrist, which had scabbed over, started to itch.

The cat stared at him, back arched. Then it jumped with feline grace onto the seat of the wingbacked leather chair, the chair he had sat in earlier that evening, as though daring him to claim it again.

The sound of cups rattling in their saucers shocked him into awareness. Shit. Morrighan had left the kitchen and was inside the dining room. Her shadow was already at the door. He dropped the screwdriver into his pocket and pushed the keyboard back into place. Somehow he managed to place six feet between himself and the computer by the time Morrighan entered the room, in her hands a tray with a cafetière, cups and a plate of biscotti.

"Let me help you with that."

"Thanks." She relinquished the tray. "I see Bruno has taken over your chair."

"Well, he looked so comfortable, I did not want to disturb him." In fact the cat did not look comfortable at all. It was still standing on tiptoes on the seat of the chair like a nervous ballerina, narrow eyes fixed on Gabriel with chilling intensity.

Morrighan leaned down and scooped the cat into her arms. "Hey, you," she said and buried her face into its fur. "Where are your manners?" Bruno meekly placed his chin on her shoulder, but his tail was swishing.

Minnaloushe walked hastily into the room. "Sorry, you two. That was Katrina," she said to Morrighan by way of explanation. "You know what she's like. You simply can't get her off the phone."

Morrighan set Bruno gently on the ground. Kneeling down in front of the coffee table, she started pouring coffee into one of the cups. "Gabriel, biscotti? And you haven't had any of your brandy yet."

He sat down in his chair again, Bruno having mercifully disappeared behind the sofa, and picked up the big-bottomed glass. The adrenaline that had poured through his body while he was working on the keyboard was starting to subside, and in its place was that heady mixture of relief and satisfaction he always experienced after pulling off a job without being caught. Face it: he liked the rush. He looked past Morrighan to where the Macintosh stood on the table, keyboard neatly centered in front of the screen. Good work. He really had to give himself credit. Three minutes was just about a personal best.

He relaxed deeper into his chair. Minnaloushe was busy at the music system, slipping a CD into the player. As the first notes filled the air, he recognized the music. Tchaikovsky. "Andante Cantabile," String Quartet no. 1, opus 11. The soaring violin notes almost unbearably poignant.

Minnaloushe sat down on the sofa and picked up her brandy glass. "Here's to the future."

"And to new friends," he added expansively and raised his glass. The gleam of the candle flames filtered through the amber-colored brandy, making it appear as though the liquid was magically glowing.

"New friends," the women repeated in unison.

They smiled at him and their smiles were full of promise. Their eyes looked like jewels. Morrighan lifted her glass once more in a final toast:

"To us. To getting to know each other . . ."

G surprised me tonight. Behind the carefully crafted smile lies something quite disturbing. A coolness. A cruelty. Sometimes I glimpse it in his eyes. He does not realize it himself, I don't think. There is no sense that this quality is cultivated; it is more a kind of unconscious power. Dangerous. Very sexy. This guy comes from deep within the forest of a woman's fantasies.

Only once before have I encountered someone like him: a man who gave the same impression of lazy ruthlessness. And maybe my memory of him is no longer accurate. I was only thirteen years old, after all.

I remember I was at a wedding reception and I was bored. The ceremony in the church had been beautiful—the bride in a shimmering white dress and gauzy veil. The groom looking adorably nervous. The bridesmaids smiling. Joyous music.

But the reception itself was utter boredom. Inside the marquee in the garden it was steaming hot, and I recall the smell of deodorized sweat and melting makeup. Sentimental speech following sentimental speech. And I remember that M and I had quarreled. She had tripped me and I had pushed her. It was one of those fights. I could not bear to be near her any longer so I had slipped away from the table at which M was sitting with Mum and Dad and had entered the house.

It was quiet inside. I crept up the stairs, hoping to find a place to hide out for the afternoon. The bedrooms were on the top floor. As I walked down the carpeted passageway, I heard a noise. A whimper. I felt the hair on my arms rise—not in fright, but in anticipation.

The door was ajar. I pushed it open even wider. It did not creak, and the two people inside the room did not notice me as I stood there watching avidly. They were making love. A blond woman and a black-haired man I recognized as wedding guests.

They had been sitting in the pew in front of me during the service. The woman's hat had formed a perfect frame for her delicate face. She was beautiful in a languid, slightly bloodless way. The man, on the other hand, had a devil-may-care smile and his life force was palpable. He was dressed as soberly and as formally as you could wish for, but there was something about him that was untamed. You had the feeling that with this man you shouldn't press too far. He could be dangerous. But is risk not the ultimate aphrodisiac? Even at that age I knew it instinctively.

When the bride entered the church, he turned around and for a few moments his eyes locked with mine. His face was fascinating: the full lips, the dark stubble pushing underneath the skin, the black eyes framed by long lashes. He had looked at me appraisingly—probably not the way an adult male is supposed to look at a girl barely in her teens. But it was not a lecherous look—more a nod, a recognition of the woman I was becoming. Admiring, approving. A jaunty salute. It made me blush. It was also the first time I had felt the power that comes with being a woman.

As I stood there in the door of the bedroom, my breath was caught inside my chest in pleasurable suspense. The blond woman was sitting on the man's lap. Her legs were clenched behind his back and her full, rounded breasts were squashed slackly against his chest. His skin was dusky from the sun, hers was cream. He held her by the nape of her neck as though he had to subdue her forcefully. The sight of his arm demanding submission and her bowed head resting against his shoulder spoke of delicious mastery and subjugation. I felt my own limbs tremble. She was moving herself against him slowly, languorously. The smell in the room was like buttermilk. Warm. Curdled.

He moved away from her and gripped one breast in his hand, rolling the nipple roughly between his fingers. She made a small mewing sound and her head drooped against his shoulder even lower. And now he was stroking her hair, her neck, the side of her cheek, his lips murmuring against her ear. She was moving ever more quickly against him. I could see where he had entered her and the sweaty nest of hair and crumpled skin at the base of his shaft. I stared, fascinated, my own body flushed. And then the woman suddenly screamed through closed lips and arched her back. I felt my own body shudder in recognition.

So this is it, I thought. This is what people risk hell for. This agony and ecstasy of the flesh.

How sad, then, that I have never again captured quite the same sense of delight as I felt that day standing in the door of a bedroom in a strange house—not yet a woman, no longer a child. Years later, when I became a participant in the game of love myself and not a mere onlooker, I had expected smoke, honey, crystal, fire. But reality never seemed to fully match the power of that first, vicarious experience when I watched from the bedroom door.

Is it because G reminds me of that unknown man from my youth that I am so attracted to him? A sexual imprint—a hidden trip wire planted in my brain years ago?

But G has been chosen as a player in the game, not as a partner for my bed. He is to follow in R's footsteps. Transcend them. Solve et coagula.

I must meditate upon my name.

CHAPTER THIRTEEN

"Inhale. Exhale. Stretch."

This was a hell of a lot tougher than he had thought it would be. Gabriel sneaked a look at the woman who was occupying the mat to his left. She was performing the exercise effortlessly; back straight, legs firm but not rigid. The woman must have core muscles like piano wire. He, on the other hand, was wobbling all over the place like a happy drunk.

"And down." The yoga teacher's voice was soothing. "And relax. Good work, people. See you all next week."

Gabriel turned his head painfully and caught a glimpse of himself in the full-length mirror covering one wall of the gym. His face was red. And were those bubbles coming from the corner of his mouth?

For a few more moments he continued to lie spread-eagled on the mat, exhausted. Apart from the fact that he was hurting in places he never even knew he had muscles, he was also suffering from the effects of the previous night's dinner party at Monk House. He knew he shouldn't have had that last Cognac. The way he felt now, he could go to sleep right here this minute.

But the yoga teacher was starting to roll up his mat and was obviously getting ready to leave. Move your ass, Blackstone. Time to go to work.

"Mr. Scott . . ."

The yoga teacher turned toward him. "Ariel, please."

"Uh, right. Ariel."

"Is there something I can help you with?"

"I understand from the front desk that this class is full and that I will not be allowed to attend it again. Do you offer another class, by any chance?"

"Indeed. Every Tuesday morning at six-thirty."

Gabriel shuddered. Six-thirty. Oh, man. That was brutal.

His expression must have given him away, because the yoga teacher said apologetically, "I realize it is very early but I teach only part-time. I have a day job as well."

Gabriel almost smiled. Yes, he knew all about Mr. Scott's day job. It was the guy's day job that interested him. He couldn't care less about lotus positions and mantras. But yoga was to be his way in. If it meant learning how to twist himself into a pretzel and getting up at some ungodly hour, then so be it.

Ariel was opening his gym bag and was taking out a truly extraordinary piece of clothing, which he proceeded to pull over his head. Gabriel stared. Could it actually be a poncho?

"Well, good-bye." Ariel nodded at him. "I hope I'll see you in my class on Tuesday."

"Wait." Gabriel touched the man's elbow. "I would love to talk to you about yoga. I don't know all that much about it. But after today's class, this is something I know I can get passionate about." He managed to keep a straight face. "If you have the time, would you allow me to buy you a cup of tea? I was about to have a cup of tea myself. Green tea," he improvised. The yoga teacher looked like he could be a green tea kind of guy.

"Of course," Ariel nodded. "Thank you, yes."

As they sat down at a table inside the café and placed their order, Gabriel quickly went over in his mind what he knew about the man opposite him. Ariel, not surprisingly, was not the name the yoga teacher's mother had given him. He had been christened Donald Michael Scott and was a low-level human resources clerk at a pharmaceutical company called LEVELEX. And it just so happened that Gabriel and Isidore had been retained by LEVELEX's competition to hack into the company's research database.

The money for this job was excellent—if they could pull it off. And that was nowhere near certain. The security at this company was super tight. Again and again he and Isidore had been stopped cold. No hack possible. Isidore was about to call it quits, but Gabriel was not. He had another plan in mind.

A plan that involved Mr. Scott.

Gabriel watched the yoga teacher take a cautious sip of his tea, puckering his lips. This unassuming little man with his polka-dot poncho was going to provide him with the information they needed, without even knowing he was providing it. A coconspirator . . . but an oblivious one.

It was going to be easy. As he listened to the man prattle on about asanas and Ayurveda, Gabriel had no doubt the guy was the perfect mark. And even though he had to say so himself, his strategy was brilliant. When he researched the employees at LEVELEX, Donald Scott's name had stood out simply because he also happened to be a member of the same gym where Gabriel worked out. When Gabriel discovered that the clerk was also a yoga teacher, he had immediately signed up for his class. By casting Scott in the role of mentor, he had lowered the man's natural inclination to be wary of strangers. After all, teaching required you to be approachable.

The only problem he could see in this whole setup was Isidore. Isidore did not like this kind of social engineering. "Scumbag tactics" is how Isidore described co-opting an employee without the employee consciously being aware of it. But what Isidore didn't know wouldn't hurt him.

"Some more tea?" Gabriel smiled at Donald Scott.

"Yes, thank you."

Gabriel pushed the earthenware teapot toward the yoga teacher. "So what do you do when you're not teaching yoga and inspiring your students?"

"Well, actually, I work for a pharmaceutical company . . ."

It was all too easy. Like a lamb to the slaughter.

After saying good-bye to the yoga teacher and promising to sign up for his Tuesday morning class, Gabriel got into the Jag and took out his mobile phone. Time to check in with Frankie.

He caught her just as she was about to step into the lobby of her hotel in Paris. The cell connection made her sound as faraway as though she were in the Arctic, not a mere hop, skip away over the Channel. But at the sound of her voice, he felt a sharp surge of pleasure. He missed her.

"Talk," she said economically.

"Well, good morning to you too."

"Sorry." She coughed discreetly. "But William and I are just about to check in. He's fine," she added before Gabriel could ask. "And the doctor he consulted seemed convinced he could add up to a year to the prognosis."

"That's great."

"Yes, well. We'll have to see. So how did it go with the sisters last night?"

"Pretty good. They want to be friends."

Something that sounded suspiciously like a snort was her response. Then, "Any idea who the remote viewer is?"

"Not a clue. I couldn't pick up anything from either of them."

"Watch out, anyway."

"I will. Don't worry about me. I plan to enjoy myself."

"That's what I'm afraid of," she said cryptically and disconnected.

Gabriel smiled as he dialed Isidore's number. He would have to wait for the women to invite him back to the house again before he'd be able to retrieve the logger he had installed inside the Mac's keyboard. But until they did, he was not about to sit idle. Isidore's virus should have done its work by now on the IBM, which meant that even though *The Promethean Key* was to remain a mystery for a while longer, the diary was about to give up its secrets. Of course, it all depended on whether Minnaloushe had downloaded the attachment. He was confident that the bait had been a good one—the chance to obtain another *Makishi* mask must be pretty irresistible to her—but you never knew.

But the news was good. "Your plan worked," Isidore said without preamble. "We're in."

* * *

Smith's at Smithfield was packed. The huge loftlike space was buzzing with conversations from many voices, the windows steamed up. From the kitchen came a steady stream of plates filled with baked beans, thick steaks, fried eggs and slices of white toast. Gargantuan portions and no low-fat options in sight. Smith's was only a few blocks away from Isidore's house and one of his favorite hangouts.

Isidore was slumped over one end of one of the big kitchen tables, long legs tucked underneath the low wooden seating bench. The expression on his face was that of a cat having stolen a particularly rich bowl of cream. There was also a glint in his eye, which gave Gabriel pause. He lowered his backpack and looked at his friend suspiciously. "You look happy."

"Living a clean life and thinking healthy thoughts will do that for you. You should try it sometime."

"Yes, oh Yoda."

"Did you hang with the ladies last night, my man?" Isidore still had that Cheshire cat grin on his face.

"I did."

"And?"

"They said they wanted to get to know me better."

"Did they really. Why is that? I wonder."

"They're attracted to my brilliant mind. They can't get enough of it."

"You're sure that's all it is." Isidore's voice was heavily sarcastic.

"No, you're right. It's my body, as well."

"Conceited sod." Isidore looked at him disgustedly for a moment. But then he smiled creamily and reached into his own backpack. Extracting a paper folder, he placed it neatly in front of him, pushing a sugar bowl out of his way.

"Actually, I know quite a bit about your visit to the girls last night." Something was amusing Isidore greatly.

Gabriel watched him warily. "OK. Spill it. The diary. You've read it?"

"Oh, yes. Well, parts of it, anyway."

Gabriel waited. Isidore clearly wanted to make the most of the moment.

"The diary goes back years—it's going to take ages to read through it all. So I've just skimmed through some of the more recent entries, you understand."

"And?"

"There's some weird shit in there, man. Some off-the-wall descriptions and really esoteric stuff but," Isidore paused, enjoying himself, "there are also more personal observations—especially last night's entry, you'll notice—and that's where it gets really interesting."

"What do you mean?"

"I'm talking about you, bro. You figure strongly, my man. The writer is obviously intrigued by you. When you get back to your computer, you can browse the diary at your leisure. But just for now, I've printed out a few pages for your information." He pushed the folder across to Gabriel. "I've highlighted some of the choice bits, you'll see."

Gabriel opened the folder. Inside were a few sheets of paper. Certain parts of the text had been highlighted with a pink Magic Marker. The date at the top of the first page was yesterday's. As he began reading, he could feel his face getting warm.

G surprised me tonight. Behind the carefully crafted smile lies something quite disturbing. A coolness. A cruelty . . . Sometimes I glimpse it in his eyes . . . Dangerous. Very sexy. This guy comes from deep within the forest of a woman's fantasies . . .

"They're not all rave reviews, though. As you can see from this bit here . . . and here." Isidore leaned over helpfully, one long finger pointing out the two relevant paragraphs.

G possesses an overweening vanity. It manifests itself in every gesture, every elegant move. Even the way he dresses. I have to admit, he has graceful hands. A cute tush! Pity he knows it.

There is undoubtedly a strong streak of narcissism there. And with G it is more than just personal vanity; it is also a vanity of the mind. A deep belief in his own ability. A conviction that he can take on anyone, on any terms.

Isidore sat back in his chair. "Now, that's what I call penetrating prose. And did you read the racy stuff in last night's entry? Seems as though you remind her of some sexual fantasy man she met in her tender years."

"Who wrote this? Minnaloushe or Morrighan?"

"Ah well, this is where it gets tricky. I don't know. Everyone in this diary is referred to by initials. Which means the author keeps referring to her sister as *M*. And that is no help at all, of course. So far I can't find anything that gives an indication of whose voice it is. The ironic thing is, this woman has an obsession with her own name . . . See, almost every entry ends with *I must meditate upon my name.* Wish she'd stop meditating and start talking."

"Does the diary mention anything about remote viewing?"

"Yes. Here—one page back where she calls you 'multi-sensory man.' Catchy name, don't you think? Beats Batman and Superman anytime." Isidore sniggered. "She thinks you represent the next step in evolution. Man, if you're what's waiting for mankind in the future, I'm worried."

Gabriel sighed. "Get serious for a moment, will you? Is the writer the viewer?"

"I have no idea. She keeps talking about how amazed the two of them were to discover that you're a remote viewer, but she doesn't say who actually does the scanning. Like here: *The scan will be as delicate as Goliath moving on silk. No imprint. A phantom ghosting through his thoughts.* It still doesn't say who'll be scanning like Goliath. Who is Goliath anyway?"

"A spider."

"Huh?"

"Never mind. What about Robert Whittington? Does the diary mention him?"

"A lot. When you get to your computer, go back about eighteen months: that's when his name first surfaces. Or rather his initial—I imagine *R* stands for Robert Whittington. The author always sounds regretful when she talks about him. And she says again and again how much she misses him. But no chilling confessions or murderous thoughts. Which is not to say that parts of the diary aren't spooky, bro. Some of it freaked me out big-time. This is not your ordinary garden variety 'Dear Diary,' believe me. It has almost no 'this is what I did today' kind of detail. No real specifics."

"Did you check to see what she wrote during the week the boy disappeared?"

"Of course. But it was no use. During that week she never wrote in it. And the next time she mentions Robert, it is only to say that he has 'left.'" Isidore added imaginary quotation marks with his fingers.

Gabriel stared at the printed pages. "So you found no indication that the boy was harmed."

"Well, no. Just that he left because he wasn't up to the challenge, whatever that might be. And that he wasn't strong enough. I suppose she could be using euphemisms, like when she says 'he left,' maybe she means he checked out. As in permanently."

"But nothing about drowning?"

"Nada." Isidore shook his head. "But they're into something weird, Gabe. And whatever it is, they managed to get Whittington hooked onto it as well. Take a look at this page. The second paragraph."

The three of us are about to engage in the most sublime form of play. We told R about the game today. He is so keen, bless his sweet heart. It will be fun playing with him. R is a seeker. He has already searched for the white light elsewhere. But now his journey will truly begin. Passion. Death. Rebirth.

"I can't make up my mind if they were planning some erotic orgy for the boy or if they wanted to take him to church. And all those references to 'playing' with him?" Isidore drummed his fingers on the tabletop. "To tell you the truth, I find that creepy as hell. Like he's a doll or something. What does it mean?"

"I don't know."

"And what is this 'game' and the 'white light'?"

"Isidore, I don't know."

"Well, I'd better warn you, the ladies have plans for you as well. When you start reading the diary properly, you'll see they've decided that you're to be their next playmate."

"Is that a fact?"

"Oh, yes indeed. You're the chosen one."

"I suppose I should feel flattered."

"No, my man. You should feel apprehensive."

Gabriel dropped his eyes again to the pages in his hands.

M and I are convinced that G is perfect for the game. But unlike R, G is no spiritual seeker after truth. Feeding the soul is not high on his list. Instant gratification. Materialism. Those are his gods. A peddler of information. He sells it and moves on. Out of sight, out of mind. No spiritual footprint.

It will be a challenge and a great adventure. Everything points to this guy liking to push the danger button. Risk equals self-knowledge. My kind of man.

Gabriel frowned. "This doesn't help very much at all." He closed the folder and pushed it away from him. "Damn."

"Maybe the answer lies on the second computer. In *The Promethean Key.*"

"Maybe."

"So get me the keylogger and I'll get you the password."

"I plan to. As soon as they invite me back." Gabriel stared moodily at the folder. "I wish I knew who the author of the diary is: Minnaloushe or Morrighan."

"Well, don't despair. You'll now be able to access this diary whenever you feel the urge. Maybe the writer will reveal herself in future entries."

"Here's hoping."

Isidore grinned. "And maybe she simply won't be able to keep her hands off your 'cute tush.' That would be a dead giveaway." He laughed and ducked the sugar cubes Gabriel threw at him. "So, what's next?"

"As they're so keen on spending time with me, I don't think I should disappoint the ladies. I will give them every opportunity to do so. The three of us will hang some more, to borrow a phrase from your vocabulary."

"Do you think it wise?"

"Probably not." Gabriel grinned suddenly. "But who wants wise when you can have fun? In the meantime . . . I have some reading to do."

It took Gabriel almost a week to read through the entire diary. The diary was voluminous and covered a time span of close to five years. Some of the entries were thousands of words long. Others, only a few sentences. The writer did not always write in it every day, but she rarely skipped more than a week. She was obviously committed to keeping some kind of record of her thoughts and the passage of her days.

With the help of Isidore's Trojan virus, he was able to access the diary's electronic pages whenever he felt like it. It allowed him to read not only past entries, but also brand-new entries made in the present. Once, he even found himself logging in on the diary at the exact moment she was busy keying words into it. It was an odd sensation, watching the disembodied words float across the screen, knowing she had no idea he was on the other side of the looking glass, looking in.

Much of what he read was obscure. *The white light. I will search for it as for an enchanted city lost beneath the waves, following the water-heavy sound of bells tolling in their drowned cathedrals.*

Some ideas surfaced again and again. *White light, journey, game.* The language used to describe these concepts was frustratingly opaque.

What to make of this, for example?

Why try to find sublime purpose in the haziness of dreams or the an-archic lines in the palms of your hands? Play the game. That is all that is required. Follow the path that does not wander.

The images and observations made little logical sense, but she had created a magical world within the diary's pages, a wild world. The entire diary was a celebration of an extraordinary imagination: poetic, haunting, evocative.

Can you hear the sun set?

What is the color of seduction?

The easy answer is red, but that does not ring true. Red is full on. Seduction is a feather brushing against the skin of the inner thigh. Subtle. Teasing. I think the color of seduction is cappuccino. Dark coffee diluted with cream.

From love to death:

Death should not be turkey-necked, flaccid, trying to speak profound words through a toothless mouth. Death should be strong and virile and grab you by the hand as you run into a windswept darkness stalking flame after flame.

And then there was the instruction to herself, like a running leitmotif: *I must meditate upon my name.*

But she never gave it.

Not every observation was mystical or nebulous. There were pragmatic, everyday observations as well: ruminations on politics, local events, pop culture—even trivia read in newspapers and magazines. These observations were irreverent and witty. Often deliriously dark. Sometimes sly.

Not your ordinary garden variety diary, Isidore had said, and this was certainly true. The voice in these pages belonged to a complex woman.

Though much of what she wrote had a spiritual dimension to it, the author of the diary clearly did not deny herself the pleasures of the flesh. She possessed a mind aggressively sensual. The pages were studded with sexual encounters: the men, always referred to by their initials only, were usually spoken of fondly, but ultimately dismissively, warranting only a few words. In the diary's pages her male partners were reduced to alphabet soup. It was the act of love itself that she celebrated.

The Egyptians believed love to reside in the brain, not the heart. But I believe love should be vehement, physical, blotting out rational thought. Bathing in his maleness: his smell, his touch, his exquisite violence. The next morning a bruised body, a disheveled bed. And that searing sense that life is joy and passion.

Another entry:

Why is it that women find men's hands so attractive? Is it the strength implicit in the powerful fingers and wrists, or just because of the role hands play in the making of love? Hands, which may caress, tease, grip in ecstasy. Smoothing the hair from my face, opening my mouth, quietening me.

He knew he should feel guilty: these sentences were not meant for his eyes. He told himself he had no choice—it was a necessary step in his investigation into Robert Whittington's death—but he knew there was more to it.

And it wasn't just the surreptitious thrill of being a voyeur, a Peeping Tom. It went deeper. The more he read, the more captivated he became by the person behind the words.

She usually entered her thoughts into the computer late in the evening. Writing in her diary was possibly the last thing she did before going to bed. Gabriel pictured her, already dressed for sleep: feet bare, her face innocent of makeup, her brow slightly furrowed as she tapped the keys, hesitating over this word or that. He saw where she sat at the long living room table in the uncertain light of a lamp, her hands resting lightly on the keyboard, her face turned away from him. He had a glimpse of the outline of her figure underneath the wispy nightdress, saw the shadow hugging her feet. And then she looked his way, and immediately her features dissolved and he was unable to even see the color of her eyes.

Minnaloushe? Or Morrighan?

The raw sensuality, which burned up many of the sentences like brush fire, reminded him of Minnaloushe. But that wing-brush of darkness—the relentless pursuit of risk—was pure Morrighan.

Risk leaves our senses quivering. Danger is erotic. We are most aware when we find ourselves in the shadow of death.

Was it possible to fall in love with a voice in a diary?

The woman speaking from these pages was irresistible. He couldn't get enough of her. He read the diary, and it was like watching a beautiful dancer strip off her clothes. Like the sultan and Scheherazade, he thought, self-mocking. Getting turned on by the power of words. A power far more subtle than a pretty face.

She was keeping him spellbound.

Bewitched.

CHAPTER FOURTEEN

"You're obsessed."

Gabriel turned his head to look at his friend. They were in their van, a block away from Pittypats's offices. But before they could get to work with their Pringle can, they needed a place to park. Gabriel sometimes thought the most challenging part of their job was simply finding suitable parking space.

"You've fallen in love with the woman in the diary. You're smitten, Gabe. Admit it."

"The lady has an appealing voice."

"You do realize that this appealing voice might belong to a woman who drowned someone? A murderer?"

"No way." Gabriel shook his head. "No way."

"You don't know that," Isidore warned. He glanced over at Gabriel before changing the gears noisily. Isidore was not the most accomplished of drivers. "And if she didn't kill him," he continued, "the diary makes it clear that she was—at the very least—engaged in playing this weird game with Whittington, whatever it was. She and her sister both."

"There's nothing to indicate that the game led to his death."

"There's nothing to indicate it didn't." Isidore was impatient. "For God's sake, she talks about walking through that creepy house of many doors—how weird is that?"

"So?"

"Don't you get it? By her own admission, it puts her in the same location as the woman who drowned Robbie Whittington."

Gabriel was silent. Isidore had put his finger on the one aspect of the diary that distressed him. There was no doubt that the writer of the diary was familiar with the house of a million doors. The house in which Robert Whittington had encountered the woman responsible for his death. And the house was not just familiar to her, she walked through it regularly. *The journey continues. Every day I climb the unfathomable staircases, walk down the tilting corridors, cross the treacherous drawbridges and open deceiving doors.*

Deceiving doors. Not a bad description, if a little understated. Behind one of those doors lay screaming madness.

He looked out the window of the van. "She's not a murderer, Isidore. I know it."

"You're kidding yourself, my friend. But even if she didn't kill him, she probably helped her sister cover it up."

"I think she doesn't know her sister has killed. Sisters don't share everything, you know. Especially not murder."

"You're rationalizing." Isidore put his foot on the gas a little too emphatically and the van jerked into motion again. "You're infatuated."

Yes, Gabriel thought silently. I am. I am infatuated with a woman who has glowing poppies growing in her heart. With a woman who wrote a poem—in rhymed stanzas, no less—to her big toe. "Ode to Lord Magnipus." How can you not love a woman who names her toes and writes poems in their honor?

He suddenly noticed a free delivery bay right outside the squat sixties building opposite Pittypats. Miracles never cease. He tapped Isidore's arm.

"Well spotted." Isidore turned into the bay with alacrity. "Although the chances that we'll be chased by the building's security guards are pretty high."

"So let's get cracking, then."

As Isidore reached behind his seat to extract their goody bag, he said complainingly, "Man, I'm not up for this today. To think I could be in Hawaii right now."

"Chin up. Whistle while you work, that's my motto."

"Hi ho. Hi ho."

"Most men lead lives of quiet desperation."

"No shit. I take it you're not the author of those immortal words?"

"No. Thoreau. But I can be almost as poetic. How about: Life sucks?"

"Works for me." Isidore dragged the bag onto his lap. "By the way, I think we should call it a day on the LEVELEX job. That place is Fort Knox, man. Let's cut our losses."

Gabriel shook his head. He was still grooming Mr. Ariel Scott, and he and the yoga teacher had shared another pot of green tea only yesterday. It was just a matter of time before he'd be able to get some workable info off the man. Isidore knew nothing of this, of course.

"Let's hang in there awhile longer."

"OK. You're the boss." Isidore tapped the digits into the key lock of the bag. "To get back to the sisters—when are you meeting up with the girls again? It's been a week since the dinner party. You still need to retrieve the keylogger from their computer. It's going to be difficult if they don't invite you back."

"Don't worry on that score."

"I hope you're right. I need to give that logger back to my friend. It's just on loan, remember. And even though he's a buddy, this guy can get seriously aggressive when he's pissed."

"Isidore, relax. It's a sure thing."

"How do you know?"

"I've been reading the diary. And it tells me they have not forgotten about me. I expect to hear from them any day now." On the other side of the big plate-glass windows fronting the lobby, Gabriel could see a capped security man sharing a desk with the company's receptionist. The man seemed to be looking in their direction.

"OK." Gabriel pulled the bag toward him and rolled down the window. "Focus. We need to get to work before they send Fido over there to check us out."

"Yeah. Yeah. But you're *sure* they'll invite you back?"

"Believe me. It'll happen."

And he was right. The next morning, when he logged onto the diary, Gabriel felt his pulse quicken.

* * *

Entry Date: 20 July

M *thinks it's time to contact G. I can't agree more.*

When I think of him, I feel my entire body turning on. Moist palms, crackling neurons, electric storms in every cell.

Watch it, girl! M will not be amused. And she's right. G has not entered our life as a romantic interest. He will walk another path.

And we will need to take it slow, this time. R signed up for the game. G did not. He will have to be seduced into playing.

And then we can give G his name . . .

So no rushing things. The approach will need to be far more circumspect. A leisurely dance. A courtship.

He was still staring at the screen when, as if on cue, the doorbell rang.

It was a courier with a letter. The handwriting on the envelope was feminine but strong: delicate connecting strokes but luscious loops to the *g*'s and *l*'s. Inside was a sheet of delightfully scented rice paper folded in half. The message was short but sweet: *Two ladies in need of a dashing escort. May we prevail upon your sense of gallantry? Ticket enclosed. Dress glam.*

A buff-colored ticket was attached to the note with a paper clip. A grand tier seat for the premiere of *Romeo and Juliet* at Covent Garden.

The courtship had begun.

ENCHANTED SUMMER

Knowledge is power.—Nam et ipsa scientia potestas est.

Francis Bacon, *Meditationes Sacrae. De Haeresibus*, 1597

Power is not knowledge. Power is code.
Erik Davis, "Techgnosis, Magic, Memory"

CHAPTER FIFTEEN

Romeo and Juliet was an evening of penguin suits and champagne. But, as Gabriel was about to discover, the tastes and interests of the sisters Monk were eclectic.

Within the week he had also escorted them to an open mike poetry evening, a kickboxing tournament in Essex and a picnic in a graveyard. The graveyard, it had to be said, was not just any cemetery, it was Highgate: final resting place of Marx, Christina Rossetti, George Eliot and Michael Faraday.

"And the haunt of Lucy Westenra," Morrighan added. She was sitting cross-legged on the grass with a plate of sandwiches on her lap, her finger hovering between cucumber and egg-mayonnaise.

"*Dracula*," she explained in response to the query on Gabriel's face.

He looked down at her where she sat, her posture at ease but her back straight. Morrighan seldom slouched. Even at her most relaxed you had the feeling of leashed-in energy. Kneeling next to her, was Minnaloushe, red hair fastened in a careless knot. She was worrying the cork from a wine bottle. He knew he should offer his help, but Minnaloushe looked so cute, bottle clutched in one fist, tongue slightly protruding with effort, that he refrained. And as he looked at the two women, side by side, he felt his heart lift.

"*Dracula?*"

"Yes. Highgate was where Bram Stoker got his inspiration from."

Morrighan closed her eyes and intoned in a deliberately doleful voice: "*He is young and strong; there are kisses for us all . . . The girl went on her knees, and bent over me, simply gloating. There was a deliberate voluptuousness which was both thrilling and repulsive, and as she arched her neck she licked her lips like an animal, till I could see in the moonlight the moisture shining on the scarlet lips and on the red tongue as it lapped the white sharp teeth . . .*"

She stopped and opened those startlingly blue eyes. Before he could gather his wits, Minnaloushe started speaking, obviously taking up where her sister had stopped. "*Lower and lower went her head as the lips went below the range of my mouth and chin . . . I could hear the churning sound of her tongue . . . I could feel the soft, shivering touch of the lips on the super-sensitive skin of my throat, and the hard dents of two sharp teeth, just touching and pausing there. I closed my eyes in a languorous ecstasy and waited—waited with beating heart.*"

"Holy shit." He looked from one woman to the other. "What the hell was that?"

"Poor Jonathan Harker. Fighting off Count Dracula's succubae. Erotic, don't you think?"

"I'll say. That was from the book?"

"Uh-huh." Morrighan nodded. "Those Victorians knew about the allure of sexual mastery and submission, you have to give them that."

"Well, it's obviously a favorite. Do you keep it next to your bed?"

"Maybe Minnaloushe keeps it under *her* pillow. It wouldn't surprise me. But I haven't read *Dracula* since high school."

"Me neither." Minnaloushe shook her head. "I have to admit, when I was fourteen the Count was top of the pops for me. Dark, handsome, good teeth. But I'm happy to say I've grown up and no longer require my men to be quite as exotic." She laughed and leaned over to high-five her sister.

He joined in their laughter, but he was slightly taken aback. Whereas he had difficulty remembering his phone number, these women apparently had word-perfect recall of entire paragraphs of text. From a book they hadn't read in years. Impressive . . . and weird.

From the bottle in Minnaloushe's hand came a satisfying squeak as she finally succeeded in removing the cork.

"Gabriel, wine?"

The wine bottle, he noticed, had no label. He sniffed suspiciously at the dark red liquid. "What's this?"

"Berry wine. It's Morrighan's brew."

He took a gingerly sip from his glass. It was unexpectedly wonderful. "I could get used to this." He took another swallow.

Minnaloushe smiled slowly. "Good. It's very healthy. It will build up your immune system. Make it part of your daily diet."

"Maybe I will." He drained the glass. The liquid left a red sediment circle at the bottom.

She nodded again, satisfied. "Another glass?"

"Why not?"

"To us." Minnaloushe smiled.

"To getting to know each other," Morrighan added. She squinted her eyes against the glare of sunshine. Her glass when it touched his pinged so pure it sounded like joy.

Good for your health it might be, but Morrighan's berry wine also packed a kick like a mule. When he got home Gabriel fell asleep in front of the TV. When he woke up it was to find himself slumped onto the sofa at a very uncomfortable angle, drool staining the cushion under his head. The TV was still on. The phone on the coffee table was ringing.

He glanced at his watch. 11:53 P.M. Too late for a social call.

He clicked the mute button on the remote and picked up the receiver.

"Did I wake you?" Frankie's voice was so clear, it sounded as though she was standing right next to him.

"It's OK. What's up?"

"Nothing much." A long pause. "I just wanted to chat. I was wondering how you're doing."

He frowned. "I'm good. You?"

"I'm OK." But there was something in her voice that was off.

"What's wrong, Frankie? It's late. Why aren't you in bed?"

"I am in bed."

"Oh. And William?" Surely she wasn't calling him just for a chat with her husband lying next to her.

"He's sleeping. Since his illness started, he sleeps in his own room. He doesn't want to worry about disturbing me." A pause. "I was dead set against it, at first. But he insisted. And maybe it's easier for him that way."

"I'm sure." Gabriel wondered how much physical intimacy there still was between Frankie and her husband. He knew he shouldn't be speculating about something like that, but under the circumstances it was hard not to.

"Gabriel . . ."

"Yes?"

A long pause, so long he thought for a moment she was no longer on the line.

"Have you ever thought what it might have been like if . . ."

"If what?"

"If we had stayed together?"

He rubbed his forehead. "Of course I have." Not only that, he thought silently, but since she came back into his life, there were times when he had wondered if they might have a second chance. He hadn't felt good about it—it was as though he were wishing William Whittington dead. Which emphatically was not the case. But the fact of the matter was that Frankie would be a free woman again in the not so distant future.

A long, drawn-out sigh. Her voice muffled now. "I love William. With all my heart. I need you to believe that."

"I do, of course."

"But sometimes I can't help wondering . . . I'm sorry; I shouldn't be saying these things. And I shouldn't lay this on you. It's not fair."

"You know you can talk to me about anything."

"It's too soon, you know? He and I haven't had enough time together. And now that he's ill, he's withdrawing. He's already said good-bye. I can't reach him."

"Frankie, I'm so sorry."

"You, I could always reach. You were a bastard in many ways, but I knew what you were about."

"Well, thanks, I guess."

"I feel disloyal. Talking like this."

"We all need a shoulder to cry on."

"I know."

"Frankie . . ."

"Sorry I woke you." She was in a rush now. She was regretting calling him, Gabriel could tell.

He sighed. "Anytime."

He replaced the receiver and stared at the phone. Two weeks ago he would not have believed a conversation like this to be possible. Frankie opening up to him, talking about the past, reaching out. And two weeks ago, he would have been thrilled to receive this call. But now, he was not quite as excited as he would have expected, and he did not need a shrink to tell him why. For a moment he thought of the hapless Jonathan Harker on the verge of turning into neck candy for Count Dracula's brides. *I closed my eyes in a languorous ecstasy and waited—waited with beating heart.*

Oh, man. Why the hell did everything always have to be so complicated?

Complicated, of course, did not even begin to describe the situation in which he found himself.

In the eight weeks that followed he and Minnaloushe and Morrighan Monk became virtually inseparable. And as he got drawn deeper and deeper into the sisters' world, he was losing his ability to think about them with any kind of objectivity.

He knew they had an agenda. The diary made that crystal clear. Should it have kept him watchful? Undoubtedly. Did it? Hardly. The more time he spent in their company, the more difficult it was to keep up his defenses. This was a slow seduction. To be the object of attention of two extraordinary women was heady stuff.

And they were extraordinary. Even though he saw the sisters almost every day, and sometimes in the most mundane of situations—doing the laundry, or early in the morning still dressed in their bathrobes with hair mussed and lips pale—they remained exotic creatures, their ways mysterious. They were undoubtedly women of their time, but there was a twist to their thinking, which was not modern in the least. It was even evident in their immediate environment.

"Do you still use this?" he once asked Minnaloushe, pointing at the ivory-beaded abacus.

"Of course," she replied, as though astonished by the question.

And then there was their interest in alchemy. It carried with it a whiff of witchcraft, old dusty books and divine insanity.

He was starting to neglect his work. He had always worked as hard as he played, but the balance between the two was slipping. Every day saw him squiring Minnaloushe and Morrighan Monk around town. The two ladies made an impact wherever they went, and it was flattering to enter a room with a stunning woman on each arm. Everyone watching. He would feel pride and even a certain sense of possessiveness. They're with me, he'd think, noticing the sidelong glances. I'm their guy.

But it wouldn't be the gala evenings, the polo matches or the dinners at restaurants he'd remember when later he thought back on those two months. What he would remember best were the evenings spent quietly at Monk House. Lovely long dusks in the darkening garden watching the humpbacked tree with its fiery petals turn to black; breathing in the fragrance of the star jasmine smothering the rows of trellis. At other times finding himself slouched in one of the creased leather armchairs in the living room, a glass of Morrighan's berry wine in his hand. Morrighan would be curled up in the peacock armchair, reading with fierce concentration. Perched on a high stool at the workbench was Minnaloushe, fairy-sized chisel in her hand, working on restoring a weathered mask.

There would always be something beautiful playing on the state-of-the-art Nakamichi music system. The sisters had a vast library of music, but their favorite piece was "Andante Cantabile," Tchaikovsky's String Quartet no. 1, opus 11. When later he remembered those long days of summer, he would always recall the bittersweet violin notes: a musical leitmotif running through their days like golden thread.

But he was leading a deeply schizophrenic existence.

To us. To getting to know each other. Except . . . their tight little group had a fourth member. Invisible but ever-present. When they filled their glasses with wine, he too would be at the table, raising his glass in a silent toast. When they were in the garden, soaking up the sunshine, he was stretching out his lanky legs to catch the rays, smiling a sweet uncomplicated smile, his eyes—those absurdly innocent eyes—crinkling at the corners.

Robert Whittington. Who had died screaming, his mind shattered.

On the surface Gabriel laughed with the sisters, flirted with them, teased them affectionately. But all the while, beneath that gleaming river of friendship lurked the knowledge that one of them was a killer.

He sometimes forgot that. Or maybe he simply didn't want to think about it. One of these women walked through his dreams every night. The bizarre fact that he didn't have a clue as to which of the two women she was meant he did not want either one of the sisters to be guilty.

He had thought it inevitable that he would be able to put face to voice as he got to know both sisters better, but as each day passed, the identity of the diary's owner remained tantalizingly elusive.

Minnaloushe, despite her warmth and copious charm, had an opaque quality about her. She made him think of smoke on water. Of mist, fog and hidden places. Her femininity was full on. The long golden red hair cascading over her cheekbones, the full breasts and rounded hips and the generous gypsy mouth were elementally female.

Morrighan's personality was less diffuse. Everything about her seemed pure and clear-cut. Her features were as elegant as a profile on a Grecian urn. The black of her hair so black it gleamed blue with a midnight sheen. The white of her eyes so white it looked almost artificial. She carried herself with feline grace. You had the impression that what she wanted from life—and from love—she took. No hesitation.

With Minnaloushe you were aware of a slow, throbbing erotic energy. He recalled one of the diary entries: *I am addicted to experiencing love with all my senses open.* Surely the voice in the diary must belong to Minnaloushe.

Love is extreme sport. It exercises the muscle of the mind with the same intensity as climbing a mountain exercises the muscle of the heart. And it is just as dangerous. Was the voice Morrighan's?

Each day Gabriel watched the sisters: evaluating their behavior, trying to match it to the template of the diary's enigmatic text. If he watched closely enough, maybe he would get lucky. All he needed was one giveaway gesture; one word to betray her true identity.

It did not occur to him that his search for the diary's owner had taken precedence over his quest to find Robert Whittington's killer. He told himself the two goals were inseparable. Once the identity of the writer was established, the identity of the mysterious M she referred to in her pages would also be revealed. And he would have found his killer.

The possibility that the diary's writer might be the killer herself was a possibility he simply refused to consider.

CHAPTER SIXTEEN

There was another way in which the identity of the killer could be established, Gabriel knew. The answer might lie in the mysterious file *The Promethean Key*. And so, within days of escorting the sisters to *Romeo and Juliet*, he had made sure to retrieve the tiny electronic spy he had installed inside their keyboard.

Isidore was much relieved. The logger's rightful owner—a wizard named Aaron—had the brain of a techno nerd but the arms of a cage fighter. Messing with him was to be avoided. But before returning the logger to its owner, Isidore analyzed the keystrokes it contained.

He called Gabriel with the password the very next day.

"The password to *The Promethean Key* is a name: Hermes Trismegistus. T-r-i-s-m-e-g-i-s-t-u-s."

Gabriel wrote the words down carefully. "That's a mouthful."

"Now that you have the password you can take a peek at that file, bro. Just make sure they don't catch you at it."

"I'll do it as soon as I can."

At the time, when he said those words, he meant them. But as the days passed, he kept putting it off. To be fair, the perfect opportunity to access the Mac did not immediately present itself. But when he finally got his chance, he did not take it.

It was a Saturday afternoon. He was in the kitchen slicing up a lemon to add to some freshly made granita. Minnaloushe and Morrighan were in the garden, sharing a hammock, balancing it between them effortlessly. He had been sent inside by Minnaloushe to find her something to drink.

After slicing up the lemon, he took the jug with granita from the fridge and poured the mixture into a tall glass. As he replaced the jug, he paused.

The door of the fridge was covered with photographs drooping lopsidedly from colored magnets. Many of the snapshots were of himself. There he was, looking decidedly goofy doing an Ali G impersonation. Man, that was embarrassing. He must have had way too much to drink that night. But in all these pictures he looked amazingly carefree, he thought. Happy.

Just as Robert Whittington had looked happy.

He frowned, remembering the photographs of the boy tacked to the wall in the bedroom upstairs. He wondered if they were still there. After that first clandestine visit to Monk House, he had not had the opportunity to visit the top floor again. Certain things were still off-limits to him despite his friendship with the women. Bedrooms were definitely out of bounds. Sadly so.

He picked up the glass and headed out of the kitchen. As he walked through the living room, his eye fell on the Macintosh. The screen saver was on, the woman with the flowing hair and swirling robe smiling gently at the exploding sun waxing and waning in her hands.

He stopped. The ice cubes inside the glass tinkled lightly.

Through the slatted shutters he could see the hammock and its two occupants. Morrighan had covered her face with her hat and seemed to be napping. Minnaloushe was reading her magazine.

He looked back at the machine. All that was needed was for him to type in the password. Open the file. Steal one of the spare CDs in that plastic holding case over there and download the data.

Easy.

So do it.

He was dimly aware of a trapped bumble bee desperately buzzing against the windowpane. In his glass box on the shelf above the computer, Goliath stirred, long legs moving restlessly.

He waited, his mind oddly blank. Inside his chest a sick feeling.

The contents of that file could tell him who Robert's murderer was.

Do it.

Teardrops of condensation were forming on the sides of the glass. His hand was wet.

He transferred the glass from one hand to the other and wiped his hand dry on his pants. Pushing the French doors wide, he walked back into the heat of the garden.

CHAPTER SEVENTEEN

At about this time Gabriel started having the dream.

He was in the portal. The room in which Robert Whittington had opened a door and discovered madness. And even though he had come to know it well, each time he entered the vast circular space, the sense of awe was as sharp as though he was seeing it for the first time. The blinding light illuminating the dome. The massive concentric stone walls covered with symbols. The feeling that he was entering sacred space.

At this point in the time line of the dream Gabriel would be happy, a sense of expectation lifting his heart. If only the dream stopped there, but it never did.

The door. The door that was open a crack. He knew he should keep his distance. He knew what was lurking behind it. Pain and an avalanche of images and sounds that would crush his mind to pulp.

He was sweating. Turn away. Turn away. But he kept moving forward, his fingers reaching for the door.

He had once read that dreams could be harbingers of what was waiting down the road. Patients dreaming about mutilation and death have been shown to have serious health problems. And the more nightmarish their dreams became, the more their condition had worsened, even though they might not even have been aware of their illness. Progression in the dream mirrored progression in the disease.

Gabriel's dream was also progressing. Every time, he knew he was one step closer to opening the door. With every installment he was moving closer to that moment when his fingers would not just reach for the door but open it fully.

But if his dream life was progressing, the same could not be said for his waking life. He was still no closer to identifying the siren voice who kept him in a state of invisible intimacy. It sometimes felt to him as though she was engaged in a game of cruel, perpetual arousal. Here I am, she seemed to say. You may look, but you can't touch.

It was driving him crazy.

Last night in bed I thought of G. I fantasized. Touch me here, I said and placed his hand against my breast. And here, and I guided his fingers between my legs.

He read her words—cool black against white—and his body was sweating and restless and he ached with wanting to know who she was.

"Who would you like it to be?" Isidore asked him.

"What do you mean?"

"If you had a choice," Isidore asked, half-serious, half-mocking, "who would you like your mysterious anima figure to be? Minnaloushe or Morrighan?"

But to that question he was unable to give a straight answer. "I would like it to be the one who did not murder Robert Whittington, that's who."

"So you admit the writer of the diary could be the guilty one. The last time we talked you said it could never be."

"I still think that . . . most of the time."

"You haven't answered my question. If you had to choose between Minnaloushe and Morrighan—who would you choose?"

"I don't know."

"You can't like both of them equally, Gabe. Come on. Go with your gut."

"Isidore—I don't know."

"What do you like most about Minnaloushe?"

"Her warmth. Her sense of play."

"And Morrighan?"

"Morrighan . . . Morrighan is intrepid."

"OK. Let's try this. If you had to live on a desert island for the rest of your life—who would you rather want to be with?"

In his mind came an image of Minnaloushe, stretching lazily like a cat, curling up in the sunshine that is striking the padded window seat where she is sitting. The hair at her temple is gold and her eyes are turquoise flecked with bronze. Her breasts are full and heavy underneath the silk blouse. She catches him looking at her and strikes an exaggerated pose—a model performing for the camera—before blowing him a kiss.

But even as he smiled at the memory, another memory came crowding in. Morrighan drying her hair, her forearms pearling with drops of water after her shower. Her robe is clinging to the dampness of her skin, accentuating the lovely V of her back. The robe is thin and the light such that he can see the outline of her narrow hips, a shadow between the long legs. She combs her hair with bowed head and catches a glimpse of him through the triangle of her arm. She smiles—the delighted smile of a woman who knows she is being admired.

He sighed. "I can't choose. It's too hard."

"You know you're playing with fire."

"I know."

"You've got balls of steel, my friend. And even if your diary writer isn't the murderer, she *must* have known what her sister was up to. They're close, those two."

Yes, they were close, Gabriel thought, but it was a closeness that was not trouble-free.

M's arrogance. That pure, bright arrogance that burns within her like a flaming sword.

The diary had exposed a relationship that was a tangled bond of affection and aversion. In fact, the writer's feelings for her sister sometimes seemed to vacillate between extreme admiration and outright hostility.

I am in awe of M. Her thoughts are like hammer blows. Powerful enough to crack the world wide open.

Another entry: *Sometimes I cannot abide it. I look at M and my skin starts itching as if from a toxic rash. Her obsession is like a growth sucking*

all the oxygen from the air. I feel strangled. I feel like screaming at her,
over and over again: Stop! Stop! Stop!

But it wasn't only the diary that told him that not everything was
smooth sailing between the sisters.

"She can get anyone to do anything she wants." Morrighan's voice
was casual, as though she were mentioning some trivial fact of no
real importance.

Gabriel turned toward her, surprised. She caught his glance and
smiled faintly. "You can't blame me for being envious. Minnaloushe
has always been able to twist people around her little finger. And
once she wants something from you, she won't stop until she gets it."

He felt awkward.

"Minnaloushe is beautiful, Gabriel. Don't you think so?"

"Morrighan, you're beautiful too."

"I know," she said without any pretense at mock modesty. "But I
don't have her charm. That devastating charm. She can make you follow her into a burning house." And her voice was no longer casual.

The rivalry wasn't one-sided. Once, quite by chance, he had pulled
a photo album from one of the bookshelves at Monk House. It contained newspaper clippings and photographs of Morrighan's more ad-
venturous exploits. Morrighan skydiving. Morrighan free climbing.
Morrighan picketing outside a nuclear facility in the Ukraine, con-
fronted by baton-wielding security guards with menacing shoulders.
As he paged through the album, fascinated, he was joined by Minnaloushe. She looked over his shoulder and watched in silence as he
turned the leaves.

"Your sister leads quite a life."

"Yes. I envy her."

"Envy?"

"I envy Morrighan her fearlessness. Look at this picture." Minnaloushe tapped against a black-and-white close-up photograph.
Morrighan's head was thrown back and her face was sooty. Her hair

lay sweatily against her forehead. Across one cheekbone was a clotted scratch. Her eyes were challenging, but there was a smile on her lips. The overall impression was piratical.

"When was this taken?" he asked. "What was she doing?"

"God knows. I can't remember. Something that required guts and a total disregard for safety, you can be sure of that." She sighed. "I am convinced that in a previous life Morrighan was a great warrior who led armies into the night. Or maybe a Joan of Arc. I can see her embracing the pain."

"And you?"

"Me? I'm feckless." She repeated the word as though she liked the feel of it on her tongue. "Feckless."

Sometimes the fault lines in their relationship erupted into open warfare.

He was taking a nap outside in the garden when he woke suddenly feeling inexplicably anxious. It was as though someone had shouted into his ear only a moment before. But when he looked around him, there was no one.

He tipped himself out of the hammock and started walking toward the house. As he approached the French doors, he could see the two sisters inside the living room. They were facing each other. There was something about the way they held themselves—the rigidity in Minnaloushe's shoulders, the jut of Morrighan's chin—that made him slow his steps.

"You did it on purpose." Minnaloushe's voice was hard, accusing.

"No."

"Yes. You knew it would upset me."

Morrighan made a sharp, disgusted noise. "I know you find this hard to believe, Minnaloushe, but the idea of what you like and might not like does not always occupy my mind. You think the world revolves around you. It doesn't."

"Sometimes . . ." Minnaloushe's voice was now trembling. "Sometimes I think I should leave this house."

"And sometimes you're so childish I can't stand it."

He shouldn't be witnessing this, Gabriel thought. He should get the hell out. He took a long step backward, trying to be as quiet as possible.

But at that moment, Minnaloushe turned her head sharply in his direction. Even though it had not been his intention to eavesdrop, Gabriel felt embarrassed.

Her lovely face was flushed and her eyes very bright. For a second it looked as though she might say something, but instead she turned on her heel. Back held ramrod straight, she walked—stalked would probably be the better description—in the direction of the dining room and disappeared from sight. Another few moments and they heard the door to the kitchen slam shut with tremendous force.

Silence. It was as though the entire house were in shock.

Gabriel looked at Morrighan. As she caught his glance, she smiled wryly. She turned her palms upward. "Sorry about that."

He stepped gingerly into the room. "That's OK. Sorry I interrupted."

"No. It's just as well. We might have ended up saying things to each other that would have poisoned the atmosphere for days." Morrighan looked tired. Her eyes were shadowed.

"Have you guys ever thought of living apart?" he asked, his mind on Minnaloushe's last words.

"Oh, yes. I often think the best thing would be for us to go our separate ways."

"So why don't you?"

"It's complicated. We need each other. And neither one of us wants to leave this house."

She brought her hand up to the pendant dangling from her neck. He had seen her do this before, as though she derived strength from it. It was the pendant in the shape of the letter *M*.

He watched as she twirled the silver chain around her finger. She had lovely hands with graceful fingers. The nails were unvarnished and cut short.

"My mother gave me this," she told Gabriel, noticing his interest.

"Minnaloushe has one too, doesn't she?"

"Yes. Mum gave them to us at the same time. I was sixteen. Minnaloushe a year younger. Six months later my mother wasn't able to recognize us. She suffered from Alzheimer's."

"I'm sorry. That must have been hard."

"It was horror. It is the most primal of all fears, I think—the fear that your mother will forget you."

"I'm sorry," he repeated.

"It was because of my mother's condition that Minnaloushe became interested in the subject of memory. She did her Ph.D. on that topic, you know."

"Yes, I know."

"I think it helped her come to terms with the dreadfulness of it all."

"And you?"

"I wept," she said simply. "I wept for a long time." She paused. "I still weep."

For once her face was unguarded, the habitual expression of cool amusement gone. Morrighan did not like to appear vulnerable. This was the first time she had opened up to him in this way.

Gabriel touched her hand in sympathy. Her fingers twitched underneath his, and as he looked into her eyes, her pupils swelled.

His breath caught.

Morrighan's eyes went past his shoulder. He turned around.

Minnaloushe was standing in the door, smiling at them. Her smile included her sister—a clear sign that hostilities had ceased.

"Sorry, sis."

Morrighan sighed. "Me too. Sorry."

Minnaloushe looked at Gabriel. "If we promise to behave, will you stay for dinner?"

He hesitated.

"Please?"

He relaxed. "Thanks. I'd love to."

"Good." She linked her arm through his and dropped her voice to a conspiratorial whisper. "Because this morning I baked my magic chocolate cake for dessert."

"Magic?"

"Sure. Eat it and you'll become smart, sexy and psychic."

"I thought I was all of that already."

"And modest," Morrighan added, taking hold of his other arm. "Did she mention modest?"

He joined in their laughter, the discomfort of having been a witness to their argument receding from his mind. Placing an arm around the waist of each, he drew them toward him. Still laughing, the three of them walked side by side into the garden, where twilight was turning a blue sky pink.

Later that night, after he had returned to his own apartment, he logged on to the diary.

When G placed his hand on the small of my back today, my whole body reacted. I wonder if he noticed. I could feel my skin flush, sweat in my armpits. My legs becoming weak. His fingers were touching that exact spot, where a man places his hand when he guides a woman in a dance, inviting her—oh so gently, but oh so insistently—to follow his lead. And as in a dance I wanted him to lean into me. To feel the muscles straining in his thighs. To feel my hips moving to his rhythm. Sexual desire inflamed, but kept at bay by the formality of the steps.

I could see M watching me. And it wasn't just because of our argument today. I know she senses my attraction to G. Is she worried that I will falter and not give him his name? Or is she jealous?

But I can't help myself. I think about it too often. What it would be like to taste his mouth. What it would feel like to have him lying heavy and spent on top of me, to have him crush me beneath his weight.

Gabriel got up and walked onto the balcony, his hands gripping the railing hard. His heart was beating as though he had run a hundred-meter sprint. He stared into the light washed darkness.

My love. Who are you?

CHAPTER EIGHTEEN

Gabriel suppressed a sigh as he looked at the yoga teacher, who was once again wearing his polka-dot poncho. He had spent a lot of time on this guy, but it didn't look as though he was going to get anything worthwhile out of the man. Frankly, he was losing enthusiasm for the project. Ariel was not the most exciting conversationalist, and getting up at the crack of dawn every Tuesday was getting to be tiresome. As usual he had spent a late night with the sisters. Setting the alarm for six this morning had been a heroic act. Maybe he should terminate the project today. Pity, though. He'd really thought this one would come through.

The yoga teacher was moaning about having a lot of pressure at work. Gabriel was listening with one ear, not really paying attention. He wondered whether he had any Neurofens in his locker. He had a headache—he really should start watching his consumption of Morrighan's berry wine. He was getting a wee bit too fond of a dram every night.

"Sorry?" He focused fully on the yoga teacher. "What was that you just said?"

"I said, the company I work for is now providing live network jacks inside the cafeteria, so employees can access the corporate network while they're having lunch. How diabolical is that? They're putting pressure on us to work while we eat. You can't even have a sandwich in peace anymore."

Bingo. Gabriel stared at the man. "Live jacks," he repeated slowly.

"Yes. Don't you think that is putting pressure on employees to continue working during their downtime? Quite disgraceful."

"Yeah. Disgraceful." Gabriel nodded. His brain was working furiously. He had always known that in order to crack the code at LEVELEX, he would have to break into the premises. But LEVELEX hired guards who looked like marines and the premises were pretty much burglarproof. Except for the cafeteria. The cafeteria was in a low-level security sector of the building. Which made sense: nothing much of value there. But for those live jacks. All he would have to do was find his way to the food hall, which would not be guarded. Once there, he could plug in an Ethernet cable from his laptop to the wall jack. And then . . . rich pickings.

He looked at Ariel and wondered how he would react if he was told that by sharing this one tiny detail of his job—which he probably didn't even think was confidential—he had exposed his company to a deep hack. Way to go, Blackstone. He knew he'd hit the jackpot at some point.

All that was left now was to get Isidore on board.

Isidore was uncharacteristically irritable.

"So where's the report? You promised me you'd finish the analysis last night. So where is it?"

Gabriel's head was aching. After he had left the yoga teacher he had popped two Neurofens, but in the battle between berry wine and drugs, berry wine was winning hands down.

He squinted at his friend. "Why are you in such a good mood, Sunshine?"

"I mean it, Gabe. This isn't fair. You're playing Casanova and I'm working overtime. You knocked off early yesterday and you promised me the analysis this morning. Actually, you promised it to me two weeks ago already. So what's the plan? Do you even have one?"

Gabriel sat down heavily in Isidore's hideous pumpkin-colored velour armchair. He really did feel fragile. Being lectured to was not what he needed right now.

Isidore moved a stack of books from one end of his desk to another. His movements were abrupt and he slammed the books onto the desk with a bang that reverberated inside Gabriel's head.

"I've decided that we should terminate the LEVELEX project." Isidore's voice was firm. "I'm spending way too many hours on it and it's an impossible hack. I know you like the money, but we're giving the advance back."

Whoa. Gabriel sat up straight. "Don't do that, Is. I'm working on it."

"If I can't crack it, you won't be able to either." Isidore's voice was matter-of-fact.

Gabriel sighed. It was true, of course. Isidore was the master.

"I'm not talking about a hack. I have found another way in."

"Yeah? How?"

Gabriel hesitated.

"Oh, shit. No!" Isidore's voice rose. "Don't tell me you're grooming someone inside the company?"

"Isidore, calm down. The guy won't lose his job. And he doesn't even know about it."

"That is not the point. Dammit, Gabe. You know how I feel about social engineering."

"First you accuse me of not pulling my weight, and then when I come up with a solution to a problem you can't fix, you crap on it."

"Gabriel, I'm not your handmaiden, OK? I have a say in the running of the business as well. And I'm telling you, no. Manipulating people is not an option."

Gabriel flushed at the contempt in Isidore's voice. "Don't be so bloody squeamish. This is the real world—get it? And you're not the one getting your hands dirty. Go play with your little friends in *Dreadshine*. Leave the hard stuff to me."

For a moment they glared at each other. Before either one could speak again, the front door buzzer sounded.

Without asking who it was, Isidore placed his finger on the release button. Downstairs a door opened and slammed shut.

Gabriel frowned. "Who is it?"

"Frankie," Isidore answered briefly. "I've asked her to come over."

Shit. Gabriel cringed. He had been avoiding Frankie over the last couple of weeks, dodging her phone calls, leaving noncommittal e-mail and text messages. Obviously, a showdown was in the cards today.

Light steps sounded on the stairs, and the next moment Frankie entered the room. She was dressed in gym clothes and sneakers. Her hair was windblown and there was a lovely color in her cheeks. She looked vital and glowing. It made him feel even more decrepit.

"Hey you," she said, her voice friendly, and leaned over to give Isidore a kiss. Turning, she looked at Gabriel, a withering expression on her face.

"Well," she said. One word only, but it dropped the emotional temperature in the room by several degrees.

"Hi," he said feebly.

For a few agonizingly long moments there was quiet between them.

Isidore pushed a chair toward Frankie. "Maybe you should sit down."

"Thanks," she said without taking her eyes off Gabriel's face.

Silence again.

"What's up, Gabriel?" Frankie's voice was deceptively soft.

"I don't understand what you mean." He knew he sounded defensive.

"You've completely forgotten about Robbie."

He pressed his hands against his temples. "That's not true."

"Oh, really." This was Isidore, the traitor. "So why haven't you accessed *The Promethean Key* yet? I gave you the password for that computer weeks ago. You must have had plenty of opportunities by now."

Gabriel sent Isidore a bitter look.

"OK," Frankie said. "Forget about the computer, for a moment. You've been around the sisters a lot. By this time you should know who the remote viewer is. And if you know the identity of the remote viewer, you have a pretty good idea who the killer is."

He stirred himself. "I don't, Frankie. I didn't want to risk scanning either one of them and tipping the viewer off. And she hasn't tried to scan me again."

"Are you sure? Are you sure you'd know if she tried to access you?"

"For goodness' sake. Give me some credit. Of course I'd know."

Frankie's voice was tight. "Why have you been avoiding me, Gabriel? Is it because of the phone call I made that night? Did it scare you so badly?"

Isidore's embarrassment was palpable. "Maybe I should give you guys some privacy." Frankie waited until he had closed the door behind him.

"Was it the phone call? I was needy that night, I know."

"It's not the phone call."

"So it's the sisters."

The silence this time was stretched excruciatingly tight, like a rubber band refusing to snap.

"You're besotted with them, aren't you? Like Robbie was."

He didn't answer.

"Gabriel . . . what's wrong with you? One of them is a killer. And the other one probably helped her."

"You don't know that."

"What I know is that they're poison. And you're dying a slow death."

"Frankie, please. It's too early in the morning for melodrama."

"I should have known. I should have known you wouldn't be able to stay the course. You've never been a long distance runner. Not at Eyestorm and not now."

His face burned. "I don't need to listen to this." He got to his feet.

"Gabriel, don't go. We have to talk."

"I'm finished talking."

As he walked past her, she said something, her voice low.

"Please don't disappoint me. Not again."

He slammed out of Isidore's house in a foul mood. So this is what happens when you try to help someone, he thought. No good deed goes unpunished. He should have stayed the hell away from Frankie and her missing stepson.

Except . . . he would not have met the two most fascinating women he had ever encountered in his life.

A taxi, its light on, was coming toward him and he lifted his hand.

"13 Drake Street," he told the cabdriver. "Chelsea."

It was Morrighan who opened the door for him at Monk House.

"Gabriel. What a lovely surprise. I wasn't expecting you before tonight."

"Sorry. Am I interrupting?"

"Not at all. Come on in. Minnaloushe isn't here so you'll have to make do with me, I'm afraid."

As he stepped into the house, he felt his mood lighten. The house was quiet and peaceful. The scent of flowers was everywhere. He followed Morrighan into the kitchen and sat down on one of the chairs.

"Can I make you some tea?"

"No thanks. You get on with whatever you were doing."

"I'm taking inventory," she said, turning toward the pine table with the chemistry equipment. "It's long overdue. I've been lazy."

She started counting a number of tiny brown bags and plastic tubs. Muttering something to herself, she paused and made a note in a book, which lay open on the table.

"Are you OK?" She flicked him a glance.

"Of course."

"You seemed a little agitated when you arrived."

"No, I'm fine."

"OK," she said amiably and turned toward the table again.

Gabriel watched as she picked up a vial, squinting at the contents. Her movements were sure and practiced.

"So who's the alchemist here—you or Minnaloushe?"

"The laboratory is mostly my baby. But we're both interested in alchemy. I tend to go for a hands-on approach whereas Minnaloushe's interest in the subject is more cerebral." She pursed her lips. "The thinker and the doer. As always."

He leaned back in the chair. He was starting to relax. The argument with Isidore and Frankie suddenly seemed of little importance. All that mattered was that he was here, in Monk House with a lovely, fascinating woman who was happy to have his company. What more could he ask for?

Morrighan was wearing a strappy lacy top. Her black hair fell cloudlike over her shoulders. She was beautiful. He suddenly wondered what it would be like to scoop the hair away from her face, to press his lips against the soft skin at the side of her neck . . . .

Manfully he turned his eyes away to study the framed prints on the wall. Not that these prints were designed to make one think of higher things. They seemed to focus on pretty primal emotions. Naked figures hugging, touching fingertips to one another, dancing with pagan abandon in front of bubbling cauldrons. Flames, heat, sweat.

"Smell this." Morrighan held a small tub out at him.

He took a cautious sniff. "Is this perfume?"

"Yes. But solid perfume. You rub it on, you don't spray it on. We're thinking of selling it along with our other stuff. Do you like it?"

He wasn't quite sure. The scent was wild and woody and for some reason made him feel strangely anxious. But it was certainly distinctive.

"I made this perfume according to alchemical principles. Separate and reassemble. See." She lifted her brows. "Alchemy can have quite pedestrian uses as well."

He gestured at the liquid vials and the prints. "You have to admit, all of this looks very hocus-pocus."

"You don't believe in magic?" Her tone of voice was the same as if she had said, *You don't believe the earth is round?* Surprised incredulity.

"I can't say I do."

"Nothing has ever happened to you that can't be explained by the laws of physics?"

Slamming a ride probably qualified, he thought. But remote viewing was free from incantations and spells and he had never picked up even a hint of sulfur.

He shrugged. "I suppose there are things that can't be explained yet, but which will be in future. I don't think alchemy qualifies. It has already been discredited."

Morrighan shook her head firmly. "Alchemy used to be a highly respected discipline. And many of the great figures of deductive science who openly ridiculed alchemy were actually closet alchemists themselves. Copernicus, Kepler, Bacon. Even Newton tried to discover the secrets of the philosopher's stone. Some of the alchemists who practiced during the Middle Ages and Renaissance were responsible for breakthrough discoveries in metallurgy, chemistry and medicine. Just think of Paracelsus."

"Who he?"

She frowned at his irreverence. "He introduced chemical compounds into medicine and described zinc. He was one of history's greatest physicians and could heal gangrenous limbs, syphilis and ulcers." She grinned. "He even practiced an early form of homeopathy, treating plague victims with tiny amounts of their own feces."

"Innovative."

"I thought you'd be impressed." She turned around and gestured at the bottles and jars on the table. "I use many of his techniques when making my lotions and drinks." She caught the expression on his face. "Excrement-free, don't worry."

"Well, the guy sounds like a lateral thinker, I'll give you that."

"And a courageous one. To be a practicing alchemist was very dangerous in those times. They met with very sticky ends." She paused, frowned again. "No, wrong metaphor. They met with very dusty ends. *Corpus kaput.* They were usually burned at the stake. Like Bruno here." She bent down and stroked the head of the cat, which was rubbing itself against her legs. "Isn't that so, my sweetest sweetheart?"

Gabriel looked on dispassionately. He and the cat had achieved a kind of armed truce. They still disliked each other intensely, but in deference to the ladies they tried not to give in to their mutual animosity. But whenever he entered the room, Bruno's tail would start swishing as though animated by an electric current. Minnaloushe and Morrighan thought it very funny.

Morrighan looked up at him. "You know that Bruno here was named after Giordano Bruno?"

"Yes. Minnaloushe told me. She said he was a magician."

"Most alchemists were, and we're not talking card tricks. These men were adepts. And very, very powerful."

He shrugged. "Well, if they were able to turn lead into gold, they have my vote."

"Why doesn't that surprise me?" She smiled wryly. "But that's not what alchemy was really about. Material transmutation was only one part of it. Alchemy is really the transformation of the spirit into a higher form of consciousness. Enlightenment. Coming face-to-face with God and discovering his motivations for creating the universe and your own place within it. Don't you think that is a far greater secret than knowing how to exchange one metal for another?"

"Will you hate me if I say I'd still rather settle for the gold?"

She sighed. "You're a barbarian."

"It's the world we live in. It's all about money and things which can be measured, perceived and weighed."

"Oh, no," she said. "That's not the world we live in at all. Why," she placed one hand on her breast in a strangely ecstatic gesture, "don't you realize . . . the world is *imagination*. The world is magic."

His eyes were drawn to her hand. Her fingers were touching the tattoo of the *Monas* on her breast: the rose and its enigmatic sign inked into breathtakingly creamy skin. A deeply erotic bruise.

She lowered her hand. "Alchemy is fascinating."

He swallowed. "I'm beginning to think it might be."

CHAPTER NINETEEN

He was supposed to spend the day with Isidore mining the latest data they had collected on the Pittypats project, but Gabriel did not feel like facing Isidore after the verbal punch-up of the previous day. His friend's self-righteous anger was more than he could deal with right now. And so, instead of heading to Smithfield, he found himself escorting Minnaloushe to a bookstore in North London.

Minnaloushe pulled a footstool toward her and stepped onto it. Extending her arm to its fullest reach, she began to worry two books from a shelf almost out of reach. As he watched, her top rode up to reveal the base of her spine and the *Monas* in all its delicate intricacy.

It was amazing what a visual punch a few inches of bare skin could deliver, he thought. And how fortunate that he should have the privilege twice in as many days.

She looked over her shoulder and caught him looking. "Hey, you." She handed him the book. "Stop drooling and take this. And no peeping up my blouse."

He smiled. "Sweetpea, I've seen it all before. Remember? And much more besides."

She grinned. "So you have. OK. Take a good look." And without any self-consciousness, she lifted her top and bent over forward, her hair cascading in front of her face like a waterfall. On the other side of the room a studious-looking young man stared at her and dropped his book. He looked as though someone had hit him over the head, leaving him severely concussed. When he saw Gabriel looking at him, he picked up his book abruptly and started reading again. Maybe he was concussed after all. The book was upside down.

Gabriel touched the tattoo lightly. "Very nice."

She straightened and gave him a wicked smile. "It is, isn't it?"

"I noticed Morrighan has one too."

"We had them done on the same day."

"So what does it mean? Make peace not war? Ban the bomb?"

"Oh, please. Give us credit for a little originality. It represents the unity of the cosmos."

"How Age of Aquarius."

She swatted his arm. "It was designed in the sixteenth century by a magus, no less. A certain John Dee. His personal diaries are kept at your old alma mater: in the Bodleian Library at Oxford. What's really cool, though, is that he's an ancestor of mine."

"Great."

She put her head to one side. "You don't look nearly impressed enough."

"No, I am. Really. Very cool." But something about what she'd just said was bothering him. If only he could put his finger on what it was.

She was now reading from one of the books she had taken from the shelf and her face was assuming a mask of concentration. It made her look almost stern. He had noticed this about her before. There would be something in her eyes, or the set of her mouth, that—for just a moment—would give him pause. It made him wonder what lurked beneath the playfulness, the femininity, which he associated with her so strongly. There was another side to her that was cool and watchful and *determined*.

He looked away, his eyes traveling over the rows of books packed murderously tight on the long shelves. At the far end of the room the store clerk was writing something on a blackboard. She was slim and had a delicately oval face with brown hair springing from her forehead in a widow's peak. Just like Frankie. Frankie, who had looked at him yesterday with disappointment. Her face etched with strain.

No. He shut his mind deliberately to the image. He wasn't going to allow himself a guilt trip. He had nothing to feel guilty about.

Minnaloushe replaced the first book she had taken off the shelf and opened the second one. He was standing slightly behind and to the side of her and was able to catch a glimpse of the contents of the book as she riffled through the pages. They appeared to be filled with watercolors but the scenes they depicted were not exactly pastoral. Fire seemed to be the prevailing motif. And caught in the flames were women in flowing robes, their bodies writhing in anguish but their faces eerily serene. It was rather shocking.

"Witches." Minnaloushe's voice was dispassionate. She hadn't looked up from the book in her hands, but she must have sensed his reaction. "Or rather, women perceived to be witches."

"Perceived by whom?"

"Oh, men. Men scared by the idea of women wanting to know the great secrets. Scared of other things too. Like female sexuality." She slammed the book shut. "Do you know how they used to test for witches?"

He shook his head.

"They'd throw the woman in a river with weights tied to her feet. If she sank, she was innocent. If she floated, she was a witch. Or they'd throw her off a high cliff to see if she could fly. In many seventeenth-century records of English witchcraft trials you'll find the words 'not guilty, no flying.' Which means, of course, that these women literally had to die in order to prove their innocence."

She stepped onto the stool again and pushed the thick tome back into place. It was much bigger than the other books on the shelf and stuck out awkwardly.

As they stepped through the wide doors that would lead them to the outside, he looked back. Even from this far away he was still able to see the black leather book with its spine jutting out like an accusing finger.

But it was sunny outside, and the uneasiness he had felt inside the bookstore was dissipating. It was lunchtime and they bought sandwiches from Marks & Spencer to eat in Regent's Park. From her capacious bag, Minnaloushe also extracted a bottle and two plastic cups.

"I came prepared," she said, grinning at him.

"Morrighan's?"

"Of course. Drink up. Good for you."

They ate slowly and in silence. Across from them an exhibitionist type was taking off his shirt and oiling himself. Gabriel had to admit he had an imposing physique: all coiled muscles and rock-hard abs. And he had the *I'm-so-cool-can-you-stand-it* look down pat. Minnaloushe was staring unashamedly.

She glanced over at Gabriel and caught his sardonic smile. "He's cute," she admitted.

"I could tell from your expression."

"But he's still a baby. It will take another ten years or so before he's interesting. Men don't become worth your while until they're in their thirties."

"At least I make the cut, then."

"Well, it's not automatic with all men, you know."

"Right."

With women, of course, it's different. Women are born interesting." She dimpled again and flopped down flat onto the grass.

He poured some more wine into his cup, watching her. She was lying, arms spread-eagled, eyes closed. Hair like Spanish moss. Was this his love? he wondered for the hundredth time. Are you the girl who can hear the sun set? Who likes to dive to the bottom of an ocean where the floor is made of glass and where fish get lost on purpose?

What if he simply asked her? "Minnaloushe, I've been snooping on you and your sister. I think one of you is a killer. But the other one writes the most intriguing diary and I've fallen in love with her. Is it you?"

If only it were that easy.

She opened her eyes. "What are you thinking?"

He reached out a languid hand and picked up a strand of silky soft hair.

"Minnaloushe. Such a pretty name. It suits you. It's very feminine."

She smiled gently, amused. "That's very sweet of you. But it's actually a man's name."

"No . . ."

"Yes. From the Yeats poem about a cat. Black Minnaloushe who wanders and wails, his pupils changing from round to crescent, his blood troubled by the pure cold light of the moon. It was my father's favorite poem. He desperately wanted a boy after Morrighan and had the name all picked out. But he got me instead. Big disappointment. I got stuck with the name anyway. It could have been worse, I suppose. He could have had his heart set on Cuchulainn." She laughed and pushed herself into a sitting position.

"And Morrighan? That's unusual too."

"Irish again, what do you know? From Irish mythology this time. My mum was from Galway."

"So you're half-Irish."

"Oh yes. Descended from fairies and pixies and beautiful witches."

"And the great John Dee."

"Yet another wizard." She stood up and brushed herself down. "It's getting late. Morrighan will be waiting."

It was only when they arrived back at Monk House that he realized what had bothered him earlier that day when they had talked about John Dee. Dee's diaries could be found at the Bodleian Library, she had said. At Gabriel's old alma mater. Except he had never told her he had been to Oxford. So the sisters had made some inquiries about him. Which meant they probably knew about Eyestorm as well. Of course, they already knew he was a remote viewer, but Eyestorm was not something he wanted to share. He supposed he should have expected that they would check up on him, but it still made him feel unsettled.

"Gabriel?"

He looked up to see Minnaloushe holding the door open for him. "Aren't you coming inside for a drink?"

He hesitated. For the first time he was reluctant to enter. It was as if some interior seismograph were warning him of danger ahead. If he wanted to evade it, he should flee now.

The moment passed. Inside the house a light came on and a moving shadow appeared against the lace curtains. Morrighan, engaged in some or other task.

He was suddenly tired and aware only of how pleasant it would be to pour himself a drink and to stretch out on the sofa in the cool, high-ceilinged living room with its scent of roses.

"Yes," he said, "I'm coming."

That night he dreamt. It was the old familiar dream of the portal but with a difference this time. One moment he was still inside the vast circular space with its symbol-clad walls, approaching the door, which was pulling him like a magnet. As always he was sweating, shivering in anticipation of the moment when the door would open fully.

And then suddenly he was not alone. A woman was standing with her back to him. Her hair was swept up underneath her broad-brimmed hat. She turned around and he saw it was Minnaloushe. In one hand she held a large black leather volume. In the other she was holding a wineglass filled with liquid that sparkled like the magic potion in a comic book. "Here," she said holding the glass out at him. "Drink up. Good for you." But as he stretched out his hand to take the glass from her, she suddenly burst into flame, the fire enveloping her in a cocoon of light.

And then he was standing on top of a tower and he and Morrighan were preparing for a jump. She was pressed against him and he felt the tautness of her breasts, her hips moving against his. As they stepped into nothingness, she placed her arms around his neck and said something. He strained to make out the words: "Perfect like flying," she said, her voice snatched away by the wind. "Perfect like flying."

But as they continued to fall—sky and earth merging into an insane blur—he realized he had misheard. "Perfect like dying," she was saying, over and over again. "Perfect like dying."

SHADOWS

The search for enlightenment is actually like an addiction: The drug that enslaves us is the shadow itself.

—Akron, *The H. R. Giger Tarot*

I wanted to know how the human mind reacted to the sight of its own destruction.

—C. G. Jung, *Memories, Dreams, Reflections*

CHAPTER TWENTY

The second indication that the sisters were checking up on him came only a few days later.

Gabriel had arrived early for a dentist's appointment only to be told by the sour-looking receptionist that Dr. Guiley's car had broken down and that he would be an hour late. Paging through a woman's magazine did not appeal. A walk outside seemed a better proposition. But as he stepped into the street, he realized that the sky had turned sullen. A few stray drops of rain spotted the sidewalk.

He hesitated, wondering if he should go back inside. He was standing on a busy street corner, but to his right a quiet alley led off from the high street. The alley was home to three tiny shops: a florist, the windows filled with prickly cacti, a sad-looking coffee shop with metal tables and a store with a dusty sign peeping through an even dustier window. *The Pagan Wheel*. And underneath it the words *divinatory tools, wiccan art and other essentials for the magick life.*

Magic again. He was not a great believer in synchronicity, but this was getting ridiculous.

As he pushed open the door, a bell tinkled faintly somewhere above him. The man behind the counter lifted his head at the sound. He had a thin face with feral eyes and reminded Gabriel of an emaciated wolf. The back of his hands were covered in tattoos— blue spiders weaving inky webs—as were the fingers. For a moment he stared expressionlessly at Gabriel, before going back to his book.

The shop was small but the shelves were packed. The paint on the walls was peeling, and there were damp patches at the skirting boards. Among the clutter Gabriel also noticed three mousetraps with dusty bits of cheese stuck inside their steel jaws. He grimaced. If he had to confess to a phobia, it would be mice. Rats were in the realm of total hysteria. Where his fear of these rodents stemmed from he had no idea, but they represented his ultimate nightmare.

There was a faint smell in the air. Sweetish, cloying. Gabriel wrinkled his nose in recognition. This smell came straight from his youth, but was one he did not encounter all that often any longer. Marijuana. Someone in this shop had been smoking grass. Well, he thought sardonically, mysticism and getting stoned have always gone hand in hand.

He glanced over at the shop owner again. The man was still deep in his book. His elbows were resting on the counter and he had his head propped up on his hands.

On the far wall were two prints. One was in black-and-white and showed death—a grinning skeleton—holding an hourglass. The other was lavishly colored and depicted a woman with flowing hair and swirling cape looking down at a sun clasped between her hands. The picture looked familiar: he had seen this image before. Then he remembered. The same image served as a screen saver on the computers at Monk House.

He made his way over to the picture, ducking dream catchers hanging from the ceiling. And there was no doubt about it: it was the same image. The flowing hair, the cape, the long white fingers wrapped around the golden sun.

He turned and looked over his shoulder. "Excuse me . . ."

The store owner looked up, and Gabriel was once again reminded of a wolf. It was something about the eyes.

"Can you help me?" Gabriel gestured at the print.

The man closed his book deliberately.

"This picture . . . what does it mean?"

The store owner moved out from behind the counter and came up to Gabriel. A bracelet in the shape of a snake was wound around the fleshy part of one arm, which was thin but muscled. His voice was soft and educated.

"As you can see from the color of her cloak, this woman is a witch."

Gabriel looked back at the picture. The cloak was green.

"The sun in her hands indicates she is a solar witch."

"Solar?"

"Solar witches are practitioners of high magic."

Gabriel was starting to feel irritated. "As opposed to low magic?"

The man did not react to the heavy sarcasm. "Magic can be separated into common magic and high magic. Common magic is the colorful side of magic—the kind that has always attracted the man on the street. Potions, incantions, sorceries." His voice sounded bored. "Women on brooms with pointed hats. Harry Potter books. TV shows. A lot of it is based on superstition and myth. Magic for the masses."

He made a sweeping gesture with his arm, taking in the glass-fronted cases filled with dowsing rods, daggers and jewelry. "Most of the stuff you see here is for dabblers in common magic. I have to make a living, yes?" He lifted his eyebrows as if astonished at himself for making the admission. "But high magic . . . high magic is rooted in the Hermetica, the Kabala and oriental mysticism. High magic is something else altogether."

Gabriel waited. The sky outside the window had darkened considerably and raindrops were spattering the window.

"If you want to practice high magic, you're in for a rough ride. You will have to undergo a purification process. At the end of it, your consciousness will be irrevocably altered. It is a rigorous journey, traveled by few. If I were you, I would not even think of attempting it."

Why the hell the man would think he'd want to attempt something that kooky was beyond him. Besides—Gabriel looked back at the picture—green was not his color.

"Would I have to wear a cloak?"

The store owner did not acknowledge his feeble attempt at humor. He looked at Gabriel expressionlessly.

"During the Middle Ages and the Renaissance, high magic was practiced by secret societies and lodges. The Church tried to stamp it out, of course. It was considered the great heresy." The store owner gave a curious half-shouldered shrug. "Practitioners of high magic were witches and wizards who sought to know the secrets of the universe. They were ready to look God in the eye without flinching. That takes a lot of guts, yes? The Church liked to keep the masses obedient. And scared. Alchemists had a rough time of it. If they were caught, they died truly horrible deaths at the hands of their inquisitors." He touched his forefinger to his lip as if in secret. "You know one, don't you?"

"Know who?"

"A witch."

"I don't know what you mean."

The store owner smiled suddenly, his lips pulling away from his teeth to show very pink gums. "I think you do. I knew you'd been touched the moment you walked in here. I can sense her fingerprints on the tissue of your brain."

Even though he told himself the man was simply messing with him, Gabriel was conscious of a chill settling at the base of his spine.

He tried to be flippant. "Does she at least practice good magic?"

"There is no such thing as good or bad magic. Magic is amoral. It is the intent of the witch that is good or evil."

"Well, is her intent good?"

"I don't know." The store owner shrugged again. "I sense . . . ambivalence. So be careful."

"What is it you're saying?"

"I'm saying, don't make her angry. Don't make her feel threatened."

"Or what?"

"Magic has three functions." The store owner ticked them off on his web-covered fingers. "To produce, protect and destroy. Even a good witch will sometimes make use of destructive magic in self-defense. So if this woman feels she needs to defend herself against you . . . well, watch out."

The tiny shop with its mildewed walls was crowding in on Gabriel. And for a split second he thought he saw something small and dark dart along one of the shelves. A mouse?

"I have to go."

"Wait." The store owner walked over to one of the glass cases and opened the hinged lid. Reaching inside, he removed a silver-colored circle pinned to the felt board.

"Here, take this. On the house. It's an amulet."

Gabriel took the object from him. It was small but surprisingly heavy.

"Iron," the man said as though Gabriel had asked a question. "A good metal for protection against witchery."

"I thought you said this kind of thing was common magic?"

"Common magic has its uses."

Gabriel slipped the amulet into his pocket. "Thanks. But let me pay for it."

"No. This will be my good deed for the month." The store owner smiled again, the pink gums reinforcing the vulpine quality of his features. "And good luck on the journey ahead. You do not live the magic life yourself, but you are within its orbit. It will draw you in. Soon."

Gabriel looked at him, perturbed. The decaying shop, which suddenly seemed full of tiny moving shadows, and the proprietor with his heavy eyes were starting to creep him out.

The store owner had settled himself behind the counter again and was reaching for his book. "The journey will test your sanity." He spoke in a matter-of-fact tone, as though there were nothing extraordinary about his words. "And once you start walking down that road, there is no turning back. You will start craving the rush. One can become addicted to madness, you know. Develop a taste for it." He looked down at the book in his hands, frowned and turned a page.

Gabriel waited, but it was clear the store owner had lost interest in him. "Shut the door tightly behind you, please." He spoke without looking up. "It has a tendency to slip open."

Later that afternoon, after the rain had cleared, Gabriel went for a run. As he started jogging down the Embankment, the day was dissolving into blue dusk.

He was moving at a fast clip. Sweat was running down his forehead and he pushed his arm angrily across his face.

He knew the reason for his anger. He was spooked. He had allowed himself to fall for the deliberately enigmatic warnings of a pot-smoking weirdo who probably enjoyed putting the wind up gullible customers.

He did not believe in witches. He did not believe in witchcraft.

And yet, and yet . . .

Solar witches were witches in search of self-knowledge and enlightenment. He was unable to see how this quest could be construed as sinister or threatening. But somehow it had led to the death of Robert Whittington. Why?

And how? There was little doubt in his mind that Robert Whittington had tried to become a solar wizard himself. And that this journey had involved walking through the house of a million doors. Maybe this was what the "game" was that she kept referring to in the diary. But what exactly *was* the house of a million doors?

One can become addicted to madness . . . Develop a taste for it.

The writer of the diary was not insane. But—and he was facing up to this truth for the first time—some of the passages in the diary read as though the mind behind the words was calibrated too finely. As though the writer was inflamed with a vision of such fevered beauty, the heat might cause her to burn herself from the inside out.

Had she snapped? Had her frantic quest for enlightenment somehow tipped her over into shadow?

The thought was so unpleasant that he involuntarily slowed his pace to a walk. In front of him was a wooden bench. It was sprayed with graffiti and encrusted with bird droppings, but he nevertheless lowered himself heavily onto the seat.

He might be in love with a murderer.

For a long time he simply sat there, staring at the river. The algae smell rising into the night air was strong here and fetid. He loved the river, but every day the newspapers carried a roll call of horror. The broken-boned body of a jumper. A severed head bobbing on the water like a fleshy bowling ball. Syringes. Crack vials.

Was he in love with a killer?

Even more shocking: did he really want to know the truth?

In his mind's eye he saw himself standing in the living room at Monk House with its high, shadowed ceiling, a sweating glass of water in his hand. Inside his chest a feeling as though his heart were being squeezed to dust. On that day he could have accessed the computer holding the file of *The Promethean Key* and he hadn't. He hadn't had the guts. If the woman in the diary was the same woman who had pushed a boy's head under water till he drowned, he did not want to know it.

He felt cold. There was a chill in the air that warned summer was drawing to a close. It was time to go home.

In the communal entrance hall of his apartment block he stopped to check on his mailbox. It held two invoices—gas and electricity—and a mail order catalog. He dropped the catalog into the open bin provided for residents to get rid of their junk mail. It held some bus ticket stubs and a take-out menu. *Babbaloo.* He recognized the bold lettering and distinctive logo. This restaurant was only three blocks away from Monk House. He was slightly surprised to see the menu here. This was not SW3, and as far as he knew, Babbaloo only delivered locally.

The entrance hall was brightly lit, and the lamps on the landings should have been burning as well, but for some reason the stairs were dark. He hesitated for a moment before heading for the elevators.

Just before pressing the button in the wall to summon the cage, he looked up at the row of numbers in circles above the elevator door. The very last circle was lit. It made him pause.

The building had only eight apartments arranged over four floors. The top floor held one apartment only. His.

The elevator was open on the top floor.

He stared frowningly at the lit circle with the letter *P. P* for "penthouse." Someone had taken the elevator to his apartment and must still be up there.

He turned away and headed back to the unlit stairwell. As he mounted the stairs two by two, holding on to the railing for support, he wondered why he was feeling so anxious. It could be anyone up there. The superintendent. A messenger. Even a neighbor—although the residents of the warehouse tended to keep themselves to themselves. Well, he would know in a moment.

As he stepped onto the landing of the third floor, however, he heard the unmistakable whine of the elevator starting up. It was on its way down.

He turned around and started racing down the stairs. But as he approached the first landing, the elevator whine ceased and was replaced by a juddering sound as the cage reached the ground floor. He would not make it in time. He stopped, breathless, and leaned out over the balustrade, looking down the well and straining to catch a glimpse of the occupant.

He heard the door open. A shaft of light fell across the floor. The merest hint of a black wool coat. Light steps. The next moment the muted whoosh of the revolving glass doors in the front hall. Silence.

Well, so much for that, then. He straightened, feeling disappointed and almost angry.

The front door of his apartment was closed and locked. But even as he turned the key, he knew that someone had been inside.

Not that there were any clear signs of disturbance. The papers on his desk were still neatly stacked. As far as he could see, nothing had been taken. The data on his computer was what concerned him most, but fortunately, he had been carrying his notebook around with him all day and had not had the chance to set it up again before he went for his run. It was still in his satchel inside the safe, and the combination lock was fast. His CDs were out of harm's way inside a

beautiful eighteenth-century fruitwood cabinet with a very sophisticated twenty-first-century lock.

But there were signs nevertheless. The broom cupboard in the
kitchen could not be closed unless you deliberately pushed against
the door, and he never did that because once closed, it was murder to
open again. He had once ruined two perfectly good table knives trying to pry the door open, and ever since he never forced it. He had
been meaning to get the locking mechanism fixed but hadn't got
around to it yet.

The door was immobile. He pulled on the knob but it stayed
closed. Someone had walked past this cupboard and inadvertently
pushed the door shut, not realizing it would be a dead giveaway that
an intruder had been inside.

The second sign was in the bedroom. Before setting out for his
run, he had changed his day clothes for his running shorts and a
T-shirt and had simply dropped jacket and trousers on the bed without bothering to put them away. The clothes were still where he had
left them. He had also dropped his long-sleeved shirt into the open
laundry basket and the shirt was inside the hamper. All as it should
be. But on top of the shirt were two socks and that was wrong.
When he had taken them off, he had, as usual, tried to pitch his
socks into the basket. He averaged a 98 percent success rate but today
his aim was off and one of them had ended up outside the hamper.
He remembered feeling annoyed about it. When he left, one sock
had been inside the hamper. One outside. No longer.

The footsteps downstairs had been unmistakeably those of a
woman. And only a woman would tidy up a stray sock. And then
there was the Babbaloo menu in the bin. Taken together, all these
signs gave him a pretty clear indication as to which direction he
should be looking.

He had never invited the sisters to his apartment: it was as though
he realized that he needed to keep this part of his life separate. But
tonight one of them had paid him a visit.

Both sisters were interested in transformation and alchemy. But only one had stepped over into darkness. Magic was amoral, his tattooed friend of this morning had assured him. It was the intent of the practitioner that was key. So who had been inside his apartment tonight? The good witch, or the witch with evil intent? He smiled, grimly amused that he now seemed to be able to use the word "witch" without any sense of irony.

A thought suddenly entered his mind and he went cold. The picture of Robert Whittington and the two women on Hampstead Heath. The one he had stolen during his very first visit to the house. Where was it?

He walked swiftly to his bookcase and pulled down the heavy volume of *The Oxford English Dictionary*. Placing his thumb on the tab marked R, he opened the filmy pages.

The picture was still there, along with the headshot of the boy Frankie had given him. He gave a deep sigh of relief. His secret was safe.

Which still left the main question unanswered. Who had entered his apartment tonight: his love or his adversary?

And what if they were one and the same?

He was still standing there, the dictionary heavy in his hand, when the phone rang.

Gabriel recognized the voice immediately. He tried to keep his own voice cool. "What can I do for you, Mr. Whittington?"

"I would like to meet with you at my house, Gabriel. Tonight, if possible."

Oh, no. The last thing he felt like doing was talking to a dying man about his dead son.

When he didn't answer, Whittington continued, "Please. It will just be you and me. Cecily will be at a charity dinner."

Well, at least he wouldn't have to face Frankie. He hadn't seen her since their argument five days ago in Isidore's house. He and Isidore were back on speaking terms, although relations between them were still strained. But Frankie . . . the disappointment in her eyes had been bad enough. Worse, though, had been the resignation he had read on her face—as though she had hoped he wouldn't fail her but was not really that surprised that he had.

"Please," Whittington repeated. "Around eight. I'll be waiting for you."

CHAPTER TWENTY-ONE

The butler who opened the door of the Whittington residence for him wore an expression of long-suffering patience mixed with faint nausea.

"Mr. Whittington is expecting you," he said, managing to inject an inflection of pained surprise into his voice. "If you would come this way."

Gabriel followed silently, even though he felt like kicking the man's imperious arse. Who still employed butlers anyway? Hadn't they gone the way of the dodo?

They passed through the impressively domed entrance hall, which smelled of furniture polish, and entered a room that was obviously used as a study. It had a very masculine feel to it: all leather club chairs, hunting prints and tooled calfskin books.

Set within the bay window was a gigantic kneeholed desk. A gilt-framed photograph sat in the extreme right-hand corner. The back of the photograph was facing the room and he was unable to see who or what it depicted. Hanging above the fireplace was a life-sized oil painting of Frankie. It was an excellent rendition: the artist had managed to capture the essence of his sitter. The painted eyes were lifelike and reflected her levelheadedness, compassion and humor.

Gabriel turned to the butler, who was watching him over his nose. For a moment he thought the man was going to tell him not to touch anything, but all he said was "Please wait here. Mr. Whittington will be with you shortly."

Gabriel sat down in one of the club chairs and crossed his ankles, trying to relax.

A sound at the door made him look up. William Whittington had entered the room, and once more Gabriel was aware of the force of his personality. It wasn't the in-your-face arrogance of the typical corporate alpha male—it was far more subtle than that. But there was no mistaking that this was a big, big jungle cat even if it walked softly.

"Gabriel. Thank you for coming." Whittington held out his hand, and as Gabriel took it, he noticed the raised blue veins under the skin. And did he imagine it or was the grip less firm than the first time they had met?

"Can I fix you a drink?" Whittington approached a glass-fronted bookcase and placed his hand against the door. It swung open to reveal a bar area with a mirror, glasses and several rows of bottles.

"Whisky, thank you."

"Bourbon or Scotch?"

"Scotch, will be good."

After handing Gabriel his drink, Whittington sat down in his swivel chair behind his desk. A grimace of pain flitted across his face and Gabriel felt a stab of pity. Not that Whittington was the kind of man who would welcome his concern.

Whittington raised his glass. "Cheers."

"Cheers." Gabriel took a sip of the smoothest whisky he had ever tasted. He glanced over at the bottle. The label was unknown to him, some unpronounceable Scottish name. Probably at least ten pounds a shot.

"First," Whittington looked steadily at Gabriel, "I'd like to thank you."

Gabriel moved his shoulders uncomfortably. "I haven't been very successful so far."

"You've brought us much closer to the truth than anyone else. That's more than the police and private investigators I've hired have been able to do. At least we now know where the evil lies. In Monk House."

Gabriel was jarred. Evil? When he thought of Monk House, he thought of flowers, laughter, beautiful music and . . . friendship.

Whittington was watching him keenly. "They're fascinating women."

Gabriel made a noncommittal sound.

"Someone once said: 'Everything that deceives may be said to enchant.'"

"Plato, actually." He could be erudite too.

Whittington smiled faintly. "Yes, indeed."

"Mr. Whittington—"

"William, please."

"William. I wish I had more to give you but I can't really tell you all that much." Gabriel suddenly realized he had a headache. It had come from nowhere but it was now pulsing just behind his eyes.

"Tell me this. Is my son still alive?"

He took a deep breath. "I'm sorry. I don't think so."

"You don't think so or you know so."

"I know so."

It was very quiet in the room. Whittington sat in his chair with extraordinary stillness. Gabriel looked away, unwilling to witness the grief in the eyes of the man opposite him. His gaze went past Whittington's shoulder and out the curved bay window and came to rest on the spotlit statue of a naked female. She was standing inside a niche in the garden wall and had flowing hair curling coyly around her hips, only barely concealing the mons veneris. Her breasts were full and her shoulders beautifully rounded. But her features were weathered and pitted, the eyes shallow indentations in a blank face.

When Whittington spoke again his voice sounded exhausted. "Frankie tells me Robert might have been drowned."

"Yes. The impression I got during my ride was of death by drowning."

"My son was an excellent swimmer. He loved water."

"I know. Frankie told me. But something happened to your son before he drowned. Something that affected his brain and which induced partial paralysis of his body. What, I don't know. But I think that was why he was unable to defend himself. I'm not going to lie to you. At the moment everything is a muddle. I don't see clearly at all. The only thing I am convinced of is that your son is no longer alive. I'm sorry—I wish I could say different."

Whittington inclined his head. "Frankie has been trying to prepare me but I needed to hear it from you myself. Thank you for your honesty." He reached out to the photograph on his desk, and as he pulled it toward him, Gabriel had a glimpse of the picture. It was a copy of the one Frankie had given him when she first visited the loft. Robert Whittington. Smiling.

Alive.

Whittington touched the picture with his thumb. He looked up, and the expression in his eyes was no longer one of sadness but of determination.

"Now I want to ask you something else. Will you be able to find out what happened?"

Some things are better left to mystery. The words popped into his mind unbidden, and for one horrified moment Gabriel thought he had actually uttered them out loud.

But Whittington was no fool. "You think it best to let sleeping dogs lie."

"No." Gabriel pressed his fingertips against the spot above the bridge of his nose where the headache had settled. Man, he felt tired. And he was aware of an unheard sound vibrating through his skull, faint but insistent. It was as though . . . as though something were scratching at his mind, trying to get in . . .

"Gabriel?" Whittington's voice interrupted his thoughts.

He looked at Whittington where he was sitting behind his desk and was surprised to find that he had trouble focusing. "I won't stop searching. You have my word. As long as you want me to keep looking, I will. I'll only stop if you tell me to."

"I'll never give up," Whittington said. "Not as long as I have breath in my body."

The words might have come across as overly dramatic, but for the fact that Gabriel knew he was looking at a dying man. With things as they were, the words sounded poignant. And for one disconcerting moment—as he looked into the other man's face—he thought he glimpsed the stark sheen of Whittington's skull glowing through his skin like a premonitory hologram.

Whittington opened his mouth and said something else, but Gabriel was unable to concentrate on his words because for just a moment the image of a spider flitted across the transom of his mind and a fragrance of musk and frangipani stirred a memory . . .

NO! He slammed down on his inner eye and a massive bolt of pain shot through his head. It was so shocking he almost let go, but then he clamped down even tighter, shutting out the intrusive presence that was probing his brain. A burst of heavy fragrance—the musk and frangipani smell now almost unbearably intense—exploded in his mind as the intruder withdrew with an almost audible squeal. He was bathed in sweat and wanted to throw up.

"Gabriel?" Whittington had moved out from behind his desk and was standing beside his chair, a glass of water in his hand. "Drink this. Are you all right? Shall I call a doctor?"

"No." He pushed Whittington's hand away. "I'll be OK. I just need to get home." He felt intensely nauseous, and for a moment he thought he might vomit onto the priceless Tabriz carpet. He gulped several deep breaths, trying to settle his pitching stomach.

"I'll ask Flannery to call you a cab." Whittington walked out the room hurriedly, and a few moments later Gabriel could hear him talking to someone in the entrance hall. As he waited, he closed his eyes. His head was throbbing wildly. He didn't want to look at this room in which the light now seemed acid-color bright and the furniture horribly lopsided. His one overriding desire was to get to his bed and pull the covers over his head. He opened his eyes briefly, and for one awful moment it seemed to him as though Frankie were trying to step out of the heavy gilt frame above the fireplace and into the room, her painted figure elongated and strange. Hurriedly he closed his eyes again.

When the cab finally arrived, Whittington accompanied him into the street. As he shut the cab door on Gabriel, he leaned through the open window. "Are you sure you're all right?"

Gabriel nodded, then winced. Nodding was definitely not in the cards yet. "Don't worry." He tried to smile. "I'll be fine." He hesitated, searching for words. "And I'll keep my promise. You have my word. I won't stop searching for your son until you do."

Whittington stepped back. He lifted his hand—in a gesture of thanks or farewell, Gabriel couldn't tell. And then the cab pulled away from the curb, leaving the tall, thin figure behind.

His brain felt battered. There was no other word for it. As though someone had taken a swing at it with a blunt object.

Gabriel lay in his bed watching the play of shadows on the ceiling. Light from outside filtered in through the half-open drapes. He had left the window open even though the wind was fresh. It blew into the room at irregular intervals, chilling his face and exposed shoulders.

The alarm clock next to his bed blinked crimson seconds: 2:00 A.M.

The first thing he had done upon his return to the apartment was to check the diary in the hope that the writer had added an entry tonight, which might give him a clue as to what had happened to him at Whittington's house. But there was nothing. He had checked again half an hour ago. Still nothing. The last entry was keyed in fully three days ago. She was not in the mood to write.

Again and again he relived his visit to William Whittington and the moment he had realized he was being viewed remotely. It had been a very skilled scan. It had started out so gently, he had almost missed it. The remote viewer was testing the terrain, but what had started out as a kind of scouting expedition had turned into an assault as soon as Gabriel tried to get the intruder out of his mind. The RV who had accessed him sure as hell did not like to be denied entry.

For a moment he thought back to his years at Eyestorm and the scans remote viewers had run on one another. Sometimes the exercise was conducted in stealth mode—the idea being that the scan should be done surreptitiously without the other viewer knowing about it. But he had always been able to sense immediately when he was being accessed, and he never had the slightest trouble shutting the scan down. But tonight he had almost missed the signals—the scan had indeed been spiderlike, the viewer leaving hardly any prints behind. Only that signature of musk and frangipani. And when he did finally catch on and tried to clamp down, it had felt like trying to shut the door on an avalanche. And it hurt.

Who was it?

Someone with truly extraordinary remote viewing skills. Rivaling his own. No, surpassing them. He had never before encountered an RV who could wield his talent like an actual weapon, inflicting physical pain on the subject who was being viewed. *He* certainly wasn't able to do so.

Uneasily he remembered the agonizing pain that had shot through his head when he had clamped down. His overwhelming impulse had been to let go, to allow the scan to continue. Anything to stop the pain. What if next time he wasn't able to hold on?

Stop being a wimp. No one had ever bested him before. And next time he'd be prepared.

But it was an odd feeling, knowing he might have met his match. At Eyestorm no one had been even remotely in his league. What had Frankie called him? Mr. Super Remote Viewer.

Ah, Frankie. Suddenly he missed her fiercely. Among all the weirdness, she had always been the sane voice. He wondered what she was doing at the moment. Had she returned from her event yet? Was she sleeping? He remembered how, when she slept, there was always the hint of a frown between her eyes. It had amused him when they were still together, the way in which she would seem to be concentrating even while in the land of Nod. *It's as though sleep is an activity for you*, he'd tease her. *Not a release.* And he had pressed his lips to the little frown between her eyes, smoothing out the lines with a kiss.

But she had lost faith in him. Again. She probably wished she had never asked for his help with Robbie's disappearance.

I won't stop searching for your son until you do. His promise to

William Whittington. He still did not understand why he had made that promise. He had just about decided to tell Whittington tonight that he was quitting.

In his mind's eye he saw Whittington's face. The taut, papery skin. The intelligent eyes. The bone beneath the flesh glowing like a holographic omen.

This was a man in danger.

Warn Frankie.

Danger? The thought had floated into his mind. Whittington was a sick man. A man who was close to dying. But "danger" hardly seemed the appropriate word. And no use upsetting Frankie. She already had too much to deal with.

A gust of wind pushed gently against the curtains as though an invisible hand were trying to find a way in. He pulled the covers over his shoulders and closed his eyes. Tomorrow was Minnaloushe's birthday and the sisters had invited him to Monk House for a private celebration. A celebration for three. Waiting for him at the birthday table would be his love.

And his foe.

CHAPTER TWENTY-TWO

Whenever Gabriel tried to remember that last evening at Monk House, he would be unable to give a chronological account of the night's events. The details were as blurred as a badly developed photograph. Did they start the evening with dancing or did that come later? Was Morrighan's dress green or blue?

He'd arrived to find the living room illuminated by candlelight. Incense burning in earthenware pots. Champagne on ice. A birthday cake made of ice cream, which, on a whim, they decided to eat before the main meal. He and Morrighan singing "Happy Birthday" while Minnaloushe opened her presents. He had bought her a signed volume of Leonard Cohen's *Stranger Music*, and she seemed delighted with the gift.

"And we have something for you too." Morrighan handed him a small package wrapped in blue tissue paper tied with silver tinsel.

"For me? Why?"

"Because."

"That's not an answer," he said lightly. He was holding the package between forefinger and thumb, strangely hesitant to open it.

"OK. Because pigs might fly."

"And zebras wear pajamas," Minnaloushe added.

"Take a look."

It was a locket on a silver linked chain. Engraved on the outside was the *Monas*. The craftsmanship was superb. Inside were two strands of silken hair, the shiny filaments intertwined. Red and black. Curled in the shape of a question mark.

He rubbed his fingertips across the surface of the locket, feeling the scored lines of the engraving. He had never been one for the jewelry thing, but as he looked into their expectant faces, he felt almost emotional. "Thanks," he said. "I shall treasure this always." And they smiled.

Later he could never recall much of the birthday meal. But he remembered well how his glass was filled again and again—first with champagne, then with Morrighan's berry wine. He supposed he should have paced himself, but it was a party after all, and he was gripped by an odd feeling of recklessness.

There was dancing, he recalled—Chris Isaac singing "Wicked Game"—and he remembered partnering Morrighan, while Minnaloushe looked on. Morrighan smiling at him with her blue eyes, her lovely mouth aglow. Her hip and thigh brushing his, his hand resting on her bare back, feeling the fine muscles of a true athlete underneath his fingertips as they moved from one end of the room to the other. "Wicked Game" giving way to "Heart-Shaped World." The songs to which they danced forever after locked inside his mind with the memory of looming, distorted shadows flitting across the wall.

It was then that the events of the night started to run into one another, dissolving into a blur of crazy color, fantastical images and heightened emotions.

He had a fractured recollection of lying supine on the couch with no idea of how that came to be. The two women bending over him. The fragrance of their hair and the scent of their skin mingling with the maddeningly sweet smell of the smoldering joss sticks. Minnaloushe's hands running through his hair, Morrighan's fingers stroking the inside of his wrist. Soft hands undressing him. The inside of his mouth tasting of berries. His tongue thick and sluggish.

We want you to play with us, Gabriel. We want to show you heaven.

Was he dreaming? Was this just a lustful, alcohol-hazed dream? Fingers like velvet, their touch firm, undoing the buttons of his shirt, quite unhurriedly. Pale hands in the almost darkness, stroking, cupping. Minnaloushe's hair silken bonds around his wrists. Morrighan an ephemeral vision of porcelain skin and blue-gemmed eyes. The wet pressure of slippery lips of flesh. The bonding of damp skin with damp skin. Who was in his arms? Morrighan? Minnaloushe?

The fluttering of a wet tongue across his body, tiny flicks driving him mad. He groaned, his skin unbearably irritated. She was kissing him, drawing him inside her wet, slick mouth.

Look into my eyes . . .

And at that moment he knew he was being scanned. He sensed her presence, her signature. It smelled of frangipani and musk. A tiny portion of his mind was screaming at him to man the boats, pick up arms, guard himself . . . but he was powerless. Unlike the blunt-force power of the previous scan, this was a languid, slow probe. He could feel his inner eye opening. Slowly, slowly widening until it was at its fullest extent. He tried to clamp down but he was paralyzed. No control. No protection reflex. His inner eye was slack, wide open, completely vulnerable. As vulnerable as a normal eye staring into a dust storm without the ability to blink.

Someone was walking through his mind calmly, softly.

Don't fight it, Gabriel.

Why? The question formed sluggishly inside his head.

Follow me . . .

Her invitation a gentle caress. So good. His groin tingling, his legs heavy, his mind soft, soft, soft. The softest wax.

Who sent you, Gabriel?

"William Whittington." No hesitation.

As long as he's alive, the search continues?

"Yes. As long as he's alive the search continues."

No response from her this time, just a lingering feeling of regret and disappointment enfolding his thoughts like a thin fog.

Such a waste. It could have been good. We could have played with you, Gabriel; given you your true name. We could have changed your life.

Changed my life. Changed my life. The thought repeating itself in his head like a needle stuck on a vinyl record. Changed my life.

Let me show you. Look. This could have been yours.

He groaned. Sounds and images streaming through the receptacle of his inner eye unhindered, an avalanche of sensation.

Do you like it?

Oh, God. Such wonder. So incredible.

He saw a sparrow fall a thousand miles away, heard the moan of solar winds. The sky above his head a blue apocalypse, his feet standing on a million unborn suns. He heard the rush of angels' wings and around his ankles curled serpents with velvet eyes.

He knew he was close to understanding the speech that cannot be grasped. He was about to meet the mute who does not speak but whose multitude of words was great. And still his consciousness kept expanding. He was flying, soaring. How wonderful to possess the power of flight. He found himself giggling uncontrollably like a patient on laughing gas.

But then he was suffused with great sadness. The sadness of the suffering endured by millions of souls. Grief poured into his mind, obliterated him, a vast ocean of sorrow drowning him, and he sobbed, his heart was breaking.

It's all right, Gabriel. Don't cry.

Comfort. He reached out to the woman who was lying with her back to him. He wanted her to turn over so he could place his head against her breast.

Her skin was deathly white. He placed his hand on her flaccid shoulder. As her head flopped around, he saw it was Melissa Cartwright. Ash blond hair dirtied with mud and dried blood. Behind her violet eyes a darkness. He shrieked, tried to roll away from the weight of her lifeless body, on top of him now, and his mind went black with horror.

And then he was suddenly alone, a stick figure drawn on a blank white page.

I'm sorry, Gabriel. I have to go.

She was disengaging; he could feel her withdrawing. The fragrance of musk and frangipani was fading. This was even worse than coming face-to-face with Melissa Cartwright's dead eyes. Loneliness: he had never felt such terrible abandonment.

"NO!" It burst out of him, the thought filled with desperate longing. "Stay with me."

But she was gone.

Now he heard voices quarreling and a woman weeping and a long time later someone standing next to him. He could barely see the outline of her figure in the dark. As she placed a light blanket on top of him, he struggled to sit upright, but his limbs were still scarily numb. "Shh." He guessed rather than saw her hold a finger to her lips. "Go to sleep, Gabriel. It's over." She was whispering.

He closed his eyes like a child, feeling greatly comforted. His mind was suddenly still. At peace. Outside was the moonless night, trees rustling in the cold wind. Small creatures burrowing in the underbrush. A night bird singing.

He woke up to the most horrific hangover he had ever experienced in his entire life.

Opening his eyes was painful. Running his coated tongue over his parched lips was painful. Lifting his head was incredibly, horrendously painful. And he hadn't experienced hangover nausea like this since his student days.

He sank back against the cushions again and took stock. He was lying on the couch in the living room in Monk House. A pink throw with tiny purple flowers covered his body. The windows were closed, and the air was musty with the smell of faded incense and alcohol. Even the sunlight seemed stale.

It was quiet. From the opposite wall, Minnaloushe's masks stared down at him through an ephemeral veil of slowly twirling motes of dust. In his glass box Goliath rested motionless.

Slowly Gabriel raised himself upright, swinging one leg gingerly over the edge of the couch to steady himself. Shit. The slight movement brought on a fresh wave of queasiness. He squinted at his watch. 11:04 A.M. The day was almost half over already.

His bladder was bursting. He got to his feet, slightly surprised to find himself barefoot, and started in the direction of the guest bathroom, weaving across the floor like a sailor who was trying to adjust to dry land after months at sea. The guest bathroom was located just off the dining room and next to the kitchen. The door to the kitchen was closed, but as he approached it, he heard a low murmur of voices. He turned the knob.

Minnaloushe and Morrighan were sitting at the kitchen table. As he opened the door they looked up at him.

He hesitated. He suddenly realized that his shirt was flapping open and his trousers had no belt. A blush crept across his neck and warmed his ears and he felt as awkward as a teenager. His fingers started to button his shirt automatically.

The women were watching him with cool, impersonal eyes.

"Good morning." This was Minnaloushe.

"Good morning." He looked around him. The kitchen still showed the ravages of the previous night's feast. Unwashed plates and glasses. A half-empty bottle of berry wine on the kitchen table.

"Have a seat."

He gestured with his thumb behind him in the direction of the guest bathroom. "I'll be right back. I just need—"

Morrighan cut him off. "There's a fresh towel and soap in the cupboard."

In the tiny bathroom area he looked at himself in the mirror and shuddered. Bloodshot eyes. Black stubble on his jaw. Sweaty skin. He breathed against his hand and almost gagged at the smell.

For a moment he closed his eyes and steadied himself against the washbasin. Echoes of the previous night's happenings were stirring in his memory, but did it all take place? Or was it just one hell of a wet dream? He touched the locket around his neck. At least this was real.

But he couldn't stay shut away in the bathroom all morning trying to work out what had happened. He opened the cold water tap, splashed his face with water and rinsed his mouth. He had no comb, and running his fingers through his hair made it stand on end even more. Very attractive.

When he returned to the kitchen, he found Minnaloushe still sitting at the table and Morrighan pouring boiling water from the kettle into a mug. Reaching up to one of the shelves, she took down a slim test tube and emptied the contents—a pinkish powder—into the mug.

"Here." She held the mug out at him. "Drink this."

He hung back. "Come on," she said impatiently, "it's only rose hip and chamomile. Best cure for a hangover. You'll feel better."

As he brought the cup to his mouth, his hand was shaking. But after a few sips he did indeed feel better. He wasn't sure if it was only the power of suggestion, but he was feeling decidedly more clear-headed. Not well, mind you, but at least he was able to focus on the world around him without wanting to narrow his eyes into slits.

For the first time that morning he took a good look at the two women. They were dressed almost identically in black trousers and jerseys. No makeup—innocent lips and eyes—hair tied back in loose knots.

And there was tension in the air. But whether it was tension between the two of them, or hostility directed at him, he wasn't certain.

It didn't take him long to find out.

"We'd like you to leave." Morrighan's voice was low.

"And we don't want you to come back." Minnaloushe.

The words hit him between the eyes like a hammer blow. "Why?"

"You really are nothing more than a common snoop, aren't you, Gabriel? No, don't bother denying it. We know it's you who's been hacking into our computer. How could you? You've abused our trust. Our hospitality . . . Our friendship."

The contempt in Minnaloushe's voice made him cringe. But the next question literally took his breath away.

"Do you really think one of us killed Robert Whittington?"

He was so shocked he couldn't find his voice. They knew he was investigating them. That he suspected one of them of murder. How did they know?

Only one answer to this question: the scan last night had revealed everything.

"Did you?" he asked challengingly, suddenly angry.

"Who the hell do you think you are?" Minnaloushe's voice was trembling.

"I'm someone who wants answers, someone who is tired of being led around by the nose." His anger was growing.

"We loved Robbie." Morrighan leaned forward, palms pressing down on the table in front of her. "We helped him find what he was searching for."

He made a disgusted movement with his hand. "Yes, I know. You 'played' with him. I'd like to know what kind of game."

"Of the most sublime kind. Robbie was a seeker, on a journey to transformation. We assisted him."

"Transformation. Really." His voice was heavily sarcastic.

"We could have done the same for you." Morrighan stared at him, her eyes glacial, the pupils narrowing to two tiny points of black.

"What the hell are you talking about?" He uttered the words through clenched teeth. "Excuse me, but I don't recall asking either one of you to be my spiritual guru."

"If there's anyone who needs help it's you, Gabriel. Your arrogance is breathtaking."

"If I'm arrogant that's my business and no one else's."

"It's not when people get hurt." Minnaloushe's tone was challenging. "Like Melissa Cartwright."

So they knew about Melissa as well. How the hell had they scanned him so thoroughly? He was a master at blocking. One of them had accessed his mind with the ease of a key turning a lock. How? Even as the question formed inside his mind, his eyes fell on the empty wineglasses in the sink. The glasses were unwashed, red rings staining the bottoms.

"You drugged me." He spoke slowly, but his anger was now so great, he felt light-headed. Picking up the half-full bottle of berry wine that stood on the kitchen table, he sniffed at it.

He glared at Morrighan. "Did you lace this with one of your potions?"

No answer.

"But it wasn't just the potion, was it? Tell me, who is the remote viewer?"

"Remote viewer? What are you talking about?" Morrighan.

"You're delusional, Gabriel." Minnaloushe.

The sound of his pulsing blood filled his ears. He tried to steady his voice: "I need to know one thing."

"Know what?"

"Whose diary is it?"

Silence.

He felt like throwing the bottle against the wall, but forced himself to breathe slowly. "Please. Please tell me."

No change in their expressions. Smooth, masklike faces.

"Is it yours?" He turned to Minnaloushe. She stared at him unblinkingly with limpid green eyes. They gave nothing away.

"Or yours?" His eyes fixed on Morrighan. "Tell me, damn you." He grasped her by the wrist with such violence, he felt her bones creak underneath his fingers.

"Don't." One word only but it stopped him like a bullet. Wisps of black hair fell across her forehead, which held the slightest sheen of sweat. There was something in her eyes that made him feel sick with shame.

He released her and stepped back. His mouth was stale with misery.

Morrighan cradled her wrist in her hand. "Now go."

He tore at the locket around his neck and threw it onto the table. "It doesn't stop here. I'll keep looking for that boy. His father deserves to know what happened to him."

Silence. Two pairs of eyes watching him inscrutably.

He stumbled a little as he turned away. There seemed to be a haze in front of his eyes as he made his way through the living room. When he opened the front door, he blinked. The soft autumn sunshine seemed oddly harsh. Everything outside appeared sharp-edged; every blade of grass a razor blade.

He resisted the impulse to look back over his shoulder to see if they had followed him. In his heart he knew they had not. They wanted him gone.

He stepped out onto the porch and pulled the door closed behind him, shutting himself out of the house. It wasn't until he was standing on the sidewalk, feeling nauseous and confused that he realized he had forgotten his shoes and his wallet. In his hand, he still clutched the half-full bottle of berry wine.

He wasn't hopeful, but the very first taxi he tried to flag down did actually stop, the driver studiously avoiding making any remarks about his bare feet. The man also waited patiently outside the apartment building, meter turned off, for Gabriel to go upstairs to get money.

When Gabriel entered the loft, he immediately noticed the blinking light on his answering machine. He pressed the button, heart racing. Maybe they had called in the meantime? Maybe they wanted to talk everything over and make up?

"Gabriel." Even the tinny quality of the machine could not disguise the hysteria in Frankie's voice. "Please call me. William is dead!"

CHAPTER TWENTY-THREE

William Whittington III was cremated on a beautiful autumn day. The service was a private affair. Afterward Gabriel drove Frankie back to the house in Holland Park.

Frankie looked ill. She was impeccably groomed, but her skin was sallow and her lips so dry they were flaking. When Gabriel took her hand to help her out of the car, her fingers were ice cold.

For a moment she stood looking at the imposing facade of the house. "I love this house. It's home to me. But the idea of living here without William . . ." She stopped, drew a shuddering breath.

"Frankie, I'm so, so sorry."

"He was a great man. Oh, I know all the whispers when we got married. Gold digger. The age difference. How could this possibly be a love match? But I loved him." She inclined her head. "These last few months he started shutting me out. He thought he was making it easier for me. And now he's gone. And there's still so much I want to say to him. Oh, God." She pressed her fists hard against her eyes. "How will I bear this?"

He drew her close. A chilly wind had sprung up, and he draped one side of his coat around her so that she was cocooned in warmth. She started to weep: ugly dry sobs, her body shaking against his. The rawness of her grief was devastating. His own eyes wet, he stroked her hair, murmured words of comfort. "Frankie. My brave girl. Don't cry like that. Don't cry. You'll break my heart."

When she finally grew quiet, she pulled away from him and extracted a wad of tissues from her purse. She dabbed at her face. "Sorry." Her voice was hoarse.

She was so very pale. And the expression in her eyes . . . "Frankie, why don't I call a friend to stay with you tonight? Isn't there someone you'd like to be with you?"

She shook her head vehemently. "No. But I think I might go away for a while."

His heart gave a wrench. "Go away? Where to?"

"I don't know. Someplace warm."

Every object in her house would remind her of the man she had loved, he realized. No wonder she wanted to run away. But the idea that she might leave was unthinkable. He wanted to keep her close. Safe.

"I don't want you to go, Frankie. You shouldn't be alone."

"I *am* alone." The terrible sadness in her voice filled him with despair.

"You can't just disappear." He placed an urgent hand on her arm. "You have to keep in touch."

"Don't you think it's time for us to give each other some breathing space?"

"You're disappointed in me—I know you are. And I understand that." His fingers tightened on her elbow. A feeling of panic was rising inside his chest. "But, Frankie—please, please don't give up on me!"

"I'm confused, Gabriel. You're probably confused too. Besides, it's over, don't you think? I wanted William to know what had happened to his son. But now he's dead. And revenge seems pretty pointless right now."

"I gave your husband my word that I wouldn't stop searching." But as he said the words, he realized how futile they sounded. How was he going to accomplish this goal now that the sisters had kicked him out of the house? His wallet, shoes and belt had been couriered to his apartment in a neatly wrapped package. No accompanying note. There was no indication at all that they were interested in resuming relations. He was filled with rage at their indifference—how could they simply cut him out of their lives as if they had canceled the subscription to a magazine? But for all his anger, he knew that if they so much as lifted a finger in his direction, he would come running. What a needy pathetic fool he was.

"William told me about your promise." Frankie sounded weary.

"But the way I understand it, you told him that once he stopped looking for Robbie, you would too. Well, I guess that lets you off the hook."

Gabriel winced. But there was no bitterness in Frankie's eyes, only sorrow.

He watched hopelessly as she searched for her keys. Nothing he could say was going to change her mind, he realized. He was going to have to stand here and simply watch her walk away from him.

"I'll call you," she said. "Really, I will. But I need to be alone for a bit. Sort out my head." She touched his cheek briefly. "Don't look so worried. I'll be all right." But as she walked down the garden path toward the front door, her gait was hesitant, as though she wasn't able to see well.

The wind was becoming gustier. Earlier in the day, the sky had been achingly blue, but as Gabriel got back into his car, dark clouds were drifting over, shutting out the sun.

Summer had gone. In the garden at Monk House the roses were probably turning brown, he thought. Or maybe they were still flowering desperately in a last-gasp effort before withering away. Deep inside of him, he sensed that the change of seasons was mirroring a transformation within himself. He was still not exactly sure what he was leaving behind; wholly uncertain as to what he was to become.

By the time he parked around the corner from Isidore's house, water was sluicing from the sky. He had no umbrella with him and had to sprint from the car to Isidore's front door. As he rang the doorbell, he realized he was soaked to the skin.

Isidore opened the front door. For a moment they simply stared at each other.

"I need your help."

"You have it," Isidore answered without hesitation. "Come on in."

Isidore handed him a grimy towel. "How's Frankie?"

"Not good." Gabriel rubbed the towel over his head.

"Well, I suppose that's to be expected." Isidore pressed a mug of steaming something into his hand. "Here. It will warm you up."

"What is it?" Gabriel took a sip. The liquid was so hot it scalded his palate.

"Cup-a-Soup. Good stuff."

The brew was gritty and bland, but it was strangely comforting to sit there in Isidore's ugly chair, the warmth of the soup burning his throat, watching Isidore as he pottered around the room. The TV was on, the sound turned low. Another rerun of *CSI*. Isidore was still infatuated with the seductive if steely Catherine Willows.

Gabriel emptied the cup and placed it carefully on top of a spread-eagled comic book.

"What's wrong, Gabriel?"

He looked up. Isidore was watching him steadily.

"I think . . ." He stopped, looked back at the comic book. The cover featured a big-bosomed, kick-ass superwoman in a tight-fitting dominatrix suit squaring off against a lizardlike villain with three eyes. The lady looked as though she'd be able to kick the crap out of any scaly-skinned guy.

"Gabe. What is it?" Isidore was starting to look alarmed.

He took a deep breath. "I think Whittington was murdered." Now that the words had actually left his mouth, Gabriel felt relief.

"What are you talking about? The man was terminally ill. It's sad that he's gone but it was totally in the cards."

"Isidore, Whittington suffered from cancer. But he died of a brain aneurysm."

"If you're sick, your body's immunity is down. You're much more open to other things that can go wrong as well."

"That's not what happened. I know it."

Isidore stared at him for a few moments. "You say he was murdered. Well, explain to me how the killer deliberately triggered an aneurysm in the guy's brain. It's simply not possible."

"I think she did it through remote viewing."

"She? The woman who drowned Robbie?"

Gabriel nodded. In Isidore's eyes he saw horror. His own mind was feeling eerily at peace. As if by finally putting his suspicions into words, he had lanced the boil. But as he looked down at his hands, he saw they were shaking.

"Why? It doesn't make any sense. Does she just have it in for the Whittington males?"

"She scanned me the other night, remember? So she knew I'd keep searching for Robbie as long as his father wanted me to. With him out of the way, there is no reason for me to continue the investigation."

Silence. Isidore looked shell-shocked. In the background Gil Grissom was saying to a sad-eyed Sara Sidle, one eyebrow arched quizzically: "The best intentions are fraught with disappointment."

Isidore moved agitatedly in his seat. "I get the impression that's not all that's bothering you."

Why couldn't he stop his hands from trembling? Gabriel balled his fingers into fists. But the shaking was traveling from his hands and taking hold of his entire body. He was suddenly shivering violently.

"I feel responsible."

"Responsible? For Whittington's death? Oh, come on, Gabe, take off the hair shirt. You were tricked into a scan. Those women drugged you."

He didn't answer. He had given Isidore a fair account of the events of that night, but he had omitted the more salacious details. He still wasn't sure if there had been an actual exchange of bodily fluids between him and one or both of the women. But what he did know was that the scan itself had been a deeply erotic experience—both pleasurable and terrifying in equal measure. Bliss and peril. The sense of danger a goad to his lust. He was drugged, but if he hadn't been, would he have put up a fight? Remembering that slow, slow probe, he knew he would not have. One of the sisters had sparked a firestorm in his brain, and every nerve ending in his body had responded. He had wanted to give himself up to her control completely, allowing her to do with him what she would.

"Hell." Isidore's voice rose. "I just realized. If this witch is able to pop veins in people's heads whenever she feels like it, then you're at risk as well."

"Don't think I haven't thought of that. But I'm not Whittington. I'm an RV myself. I know how to block."

"That did not help you the other night. You were pretty much at her mercy."

"As you yourself pointed out: I was drugged. That won't happen again."

"Gabriel, don't do it. Frankie isn't holding you to your promise. Why this quest for justice?"

Silence.

Isidore spoke slowly, disbelievingly. "This isn't about justice, is it? You want to know who it is. All you're interested in is finding out if the woman you love is a murderer."

Gabriel didn't answer.

"I can't allow you to continue with this."

"You can't stop me."

For a few moments they stared at each other. "Oh, what the hell." Isidore shrugged in resignation. "What's next, then?"

"Well, the diary is closed to us now. There's no way we'll be able to hack in again from the outside. She'll be too much on her guard. But we still have to find out what the hell is in that other bloody file."

"*The Promethean Key.*"

"Exactly. And yes, go on, say it. I should have accessed the damn thing ages ago. And you're right: I had the opportunity to do so and I let it slide."

"So what are we talking about? Breaking and entering again?"

"I'm afraid so. At least it will be quick this time. I have the password so it will literally be a hit-and-run."

"When?"

"Tonight. After they've gone to bed."

"Well, I'm coming with you."

"No, you're not."

"Yes, I am. Someone has to be there to watch your back."

Gabriel looked at his friend—the concerned eyes, the blond hair falling untidily over his forehead, the bony shoulders drooping into a hacker's slump. He felt suddenly emotional.

"You're a good friend, Isidore."

"I know. You don't deserve me." Isidore grinned.

"OK, you can come along." He held up his hand as Isidore's eyes lit up. "But you stay in the van while I slip in and do my thing. Quick and clean."

CHAPTER TWENTY-FOUR

By nightfall the weather had deteriorated even more. A gale-force wind was making the trees sway, and the rain came down in a steady curtain. Even inside the van, Gabriel could hear the sound of the raindrops striking the hood like a drumbeat.

They had been sitting inside the darkened van for two hours, staring at the subdued light peeping through the half-drawn curtains on the top floor of Monk House. The rest of the house was dark, but that one light was burning steadily, a diffuse orange glow through the driving rain. A few times Gabriel had contemplated entering the house anyway. She was on the third floor and he would be confining his activities to the ground floor. If he was very quiet . . .

But Isidore wouldn't hear of it. "We're playing it safe," he insisted firmly. "This woman should not be messed with. I don't want you ending up like Frankie's husband. I don't want her to even begin to suspect you're inside the house."

And so they waited, spending the time eating Krispy Kremes—Isidore's contribution to their stakeout—and drinking black coffee from the thermos flask Gabriel had filled before leaving his apartment. But what with the caffeine and the sugar rush, it was getting very difficult for Gabriel to contain his impatience.

There were two bedrooms on the top floor, and the light came from the corner room, but unfortunately, during the time he'd spent with the sisters, he never got to find out which bedroom belonged to which sister. The top floor had always been off-limits, so he did not know who the night owl was: Minnaloushe or Morrighan.

He glanced at his watch. It was half past midnight. Witching hour.

"What was it like?" Isidore's voice was casual.

"What was what like?"

"That whole thing that happened to you at the birthday party. Flying through the air and hearing angels sing and so on."

"Why do you ask?"

"I don't know. I sense something different about you. Hard to explain. I was wondering if there's a connection."

Gabriel looked ahead into the darkness. "It was the most incredible experience I have ever lived through in my entire life." He hesitated. "And . . . and it's like I've had a taste of something, which I now crave."

Except he did not know how to satisfy his craving. How to regain that feeling of omnipotence? He had felt strong enough to explode right out of his body and take flight. The pull of earth and mortality had ceased to exist for him that night. Was this what Robert Whittington had been searching for? If so, he understood the boy's hunger. The same hunger had now become an integral part of his own makeup; it had become hardwired into his brain.

"I'm worried about you, Gabe."

"Don't be."

"Cravings are dangerous."

"It was only one taste. It will never happen again." And didn't the idea that he would never have another opportunity just tear him up? He wasn't going to tell Isidore exactly how much he was yearning for another hit. He did not even want to admit it to himself. But he was dreaming about it obsessively.

The rain continued to batter the van, sluicing down the windshield. Every now and then they heard a faint, high moan as the wind increased in strength.

"Look." Isidore's voice was tense with excitement. "It's out."

Gabriel turned his head to look at the house. The lighted windowpane was dark.

He placed his hand on the inside door handle, but Isidore grabbed his wrist. "Give it another twenty minutes. Let her fall asleep first."

They waited. The rain continued to pour down.

"OK. I'm off." Gabriel lifted the hood of his waterproof jacket over his head, pulling the strings tight underneath his chin.

"Is your cell phone on vibrate?"

"Sure." Gabriel patted the pocket of his jeans. The cell phone would allow Isidore to contact him in case of an emergency. Such as the top-floor light going on again. Or a cop on his beat. It wouldn't do to creep through the back door leading to the alley only to find a policeman interrupting his stealthy getaway.

"And you're sure of the spelling of the password?"

Gabriel gave his friend a withering glance.

"OK. OK. Just checking."

Gabriel pushed the door open and grimaced as the force of the wind shoved against him and the rain hit his face. Not a good night to be outside. He jumped out of the van and slammed the door shut.

The street was completely deserted. He walked quickly into the alley at the rear of Monk House just as he had done that summer's evening nine weeks ago when he had made his first clandestine visit to the house. Nine weeks. A lifetime.

The garden door was unlocked, as he'd expected it to be. The sisters made use of the alley to take out the rubbish and he knew they hardly ever bothered securing the door afterward. The French doors, on the other hand, were sure to be locked, and since the last time he broke in, they had replaced the lock with something more sophisticated. And to think that over the past two months he could have had a duplicate key made at any time.

He had been delinquent in his duty, he thought bitterly. He had been sure he was engineering them when he was the one who had been seduced, manipulated and flattered into submission. No steel in his spine, which was why he was now standing in sodden shoes in a rain-drenched garden, shivering with wet and cold and wishing with all his heart he did not have to be here.

The garden looked forlorn. The humpbacked tree next to the swimming pool had lost its fiery petals. The house waited, dark and still.

He approached the French doors with their stained glass panels. Placing his pencil flashlight between his teeth, he freed his hands and reached into his jacket pocket to extract the pouch holding his picks.

The new lock was a tougher proposition than the old one, but not impossible. Picking locks was his forte. However, doing so in pouring rain was no picnic. Working on the lock, he tried to ignore the rain on his neck. But even so he couldn't stop himself from shivering.

He glanced up uneasily at the silvery windows of the house rising into the night sky above him. But everything was quiet. Nothing stirred.

At last. He felt the lock give. He shoved the flashlight back into his pocket and pushed the door open.

The bloody thing creaked like the gate to an abandoned crypt.

He froze, then quickly moved into the house, clicking the door shut behind him.

The sudden quiet was unnerving. For a long moment he waited, expecting at any moment to see a flood of light cascading down the staircase. That creak had been loud enough to wake the dead.

The house remained dark.

Slowly he released his breath. For a few moments he continued to stand still, allowing his eyes to get used to the inside gloom. And there, on the far side of the room were the two computers, their screen savers on: two solar witches with their waxing and waning suns floating in the surrounding blackness.

For a moment an image of the sleeping women, two storeys above him, entered his mind. They would be breathing deeply, caught in the embrace of dreams. Hugging their pillows, the bedclothes twisted around their bodies. Bare arms, bare shoulders, long bare legs. Hair spread across the pillows like seaweed. And one of them might be dreaming of him . . . Maybe he should creep up the stairs, stand outside the doors, listen to their soft breathing . . .

Stop it, he told himself savagely. God, he was pathetic.

He switched the pencil light on again and flicked it up and down the room a few times. Cautiously, he took a few steps forward.

He stopped. His shoes were making squelching sounds. He shoved the flashlight into his pocket, stooped to untie his shoelaces—not the easiest thing to do when they're wet—and worried the shoes off his feet. His feet were now clad in socks only and he made no noise.

Softly he padded past the bookshelves, the mounted bird skeletons, the abacus with its ivory beads. He was intimately familiar with this room and its objects, but tonight in the near darkness, with the rain driving against the pale windowpanes, the place felt alien. This was a room he associated with flowers and beautiful music. But it was as though he were looking at a distorted black-and-white print of a full-color memory. A half-remembered image surfacing in a bad dream. Any music playing in this room was sure to be off-key.

Masks. The dark shapes lining the wall. He could feel their eyes on him.

He had reached the long table with the two computers. He touched the space bar on the keyboard of the Mac. The screen filled with desktop icons. He clicked on the only document name: *The Promethean Key.* The screen blinked and the prompt appeared, asking for the password.

Without hesitation he keyed in the words: HERMES TRIS-MEGISTUS.

For an agonizing moment the cursor kept blinking. But then the screen cleared. Open sesame.

On the screen in front of him was a menu. *The Promethean Key* consisted of four subfiles:

East : Mind
West : Body
North : Spirit
South : Portal—Chi

Each of the names was followed by a tiny square. Gabriel placed his hand on the mouse and ticked each box in succession.

He had brought a writable CD with him. Slipping it into the computer's disk drive, he gave the command to copy the four components of *The Key* onto the disk.

The light on the disk drive blinked and he could hear a soft whirring sound. The download started.

He swiveled the chair around so that he was now facing the IBM. He tapped the enter key and the desktop appeared.

Diary.

Ever since they had kicked him out of the house, the diary's pages had been closed to him. They had killed off his Trojan. But at this moment he had direct access to the machine and it was still connected to the Internet. He would be able to reactivate his fallen warrior.

He started working the keyboard. He hadn't told Isidore that his plan for tonight also included taking one last, final look at the diary. Isidore might have accused him of breaking and entering into Monk House merely to get to the diary—not to find out what was hidden inside *The Promethean Key*.

His fingers raced across the keys.

Entry Date: 7 October

Betrayal is the saddest word there is . . .

For a moment he closed his eyes. He was in.

Betrayal is the saddest word there is . . . To trust someone and then to have him fail you. Treachery.

He took advantage of us. Could we have been more naive? We gave a professional hacker the run of the house and we never considered ourselves at risk? Such is arrogance. And vanity. The thought never occurred to us—why? Because we thought we were playing him. Instead, he was playing us. Smiling at us with friendly eyes and all the while keeping his heart cold and his mind suspicious. A spy.

I should be furious. He's read my diary. But instead of rage, I feel longing. I miss him. On the one hand I feel violated. On the other— every woman wants to share herself with the man she loves; to have him truly know her.

M is angry and disappointed and that makes me afraid. Anger and disappointment is a potent brew and M is on the boil. I am afraid for G. I am afraid what M might do to him.

What am I really saying?

G thinks R was murdered. Is he right?

I am finally admitting it. I am allowing myself to think the unthinkable. That R did not leave of his own free will, but came to harm. And that M might be responsible.

Is M a killer?

I am concerned that G might be in danger too. I am afraid that he will be hurt without my knowing about it. What if M tries to harm him and I'm not there to protect him?

The cell phone suddenly started to vibrate against his hip. Gabriel grabbed at it and brought it to his ear. He cupped his hand around his mouth and lowered his voice to a whisper.

"What?"

"Get out of there." Isidore's voice was taut. "She's awake."

Gabriel glanced toward the staircase, which, though in shadow, was clearly visible from where he sat.

"I don't see any light."

"She turned it on for just a moment and then killed it again. Bloody hell! Don't argue. Get out now!"

He shoved the phone back into his pocket and turned to the Mac. The download was not complete. East, West and North had been copied but the copy process for South—the Portal—had only just started.

He looked back at the shadowed staircase in an agony of indecision. It wouldn't take long for her to get from the top floor to the bottom. But who was to say she was coming this way? Maybe she simply wanted a drink of water and had gone back to bed again.

The staircase remained dark. The disk drive whirred softly.

And then, suddenly, she was there. Like a ghost.

She was standing on the first landing, her hand resting lightly on the balustrade. Her face was in deep shadow but she was wearing a long, wide floating nightdress in a pale color, which intensified the feeling that he was looking at an apparition—something not made of flesh and blood.

He reacted instinctively. He clicked on the cancel icon and almost simultaneously pushed his finger hard on the eject button of the disk drive. The tray slid gently outward. Even as he grabbed the disk, she was coming down the stairs.

He turned around and ran in the direction of the French doors. In his haste he bumped against a footstool and grunted in pain as the sharp edge of the stool cut into his shin. As he continued toward the doors, his eyes searched the shadows for his shoes. Where were his shoes? He couldn't see them anywhere.

Too bad. Too late now. He had reached the door. Placing his hand on the handle, he wrenched it open and ran into the rain.

His mad rush carried him through the garden, and he didn't stop until he reached the door that would give him access to the alley. Out of breath, adrenaline coursing through his body, he turned around to look back at the house.

At first he couldn't spot her. But then, peering through the slanting rain, eyes straining, he made out the shape of her figure where she stood at the window looking out. He couldn't see her eyes or her face, but the force of her presence played over him like a tracking beam.

For a long, long moment they stared at each other through the darkness and the rain. He turned his back on her and slipped out into the alley.

Isidore poured water from the kettle into the makeshift plastic footbath. "Place your feet in here."

Gabriel dipped a cautious finger into the steaming water and yelped. "Add some cold water first."

"Lion heart." But Isidore obeyed and emptied a jug of tap water into the container. "Better?"

Gabriel grunted. His feet felt like blocks of ice, and they had turned a rather weird shade of aquamarine. The sole of one was cut and bloodied where he had stepped onto the jagged edge of an empty can during his dash out into the alley. His shin, where it had connected with the footstool, was starting to bruise quite spectacularly. He felt as though he had been through the wars.

Isidore had conjured up a bottle of Dettol and now proceeded to pour a long stream of the amber liquid into the water, turning it milky. "To stop infection," he explained. "That can was probably filthy."

Gabriel gasped slightly as he lowered his freezing feet into the water. It was still hellishly hot.

Isidore stirred the water with a wooden spoon. "That's the second pair of shoes you've left at their house."

"True."

"And this time I don't think they'll send them back."

"It doesn't matter."

"What matters is that our killer now has a very good idea of who the midnight intruder was, and who hacked into the Mac."

Gabriel thought back to that moment when they had stared at each other sightlessly through the dark and the rain. Eyes blinded but their minds connecting.

"She would have known it was me even without the shoes."

"And you weren't able to identify her."

"No. She was in shadow all the time and the nightdress she was wearing was voluminous, so I couldn't tell from her figure. But . . ." Gabriel smiled. "I did establish one thing tonight." He stopped and smiled again. "While I was waiting for *The Key* to download, I accessed the diary."

"No shit. And?"

"Well, one thing's clear as day. The writer is not the killer. And she doesn't know what happened to Robbie Whittington. But she's starting to get suspicious. And she's scared of her sister—or rather, she's scared of what her sister is capable of. She wrote it in as many words."

Isidore leaned over and punched Gabriel on the shoulder. "Way to go, brother. I don't mind telling you I had my doubts. I know you love that diary, but I think it plenty creepy. I did not find it such a stretch to think its owner might be capable of murder."

"Well, she's not. And what's more, she has feelings for me."

"I'm happy for you. Now if only you knew who it is who has these feelings."

Gabriel sighed. "That would help."

"Well, I have some news too. You remember my cousin Derek? The pharmacist? You met him at that Science Con in Northampton a year back."

"Vaguely."

"Well, I gave him the bottle of leftover berry wine you took with you the day the girls kicked you out and asked him to analyze it."

"Did you now?" Gabriel was surprised.

"It's potent shit, man. Apparently there's belladonna in there and hemlock and ashwagandha and a crapload of other stuff. Derek was fascinated. He said if the person who had put this potion together hadn't been such a skilled chemist, you'd be dead."

"Really. How comforting."

"Apparently a mixture like that is capable of altering the rhythm of the heart. It will almost certainly induce dizziness, hallucinations and an impression that you're falling or flying. And it is sure to lower your inhibitions. Also, it has a cumulative effect. So the longer you use it, the more susceptible you become to its effects. You've been drinking this stuff for a while now, haven't you?"

Gabriel thought back. "About eight weeks."

"No wonder you weren't able to resist the scan. They were marinating you like a piece of tough steak."

"That sounds about right."

"Derek also said to watch out for the stuff as it could give you a hard-on that just won't quit. The Makonde of Tanzania use something similar as a kind of homegrown Viagra."

"Uh-huh."

Isidore gave him a sardonic look. "All right. Let's see what this baby can tell us." He picked up the CD with the downloaded *Promethean Key*.

Gabriel removed his feet from the water. As he started to towel them dry, he sneezed. Reaching into his pocket, his fingers hunted for his handkerchief but instead found something round and hard.

It was the amulet given to him by the owner of the magic shop. He had forgotten all about it. As he turned the tiny object over in his palm, he was again surprised by its weight. Iron, if he remembered correctly. A defense against witchery, the man had said. Well, he supposed it had done its job tonight.

As Isidore worked the keyboard, he spoke over his shoulder. "This disk is not complete, you know. When you made your dash for freedom, the download of the fourth component—the portal—was aborted. So we only have the first three components to work with."

"Maybe that will be enough."

"Wow." Isidore's voice was a whisper. "Check this out."

Gabriel clumsily shoved the amulet back into his pocket and got to his feet. He stared over Isidore's shoulder.

The computer screen was covered with graphics—enigmatic icons, idiosyncratic symbols. As Isidore scrolled down the pages, it looked like some kind of strange, mysterious tapestry.

And there were sketches. Architectural sketches. Meticulous drawings of passageways, drawbridges, flights of stairs, ceiling details, galleries. And doors. Many doors. Paneled doors. Doors with hoods in the shape of shells. Tall, formal doors framed with architraves and pilasters. Small, unassuming doors. The rooms to which they led were labeled; the labels in code and unintelligible. Even so, as Gabriel looked at the plans, he felt himself grow cold.

"I've been inside this place."

"What?" Isidore twisted around in his chair.

"This is the blueprint for the house of a million doors."

"You're kidding."

"Or at least a partial print. Obviously this is only a tiny, tiny section.

But there's no doubt about it: I've walked through those rooms. See that door there? It gives access to a room stacked from floor to ceiling with broken violins. And that long, oblong room there is a conservatory filled with carnivorous plants. I remember it exactly."

"So what the hell is this place, then?"

"I don't know." As he looked at the plans, Gabriel was surprised to feel the hairs on his arms rise. "But believe me, walk through it . . . and you can go insane."

THE PORTAL

Seeking the mysterious portal, you must . . . render yourself invisible, that you may slip through unnoticed.

—Nei Pien of Ko Hung *(ancient treatise on alchemy, medicine and religion, 320 A.D.), as quoted in* The Invisible Fist, *Ashida Kim*

CHAPTER TWENTY-FIVE

The nightmare descended on him the day after the burglary.

After leaving Isidore, Gabriel returned home and worked for four hours straight, trying to figure out the information on the disk. If he looked closely enough, surely he would find a clue.

But it was hopeless. It was like trying to read a foreign language. He fell asleep at his desk just as the sun came up, his computer still open on one of the pages of *The Promethean Key*.

When he woke up, his watch told him it was 9 A.M. His head felt woolly. He glanced at the computer screen and shuddered. Oh, no. He simply couldn't face working on that treacherous, enigmatic text right now. Maybe he should head for the gym. His foot was still sore from the can he had stepped on the night before, but not so much that he wouldn't be able to train. A workout might get his synapses flashing again. Allow him to come back to the document fresh.

He was running at a relaxed steady pace on the treadmill when it happened. One moment he was watching a good-looking blonde with imposing pecs as she assaulted the rowing machine with terrifying ferocity. The next moment he had collapsed, the treadmill rushing along underneath his body at 8.0 mph, dragging him sideways. He was unable to right himself. The only thing he was aware of was that his head had turned into a fireball of pain. And then, nothing.

"I think he's having an epileptic fit." A female voice, sounding apprehensive.

"Give him air." Another voice. A man, trying to sound authoritative.

Gabriel opened his eyes. He was flat on his back. Around him a circle of faces looking down at him. Just like in the movies, he thought. When the hero goes down. His next question should probably be: *Where am I?*

But he knew where he was. His head hurt fiercely but he was not disoriented. He knew exactly what had happened to him. And who was responsible.

He placed his hands palms down on the floor and pushed himself up.

"Easy there." The man who had spoken before—one of the trainers at the gym—placed his arm around Gabriel's shoulders and helped him get to his feet.

"Are you all right, guy? Should we get you a doctor?"

"I'm fine."

The trainer gave him a dubious look. "Maybe you should sit down, what do you say? I'll get you some water."

He pushed Gabriel onto the seat of one of the weight machines and strode off purposefully in the direction of the water cooler.

Gabriel touched his forehead. It was creamy with sweat, whether from his run or from the pain was difficult to say. But inside his skull a little man had taken up residence. A little man with an enormous pickax, swinging away, digging up soft clods of brain tissue.

"Here you go." The trainer thrust out a burly fist holding a plastic cup filled with water.

"Thanks." Gabriel noticed that a few of the other gym members were watching him from the corners of their eyes. Some looked sympathetic. A few of the men seemed scornful.

Gabriel took a sip from the plastic cup. But even the simple act of swallowing appeared to kick the little man with the pickax into overdrive.

"I think I should go home," he said to the trainer, who was still eyeing him with trepidation.

"Yeah, man." The trainer looked relieved. "Have a rest, OK?"

In the men's changing room, Gabriel removed his gym bag from his locker. But instead of heading outside, he sat down on one of the wooden benches. Leaning his head against the wall, he closed his eyes. Time for a recap. He thought back, trying to slow down the experience in his memory: to recall what had happened one still frame at a time.

Running. The treadmill moving smoothly. The blonde working

the rowing machine. Feeling nauseous, not much at first, but with ever-increasing intensity. The sounds in the room receding. Then the extraordinary sensation that a window had opened inside his brain. An aperture, giving access to a massive cascade of images flooding through his mind with the ferocity of an avalanche. The protection reflex kicking in. His brain screaming at him to clamp down. The tidal wave stopping but his head gripped by pain. Pain such as he had never experienced before in his entire life, blowing out his consciousness. His brain crashing like a computer on overload. Blackout.

Mind attack. The same experience that had left Robert Whittington brain damaged before he drowned, and which had killed his old man. And now it was his turn.

She had entered his mind twice before but those had been scans: explorations, fact-finding missions. "Getting to know you" exercises.

This had been no scan. This had been an assault.

For a few seconds he continued to sit quietly, trying to come to terms with the implications. But it was difficult to concentrate. The little man inside his head was still wielding the pickax with great gusto. The little guy must be in pretty good shape: he hadn't slowed down since he started on his mission of destruction. Gabriel knew he should make an effort to get to his apartment, but it was peaceful here and he felt so damn tired. The idea of having to make the journey home seemed overwhelmingly daunting.

On your feet, Blackstone. You can't hide out in the men's changing room for the rest of your life.

Outside the sun was shining. The storm of the previous night had disappeared and there were no clouds in the sky. But it was very cold. Or maybe it was just that he was still suffering from shock.

He had used his bicycle to get to the gym. For a moment he contemplated leaving the bike where it was and taking a taxi home. The way he felt now, a stretcher would not be unwelcome. But it was difficult to find a cab around here, and if he took one, he'd only have to come back for the bike later. Better to bite the bullet. It wasn't that far to his apartment.

He pedaled slowly, keeping well to the left side of the road, traversing intersections with care. Taking no chances. Only a few minutes more and he'd be home. Sanctuary.

And then it happened again. And this time it almost killed him.

One moment he was pedaling slowly and deliberately, keeping his eye on a worn-out MG, whose driver was signaling that he wanted to change lanes. The next moment his entire body was gripped with pain and nausea. The force of it was so great, he almost crashed his bicycle there and then. He swerved violently and a car hooted angrily behind him. For a few agonizing moments, it was as though he had entered a fun house in a carnival. Everything ultrabright. Nothing making sense. The traffic around him frightening chaos. And then someone was emptying a giant container of violently animated images into his brain: the flood roaring through the window in his mind at warp speed, too fast to process; a sick, psychedelic blur.

Clamp down! Clamp down! The nauseating flood of images was arrested midstream, but at the same time a bolt of pain ripped through his head with gut-wrenching violence. Vaguely, he was aware of the bicycle wobbling underneath his hands like a thing possessed—but it seemed to be happening to someone else, not himself. Someone else . . .

The hissing of giant brakes and the urgent hoot of a bus shocked him out of his stupor. He had strayed into the bus lane—right into the path of an oncoming double-decker.

Gabriel screamed. He swerved his bicycle violently to one side and plowed onto the sidewalk and into a crowd of pedestrians. As the bike went down, he could hear shouts of alarm and anger.

He lay where he fell. He could hear voices, but no one came over to find out if he was hurt. Someone said something in a low, disgusted voice and he thought he caught the word "drunk."

He did not know for how long he remained on his back staring stupidly at the sky. When he finally pulled himself upright, he was a lone island in a river of pedestrians. People were giving him a wide berth, keeping their faces averted as they passed him by.

The bicycle's wheel was bent. He would not be able to ride it home. He started pushing it next to him, an automatic act. He wasn't able to concentrate. Everything around him fragile and impermanent. His thoughts incoherent.

Mind attack.

She was through playing around. He was in her kill zone.

He spent most of the rest of the day in bed. After arriving home, he swallowed a handful of Neurofens and two sleeping tablets. Time enough later to come to terms with what had happened to him and to devise a plan of action. Action was the last thing on his mind right now. All he wanted was relief from the ocean of pain inside his skull.

But when he woke up a full five hours later, his head was still throbbing. Not nearly as badly as earlier in the day, but the pain was there, lurking slyly among the ganglia.

It was only four o'clock in the afternoon, but already the sky was a cold, dirty yellow and the sun was disappearing. His bedroom was gray with shadows.

He pulled the blanket closer around his shoulders and tried to focus.

He needed to decide what to do. Even though his clamp-down reflex was highly developed, he would not be able to continue to defend himself against the kind of battering his mind had received earlier in the day. The second time, on the bicycle, he had felt his brain *sag*.

Why now? The night of the birthday party he had been at her mercy but she had not harmed him, she had only scanned. So what had changed? What made her decide to go on the rampage?

The Promethean Key. His retrieval of *The Key* had infuriated her into launching a full-out assault. There was no other explanation. The architectural sketches definitely came from the house of a million doors, but what *was* the house of a million doors?

He got up from the bed and shuffled over to his computer, clutching the blanket to him as though he were some homeless person.

He started to scroll down the pages, his eyes skimming through the unintelligible symbols and cryptic references. Somewhere in these pages there must be something that would make sense . . .

He stilled his hand.

Memory Palace. Power station = portal.

He stared at the blinking cursor, which was resting on the word "Memory."

Maybe the house of a million doors wasn't a house. Maybe it was a palace.

But a *memory* palace? What was a memory palace?

No. He was asking the wrong question. The question he should be asking wasn't what, but *who*. Who would be able to design such a palace of the memory? Who would be able to build this place where a boy could be lured to his death?

The answer lay in the word "memory." And he knew of only one person who had studied the concept of memory with the rigor of a scholar and the commitment of a mystic.

Minnaloushe.

Minnaloushe was the architect of the memory palace. The place in which Robert Whittington had followed a woman who had led him to his death.

He had finally identified her.

Oh, Minnaloushe. Why?

CHAPTER TWENTY-SIX

Minnaloushe had murdered Robert Whittington. Had held his head under the water until the boy had choked to death.

Gabriel breathed shallowly. He felt sick.

OK. This was not the time to get emotional. Think.

One question has been answered. Who.

That left why. Why did Minnaloushe kill Robert Whittington?

The answer to this question was tied up with the memory palace. But he still did not know what this was. And until he did, he would be unable to solve the puzzle.

The answer could be just a click away. As he logged on to his favorite search engine, he could feel his heart pounding inside his chest.

"Memory Palace"

The first link he clicked on opened onto the personal Web page of one Adrian Stallworthy. There was no picture of Mr. Stallworthy and his personal details were sketchy, but there was enough information on the page to convince Gabriel that this was a man he would like to meet.

Adrian Stallworthy. Professor in Medieval Codes, Cambridge University. Author of the definitive work on Memory Palaces, *Theatres and the Art of Memory*. Published 1997, Cambridge University Press.

There followed a long list of journal publications, all of them sounding dauntingly esoteric.

Gabriel glanced at his watch. It was still early enough in the afternoon for a hardworking academic to be in his office.

The professor's office phone number was on his Web page, and sure enough, the phone rang only once before it was answered.

"Adrian Stallworthy." The voice was pleasant.

"Professor Stallworthy, my name is Gabriel Blackstone. I have a disk, which I believe to hold the plans for a memory palace. I was hoping you might be able to interpret the plans for me."

"A memory palace? From which period?"

"Uh . . ."

"Classical Greece? Middle Ages? Renaissance?"

"No. I think it's a modern-day palace."

A long pause. When he spoke again, the interest in Stallworthy's voice was unmistakable. "If it is, Mr. Blackstone, it would be unique. Why don't you send it to me via an attachment and I'll take a look."

"I would rather not send it via e-mail, Professor." Until he knew what he was dealing with he was not about to let *The Key* loose on the Internet. He didn't want any stray copies floating around cyberspace. "Maybe we could meet in person?"

"Well." Stallworthy paused. "I could see you in my office, I suppose. How about seven o'clock this evening?"

"Thank you, Professor. I appreciate it. If you could give me your address?"

Gabriel replaced the receiver with a heavy hand. Cambridge. Fifty-four miles through rush hour traffic on the M11. Not an appealing prospect. Especially as he still felt like death warmed over.

Fear suddenly knotted his stomach. What if Minnaloushe launched another mind attack? What if what happened to him this morning on the bicycle happened again while he was behind the wheel of his car? Twisted metal, sirens, flashing lights, ambulances.

Death.

For the first time he thought about it straight up. He could die. She could kill him.

But if he didn't get answers, he would never be safe. She had him in her crosshairs. Without knowing what he was up against, he would have nowhere to run. Know thine enemy.

He could ask Isidore to drive him. It would minimize the risk to himself and to others on the road. And the thought of company was attractive. But he did not want to put Isidore in danger. Letting his friend come with him to Monk House last night had been a stupid thing to do. He didn't want Isidore to surface on Minnaloushe's radar screen. From here on he was going to leave Isidore out of this mess. And for the first time since she had left, he was glad Frankie was out of the country as well.

Now that he had made up his mind to go, he wanted to get on the road as soon as possible. He would drive very slowly, and at the first hint of a scan, he'd pull off.

In the bathroom he washed his face and combed his hair. His eyes were bloodshot. His head hurt. A tiny tick pulsed underneath one eyelid. Just a tremor, but he couldn't seem to calm it down. He placed his fingers on the spot underneath his eye where the nerve was twitching, willing it to stop. But when he removed his fingers, there it was again, the tiniest of movements.

He shrugged into his coat, collected his car keys. But as he pulled the front door shut behind him, he hesitated. He was aware of menace lurking, something lethal hovering in the air.

Instead of taking the elevator—the idea of getting into that confined space was suddenly unthinkable—he chose the stairs.

He couldn't shake the feeling that he was being watched. The sense of some sly, malevolent presence following him, waiting somewhere in the shadows, was strong and deeply unpleasant. Perhaps it had been waiting for him to leave the safety of his apartment all along.

The hair on his neck was standing up. He continued to walk down the stairs doggedly, looking straight in front of him. The pain in his head was a low, aching throb. His heart beat wildly.

At a bend in the stairs he forced himself to look up. Was there a movement up there? The blur of a white face? Had someone leaned over the railing only to jerk back when he looked up? For a long moment he waited. Nothing stirred. But instead of relief, dread slipped around his throat like a noose. Any moment now he would hear the whisper of a footfall. A hand would come to rest on his shoulder . . .

And suddenly he was running, running—sprinting down the stairs two at a time. His heart was beating so hard he thought he might pass out. As he reached the lobby, he caught a glimpse of his reflection in the hallway mirror and what he saw shocked him: the staring face of a man hollowed out by fear.

CHAPTER TWENTY-SEVEN

The drive to Cambridge took ninety minutes and was completely un-eventful. The sense of foreboding, however, did not let up. When Gabriel finally parked his car in one of the city center car parks, his neck was stiff and his back cramped from the continued apprehension.

The professor had given him the address of the college but no di-rections. After getting lost twice, he was finally steered right by a pretty student. He glanced at his watch. Ten minutes past the hour. He was late for his appointment.

As he followed the girl's instructions, he wondered about the man he was about to meet. Medieval codes. Not exactly a run-of-the-mill specialty even in the rarefied corridors of academia. The man was probably more than a little eccentric.

But Adrian Stallworthy turned out to be nothing like Gabriel had imagined. Instead of the caricature of the academic professor—stooped, balding, nearsighted—Adrian Stallworthy was quite the hunk. He had blue eyes, broad shoulders and slender hips. A photo-graph of the professor standing in front of a rowing boat, an oar clutched in one fist, explained the impressive physique. Gabriel guessed the man had no trouble attracting female students to his classes.

Stallworthy's grip was firm and his smile genuinely friendly. "Mr. Blackstone. Have a seat." He waved at a battered armchair.

Gabriel sat down. The springs of the seat were drooping and he sank almost to the ground. But once you got the hang of it, the chair was surprisingly comfortable.

On the professor's desk was a scuffed cardboard notice saying, *Please switch off your cell phone!* Stallworthy saw him looking at it and said apologetically, "Cell phones are my pet hate."

"Understandable." Gabriel reached into his jacket pocket and extracted his mobile. Pressing his thumb on the off button, he waited for the lighted display to darken. "There."

"Thank you." Stallworthy inclined his head.

Gabriel leaned forward and pushed the disk with *The Promethean Key* across the desk. "If you could explain to me what's on here, Professor, I would be in your debt."

Stallworthy picked up the CD and slid it into his disk drive. "This may take a while."

"No rush."

Gabriel looked around him. Stallworthy might not be your quintessential dried-up academic, but his digs were decidedly conventional. Shabby Oriental carpet with bald spots. Hideous sludge brown curtains. Books everywhere. A replica of this office could be found on any campus anywhere in the world. The room was also distinctly chilly, the fire in the soot-stained fireplace creating more smoke than heat.

Stallworthy made a slight sound. Whether of surprise or incredulity, Gabriel couldn't tell. But whatever it was the professor was looking at, it certainly held his attention.

After about twenty minutes, he leaned back in his chair and looked at Gabriel.

"Mr. Blackstone—I have to confess, I haven't been this excited in years."

"So you do know what it is."

"Something truly unique. Very special indeed." Stallworthy pressed his finger on the button of the disk drive and removed the CD, placing it delicately on the desk in front of him as though afraid it might break.

"Have you ever heard of something called the Art of Memory?" There was reverence in Stallworthy's tone. Gabriel could hear him virtually capitalize the letters *A* and *M*.

"I can't say that I have."

"It's a technique that originated with the ancient Greeks. Later, in the Middle Ages and the Renaissance, it became a tool in the hands of alchemists and Gnostics."

Gabriel felt a sense of inevitability descend on him. "A tool. A magic tool, of course."

"Indeed. By practicing the Art of Memory, practitioners were able to amplify their memory skills to unimaginable levels."

Gabriel frowned. "I'm not sure I understand. You mean, their memories were improved?"

"Improved is far too mild a term to describe what happened to these men. Their memories were rocket boosted."

Stallworthy steepled his fingers. "Let me try to explain it this way. We're all born with natural memory. But our memory spans are limited. So we use little memory tricks to aid us. You know how some people make use of mnemonics to help them remember names? Well, the Art of Memory is a very highly developed form of mnemonics. When someone practices the Art, he builds artificial memory in his mind, which is capable of handling infinitely bigger chunks of knowledge than he'd normally be able to absorb. You could almost say his mind becomes computerized, adapting itself to processing vast quantities of information."

Gabriel didn't bother to hide his skepticism. "A computerized mind. Really. How?"

"Well, there are several ways. One way is by constructing a memory palace, of which this is an example. A truly astounding example."

"So how does it work?"

"Well, a memory palace, such as this one, is an imaginary space."

"Like a building?"

"Exactly. And even though it is imaginary, the practitioner who built it will have constructed it very carefully indeed, right down to the exact size of the rooms. Even the correct lighting."

"You said it is imaginary. What do you mean by that?"

"The palace exists only in the mind of the practitioner. It will never be constructed in the real world. It is an architectural space that is embedded in memory. And that's where it will stay."

Gabriel flashed back on the ride. "Inside those rooms . . . are there objects, images?"

"Oh, yes. Thousands upon thousands of images. Some of these images will be fantastically beautiful, others quite horrendous. As in this memory palace here." Stallworthy tapped the CD with his forefinger. "In some of these rooms are beautiful things such as butterflies and glowing moons. And then right next door, there's a room used as a slaughterhouse. Gutted pigs. Or a self-mutilating monk."

"What do the images stand for?"

"They're symbols. Each one represents a chunk of information. The idea is that the practitioner can walk through the palace, locate the various images and recover the information associated with every symbol. In other words—to use computer terminology again—he is walking through coded space. It is like opening the desktop on your PC and clicking on an icon, thereby retrieving the info attached to the icon. But instead of pointing and clicking a mouse, someone practicing the Art of Memory would be walking through imaginary rooms created inside his own mind. And while he is moving from room to room, he will be accessing images and their stored information in order."

"The order of places, the order of things," Gabriel parroted.

"Exactly." Stallworthy nodded. "That was the rule. Every time the practitioner walked through the palace, he had to access the rooms and images in order. This was very important. Otherwise he'd get lost and the information he tried to access would be scrambled."

Gabriel sat quietly, trying to absorb what Stallworthy had told him. The house of a million doors was an imaginary building. That was what he had accessed during his ride inside Robbie Whittington's mind. The kid had not been on drugs. He had been walking quite deliberately through an imaginary palace inside his head. A palace constructed by an expert on the subject of memory: Minnaloushe Monk.

Gabriel looked at Stallworthy. "You said the images inside the rooms of the memory palace should be either beautiful or horrendous. Why?"

"Simply because visual images, which evoke a strong emotional response, are easier to remember than bland ones. You're more likely to remember a solar eclipse than a lightbulb. Striking images are an aid to memory."

For a moment Gabriel remembered some of the bizarre objects he had encountered inside the house of a million doors. An eyeless monk. Phosphorescent lilies. Bloodied doves. Crucified babies. Pulsating galaxies. Stallworthy was right: those images were hard to forget.

Gabriel frowned again. "Does this memory palace thing really work? It seems to me as though it would be impossible to remember all those thousands of images—never mind the information attached to them."

"Quite frankly, the modern mind isn't up to it anymore." Stallworthy sighed. "Our memories have become flaccid because of all the technological tools we use. The photocopier. The Internet. Television. We're using them as props. You told me you're a computer specialist. That must mean you are used to working with information. However—correct me if I'm wrong—your long-term memory is probably quite feeble. Citizens of Ancient Greece and Rome would find your attention span laughable."

The contemptuous tone was unexpected. For a moment Gabriel was taken aback. "Citizens of Ancient Greece did not encounter a tenth of the ideas I'm exposed to every day, Professor," he objected. "Communications technology is making incredible demands on our brains. Personally, I think we are evolving into far more complex human beings than even our grandparents."

"I don't agree." Stallworthy was emphatic. "Modern man is increasingly incapable of internalizing knowledge. Our memories have become shallow. We surf the Internet obsessively but forget what we've read almost as soon as we've read it. Information in newspapers and the TV is fed to us bite-sized for easy consumption. Yes, we do receive enormous doses of information every day. But it's in the one ear, out the other. We never memorize it and make it our own."

"Yet our multitasking abilities are far superior to our grandparents'."

"Of course. But our multitasking ability is a facile skill, allowing us to skim the waves of chaos, not swim through them. We're all born with natural memory. But instead of strengthening that memory throughout our lives—training it the way you would your body in a gym—we allow it to become flabby. Did you know Simplicius could recite Virgil backwards? And that Seneca the Elder could hear a list of two thousand names and then repeat them in exact order? We're talking around 40 B.C."

"Impressive. But that's rote knowledge."

"Maybe. But in the days before the printing press people had to remember everything. *Everything.* Students listened to their teachers and would pass on knowledge gained by word of mouth. Their memories were *muscular.*"

For a moment Gabriel thought back to a summer's day and two women drinking wine in a graveyard, the sun in their hair. Quoting from a book, which they had not read in years. Their recollection word perfect.

Gabriel looked at the CD on Stallworthy's desk. "So you're saying the person who constructed that building has a good memory."

"Not a good memory. A magical one."

Stallworthy's voice had changed: the reverence was back. "The person who created this memory palace is a magician and a mathematical genius. It is someone for whom the concept of memory is a passion. Do you know him?"

"Her."

"A woman?"

"Yes."

"Really? Now, that's fascinating. All the great practitioners of the Art of Memory that we know of have been men. Trithemius. Fludd. Ramon Lull. Giordano Bruno. Giulio Camillo. Magicians all of them."

"So this woman is a witch as well."

"Oh, yes."

Gabriel closed his eyes. Minnaloushe holding a book with pictures of women burning like torches. Her hands pale, her hair a glistening cloud of Spanish moss.

"You see," Stallworthy leaned forward, his handsome face intense, his words flowing rapidly, "at first the Art was merely an aid to memory—that's how the Ancient Greeks conceived it. But during the Middle Ages and Renaissance, the Art changed when it fell into the hands of men who were interested in obtaining divine powers."

"You're saying it turned into witchcraft."

"Absolutely. These men—men such as Giordano Bruno and Ramon Lull—built memory palaces that were appallingly complex. They were supposed to hold information about every aspect of the universe—the entire history of human civilization. So the palace represented the cosmos, and the images inside it knowledge of the cosmos. These buildings were really vast information systems constructed according to techniques of numerology and cryptology infused with magic—a kind of mystical mathematics—but still based on the ancient principle of the order of places, the order of things."

Gabriel was struggling to come to terms with Stallworthy's words. "But what on earth did they hope to achieve?"

"Their highest aspiration was gnosis—divine knowledge and universal memory. They believed they could produce a kind of memory machine capturing all the knowledge in the universe."

"Like a universal computer."

"Yes. But a computer located firmly in the mind alone. Wetware. Not hardware. Their ultimate goal was to tap into this mind computer and access all universal knowledge at once. In one single gigantic blast of data."

"Why?"

"Because at that instant of total knowledge, they would experience enlightenment. They would become one with cosmic consciousness. *Anima mundi.* When that happened, the magus would comprehend divine power. Become godlike himself."

Gabriel stared at Stallworthy. "Madness."

"Divine madness.

"It's not possible."

"Who's to say what is possible? There are reports of alchemists walking on water. Becoming immensely old. Seeing into the future."

"This can't be anything but superstition and mythology. A product of the dark ages."

"Mr. Blackstone, the search for enlightenment is one of the oldest quests of mankind. It is indeed the Holy Grail. Even today there are people all over the world, from different philosophies and widely different cultures, who pursue exactly the same goal. Martial artists partake in *shugyo* or fearsome rituals designed to break down body and spirit. North American shamans use meditation and drugs to achieve enlightenment. Right at this minute there are people staring at a blank wall or sitting on top of a very tall pole—who have done so for years—in order to expand their consciousness. This may seem ridiculous, even laughable to you, but seekers of enlightenment are willing to sacrifice everything for a moment of true illumination. *Everything.* Memory artists were no different. But instead of using kung fu or mantras, they drowned themselves in data and built information palaces."

"The whole idea is crazy." Gabriel could hear his voice rising. "There's no way these guys could have carried around universal knowledge inside their heads. I don't care how good their memories were."

Stallworthy shrugged. "Whether any of them actually achieved the goal of universal knowledge is highly questionable, granted. But it's the journey as much as the destination that attracted these men. Just constructing the palaces and embedding them into their own memories was a stupendous feat. Such a highly strenuous journey would inevitably lead to Purgation and Purification of the Self. And as they traveled, they harnessed godlike powers. These palaces were created to mirror the immensity of the cosmos, remember. By trying to wrap his mind around one of those information systems, the magician's mind was stretched and strained—propelled into a divine change of state."

"Transformation."

"Every alchemist's dream."

Gabriel looked out the window. Behind the shiny leaded panes, the sky was sullen.

"Now, I should stress one thing . . ." Stallworthy hesitated. "Unlike the classical memory palaces, alchemists' palaces were animated by magic. The objects in the rooms weren't just ordinary symbols—they were magic symbols."

"Magic how?"

"The objects inside the rooms were talismanic images. Every single image—whether it is a gutted pig or a butterfly or a monk or whatever—was conceived according to very definite magical formulae. Each object—whether beautiful or horrific—was constructed with one goal in mind. To endow the magician with supernatural power."

"As easy as that, huh?"

Stallworthy shook his head. "True magic is never easy. The magic we're talking about is highly systematized magic. When you read the writings of memory artists, you realize you are in the presence of a different breed of men. Bruno's *Shadows* is a work of exceptional brilliance. And Lull's memory theater was a massively intricate system of wheels within wheels. His use of symbolic logic influenced Leibnitz's development of calculus. And the *Ars Magna* was translated by a German philosopher into the programming language COBOL. Some say Lull's memory system is the occult origin of modern computers."

Gabriel looked back to where the CD lay innocently on Stallworthy's battered desktop. "So that," he gestured with his head at the CD, "that is . . ." His voice tapered off.

"Yes." Stallworthy's voice was quiet. "*The Promethean Key* is a magical memory palace. And quite the most elaborate one I've ever studied."

Gabriel brought his hand up to his eyes. He was so tired. The room around him seemed edged with white.

"The woman who created this palace has combined the classical

Art of Memory with Bruno's *Shadows* and Lull's *Wheels*, refining it to the square. Within this palace hide innumerable worlds. Galaxies of information."

"And she's carrying all of it around in her head."

"She's attempting to, yes."

Gabriel was suddenly furious. "Do you realize what you're saying? You want me to believe she's trying to memorize the entire bloody Library of Congress—God knows how many terabytes of information."

Stallworthy didn't flinch. "I'm not sure why the idea should make you angry. This woman is a solar witch in search of transformation, which will lead to enlightenment. Her memory palace is the product of an exquisite mind. I find it inspiring. You, on the other hand, seem to find it frightening."

Frightening? Gabriel almost laughed out loud. A mind that strong, that rigorously trained . . . and in possession of remote viewing skills. Yes, frightening was probably an apt word.

He reached out and picked up the CD, flicking it over and over in his hand. "Surely this one disk does not carry all the information in the universe." His voice was heavily sarcastic.

"Of course not. But it holds the framework of the memory palace and the codes upon which it is based. The software, if you will."

"Will you be able to decipher all of it?"

"Hardly. It's written in green language—the esoteric language of alchemists and initiates. I don't think I'll ever be able to decode a system like this completely. It is rife with simulacra and encrypted messages. Not to mention the sigils and talismanic images. And the math underlying it all is rigorous to say the least. Besides which, the portal is missing. And without the portal, I can't work the system."

Portal. In Gabriel's mind stirred an echo of that fantastical geometrical space with its symbol-clad walls. Gateway to madness and death.

"What is the portal?"

"It is the heart of the system: the power station, if you will. It drives the entire construct. Inside the portal there is a series of concentric revolving wheels densely inscribed with magic images that can be combined and recombined in ever-changing arrangements. Most of the images will be from ancient Egyptian star lore and star magic. But you need to animate the wheels and get them to turn, otherwise the system won't work. Of course, in order to activate the wheels you also need a password."

"A password."

Stallworthy nodded. "Without the portal and the password, the disk is just a curiosity."

"And with it?"

"With it I would be able to start internalizing this memory palace. Magicize my mind."

"Become an alchemist yourself."

"Yes. An extreme magician." Stallworthy's voice dropped to a whisper. His handsome face was tight with fervor.

But then he suddenly relaxed. Leaning back in his chair, he smiled at Gabriel's expression. "You look shocked."

"I find it amazing that anyone academically trained in the twenty-first century can speak of magic so glibly."

"What else is magic but an attempt to grasp the laws governing the universe and apply them to your own ends?"

"That's not magic. That's science."

"Yes. And alchemy is the science of the soul."

Silence. The only sounds in the room the crackle of the flames and the tiny secret rushes of settling soot.

Gabriel rubbed his forehead. "This password you talked about . . . you have no idea what it might be?"

"No. Only the designer of this palace knows its true name. And that is locked away inside her mind." Stallworthy shook his head almost sadly. "Of course, even if I did have knowledge of the password, I don't think I would use it."

"Why not?"

"Because walking through such a palace is dangerous. The strain on the mind is stupendous. You can get lost inside, unable to ever return to the real world again. Once you lose the order of places, the order of things, you'll be stranded inside a labyrinth, unable to find entrance or exit. It takes a very highly trained mind to make the journey. An alchemist of the highest order. This is not for the dabbler. It should only be attempted by a magus. Or a witch."

For a moment Robbie Whittington's face came into Gabriel's mind. The sweet mouth and vulnerable eyes. An alchemist of the highest order? A magus? Surely not. And that might have been the problem. Somehow—he didn't know how or why—but somehow Whittington's attempt to walk through Minnaloushe's memory palace had damaged his mind. But why did she then also have to kill him?

Gabriel got up from his chair. "Professor Stallworthy, thank you for your time. You've certainly cleared up a quite a few issues for me."

"Not at all." Stallworthy gripped his hand firmly. "The pleasure was mine. It's amazing to think there is still a genuine practitioner of the Art out there. I rather thought they had ceased to exist. May I ask, how did you come to be in possession of this disk?"

Gabriel hesitated. "It was amongst the personal effects left to me after the lady's death."

"She's dead?" Stallworthy's voice was filled with regret. "I would have loved to meet her. She must have been a remarkable woman."

"Remarkable?" Gabriel paused. Minnaloushe's face was suddenly clear in his mind. Red hair, gypsy mouth, ocean eyes.

"Yes, I suppose you could say that."

As he walked away from Stallworthy's office, Gabriel glanced at his watch. It was already after nine o'clock. The building had gone into after-hour quiet. The corridors were deserted. No clicking of keyboards coming from offices. No voices shouting and laughing. Every door closed. A light breeze was blowing, and flyers rustled quietly on the bulletin boards lining the walls.

At the end of the passageway, he looked back. Even the light in

Stallworthy's office was now dead. The professor hadn't passed him in the corridor. He must have taken another way out.

Gabriel pushed his hand into his jacket pocket and extracted his cell phone. Switching it on, he glanced at the lighted display. Two missed calls. Both from Isidore.

The first time around, his friend hadn't left a message. But the second time, he had. "Gabe. Call me . . ."

CHAPTER TWENTY-EIGHT

Isidore replaced the receiver without leaving a message on Gabriel's cell phone. It was rare indeed not to be able to contact Gabriel on his mobile. Highly irritating. Isidore had a pressing need to talk to Gabriel right now; right this minute. He had some fantastic news to share.

Isidore felt very pleased with himself. Sometimes he was amazed by his own brilliance. Like today.

He dialed Gabriel's cell phone number again. Once more he listened to his friend's recorded voice informing him that he was not available to take the call. This time he decided to leave a message.

"Gabe. Call me. I have interesting news. No, I have stupendous news." Isidore hesitated. Should he just come right out and tell Gabriel what it was? But then he decided against it. It was best if he talked to his friend in person and explained how he had arrived at his conclusions. Besides which, he felt pretty damn good about cracking this little riddle and would like to spin out his moment of glory. So he merely added mysteriously, "Beware the crow . . ."

With this tantalizing clue, he rang off, smiling all the while. No question about it. He the man. Admittedly, cracking the puzzle hadn't required great deductive skills on his part. He had been surfing the Web rather aimlessly and had happened to scroll through a list of animal totems. And hey, presto: the answer was staring him in the face.

He swiveled his chair around to face his computer, his smile disappearing. He was worried that someone had been hacking into his machine. The cloaking device used by the snoop was pretty damn good but there were telltale signs. What he couldn't figure out was if his visitor had been merely curious, obeying the hacker's code of looking but not touching, or whether his system had in fact been compromised.

Earlier today he had stripped his system bare but found nothing wrong. Besides, most of his software was stashed in the university computers at the London School of Economics. It was his file transfer protocol site. Not that the people at LSE knew anything about this, of course. It was strictly under the wire. But it was a great hiding place, and it was highly unlikely that the snoop would have been able to track down any of his stuff. Without the FTP address, user name and pass code, his visitor would get nowhere.

But Isidore still felt uneasy. There were very few hackers around who were skilled enough to hack past his firewalls.

He sighed and decided to make himself a cup of cocoa. As he waited for the milk to heat, he picked up a small circle made of iron, which he had discovered stuck in the fold of the seat of his orange armchair earlier today when he had made a halfhearted stab at cleaning his apartment. The circle was quite heavy. He had never seen it before and rather thought it might have fallen out of Gabriel's pocket last night when his friend had been drying his feet.

He turned the tiny object over in his hand a few times. It didn't look like much. Probably worthless. Yawning, he lifted the lid on the garbage can and tossed it inside where it disappeared among yogurt cups, take-out empties and soggy tea bags.

He carried his mug of cocoa with him back to his computer. It was high time he visited his favorite MUD again. He hadn't visited the land of *Dreadshine* for over a week.

He knew Gabriel found his addiction to *Dreadshine* a little sad. And he supposed his friend was right. Instead of face-to-face contact in the real world, he preferred forming relationships in the anonymous, mapless world of cyberspace. And *Dreadshine* was where he felt most at home.

Dreadshine was a text cyber world filled with castles and knights, damsels in distress and deeds of valor. Every member of this online community had adopted a character, which they had invented themselves and which probably had very little to do with the kind of person they were in everyday life. Isidore himself had assumed the persona of the court clown and this was his handle as well. In *Dreadshine* he was known as Jester. No one knew his true identity. No one knew his real name. Which is the way it usually is in cyberspace. In cyberspace everyone wears a mask.

He logged on to the *Dreadshine* site, but before joining the rest of the gang in the castle's banqueting hall, he made a little detour to visit a friend who lived in the dungeons.

Or rather, who used to live there. Razor was a one-eyed cripple who had been tortured by evil monks when he was a child. His hideous appearance caused him to hide himself away in the dank garrets of the castle. Razor had been Jester's friend for a long time, and they had slayed many dragons and evildoers together.

But a few weeks ago, Razor had been killed in an online battle with a demonic gremlin. The combat rules of *Dreadshine* were strict. If you lost a battle, you had to pay the price and your life was forfeit. Razor had lost and had been ceremoniously buried by the other *Dreadshine* residents. The light in his garret was now switched off and a message posted for all members to see: "Razor's house is dark." This phrase was always used when a member died. The garret where Razor used to live was left intact, though, and sometimes Razor's friends would go there to pay their respects to his memory: light a candle, leave a bottle of beer.

As Isidore approached the garret, he was surprised to find someone there already. A woman—and obviously a new member. He did not recognize the name. Lady in Green.

He should probably introduce himself.

Hi,

he typed.

I'm Jester.
I know who you are.
Have we met?
No, but your fame goes before you.

Isidore smiled. She was flirtatious. This was going to be fun.

Please,

he typed politely,

would you tell me what you look like?
I am a seductress. I wear a mask but my eyes are magnificent. The
fragrance of pomegranates lies in my bones. I am shame and bold-
ness. I am knowledge and ignorance.

Wowza. Isidore blinked. This was one hot babe. His hands hovered over the keyboard.

Jester has fallen under the spell of the Lady in Green and wishes to
spend time with her.
In that case look into my eyes, Jester. Tell me what you see.
I see mystery. And tantalizing secrets.
And what do I have on my shoulder?

Isidore hesitated. How to answer this one?

What would you like me to see?
Do you see the crow?

Crow? He frowned. The next moment a steel vise gripped his
head. His brain sliced open and a massive torrent of images rushed
into his mind at lightning speed. He screamed. The pain was excruciating. His skull was on fire. He grabbed his head with both hands
as though he might shield his brain from the relentless assault. But to
no avail. His brain was being pulped by the weight of data rushing
into his mind at warp speed, and there was nothing he could do to
stop it.

The last sensation that flitted across his mind before every thought
was extinguished was one of disbelief. On the screen in front of him,
letters were appearing:

Jester's house is dark . . .

CHAPTER TWENTY-NINE

Isidore was to be buried in the churchyard of the village where he grew up and where his parents still lived.

Gabriel had taken the train. He couldn't trust himself behind a wheel any longer. He was shivering constantly and he was unable to keep his hands still. When earlier this morning he had introduced himself to Isidore's parents, he had twitched and jerked like a junkie in need of a fix. What their impression was of him, he hated to think.

In the past three days he had experienced five mind attacks. He had come to recognize the signs. The humming in the air. The nausea. His skin stretched tight over his scalp. And then the window opening inside his mind, the toxic avalanche of images and information ripping through his skull like soft-nosed bullets carelessly tearing apart the tissue of his brain. He was now able to anticipate what was coming and was usually able to clamp down before the window fully opened. But the blocking action itself always increased the pain inside his head. Every time he clamped down, it felt as though his skull was about to explode.

The last assault had happened only a few hours before, when he was busy shaving. The window inside his mind flying open. His hand with the razor jerking, leaving a thin but burning gash on the taut skin of his jaw. For an agonizing moment he simply stood there, allowing the avalanche of information and images to stream through his brain. Then, with a tremendous force of will he clamped down, and in doing so, he felt something inside his head give. He must have blacked out briefly. When he came to, retching over the washbasin, he looked at his mirrored image and his one eye was filled with blood.

If only he could keep his hands quiet. In desperation he tucked them under his armpits and tried to concentrate on the words of the minister, a diffident man with shy eyes. He was young, probably too young to have known Isidore himself when he was a boy attending church with his parents. The mourners, on the other hand, were almost all elderly: obviously acquaintances of the mother and father. Isidore did not have many friends. Correction. Isidore did not have many friends in the brick-and-mortar world. In cyberspace, his friends were numerous.

Facing Gabriel, on the other side of the grave, was Isidore's mother. She was weeping quietly. She was heavily powdered, and her crimson lipstick was bleeding into the furrows of her lips. In her youth, she would have been a great beauty. Her husband, who was standing next to her, had his eyes closed. His lips were moving soundlessly in prayer. He had his son's high forehead and thin, aquiline nose. Watching him, Gabriel knew what Isidore would have looked like in another thirty years.

After the funeral there was to be a reception, but his mind balked at the thought. He would take leave of Isidore's parents and head for home.

"Mrs. Cavendish . . ."

Isidore's mother looked up at him with tear-filled eyes.

"I just wanted to say good-bye." His hands were still twitching. His head was bobbing like a crazy man's.

If she noticed anything amiss, she did not show it. "Thank you." Her voice was heavy with tears. "And thank you for coming."

"I just wanted to say . . ." He stopped. What did he want to say? *I'm sorry for causing the death of your son?* Or, *If not for me your son would still be alive?*

Isidore had died of a massive stroke. Unusual in someone so young, the doctor had explained to Gabriel, but not unheard of. A brain aneurysm can be present from birth and lie undetected like a stealth bomb. He had listened to the doctor, nodding his head in agreement, all the while knowing what had really happened. An intruder had entered his friend's mind. An assassin. A killer who had torn Isidore's mind apart with the brutality of a butcher.

He looked into the sad eyes of Isidore's mother. "I'm sorry," he said. "I'm so sorry."

She touched his arm briefly. "Thank you. And God bless. I know Francis counted you as his best friend."

In the train, on the way back to London, Gabriel closed his eyes, but he couldn't keep the tears from running down his face. He knew he was attracting curious glances, but he was past caring. Memories of Isidore washed through his mind. Isidore in his flip-flops and swimming trunks, mixing mai tais and listening to island music in deepest midwinter. Isidore hacking code, concentration sculpting his face into a serene-looking mask. Isidore singing "Oh for the wings of a dove" with pitch-perfect intonation. Isidore. His friend.

His friend who had died because of him.

Oh, God.

If only he could speak to Frankie. He wished desperately for her presence. In a world in which nothing made sense anymore, he needed her aggressive sanity. But he had been unable to track her down. She might go somewhere warm, she had told him the last time he saw her. But she hadn't left word on where the sun was. And she wasn't answering her cell phone. He had left countless messages since Isidore's death.

He was falling into a light doze, flickering in and out of consciousness. The rhythm of the train was soporific. Clickety clack, he thought. Just as in his Tootle Tank engine book when he was a boy. Clickety clack.

Vaguely, he was aware of a woman taking the seat opposite him. She was petite and had long blond hair. Her head was bowed, she was reading a newspaper.

Clickety clack . . . clickety clack.

She shook the pages and folded the newspaper neatly along its creases. Her fair hair was hanging over her forehead, covering one eye. She lifted her head and brushed the hair away with a slim hand. And looked straight at him.

There were cobwebs in her empty eye sockets. The flesh along her jaw was green with decay.

Melissa Cartwright. Catwalk model. Trophy wife of Sir Stephen Cartwright. Kidnap victim.

You let me down. Her mouth moved and he glimpsed her rotting teeth. *You let me down.* A tiny black spider dropped out of one eye socket and ran across her lap.

Clickety clack. Clickety clack.

No. He tried to speak, but his throat worked uselessly, no sound passing his lips.

Yes. Just as you let him down.

The head with the ghastly eye sockets looked at a spot somewhere on his right. As in a trance, Gabriel turned his head in the same direction.

Isidore . . .

His mind blacked out in horror.

When he came to, the conductor was shaking him by the shoulder.

"Waterloo Station. Last stop, sir. Time to wake up."

Gabriel looked stupidly around him. The compartment had emptied. The seat opposite him was empty. As was the seat beside him. He was the only one left.

He was feeling so cold. He stepped out of the brightly lit compartment onto the platform, and his back was gooseflesh. It was just the cold, he told himself. Just the cold.

As he took the escalator up, he kept glancing over his shoulder. The third time he spotted her. Black coat, blond hair. Cobwebbed eyes.

He started to push his way past the people in front of him. But it felt as though his legs were caught in quicksand. He tried to take the steps two at a time, but he could hardly move. His breath was leaving his throat in a ragged whistle. Again, he glanced behind him.

She had disappeared.

The taxi rank. He needed to find a cab to take him home.

The cab pulled up to the curb, the yellow sign glowing. As he opened the door and ducked to get inside, he spotted her reflection in the window. She was right behind him. If she stretched out her hand she would be able to touch his shoulder.

A strange sound escaped his throat. He fell into the cab and slammed the door shut behind him. The driver looked at him with surprise.

Just a hallucination. Your mind playing tricks. Keeping his eyes resolutely away from the window he gave his address to the cabbie, who was now watching him with open suspicion.

She's messing with your mind. She's planting these images of Melissa Cartwright and Isidore into your brain like toxic seeds. Don't allow her to do that.

Her.

Why couldn't he say her name?

Whenever he thought of her, he used the words "killer," "assassin," "intruder." It was as though by not saying her name, he could avoid the truth.

Minnaloushe.

Face it. Deal with it.

And work out how you're going to tell Morrighan that her sister was responsible for the death of three people.

At his front door, he fumbled for his keys. Once inside his apartment, he would be safe.

He flicked on the light switch. The living room was empty.

Except . . . the wind chimes hanging from the ceiling in that quiet, wind-still room were swaying gently. As though someone had passed by close enough to stir the air.

No. It was just a trick.

So cold. He looked at his hands and they were shaking. Had they ever been still?

He walked into the bathroom and turned on the taps of his bath. He took off his jacket and his shirt. Steam was starting to fill the room, pearling down the mirror like tears. His own face, pale with eyes unfocused, looked like the face of a person drowning.

Something stirred behind him. Hazily swimming into his vision was the face of a woman with hair like blond seaweed. The flesh of her face decomposing, soft as a sponge.

He screamed. He sprang to his feet, in his haste slipping on the bathroom mat. Running out of the room, he slammed the door shut behind him. His fingers gripped the knob of the door firmly, as though trying to keep whatever was inside the bathroom from coming out. He stared at his hand. Any moment now, the knob would start to turn inside his palm . . . Any moment now.

Nothing happened. From behind the closed door he could hear the water flowing from the taps.

Still he waited. The water continued to rush from the taps. How long he stood there, holding on to the knob with all his strength, he did not know. Water seeped underneath the bathroom door onto his feet, but he did not move.

Someone was watching him. He turned his head, stiff as a doll, and looked behind him.

Against the wall hung Minnaloushe's African mask. The wooden face with its empty eyes and empty smile. *Protection against witchcraft.*

His stomach heaved miserably. Swinging his arm, he struck the mask from the wall. It fell to the floor with a crash. A crack ran through one eye socket. The mouth was still smiling.

The doorbell rang. The sound paralyzed him, froze him to the spot. He glanced at the door fearfully. He suddenly thought of Isidore, buried only that morning, resting in his coffin in dank soil. Maybe his friend wasn't in his coffin. Maybe he was standing outside the front door right this minute, his hand raised to press the bell once more.

The bell rang again. After a few moments someone pounded the door with a fist. "Gabriel?" Frankie's voice was muffled. "Are you there?"

He scrambled to the door and unfastened the door chain with fingers that were weak from eagerness and recent panic.

"My God." Frankie's voice was appalled. "What's happened to you?"

CHAPTER THIRTY

The MRI scan looked like a work of art. A creepy work of art, but still art.

"Lovely, isn't it?" The man on the other side of the desk was beaming at Gabriel as though he had the same thought. "The detail is stupendous."

Gabriel looked back at the scan, which was clipped up against a light box. He still couldn't believe he was staring at his own brain. It looked like a splayed white mushroom floating in a well of black ink.

Next to him, Frankie moved her chair closer to his and took his hand in hers. She had hardly left his side since she found him in his apartment the night before. And it was her doing that he was now sitting in the office of one of the most eminent neurologists in Britain.

Earlier that morning he had undergone an MRI scan. Gabriel knew that a scan—even a private one—usually took time to schedule, but Frankie had gone into overdrive. She had taken one look at his bloody eye and the shaking hands and had called the consultant who had attended her husband while he was still alive. He, in turn, had made them the appointment with the neurologist. Gabriel had no idea what other wires were pulled, but within one day he had been scanned, prodded, examined and called in to learn his fate.

The neurologist, who went by the cheerful name of Horatio Dibbles, placed two plump hands on his desktop and looked at Gabriel with eyes that were colored angelic blue.

"Mr. Blackstone. We have good news and not such good news." Gabriel half expected the medic to ask him which he wanted to hear first, but Dibbles continued without pause. "You have suffered a transient ischemic attack."

"A stroke?" For a moment Gabriel thought of his uncle Ben who had collapsed with a stroke at the age of forty and afterward had spoken with a tongue that seemed dipped in tar, dragging his left leg behind him like a useless piece of wood.

"A temporary stroke. Now, the symptoms of a TIA are the same as for a full-blown stroke, you understand. Vision can be affected. Also behavior, movement, speech and thought. Mental confusion is quite common."

Mental confusion. No shit. Melissa Cartwright's wasted face washed into Gabriel's mind.

Dibbles coughed discreetly. "A TIA's symptoms are temporary. The majority clear within an hour. Although they can sometimes continue up to twenty-four hours. But what is important to remember is that in most cases permanent damage is unlikely."

"So what's the not so good news?"

"Well, you have to realize you've had bleeding in the brain. In the artery of your brain there's a weak spot, an aneurysm. It's like a small balloon or a worn spot on the inner tube of a tire and it leaked. What concerns me is that you seem to have had repeated leaks. Each time the leak has healed itself and the bleeding has stopped. But repeated leaks in the brain are not good news."

"Is it treatable?" Frankie leaned forward, her face anxious.

"Usually if an aneurysm is identified, it is repaired with microsurgery and removed. But obviously we need to run more tests." He looked back at Gabriel. "I would like you to book into hospital so that we can get to the bottom of this. Find out what's responsible for these repeated leaks."

Not what, Gabriel thought. Who.

The neurologist seemed concerned by his silence. "Mr. Blackstone—"

"It will have to wait."

"Wait?"

"Yes. I'll be in touch with your office at a later date." Gabriel pushed his chair backward and started to get to his feet.

"This is highly unwise." Dibbles had lost his cheerful smile.

"I understand. But right now is not a good time."

Dibbles looked at Frankie. "Mrs. Whittington, I cannot stress strongly enough how important it is that Mr. Blackstone submit himself for observation."

Frankie got to her feet as well. "I'll talk to him, Dr. Dibbles. I promise we'll be in touch very soon."

The expression on Dibbles's face made Gabriel wonder if he was going to try to restrain them physically. Maybe the man had some kind of silent alarm under his desk that, at a touch, could summon an army of brawny nurses with straitjackets and needles at the ready.

But then Dibbles sighed. Folding his plump hands deliberately, he said in an emotionless voice, "I cannot force you to commit yourself to this hospital, Mr. Blackstone. However, please know that the next attack could be a full-blown stroke. It can lead to paralysis."

He paused, rearranged his hands.

"Or death."

"Cheers." Gabriel clinked his glass against Frankie's a little too emphatically.

He brought the glass to his mouth and drank deeply. It was a full-blooded Cabernet and the tannin burned his tongue. Drowning his sorrows in alcohol was probably not the wisest course of action, but he was beyond caring. Frankie was sitting in one of the leather club chairs in his apartment. She looked shattered.

He didn't even want to think what he looked like. He was now consciously avoiding mirrors. Whenever he looked into the mirror, his grandfather's face stared out at him. His grandfather on his deathbed. But it wasn't merely the fact that the sight of his own face was a real downer—ashen skin, bloodshot eyes—he was also afraid of seeing a shadow fall across the door behind him, a flaccid hand beckoning. He didn't know what was worse: the mind attacks or the hallucinations.

"How are you feeling?"

"Not bad." He had a splitting headache, but these days he always had a splitting headache. It was starting to feel normal. And the pain from the headache was as nothing compared to a full-blown mind attack.

As if reading his thoughts, Frankie said, "Why hasn't Minnaloushe launched another attack? The last one was two days ago."

"Maybe she's tired. Maybe she needs a rest period herself in order to juice up." He shrugged, took another sip of wine. "Who knows? But launching an attack probably takes something out of her as well."

"God, I hope so." Frankie's voice was savage. "I hope it's really painful for her. The bitch."

Gabriel winced at the word. Strange how he wanted to protest Frankie's use of the epithet. Which was pretty damn pathetic no matter how you looked at it. Minnaloushe was hell-bent on destroying him and here he was feeling squeamish when Frankie called her names.

But he had to be honest. The idea that Minnaloushe was a murderer still felt wholly unreal to him.

He remembered what she had looked like the night of her birthday. A figure from a religious painting. One of those beautiful women with slender wrists and radiant eyes, who inhabited the canvases of the old masters. A worshipful Mary Magdalene or a righteous Judith. Her skin bathed in light, shadows in her hair and at the corners of her mouth.

He was grieving, he suddenly realized. Grieving for lost innocence. But he was being foolish. He couldn't afford the luxury of grieving. If he didn't toughen his mind where Minnaloushe was concerned, it would be the end of him. She was sure to exploit his every weakness, and for his own sake, he had better shape up. For his own sake and for Morrighan's. She might be in danger from her sister as well.

Which brought him to the most important question: How to protect Morrighan?

He had a horrible feeling that Morrighan was in imminent peril and in need of his protection. If the danger had been physical, he would have backed her against Minnaloushe any time. Physically she was by far the stronger and the more agile of the two. But the danger wasn't physical. It was more insidious. And here he was, his brain leaking like a punctured tube, in pretty poor shape to assume the role of shining knight on a white horse.

Morrighan. How to warn her? How to protect her?

Frankie picked up the bottle of wine and filled her glass again. Gabriel waved the bottle away when she offered it to him. He was on to his third glass already.

"Frankie . . ."

"Yes?"

"I'm very grateful for everything you've done so far. But I want you to go home now. And I want you to stay as far away from me as you can."

"What are you talking about?" Frankie was scowling.

"I mean it. I'm bad news. You know what happened to Isidore. I don't want the same thing to happen to you."

"Oh, shut up, Gabriel." Frankie didn't even bother to raise her voice. "If it weren't for me, you wouldn't be in this mess. So just shut up."

"Frankie, I really think—"

"I refuse to discuss it any longer." Frankie set her mouth firmly. Her expression was mutinous. "Back off."

He backed off. For now.

"Let's make dinner." Frankie got to her feet. "And then we can talk about what to do next."

While Frankie boiled water for the pasta, Gabriel took tomatoes, salad leaves and parsley from the fridge. Placing the vegetables on a chopping board, he removed a gleaming knife from the knife stand. Global. The best. He had picked out this knife set in Divertimenti kitchen shop in Knightsbridge only a few months ago. An old girlfriend of his had been with him at the time. But he couldn't remember her name. Kathy? Carol? He tried to concentrate, but his head was splitting.

The heft of the knife fit comfortably in his hand. The blade was razor sharp. Chop. Chop. It sliced easily through the stalks of parsley.

His head was really hurting. He squinted at the chopping board. Chop. Chop. His fingers were pressing down on the parsley stalks, and for a moment the thought entered his mind that the tips of his fingers looked like vegetables as well. Like pale, smooth mushroom caps. Button mushrooms. The thought was funny, somehow, and a little giggle escaped his lips.

"Gabriel? Are you OK?"

"Sure." He didn't look up from the chopping board. The movement of the knife slicing through the green stalks underneath his fingers was mesmeric. Chop. Chop. White and green. White for his fingers. Green for the parsley. Chop. Chop. The knife edged closer to the tips of his fingers. Maybe red and green would be a better color combination than white and green. Red like blood.

Chop. Chop. He stared at the gleaming knife, at the blade edging closer and closer to his fingers. Just as the blade of that hunting knife had edged closer and closer to Melissa Cartwright's throat. Red like blood. Red like blood . . .

"Gabriel!"

Frankie's scream broke through the daze. The next moment she had wrenched the knife from his grasp and her hands were on his shoulders and she was shaking him.

"What the hell are you doing?"

For a moment he stared at her speechless. Then he started to cry. He leaned against the kitchen cabinets and threw his head back and wept with open mouth and open eyes.

Frankie did not try to hush him. She simply waited. Only when the last shuddering sob had left his mouth did she speak.

"I want us to talk to Alexander."

"No!" Gabriel jerked upright.

"Yes. It's time."

"I'm not going, Frankie. He will not have forgiven me for Melissa. I can't do it."

"Yes, you can." She paused and repeated again. "It's time."

CHAPTER THIRTY-ONE

She had been practically beheaded. Around her neck shredded tissue, and the great vessels from the heart exposed. The severed trachea white among the clots of blood. Her head was tilted backward but propped against the wall, as though she were lazily keeping watch.

Melissa Cartwright. Beauty queen. Glamour wife of Sir Stephen Cartwright.

Dead eyes should be empty of expression but hers were not. A horrible knowingness was in her gaze. Her left eyelid drooped flirtatiously. As though she couldn't help herself, Gabriel thought. Flirtatious in life. Flirtatious in death.

With a strange sense of detachment he saw that the front of her cream evening dress was soaked. She had bled out. The knobbly sequins of the bodice made the wash of blood look like crimson vomit. Her hands were resting on her lap and tied together with wire; white bone pushing through the slit skin. But she must have put up a fight. Some of her nails had snapped so violently, they had broken off right into the quick. Her long dress was rucked up, exposing her inner thigh.

"She's not wearing knickers," a voice said behind him. One of the detectives, talking to a female colleague.

"Probably didn't have any on to begin with. That tight a dress, you go commando." The female officer was smiling.

"Still looks like a sexual assault to me."

The woman shrugged, bored. "Let's wait for the vaginal and anal swabs."

Behind him, someone sobbed. Sir Stephen Cartwright was holding his hands to his face. Next to him stood Alexander Mullins. The two men had plastic covers around their shoes and were swaddled in white protective overalls, just like Gabriel himself. Like ghosts, Gabriel thought. Ghosts visiting the dead.

Mullins's eyes were filled with rage. "You don't belong here, Gabriel, but I wanted you to see for yourself. You could have prevented this from happening."

Gabriel tried to speak but his throat was tight.

"First you lied. And then when you could have helped, you refused to slam the ride because you were feeling . . . petulant." Gabriel winced at the contempt in Mullins's voice.

"Get out." Mullins's voice shook. "Get out now."

Gabriel looked back at the body. A smell was seeping from it. Oxidized blood. Urine. Feces. He knew that smell was going to stay with him. It would leach into his memories.

Memories. With time they grew blurred. As though they had been stored on a disk that became corrupted, throwing up a treacherous density of fragmented code whenever you tried to access the data.

But some things you never forget.

Gabriel would always remember the look on Alexander Mullins's face the day he told the viewers at Eyestorm that they had been retained by Sir Stephen Cartwright to assist in solving his wife's kidnapping.

"Stephen and I are friends," Mullins said, his face for once animated. "This case is personal. We all need to work together." He turned his head deliberately toward Gabriel, and the young man knew what that look meant. *Shape up. Fall in line. Be a team player.*

Except that being a team player had never suited his MO. When you slammed a ride, it was just you and your target. There was no room for group hugs or inspirational chats. Huddling together with other RVs, sharing information, talking things over, *opening up*— was all wasted energy. Besides, Gabriel enjoyed pitting himself against his colleagues. He always won and didn't they just hate it.

Melissa Cartwright was a supermodel and her violet eyes had

smiled from the pages of dozens of fashion magazines, at Gabriel and millions of others. A psychopath by the name of William Newts must have thought her smile was meant for him only. By the time Sir Stephen enlisted their help, his wife had been missing for three weeks and the media frenzy was intense.

Gabriel was excited. A success would be bound to impress Mullins.

The relationship between Gabriel and his mentor was bumpy. Gabriel knew Mullins admired his viewing skills, and the old man had once admitted that in his thirty years of studying remote viewers, he had never encountered an RV with greater ability. But Gabriel also knew Mullins considered him arrogant and a loose cannon, and his reluctance to work as part of a team was a continual bone of contention.

For his part, Gabriel thought Mullins overly cautious and sometimes outright punitive. Still, much as he hated to admit it to himself, he sought Mullins's respect in the way a son would seek approval from an emotionally reticent parent.

Maybe the Cartwright case would be a turning point. If he could bring Melissa home safely, the old man would be forever in his debt.

"What's wrong?" Frankie switched on the bedside light. The glow was feeble, leaving the corners of their tiny student apartment in shadow. Outside the window, the town of Oxford was asleep.

Gabriel sighed and plucked irritably at the bedsheet. "Nothing. Go back to sleep."

"No." Frankie pulled herself upright. "It is one o'clock in the morning and you're still awake. And I've had it with your bad temper. You've been impossible to live with for the past week. Tell me what's up!"

Gabriel stared at her sullenly.

"Gabriel, you and I are in a relationship. Re-la-tion-ship. That means you get to tell me what's bothering you and I get to listen and tell you it's OK and not to worry. And then maybe we can both go back to sleep and get some rest without you tossing and turning all night long and behaving like an ass the next morning."

If only it were that simple, he thought, looking at her flushed face. He suddenly felt close to despair.

"Gabriel?"

"The ride. I don't think I can do it anymore." He had difficulty uttering the words. His lips felt weirdly numb.

Frankie frowned. "What are you talking about?"

"I'm having trouble slamming the ride, Frankie. I think . . . I think, I may be losing the fire." Mullins had warned them. Remote viewers sometimes burned out and lost their gift. It happened to the best of them. Had it happened to him?

Frankie sighed impatiently. "Gabriel just because you struck out once—"

"Three times."

"—three times, does not mean you're losing it. You're just not seeing clearly yet."

"Frankie, I'm not seeing at all."

"But you identified three locations. You said you were sure. Alexander even called the police to check them out."

"I made it all up."

"What!"

"I . . . I just thought, if I could buy some time . . ."

Frankie's face was stiff with shock. The look in her eyes made him turn his head away. Every RV's work included speculation and conjecture, but it was of vital importance that a viewer should not embellish what he had accessed during the ride. Never pretend. Never lie. It was a mantra that had been drilled into their heads by Mullins during basic training. Gabriel had always kept the code. Until now.

The words tumbled from his lips. "I don't know what's going on. I can feel myself starting to cross over, the ride taking me. But then it stops. As though a door had been slammed in my face. Total block."

"You have to tell Alexander."

"No, not yet. It could still work, Frankie. I just need more time. I know I can work past the block somehow."

"If you won't tell him, then I will." Frankie's voice was implacable.

"You'll betray me like that?"

"For God's sake, this is not about you and me! A woman may die!"

The expression on her face made him flinch. "OK." He started pulling on his clothes. "OK. I'll go see him right now."

At the door he stopped and turned around. She was watching him and her hand was covering her mouth, giving her an alien, guarded look.

Frankie's reaction, however, was nothing compared to Mullins's rage.

"I am not surprised that you did not have the moral courage to own up to your problem earlier, Gabriel. It is always about you, isn't it? You and your vanity. Mrs. Cartwright is incidental in your scheme of things. You don't care about her. You just care about not looking stupid."

"Alexander, I am so sorry."

"No, you're not. You're just sorry you had to tell me about it."

"Please, just listen—"

"I blame myself. I bought into this ego trip of yours by thinking only your viewing was worthy. I neglected the team, did not give the reports of the others the same attention. You've lost us time, Gabriel. Time we could have spent exploring other avenues. And now we've lost the trust of the police as well."

Gabriel had no answer.

"I want you to leave."

Gabriel left. Back at his apartment, Frankie was nowhere to be seen. Without even removing his clothes, he fell into bed.

But it wasn't until shortly before dawn that he finally started to sink from wakefulness into sleep. And as he began to drift, he felt his inner eye opening. He was about to slam a ride.

He felt the soft tug of the ride. Let go. Let go. Cross over . . .

He hesitated.

Let go. Cross over . . .

Why should he? Mullins had kicked him out. And chances were he'd simply get blocked again. Why put himself through that kind of agony?

Let go . . .

No. He clamped down on the impulse, shutting his inner eye with ease. He was finished with Eyestorm. Such a relief, he thought. Such a relief to know that this part of his life was done with.

As he turned over and pulled the blankets over his head, he noticed the dark sky outside his window beginning to stain with palest light.

Melissa Cartwright's body was discovered eleven hours later in an outhouse on a farm in Yorkshire. She had died in the very early hours of the morning.

Shortly after sunrise.

CHAPTER THIRTY-TWO

"Gabriel, wake up." Frankie's hand was gently shaking his shoulder.

He lifted his head from the car seat and winced. He had fallen asleep during the drive to Oxford, and his neck now had a painful crick at the base. His forehead felt numb and cold where it had pressed up against the frosty windowpane.

He opened the car door and the coldness of the night air was a shock. As he stepped out, his breath left his lips in a ghostly cloud.

For a moment he stood quietly, looking at the house in front of him. With the exception of a brand-new shed in the garden, the place looked exactly as it had thirteen years ago.

Frankie slipped her hand into the crook of his arm. "Come on."

As they walked up the garden path toward the front door, an outside light went on and the door opened. A tall figure dressed in a worn velvet smoking jacket, flannel trousers and Nike sneakers stepped onto the porch.

Gabriel stopped walking. For a moment it was quiet. Then the man on the porch made a gesture with his hand. "Come in." He turned around and walked back into the house. After a moment's hesitation Gabriel and Frankie followed, closing the front door behind them.

Inside the house nothing had changed either. The flocked wallpaper in the entrance hall was immediately familiar. And the living room was still stuffed with porcelain knickknacks—winsome shepherdesses and pink-cheeked angels—and stacks of books and magazines. The low-wattaged bulbs inside the dusty fringed lamp shades bathed everything in a tired yellow light.

But if the house still looked the same, its owner did not. Alexander Mullins had aged. His skin was raddled with fine lines. His hair had thinned considerably. He made a clicking sound with his tongue and moved his mouth, and Gabriel realized with a sudden shock that Mullins was wearing an old-fashioned set of false teeth.

The eyes behind the cat's-eye spectacles, however, were still glacial. And the voice, even though it had lost none of its upper-crust plumminess, could still sound biting.

"Well, you're here. What do you want?"

Gabriel left the talking to Frankie. She did a good job, listing the facts of the situation chronologically and methodically, sanitizing the narrative of emotion and speculation. Just as Mullins had taught them to do at Eyestorm all those years ago when summing up a case. This was one student who had taken the training to heart, Gabriel thought wryly. No sloppy asides or personal prejudices clouding the issues. Mullins should be pleased.

When Frankie had finished, Mullins turned his eyes to Gabriel.

"So what is it you want from me?"

Frankie leaned forward in her chair. "Alexander—"

He silenced her with an abrupt gesture of his hand.

Gabriel spoke, his lips stiff. "I suppose I'm looking for help."

"Help." Mullins's voice was quiet.

Silence. Gabriel found that he had balled his hands into fists. He relaxed his fingers with an effort.

"Well, I'm sorry, but there is very little I can offer." Mullins paused. "I have never come across an RV like this woman before."

This woman. Minnaloushe. Fallen angel.

"It is clear that this woman's RV skills are exceptional," Mullins continued. "In all my years of research I have never personally encountered an RV who is able to inflict physical damage on someone else simply by using her viewing skills." He frowned. "This is truly extraordinary. I don't know what the explanation is."

"The explanation is she's a witch." Gabriel's voice was harsh.

"A witch." Mullins uttered the word with disdain.

Gabriel tried to keep his voice calm. "Yes. She is an extreme magician. She has taken her natural talent—remote viewing—and amplified it into a deadly weapon."

"And how did she manage to do that?"

"Through her practice of alchemy. Of high magic."

For a long moment it was quiet in the room. Then Mullins made a gesture with his hand as though pushing away something unpleasant.

"I'm afraid I do not feel equipped to follow you into these esoteric realms. I suggest we deal with the facts as we know them. A remote viewer is apparently able to use her viewing skills to create an abnormal pathology in a healthy brain. I have never encountered this before and therefore I have no data to share. And no magic bullet."

"There must be something we can do." Frankie's voice was low.

"Well, let's break the problem down to its basic components. Question: Is there a way to deny the attacker access to Gabriel's mind? Answer: Yes. He can block the scan. Second question: Is this a sustainable defense? Answer: No. When blocking, he sustains physical trauma."

Gabriel shrugged. "So I'll simply have to come up with another defense."

"There is nothing simple about that." Mullins took off his glasses, rubbing the lenses against the sleeve of his jacket. It was a mannerism Gabriel remembered well: an indication that Mullins was concentrating, focusing his intelligence on the topic at hand. He supposed he should feel grateful that the old man was at least intrigued enough by the situation to give the problem serious attention. This was what Frankie had bargained on. She had counted on Mullins's curiosity outstripping his personal animosity.

Mullins repositioned the glasses back on the bridge of his nose. "Explain to me what one of these mind attacks feels like." He turned his cold eyes on Gabriel's face.

"Sensory overload. That's what it feels like. It feels as though someone is tipping a giant garbage truck of violently frenetic images and sounds into my mind. As though an avalance is sweeping through my brain. And it happens so fast, I can't make out anything—the information is not discrete—the images all blur together. And it doesn't stop. It feels as though there is no end to it. And then, when I clamp down, my head feels as though it is about to explode. The pain is . . . severe." "Excruciating" was probably the better description, but he knew Mullins would find such an extravagant word distasteful.

It was quiet for a few moments. "The memory palace," Mullins said slowly. "It seems to me the answer lies there. As I understand it, this memory palace is really a vast depository of data."

"Yes." Gabriel nodded.

"It is my belief that she is channeling the contents of the memory palace into your consciousness by using her remote viewing skills."

Frankie entered the conversation. "You mean she's dumping everything inside her own head straight into Gabriel's?"

"Exactly. Her mind is obviously strong enough to contain all of that data. Yours," he looked expressionlessly at Gabriel, "is not."

A tense moment of silence. Mullins continued. "The obvious answer to the predicament is to destroy the memory palace. But how that is to be accomplished, I don't know."

"Maybe Gabriel can scan her," Frankie said. "Enter her mind."

"And do what? As far as I know he is not—what is it you called it—an extreme magician himself." Mullins smiled without humor. "So what would his weapon be? He doesn't have any information overload to dump into *her* mind. The flow only goes one way. The only thing that might happen is that he'll end up getting lost inside the palace, unable to find his way out again."

Mullins did not elaborate. He didn't have to. Getting lost inside the labyrinth of another mind was every RV's personal fear. Sometimes—not very often—an RV would find himself unable to sever the connection between his own mind and the host mind. This was very bad news. You could end up in a coma, stuck in the twilight world of psi-space: betwixt and between. It happened very rarely, but it did happen. RVs understood the risk, but because the statistical probability of it happening was tiny, it was not something they dwelled on obsessively. But the knowledge was always there. In this case, the odds of something going wrong must be pretty good indeed.

The bleep of a tiny alarm broke the silence in the room. Mullins touched his wristwatch. "Time for my medication." He pushed his hands down on his knees and got to his feet with difficulty. His body language made it clear that the meeting was over.

"Alexander, if you think of anything else . . ." Frankie's voice was without hope.

"Of course." Mullins's tone was courteous but the words sounded empty.

As he opened the front door for them, he turned to face Gabriel directly. He was standing so close, Gabriel could smell the man and it was an old man's smell. Mullins's eyelids were sagging and a watery pink in color. The signs of aging were shocking, somehow. He had always thought of Mullins as omnipotent.

He had loved this man once, had craved his approval. Gabriel knew he had arrived at Mullins's doorstep tonight with the expectation of finding salvation. Mullins would know the answer and bring an end to the nightmare. And Mullins would forgive him for Melissa Cartwright, the way a parent forgives a child unreservedly.

"I don't know if you've changed, Gabriel. I hope you have." Mullins worked his mouth, and again Gabriel saw the outline of dentures moving against the thin lips. "If you're going into battle against this woman, there will be no room for infantile self-indulgence. And this time you can't walk away."

Gabriel flinched.

"You were a member of a team once. But you considered yourself too strong for the team. You could have asked for help, but no, not you—you were the Lone Ranger. All that macho swaggering . . . and look where it got you, where it got Melissa. If you had come to the group with your problem, we might have been able to help you clear the block. But that would have been too demeaning for the great Gabriel Blackstone. And then, when you could have made amends, you didn't. If you had allowed yourself to slam that last ride—who knows what it might have revealed?

"You've always winged it, Gabriel. You've always trusted to talent. Well, this lady is not just talented. She has a trained mind."

A pause. "Frankly, I don't think you stand a chance."

CHAPTER THIRTY-THREE

The trip back to London was accomplished in near silence. Frankie's face was deeply fatigued and her hands gripped the steering wheel slackly.

When they stopped in front of his apartment building, she turned to Gabriel.

"Are you sure you don't want me to stay with you? I still think you shouldn't be left alone."

"I'm OK." He did actually feel a little better. Maybe it was wishful thinking, but it did feel as though the throbbing headache, which never seemed to let up these days, was easing somewhat. Not enough for him to do cartwheels, mind you, but enough to give relief. He didn't know why Minnaloushe was laying off, but he was grateful for the reprieve. Maybe she had given up on the whole thing. Now, that, he thought wryly, was wishful thinking indeed. When was he going to accept that Minnaloushe had no feelings for him? When was he going to replace the Minnaloushe of his memories with the cold-blooded killer she was?

He glanced at Frankie. To his horror he saw a tear fall from her eye.

"Oh, darling, no." He gently wiped the tear from her cheek with his thumb.

"I'm scared. I'm so scared for you. Aren't you terrified? You must be."

"We're going to find a way out, Frankie. I firmly believe that." Which was a big fat lie, but this was not the time to own up to the fear. "Don't cry, Frankie. Don't cry."

She said, eyes still brimming, "I'm sorry about Alexander. You were right: we shouldn't have gone. It was a total bust."

"No, that's not true. Alexander did manage to explain the mechanics of what is happening to me . . . even if he did it in his usual mordant style."

"What do you mean?"

"The memory palace. I think he's right, Frankie. I think all this stuff Minnaloushe dumps into my brain during a mind attack is information contained in the memory palace. I never thought of it that way, but it's the only thing that makes sense."

"So we need to shut down that palace."

"Yes. Too bad Alexander could only identify the problem, not solve it."

"He is still so angry." Frankie swallowed. "I never thought he'd still be so angry."

"He hasn't forgiven me yet. But he's right, Frankie. For years I've told myself I am not to blame, but the truth is if I hadn't been so arrogant she might still be alive. And if only I had allowed myself to slam that last ride, I might have accessed information which could have led us to her before Newts cut her. But I stopped the ride from happening because I was . . . *sulking*."

"You've changed." Frankie spoke slowly. "And I don't just mean this belated mea culpa. It's more than that. I've noticed it these past few days. Something has happened to you—something good. You used to be heartless, in a way. Always charming, but there was an indifference in you. A coldness."

He tried to smile. "Maybe you misjudged me."

"No. Something happened to you, which has changed you to the core. Who knows?" She sighed. "Maybe we have the sisters to thank for that."

"So it wasn't all in vain." His voice was wry. "I shall die a better man."

"Don't you dare talk about dying! I can't bear to lose someone else I love." She took a deep breath. "We're not done yet. We have one option left. What if we went to Morrighan? Tell her what we know. Ask for her help. If anyone can get through to Minnaloushe it would be her. She may not want to believe Minnaloushe is a killer, but it's worth a shot."

"She'll believe us. The diary told me that. The last entry I accessed made it clear she was having serious suspicions about her sister."

"So what are we waiting for?"

Gabriel hesitated. "I don't want to place her in danger. If Minnaloushe thinks Morrighan has turned against her, who knows what she'll do? I'll have to talk to Morrighan at some point. But I want to make very, very sure she's safe first."

"You're in love with her, aren't you?" Frankie said suddenly.

"Who?"

"Morrighan. You're in love with Morrighan. When you talked about the diary, your entire face changed."

"She's a very gifted writer."

Frankie offered a sad smile. "You're such a romantic, Gabriel. I've always said so, despite that hard-ass swagger you cultivate so assiduously. Look at you, falling in love with a woman because she writes a diary. It sounds almost medieval. Like the chaste passion burning between a lady and her knight who can only yearn from afar."

"It must look very stupid to you."

"No, it's wonderful." A pause. "If only it were me."

The silence in the car was suddenly tense.

"Frankie . . ."

"It's OK, Gabriel. I've accepted that I'm not the one you love anymore."

"I do love you."

"And you always will. But I can't compete with a woman like Morrighan Monk. I'm slippers and hot cocoa by the fire. Morrighan is an adrenaline rush." She smiled again; a smile full of sorrow. "But I want you to know that when you get tired of always being on a high, I'll be waiting. Adrenaline rushes are hard on the body."

Gabriel put out his arms and drew her close to him. For a long time they sat like that simply hugging, not speaking. What was wrong with him? He and Frankie were meant for each other. When she returned to his life, it had seemed to him as though they had been given a second chance. But that was before he read the diary. The diary had bewitched him.

Frankie stirred against his chest. "What are you going to do now?"

"Get some sleep. I don't know why Minnaloushe is laying off, but I should probably grab sleep while I can. But first—there is one thing I need to check out."

"What?"

"It may not be important. But if it is, I promise I'll call you." He stroked her hair. "Whatever happens, Frankie, I want you to know I am so grateful to you."

"I know." She smiled lopsidedly. "So get out of here. Get some rest."

Watching her drive away, he started to walk toward his apartment building. There was indeed something he should have checked out long ago. He was surprised that he hadn't followed up earlier. He prided himself on being meticulous: his success as an information thief depended on it. In his defense, it was probably fair to say that he had had rather a lot on his mind over the past few days. Like brain bleeds. Like death.

As he stepped into the elevator and punched the button for the top floor, Gabriel removed his cell phone from his trouser pocket. Pressing the call log button, he scrolled down to the last message he had received from Isidore and pressed playback.

He brought the cell phone up to his ear. The sound of Isidore's voice, so immediate, so alive, caused his heart to contract painfully.

"Gabe. Call me. I have interesting news. No, I have stupendous news." A sepulchral laugh. *"Beware the crow . . ."*

The elevator shuddered to a halt. Gabriel shoved the cell phone back into his pocket and took out the keys to his front door. A strange urgency had taken possession of him.

The apartment was in darkness, but the neon glow outside his windows was strong enough to allow him to walk to his desk without switching on any of the lights. Without even pausing to take off his coat, he slid into his work chair and tapped the keyboard.

The screen saver disappeared. He logged on to the search engine and typed in one word only:

Crow

Results one to ten of 3,920,000 filled his screen.
3,920,000? Good grief.
He tapped the New Search button again.

"Crow" AND "Magic"

The first ten entries of a mere 514,000 possibilities came up.

This was not going to be easy. Absentmindedly, he stared at the objects on his desk, bathed in the computer screen's lunar light. The damaged African mask was lying in his out tray. He couldn't remember placing it there. But then his memory was pretty shot these days. The face seemed oddly rakish with its grinning mouth and the wide crack running like a battle scar through one eye socket.

He placed his fingers on the keyboard.

"Minnaloushe" AND "crow"

o results found.
For a moment he hesitated.

"Morrighan" AND "crow"

The screen flipped over.

Morrighan: Irish mythology. Derived from the Irish **Mhor Rioghain** meaning "Great Queen." In Irish myth she was the goddess of war and death. She offered herself to those warriors she had chosen and if they accepted her they were victorious in battle. Those who re-fused her died. A shape-shifter, she often took the form of a **crow**.

For a moment he felt as though all the breath had left his body.

Morrighan. Not Minnaloushe.

Morrighan was the woman he had encountered in the house of a million doors, a black crow her constant companion.

Morrighan was the killer.

"I've been waiting for you." The whispered words came from directly behind him.

He swung around. From within the deep armchair scarcely three feet away, a figure lifted her hand and the tall swing lamp next to the chair blazed to life. The light fell on the woman's hair.

Red hair.

CHAPTER THIRTY-FOUR

The hair fell down her shoulders like a burning waterfall. Her face was pale.

Minnaloushe. The voice in the diary.

His love.

And it suddenly made immediate sense. No wonder he had had such a difficult time coming to terms with the idea that Minnaloushe was the killer. It had never felt right. His internal compass had tried to tell him he was looking in the wrong direction.

She stepped closer and glanced at the screen. "So you figured it out. I knew you would."

"Morrighan killed Robert Whittington."

"Yes."

"And his father. And Isidore."

"I'm sorry, Gabriel. I'm sorry for everything. Your friend—" She brought her hand up to her mouth. "I'm so sorry about him."

"Morrighan is the remote viewer."

Minnaloushe nodded. Her eyes seemed haunted.

"Who is the architect of the memory palace?"

"I am."

"Then I don't understand."

"I'll explain it all. But first, just hold me. I need you to hold me." She stepped forward until she was standing right in front of him. This close he could see the texture of her skin and the delicate laughter lines at the corners of her eyes.

She placed her hands hesitantly on his chest. He did not respond.

Like a young girl she stood on tiptoe and kissed him chastely on the cheek.

His breath caught. But still his arms hung like lead at his sides, as though he were caught in a spell.

She stepped back and brought a trembling hand to her lips.

Silence. Then she said one word only and he heard her voice break: "Please."

The spell broke. He reached out and pulled her roughly toward him.

He made love to her—the two of them wrapped in a cocoon of light, the edges bleeding into the dark shadows of the room.

He ran his thumb over her feathered eyebrows, across the sweep of her cheekbone and down to her chin.

She was his.

He touched her body, in awe. She was his to touch and feel and enter. The idea of it was almost too much for him to grasp. He had read her diary and he had fantasized. But the woman of his imagination had been as insubstantial as air. And now, when he had least expected it, here she was—glorious flesh and blood—her pulse racing beneath his fingers. Her eyes were languid. Her mouth was slack. As he touched her mouth, she opened it slightly and against his finger he felt the moist inside of her lower lip.

He picked up the spill of hair and kissed the nape of her neck. She smelled of attar of rose. He flicked his tongue across her breastbone and pressed his lips to the pampered skin in the hollow of her throat.

Everything about her body was amazing. The pale half moons of her nails. The underside of her arm gleaming like mother-of-pearl. The subtle slope of her shoulders with the skin so soft when he touched it he wondered if his hands were not too rough. At the base of her spine the *Monas* embraced by a red rose. Drops of blood beading on its spiked thorns. Pleasure. Pain.

Lifting her arms above her head, he licked the exposed hollows. His mouth traveled slowly down the entire length of her body: tracing the sculptured outline of ribs, the lovely rounded hip and long, smooth thigh. Around her ankle she wore a delicately linked anklet made of gold. It flicked bright in the gloom. He took her foot in his hand, kissed the raised arch, the pink rounded toes.

In his life he had loved one woman: Frankie. There had been other women, of course, and he had usually felt great fondness toward them. But as he looked at the woman who was now lying in his arms, staring up at him with eyes like bright water, he realized that of all the women he had known, he had adored—truly adored—only one.

He could be consumed by this woman. He could lose himself in her, lose his identity. The intensity of what he was feeling was over-powering. He might burn up in the boiling, spinning heat. But he did not care. How many people ever got to experience what he was experiencing at this moment?

He kissed her eyes, her nose, her lips, cupped her face in his hands. He stroked her fingers one by one. As he entered her, he immediately slipped inside her so deeply. Where did her flesh end? Where did his begin?

He sensed a purr coming from deep within her throat. Her fingers tapped against his shoulders. And then he felt her grip tighten and her nails cut sharply into the skin of his back. As he lost control he felt her shudder underneath him and he was gripped by a primitive sense of triumph. Wrapping his arms around her, he held her so tightly that she made a muffled sound of protest and laughter.

Pushing him away from her, she coaxed him onto his stomach. As she lowered herself on top of him, he could feel her breasts soft against his back. Her arms were resting on his; their fingers intertwined.

For a long while they stayed like this, not moving. Against the sensitive skin of his neck he felt her breath as it left her mouth gently. Her breathing slowed. She was asleep.

If only they could stay like this. In this safe room, inside this warm bed. The clocks stopped. No tragedy. No danger.

She stirred and made a soft whimpering sound. Her arm reached past him to the bedside table, and she turned the alarm clock toward her in order to see the time.

"It's very late."

"Or very early." He smiled and suddenly turned over and flipped her onto her back.

She gave a small shriek and laughed, clasping her hands to his shoulders. Propping himself up on one elbow, he pushed the heavy hair from her forehead.

She will age well, he thought, looking down at the lovely face underneath his hand. The intelligence in her eyes will remain undiminished; the beautiful bone structure as fine. The laughter and wisdom and quicksilver playfulness will not fade, nor that strange, wonderful luminosity that envelops her very being.

"Minnaloushe."

She smiled at him. Her smile was the smile of a woman who had made love and was now feeling satisfied and intensely feminine. She rolled her head on the pillow, pressing her face into the soft down, and stretched.

"Minnaloushe . . . will you tell me what happened?"

She stilled the movement of her body and he felt her muscles tense.

She turned her head toward him and he saw the sheen of her eyes. For a long moment there was quiet between them.

Then she said, "I will tell you everything."

CHAPTER THIRTY-FIVE

"Why did Morrighan murder that boy?"

Minnaloushe had moved to the far side of the bed. She was hugging herself, the line of her shoulders taut. The empty stretch of bed between them seemed to signify a mental, not just a physical, divide.

He tried to make his voice sound less accusing. "Why, Minnaloushe?"

"Morrighan was worried Robbie might betray her. That once I knew, I would stop building the memory palace."

"Knew what? And why is that bloody palace important enough to kill for?"

"It is the ultimate prize, Gabriel. Within its walls lies enlightenment. Behind its doors lies knowledge of the great secrets. People have killed for far less . . .

"My mother's death." Minnaloushe was nodding. Bright tears stood in her eyes. "That's where it all began . . ."

When Jacqueline Monk died at the age of fifty-three, her brain was a tangle of protein plaques interspersed with soft spots where the tissue had simply given way. She was still a beautiful woman but Alzheimer's had erased her memory and her personality. The sight of her two daughters standing at her bedside was the last impression she had before her breath finally left her body, but the image of the weeping girls made little imprint on her emotions. She did not know who they were.

The Tibetan Book of the Dead tells that the last thought at the moment of death determines the character of the next life. Looking into her mother's lost eyes, sixteen-year-old Minnaloushe Monk felt her heart break. Her mother's final thoughts . . . what could they be?

For the young girl, whose interest in mysticism was already

highly developed, her mother's loss of memory was profoundly traumatic. Memory, Minnaloushe came to believe, was what set man apart from all other living things in creation. Without memory you have no sense of self. Without memory you cannot remember the road you've traveled—can gain nothing from the present life. Even at such a young age, she began to study the concept of memory with a driving hunger.

As time went by, her studies took on an even wider spiritual significance. Not only memory, but knowledge itself, was now the object. Perfect knowledge, which could lead to direct contact with God. *Gnosis.*

It is twenty years ago. Minnaloushe Monk is seventeen years old. Outside the window, it is night. Lamplight pools on the pages of the book she is reading.

> *The founding of Gnosticism, or religion of knowledge, is widely credited to the miracle worker Simon Magus, who was branded the "father of all heresies" by his enemies. Gnosticism became a reviled practice, considered a dangerous, heretical sect in orthodox Christian circles. But even before the birth of Christ, Gnostic ideas had already surfaced in the Egyptian mystery cults and in Buddhism, Taoism and Zoroastrianism. The idea that man may gain insight into the secrets of God by striving for ultimate knowledge is an old belief.*

A movement at the door draws her attention away from the book. Morrighan has entered the room. Minnaloushe watches her sister walk over to the CD player, and a few seconds later, the sound of violin notes fill the air. "Andante Cantabile." Tchaikovsky's String Quartet no. 1, opus 11. It was their mother's favorite piece.

Minnaloushe watches warily as Morrighan lowers herself into an armchair. She is always wary where Morrighan is concerned, has long since given up on the idea that the two of them could be close. How sad, she thinks, looking at Morrighan's face—the elegant cheekbones, the black hair smoothed into a sleek French twist—to look at your sister and know that you have absolutely nothing in common with her.

But tonight Morrighan seems unsure of herself. In fact—Minnaloushe surprises herself with the word—she looks *vulnerable.* Maybe because today is the first anniversary of their mother's death. Earlier, when they had taken flowers to the grave, she had noticed tears in Morrighan's eyes.

"You're leaving for school tomorrow?" Morrighan nods at the volumes stacked up on the desk.

"Yes." Minnaloushe quietly closes the book in front of her. Let Morrighan think she was busy with schoolwork.

"I'll drive you."

"No need. I'll take the train."

"Please. I want to."

Curious . . . and unexpected. But Minnaloushe nods. "Thanks."

For a while they are quiet. Then Morrighan leans forward and says the words that change the relationship between the sisters forever.

"Minnaloushe, I have a secret to tell you."

If the death of Jacqueline Monk represented a turning point in the life of her younger daughter, it was only fair to say it had a similarly powerful impact on her eldest. At the time, black-haired Morrighan Monk was seventeen years old. For five years she had belonged to a secret society of teenaged girls: a pseudo wicca coven where the members talked about goddess, lapis, magic, boys and MTV with equal enthusiasm. Morrighan's revelation that she was descended from the great wizard John Dee conferred on her special status in the group and gave the young woman a strong sense of identity.

It was during this time that she also made a discovery about herself, which at first alarmed and then delighted her. She had a secret muscle inside her brain, which she could flex almost at will. It allowed her to "see" inside the minds of others. She was wise enough to know that such a gift would breed fear rather than admiration in her classmates and decided to keep this knowledge, unlike the story of her ancestry, to herself.

But the discovery of her gift fueled her interest in magic. Remote viewing, she was convinced, was essentially a magical act. After her discovery, the magic lite of her wicca coven no longer satisfied her, and she embarked on a serious study of the occult. Her main interest was talismans: ordinary objects turned into tools of magic through precise magical rules. Her talismanic knowledge would become all-important later in her life, as would her gift of remote viewing.

Most viewers discover their gift in childhood and share the discovery with a parent, a sibling or a close friend. Morrighan did not. It was a skill she relished, played with and refined. But kept deadly quiet. She was not about to let on to anyone. Least of all, her sister.

But then her mother died. On the first anniversary of the funeral, Morrighan found herself saying: *Minnaloushe, I have a secret to tell you*. The confession wouldn't have been made if she hadn't been grieving. Afterward, she fully expected derision from her sister. Instead, she found wholehearted acceptance.

Up till that moment, the sisters had not been close. They were jealous of each other and had little in common. Minnaloushe was the cerebral one, Morrighan the athlete. They grew up at separate boarding schools and saw each other infrequently. But on that evening, with the scent of their mother's roses drifting in from the garden and violin notes stirring memories of childhood, the sisters had the first openhearted conversation with each other they could remember. And they made a surprising discovery. Far from not having anything in common, they realized they were both mystics. They were approaching their goal from different directions, but they were on the same journey. A journey, which over the years, would metamorphose into a project that was vastly ambitious.

The project—or game as they referred to it in an attempt to make the enterprise seem less daunting—would eventually consume the women and become the driving force in their life. To seal their pact, they adopted John Dee's *Monas Hieroglyphica* as their personal sigil. It was the perfect symbol for the game.

Sibling rivalry was set aside. Each brought to the game her own special talent. Minnaloushe contributed a prodigious intelligence and a creativity that was genius. Morrighan's input was her knowledge of the occult. Eventually they would also draw on her talent as a remote viewer.

Together the two sisters aimed for the ultimate prize: *Anima mundi*. A moment of blinding illumination when they would understand the great secrets of the universe.

The way to achieve this was through building a house of a million doors. Memory was key.

In the course of her studies Minnaloushe had come across the work of such memory artists as Giordano Bruno, Giulio Camillo, Ramon Lull and others. The ingenuity, the erudition and the mind-blowing occult philosophy that lay at the heart of their memory systems took Minnaloushe's breath away. If man's mind truly was an incomplete reflection of the sacred mind, then these men's minds were approaching the divine.

It was a state of mind actively sought by the sisters themselves.

And so, over a period of twenty-two years, they built a memory palace the likes of which had never been seen before. Minnaloushe was the architect and the gatherer of information. Her mathematical skills were crucial to the design of the system. But Morrighan was the one who brought magic into play. Using occult rules, she turned the memory images inside the palace into potent talismans.

Brick by brick, door by door, object by object, the two sisters attempted to create an information system encapsulated within the gray white grooves of the brain alone: a system as wide as the universe, as deep as the human spirit.

They called it *The Promethean Key*.

But then something went wrong.

CHAPTER THIRTY-SIX

"Robbie." Minnaloushe paused.

Here it comes, Gabriel thought. Finally.

"We should never have allowed him to play the game."

"You deliberately targeted that boy." Gabriel knew his voice was harsh, but he couldn't help it. Robbie must have been such an easy touch for the women. He could imagine the boy being dazzled by the sisters, dazzled by their world . . .

"Gabriel, I want you to understand that we did not seduce him." Minnaloushe's voice was urgent. "Unlike you, Robbie was already a searcher."

"You must have known he was not up to the task, that he would fail."

She shook her head violently. "Failing or succeeding is not the point. Playing the game is like striking at a block of granite the size of the universe, releasing sparks of divine fire. Simply catching sight of the sparks is prize enough. Robbie understood that. He knew he could never hope to achieve the level of mastery of which Morrighan and I are capable. Except . . ."

"Except what?"

"About a year after Robbie started working on the Art, Morrighan had an epiphany." Minnaloushe's voice was taut. "And she changed the game. She decided to transfer bits and pieces of the memory palace from her own mind into Robert's consciousness using her remote viewing skills. So what would normally take years would be accomplished within a matter of minutes. With every information transfer, Robbie's memory would expand exponentially. A quantum leap forward every time."

"And it worked?"

"Yes. At first it worked brilliantly. We had some doubts in the beginning, you know. Transformation isn't fast food. You can't just order it like a burger." She gave a ghostly laugh. "Just plonking the palace into Robbie's mind without effort on his part would have defeated the object, to say the least. And it would have been dangerous in the extreme. His mind could have collapsed like a heap of rubble. So at first, Morrighan transferred only fragments—only a very few rooms at a time—and then Robbie had to figure out the order of places, the order of things himself. To put it very simply: he would have to fill in the blanks on his own, connect the dots without assistance. As I say, at first it worked brilliantly. It was as though the process fed on itself. With every transfer, the size of the subsequent data package that could be carried over increased enormously. More and more knowledge could be transferred at a time. It was fantastic. After every transfer, Robbie's memory skills increased exponentially."

"And then?"

"The burden became too heavy. Robbie couldn't filter any longer. He was like a constantly absorbing sponge, but the fibers were starting to unravel. There were clear signs. He was turning into an insomniac. And when he did sleep, he had dreadful nightmares."

"Why didn't he stop?"

"Robbie was addicted. Despite the side effects, he craved the rush."

"Why did you allow it to continue? Weren't you concerned?"

"Of course I was. I told Morrighan to slow down the data transfer. But without my knowing, she actually speeded up the process. Robbie was all for it. And because they knew I wouldn't approve, he and Morrighan kept the whole thing a secret from me."

"Things got out of hand."

"Things got badly out of hand. But, Gabriel, until very recently, I had no idea how badly. I knew Robbie was having problems. But I also thought he was beginning to have doubts about the game itself. I was always concerned that he wouldn't have the kind of mental toughness required for the Art. I knew if we slowed down the data transfer, there was a real chance he might become frustrated and drop out. Of course, I didn't realize the data transfers had increased and were feeding his addiction.

"Robbie disappeared while I was on a business trip to Ghana. When I got back and found him gone, I believed Morrighan when she said he had given up on the game. I was devastated that he had simply left without saying good-bye, but it fit. Robbie has a history of taking off without leaving word if things didn't work out for him. Even his father acknowledged that. So I accepted Morrighan's explanation without question."

"So what really happened?"

For a few moments she was silent.

When she spoke again her voice was hardly audible. "Morrighan decided to take Robbie into the portal of the memory palace. That should never have happened. Robbie was still an initiate of the first level, Air. He was still studying only the preliminary secrets. He was not yet a zelator. Only zelators are permitted to approach the Fire. By taking him into the portal, Morrighan broke the rules. For Robbie, it was catastrophic. Entering the portal led to a massive overload of data. His brain crashed."

"He had a stroke."

"It seems likely."

"But that's not what killed him."

"Oh, God." Her fingers gripped the sheet so tight, the knuckles stood out white.

"He drowned. Why was he in the pool?"

"Robbie loved water. We discovered his mind was at its most receptive when he was swimming. Especially at night. I don't know why—something about the rhythm of the exercise, the dark water—whatever it was, it was conducive to the interfacing of his mind with Morrighan's."

"So she interfaced with him while he was swimming. Overloaded his brain. But I still don't understand why she had to drown him, for God's sake. He was still alive."

"The overload wasn't deliberate, Gabriel, I'm sure of it. Morrighan didn't want to hurt Robbie, but she miscalculated. She pushed too hard. And when Robbie suffered the stroke, she was petrified that I would find out and terminate the game."

"Are you saying she deliberately drowned that boy to keep his stroke a secret from you? So you wouldn't stop building the palace?"

"Yes."

"And the body?"

"She buried it. She won't tell me where."

He stared at her in horror. "When did she tell you all this?"

"Earlier today. When she was drunk."

"I've never seen Morrighan drink more than a single glass of wine."

"A single glass of wine with a little bit of added something can pack a punch. And Morrighan isn't the only one who can mix a potion, you know."

For a moment Gabriel was quiet. Then he leaned over and switched on the table lamp. He wanted to see her expression clearly.

"The two of you gave me a potion the night of your birthday, I know that."

She wouldn't meet his eyes. "Morrighan insisted on it. You see, she found the missing photograph of Robbie when she snooped around in your apartment. Around the same time, we also discovered you had hacked into our computer. When Morrighan found the picture she was extremely upset. I couldn't quite understand why, but now it makes sense: she was worried that you were suspicious about Robbie's death. She wanted to know what you were up to. She had tried to scan you before, but you always managed to block, so the potion was necessary to get past your defenses. I now realize she wanted to find out exactly how much you knew about Robbie's murder. As for me, I simply wanted to know why you were interested in the diary."

He looked at her profile: a cameo of the greatest delicacy. "It was your diary that made me fall in love with you."

She smiled, kissed the palm of his hand. "Yes."

"My recollection of the night of your birthday is rather . . . jumbled.

Did we actually . . ." He paused, feeling suddenly foolish. "You know, did we make love? And, was Morrighan involved as well?" The words came out in a rush.

She blushed. He could see the red creeping up her neck.

"Gabriel—"

The phone rang stridently, the jangling sound making his nerves jump. He picked up the receiver.

"Let me talk to Minnaloushe."

The voice was cool as silk. Morrighan. In his mind's eye, Gabriel saw the beautiful heart-shaped face. The blue black hair. Azure eyes.

"Morrighan—"

"Just do it, Gabriel. Let me talk to my sister."

Without another word, he gave the receiver to Minnaloushe, who was already reaching for it.

The conversation was short. On Minnaloushe's side it consisted of a five words only. "Yes." A few moments of silence. "I'll be there soon."

She replaced the receiver slowly. "I have to go."

"No." He pushed himself upright, alarmed. "It's not safe for you."

"Gabriel, I can't hide. And remember, I'm immune to a mind attack."

He relaxed a little. That was true, he supposed. There was no way the architect of the memory palace could be in danger of an information overload herself. But still . . .

"Morrighan says she wants to talk."

"Talk?" His voice rose. "There's nothing to talk about. She's a killer. She killed three people—one of them my closest friend. She needs to be brought to justice."

"And how do you plan on doing that? Turn her over to the police? Do you really think they're going to believe all this stuff about memory palaces and information transfer? And where is Robbie's body buried? Forget about justice, Gabriel. All I'm interested in is getting Morrighan to stop the mind attacks against you. And I don't want her to recruit someone else to play with. She's already talking about looking for someone new." Minnaloushe paused. The expression in her eyes was despairing. "She thinks this is why she was blessed with re-mote viewing powers. That God wants her to introduce gnostic disci-ples to the palace through mind-to-mind transfer. She's obsessed."

"And what if she doesn't want to listen to reason?"

"She *has* to. Otherwise . . ."

"Otherwise, what?"

"Nothing." She shook her head and slid out of the bed, the sheets falling away from her. "The fact that she wants to talk is a positive sign."

He watched as she picked up her clothes from the floor and pulled her black sweater over her head, shaking her hair loose. De-spite the jeans and the pullover, she looked more than ever as though she had stepped from a Pre-Raphaelite painting. A pale-skinned, fiery-haired heroine from a Rossetti narrative. Mysterious. Powerful. Deeply sensual.

She reached into the pocket of her jeans. "I wanted to return this. Here, it belongs to you."

It was the locket, cool against his palm.

"When we gave it to you, you said you would treasure it always. Remember?"

"I remember." He noticed the silver linked chain was still broken where he had torn it off his neck the day after her birthday. The day everything started going wrong.

A feeling of dread took hold of him. "Don't go, Minnaloushe. She's dangerous."

"She can't hurt me."

"I don't care what you say. I don't trust her."

"Morrighan is sick, Gabriel, but how can I hate her? And you and she are so alike. Your remote viewing powers make you both so in-credibly special. I look at the two of you and I see the future."

"Stay with me. Please, please stay with me."

"Shh." She leaned forward and placed her lips against his. For a moment he resisted, then he lifted his arms and placed them around her shoulders. He wanted this moment to last forever, with the soft, heavy weight of her body in his arms. But even as he kissed her, Gabriel felt lonely.

He pulled away and placed a hand on either side of her head, looking into her long-lidded eyes. What lay behind those eyes? Sensations and images and worlds he could only guess at. He loved her. He had read her diary and had immersed himself in her most private thoughts. But even if he lived with her until the day of his death, she would remain an enigma. Ultimately unknowable. Her adventures of the mind too vast for him to share.

"Take care of yourself."

"I will." She nodded. "Stay by the phone."

His eyes followed her as she walked to the door.

"Minnaloushe."

She hesitated, stopped.

"Look at me."

Slowly she turned around to face him.

"I love you."

Her face lit up and she gave him a smile of such sweetness, his heart ached. And he knew he would never forget this moment. The night pressing dark against the window. The glow of the table light throwing shadows against the wall. The woman in the door with her luminous hair and pale face looking like an angel.

"And I you." Another smile and she was gone.

CHAPTER THIRTY-SEVEN

The phone was ringing

Gabriel jerked awake. Outside his window it was day, but the sky was miserably gray. How long had he slept for?

He grabbed the receiver. "Minnaloushe?"

For a moment there was silence. Then Frankie's voice came on the line. "No. But it looks as though we won't have to worry about that bitch anymore, Gabriel."

As he drew in his breath in protest, he suddenly realized Frankie knew nothing of what had happened between him and Minnaloushe the night before. She still thought Minnaloushe was the killer. He pushed himself up on one elbow, tried to focus on her words.

"What do you mean?"

"I mean she's dead."

The breath left his body in an explosive gasp. The room tilted and actual physical pain gripped his chest. He tried to speak but the words refused to come.

"Yes," Frankie continued happily. "I couldn't believe it when I opened the paper. Go check it out. It's in the early edition of the *Evening Standard*. Apparently she fell down the stairs at her house and broke her neck. Poetic justice, wouldn't you say? Gabriel, are you there?"

He did not bother getting dressed. He threw on his coat and pulled his boots over his bare feet. His hands were shaking so badly, he was unable to tie the laces, and in the end he simply pushed the ends into the ankle flaps. As he ran down the stairs, he found himself silently saying one word over and over again: *No. No. No.* Maybe Frankie had it wrong. Maybe Minnaloushe had only been injured. *No. No.*

The teenager behind the counter at the newsstand stared at him as he snatched the paper and dropped a five-pound note on the counter. He left the shop not waiting for change.

The report was at the bottom of page 12 in the Londoner's Diary section and consisted of two paragraphs only.

FATAL ACCIDENT TAKES LIFE OF WOMAN

Minnaloushe Monk (36) died instantly in the early hours of the morning when she suffered sudden loss of respiratory function after falling down the staircase of her house in London, Chelsea, and fracturing her neck. Ms. Monk was well-known for her contributions to various philanthropic concerns. Her sister, the well-known adventure sportswoman Morrighan Monk, witnessed the accident and is being treated for shock.

Every day about 1000 falls take place on stairs or steps in the United Kingdom. Three or four of these will be fatal. There are many reasons why falls happen, but the main contributing factors are thought to be poor eyesight, poor lighting or the use of alcohol.

CHAPTER THIRTY-EIGHT

The sky was gray with intermittent rain.

He was shivering violently and his face felt raw from the cold. He had been standing on the street corner for almost an hour. But the thought of leaving did not cross his mind. All his attention was focused on the big redbrick house on the other side of the road.

It was five o'clock in the afternoon and dusk was well advanced. Most of the houses in the street showed lighted windows, but the rooms in Monk House were dark. On the porch, the big tubs filled with blue chrysanthemums appeared neglected, as though no one was around to pay attention. The shallow steps, usually swept clean of leaves and debris, were dirty. A chocolate wrapper was trapped in the wrought iron work of the front gate, which was half open. The house seemed deserted.

But Gabriel knew it was not. It was occupied. He sensed it.

He sensed *her*.

The cold was intense. He became aware of his arms and legs cramping as he unconsciously fought against the shivers running through his body. A few fat raindrops fell on his face. The wind plucked at his scarf.

Blowing onto his frozen hands in an attempt to warm them, he quickly crossed the street and pushed the garden gate open to its fullest extent. He took the front steps two at a time. Without giving himself more time to think about it, he pressed the doorbell.

He waited. Nothing stirred.

The heavy velvet curtains in the downstairs window were open, the window only covered by the old-fashioned net curtains. But the two lacy panels did not quite meet in the middle, and through the gap he was just able to make out the room and, farther back in the passage, a glimpse of the elegant curve of the staircase.

For a moment the memories came flooding back. His first legitimate visit to Monk House. He was standing at the foot of the staircase, admiring its graceful proportions. Next to him Minnaloushe, cool and lovely in a summer dress. And he remembered her exact words. *I love staircases,* she had said. *I won't be able to live in a place without one. I believe they're essential to anyone wanting to live an interesting life.*

For a moment he closed his eyes, the pain of the memory so intense, he found himself involuntarily touching his chest. And on the heels of this memory, another image. A woman falling backward down the stairs, arms like pale petals grabbing uselessly at the banisters to stop her fall, rolling, rolling downward—a flurry of legs, arms, red hair, white neck angled crazily.

He opened his eyes and breathed shallowly. Turning away from the window, he placed his finger on the doorbell once again, pressing down and holding it for a full five seconds.

Nothing. Everything was quiet.

Maybe he was wrong. Maybe she had deserted this place, after all.

Something stirred at the periphery of his vision. He turned his head.

She had pushed one of the white net curtains to one side, and the darkened window now formed a perfect frame, as though she was putting herself on display. Pale face, pale dress, pale hands. Her hair a black snake falling over one shoulder.

She watched him expressionlessly from behind the pane of glass.

He wasn't sure she would be able to hear him through the window so he raised his voice.

"Morrighan, open the door!"

The movement of her head almost imperceptible.

"Please. I need to talk to you."

Nothing. No reaction. Her eyes black hollows. Behind the pane of glass she appeared as motionless as any exhibit in a museum.

"Damn you!" The anger boiled up in him, rising through his body like fast-burning acid.

She pressed her palm against the window. Her hand looked like a white moth. The gesture reinforced the idea of something on display. What did it mean: Stop? No further?

She was mouthing something. At first he did not comprehend but then he realized what she was saying. *An accident. It was an accident.*

"No!"

I never touched her.

"I don't believe you!"

She moved her shoulders indifferently. She didn't care.

"It does not end here." He didn't know if she could hear him. He raised his voice again. "It does not end here!"

He felt something touch him: a bolt of menace from her mind directed straight at him. An unambiguous warning. It had the impact of a physical blow, pushing him backward so that he almost fell.

Shocked, he steadied himself by placing his hand against the wall. It had felt as though she had reached invisibly through the window and punched him with great force in the chest. He had never experienced anything like it before.

Don't make me come after you. She mouthed the words slowly, precisely. Her eyes black as space.

She turned to go. For a moment he saw her profile: the profile of a huntress.

Then the curtains dropped, and the house was quiet once more.

CHAPTER THIRTY-NINE

London was in the grip of a deep freeze. It was the coldest December on record for twenty-five years.

Irritable shoppers rushed past with inwardly focused eyes. Shop windows were rimmed with fake frost and tinsel. Carols floated from hidden speakers, the same songs repeated with demonic regularity. Gabriel had never liked Christmas, but it seemed to him as though this year the forced jollity of the season was verging on the grotesque. Underneath the froth and mirth of end-of-year festivities, mince pies and jolly Santas lay a heart of ice, a seeping darkness.

He felt removed from it all: his mind cold, his heart cold.

In the dead of night she visits him. He opens his eyes and there she is next to the bed, looking down at him where he sleeps. Her red hair a cloud of light. Her pale shoulders smooth and glowing. Bringing her forefinger to her mouth, she places it between her lips, then touches herself between her naked thighs.

Sweat breaks out on his skin. He reaches out and pulls her down onto the bed with such force that she cries out. As he enters her, she tilts back her head and closes her eyes. He thinks he might hear the blood—hot and exuberant—pulsing through her veins.

But as he touches his hand to her breast, searching for the strong beat of her heart, she is turning into a ghost—her body becoming ephemeral, insubstantial—slowly fading from his grasp. One moment he is still holding on to flesh and blood, the next she has disappeared from his disbelieving fingers. A dream woman. A woman created from longing and want and memories.

The days passed, but time had lost all meaning for him. His computer stood untouched. He rarely answered his phone.

Minnaloushe. I had just found you. How could I have lost you?

New Year's Eve. Fresh snow on the ground.

Gabriel watched the pale flakes swirling in the darkness. The streets were deserted. The icy weather had driven even the most determined reveler inside.

He looked back at the book in his hands. He had been trying to read, but the black letters stared up from the page, the words meaningless. He closed the book and pushed it away from him.

The wind threw snow against the window. The refrigerator made a small tired sound. Silently the green neon light outside pulsed against the wall of his study, staining the desk with intermittent streaks of light. He hadn't used that desk in weeks, and he could see a layer of dust gleaming on the surface of his closed laptop. When was the last time he had logged on? He couldn't even remember.

For a moment he hesitated, then he stood up.

The laptop's hinges felt stiff when he opened the lid. Pressing the on switch, he waited for the machine to boot up.

Outside the window the drifting snow was thickening into a fast-falling blur. Opaque, smothering.

It was so quiet. You could think you were alone in the world.

The screen flashed blue and filled with icons. Mechanically he moved the cursor to the in-box and clicked.

Ninety-seven unopened e-mail messages were waiting in his in-box.

He scrolled slowly down the list, his mind dull. Some of the names he recognized; others were new: prospective clients, most likely. He did not open the messages, simply dragged the cursor down the list.

His breath caught. Adrenaline sluiced through his body. With burning eyes he stared at the screen.

The entry date was three weeks ago. The subject line was empty. The sender's e-mail address read: Minnaloushe@Monkmask.co.uk.

CHAPTER FORTY

My dearest love,

I have set this e-mail to a time switch. With luck you will never receive it because I shall be around to disable the switch before its release. But if things go wrong, this e-mail and its attachment will be
delivered to you at a pre-specified time. If you are reading this, then
I am in all probability dead, and you are mourning me.

After leaving you earlier tonight I went to talk to Morrighan. I was
hoping I could negotiate with her for your safety and I also hoped
she would give up on her insane compulsion to draw more disciples
into the game. But Morrighan is threatening us and for the first time
I am scared.

She wasn't always like this. Somewhere inside of Morrighan hides
my brave sister who believes in passion, creativity and beauty. Tomorrow, when I talk to her again, I will try to find this sister I admire
so greatly.

If I fail . . . we must go into battle.

Morrighan has become so powerful, Gabriel. You have no idea
how the memory palace has enhanced her viewing skills. They used
to be confined to wetware only, but lately she has moved beyond
mind-to-mind manipulation and is now able to manipulate inani-
mate objects in the real world as well. I thought it was amusing at
first—you know, watching her switch the TV off and on from across
the room, starting the microwave or coffeemaker. But who knows
where her skills can take her, eventually?

So we have no choice. We have to make her forget.

If we can make Morrighan lose her memory of the order of places
and things, she will be adrift—mapless—condemned to wander the
halls of the memory palace with no hope of escape.

There is a tradition in the Arcane schools that every seeker of enlightenment should have a secret name given to him by a teacher. As we did not have a teacher, I gave Morrighan her name and she gave me mine. Morrighan's secret name is a very old one and it means "Knowledge of God." It is also the password to the portal.

A secret name is very potent. It is keyed to magic numbers and marks the searcher's destiny. The owner of such a name must meditate upon his name constantly but should never speak it out loud. By keeping it silent, he preserves the name's vibration intact and it gains power. If the searcher gives voice to the name, it becomes worthless.

I am going to reveal to you Morrighan's name. You must enter her mind and make her say her name out loud. When she does, the name will be stillborn and she will lose the order of places and things. She will be hopelessly lost. No longer a witch.

I have written a spell which I have based on fragments of old gnostic texts. You will memorize this spell and release it. It is highly magicized code and it will act like a virus destroying Morrighan's inner resonance, her inner strength. It will compel her to first speak the magic numbers that are integral to her name, and then the name itself. She will try to resist, but she will fail. My code will defeat her.

What is all important is that you release the spell inside the portal itself. It will not work in any other part of the palace. It is only in the portal where Morrighan is vulnerable.

I am condemning my sister to walk through the palace of her own mind endlessly. I do not know how heaven will judge me for this. But I know heaven will not forgive me for what I am asking of you—my love, my heart. Please know that if I had remote viewing skills, I would have entered Morrighan's mind myself. But I don't. You are all I've got.

Morrighan will probably lead you to the portal herself, just as she did with Robbie. But how do you get out again? If the spell works, she'll be lost herself.

And, therefore . . . so will you.

CHAPTER FORTY-ONE

"It's impossible." Frankie sounded aghast.

Gabriel placed his finger on the down arrow of the keyboard and watched the fragments of text scroll past.

"Gabriel, you can't seriously consider going ahead with this. It won't work."

"If Minnaloushe says it will work, it will work."

"But look at it—it's gobbledygook." Frankie stared at the sentences on the screen.

I am the whore and the saint. I am the wife and the virgin.

"What the hell does that mean? It sounds like porn."

Gabriel gave a short laugh. "Quite the opposite. According to Minnaloushe's notes, those lines are from a gnostic tract describing the perfect mind. And these lines here," he pointed to another section on the screen, "are based on fragments from the Dead Sea Scrolls and ancient Mandaean writings."

"But what does it mean?"

"I don't know, Frankie. It's coded language. A spell."

"And it will make Morrighan say her secret name?"

"Yes. First the numerology of her name and then the name itself."

"This is all crazy." Frankie looked sick. You have to walk through the palace and somehow find the portal. Then, if you do manage to get there, you have to release this spell. How are you going to do that if Morrighan decides to open the door inside the portal and your brain gets pulped?"

Gabriel was silent.

"And that won't be the end of it." Frankie was thoroughly unhappy. "Assuming you survive your little adventure inside the portal, you then have to find your way out of the palace again. Which might be just a little difficult considering Morrighan's own mind will be scrambled egg by this time."

"I have no choice, Frankie."

"There's always a choice."

"No."

"I know why you're doing this. It's about revenge. You want to hurt Morrighan for what she's done to Minnaloushe."

He didn't answer.

"Revenge is the worst possible motive."

"It works for me." His voice was harsh.

"Gabriel—"

"It's not only revenge, Frankie. Do I want Morrighan to pay? Damn right I do. But it is not that simple. Morrighan is out of control. I'm the only one who can stand in her way. I know this is going to sound as though I've found religion, but for the first time in my life I feel as though my remote viewing powers were meant: not merely an accidental gift. If Morrighan isn't stopped, who knows what she'll get up to? And she'll be looking for someone new to train. Someone who will get hurt. I can't let her."

"You'll get lost. You're bound to. Think about it, Gabriel. Really think about it. Imagine the horror of walking endlessly through a labyrinth from which there is no escape."

"It won't happen."

"How can you say that!" She was shouting.

"I have a secret weapon."

Frankie stared at him in bewilderment.

"You."

They were lying in bed, hand in hand. The curtains at the windows were drawn. The door was shut. The darkness inside the room was all but absolute.

"Ready?"

Frankie's fingers tightened on his. "Yes."

"OK. Go."

Gabriel closed his eyes and willed his breathing to slow. He was doing his best to keep his body completely relaxed and to clear his mind of emotion. If he was too tense, he would involuntarily block Frankie when she tried to enter his mind. He needed to open up his inner eye and keep it slack. Clouds. Think of clouds. Clouds floating, weightless . . .

He sensed her tentative probings. She was hesitant, timid. But it felt instantly familiar. A soft, fragrant summery breeze. They used to scan each other often when they first started out. During his training at Eyestorm he had acquiesced to Mullins's scanning exercises, but he had never allowed any of his fellow RVs full access. He had never allowed his inner eye to slacken fully. Even with Frankie, he had held back.

But not tonight. For the first time in his life, he was about to place his life in someone else's care. No more going it alone. Frankie would be the first person to walk through his inner eye unimpeded.

Not the first person, he reminded himself. Morrighan had been the first. He shivered as he remembered the insolent confidence with which she had moved through his thoughts the night of Minnaloushe's birthday. That heavy musk and frangipani fragrance descending over his brain like a fog, his limbs growing weak, his groin tingling, the pleasure centers in his brain roughly stimulated so that all he wanted to do was give himself over to her completely . . .

He shuddered again and tried to concentrate on Frankie. Frankie whose signature was summery fresh, her presence inside his mind like a breeze. But it was so fragile, he thought, suddenly despairing. The thread was so tenuous—would it hold?

It *had* to hold. Frankie was the ace up his sleeve, the only way he could outwit the most ruthless opponent he had ever faced. Frankie was his one chance of navigating his way back through the house of a million doors. She was to be his anchor. With his mind tethered to hers, she would bring him back to safety. An Ariadne's thread leading him out of the maze. Assuming, of course, that he managed to survive whatever it was Morrighan had waiting for him inside the portal and if the aneurysm inside his brain tissue didn't suddenly spring a catastrophic leak.

Relax. Calm yourself. His heartbeat had speeded up again; he needed to slow his breathing. He tried to slacken his neck muscles, which had tightened in nervous anticipation.

He had spent the last hour memorizing Minnaloushe's code. He had sweated like a schoolboy cramming for an exam: the most important exam of his life. The text covered not even half a page, but he still had a rough time of it and was shocked at how weak his memory was. The mental strain to commit those lines to memory had been sobering. No mouse with which to point and click. No prompts, no icons to guide him. Just his own ability to internalize the information and draw on it at will.

Frankie was fully inside his mind now. Her hand inside his was still, and the grip of her fingers had loosened. Darling Frankie. Dapper, galant. The idea of going into the palace with him was deeply daunting to her; he knew that. But when he had asked her if she would follow him inside, she never hesitated. Such unconditional love—he felt humbled. Their destinies have always been linked, Frankie's and his. And they were about to embark on their longest journey . . .

His inner eye was now completely slack. It was time to interface with Morrighan. Would she accept him? But on that score he needn't be worried. She would accept him. Oh, yes. She was probably waiting for him already.

His right hand held Frankie's. His other hand was clutched around a locket. A locket with one black curl and one red. Red hair. Minnaloushe. For a moment sorrow washed through his entire body.

No time for grief now. No time for tears. Inside the locket was also a curl of the deepest black. Black as coal. Black as the feathers on the wings of a crow. The crow that was watching him with one beady eye. The bird so close to him, if he put out his hand he would be able to touch it.

For a moment the bird tilted its head quizzically, watching Gabriel as though debating on how to react to the intruder. But then it moved its weight from one leg to the other and started grooming its feathers.

He was inside. He was deep, deep within the palace.

Gabriel looked around him. He was standing in an enormous hall made of stone. The place had run to ruin. The tall windows, the delicate tracery of the frames still intact, were broken. There were holes in the thick walls, gaping squares of blackness, and the sweeping stone buttresses were crumbling.

There was a sound in the air. A wail. A long, falling cadence, the sound unbroken, like a frozen waterfall. He recognized it for what it was. He was listening to the sound of a mind in distress. Morrighan was grieving. He wasn't the only one who was feeling the pain of Minnaloushe's absence.

A movement at the corner of his eye made him turn around sharply. But it was only the crow. It had taken wing. It was flapping its way across the room and was heading for the open door and the passage beyond. After a moment's hesitation, he followed.

He stepped out into the stone passage. It was not really a passage, but a kind of mezzanine, bordered by a thin black railing. He placed his hand on the railing and his stomach felt suddenly hollow as he gazed down the vertiginous depths of a central shaft plunging to unimaginable depths.

The mezzanine on which he was standing was only one of many. From where he stood he could see the floors above and below: mezzanines, concentric tiers and galleries spiraling dizzyingly upward and downward, creating a disorienting distortion of perspective. And doors, millions of doors opening ceaselessly into the remotest distance: mystical replication.

For a moment his mind buckled under this visual onslaught. So many doors and no map. The previous two times that he had walked through the memory palace he had been looking through Robert Whittington's eyes. Every time he opened a door, he had been guided by Whittington's knowledge of the order of places and the order of things. But this time he had not interfaced with the boy's psi-space. This time he was on his own, walking through a mind that was hostile and cold. He had no idea where he was or how to continue. He did not know which doors to open and which to leave alone. He had no idea how to find the portal.

It didn't matter. He closed his eyes tight, shutting out the hallucinatory image of infinite doors. It didn't matter. Morrighan was sure to guide him to the portal herself. That was where she wanted him to be because that was where he would be at her mercy. He could choose any door at random and wander through this labyrinthine palace at will. She would find him.

He waited, his hand on the railing, expecting at any moment to sense her signature—that heavy scent of musk and frangipani—but there was nothing. The only signature inside his mind was Frankie's—faint, ghostly—like a shadow shimmering across a pane of glass. And again he wondered: would it hold?

He opened his eyes. The crow was sitting about three feet away from him, perched on the railing. The tiny eye stared at him pitilessly. Maybe he should follow the crow. Maybe the crow was to be his guide. But even as he made to move toward it, the bird lifted its wings and sailed soundlessly over the edge of the railing, plunging down, ever down, until the crescent of its black wings got lost in the shadows far, far below.

No guide then. Gabriel straightened. Well, a journey started with a single step. He turned the handle on the door nearest to him.

So many doors. You could go mad simply from the idea of so many doors. And as he walked from room to room, that eerie frozen wail was becoming ever more pronounced. The deep melancholia, the ice-cold anguish was overwhelming.

It seemed to have affected the physical environment as well, turning it into a weird broken-down building site. He found himself walking up staircases that hung suspended in space, leading nowhere. Winding corridors ended in blank enigmatic walls. Many of the doors opened not into rooms, but onto nothingness, so that he would step through, and find himself teetering vertiginously on the edge of empty space. And when he did enter a completed room, the proportions appeared distorted. The walls buckling, the ceilings pulled askew. The windows drooping deliriously in their frames.

And he was troubled by an indefinable sense of something missing. He couldn't figure out what it was. But then it hit him. The rooms were completely empty. There were no objects, no figures behind the doors. Where were the talismanic memory images that should have populated these rooms?

In his first two rides, every room he entered had been occupied—butterflies, blind monks, bloodied doves, giant marbles, lashless eyes—millions of potent images, meticulously conceived. But the rooms through which he was wandering now were bare except for fallen masonry. In some rooms the brick walls were raw and unplastered, as though builders had left the premises prematurely. Why?

But even as he wondered, the answer came to him. These rooms had the appearance of being unfinished because that was exactly what they were. This was a work in progress. Minnaloushe had been building this space, but she never had the chance to finish it. And Morrighan was unable to continue without her sister's help. The anguish Morrighan was feeling was not just for her sibling's death. It was also for the worlds that would remain undiscovered now that Minnaloushe was no longer there to help her sister conceive fresh horizons.

The wail was increasing in intensity. An unceasing sob. It chilled him to the bone. He was approaching a door with thick strap hinges and a highly chased lock affixed to the timber. He placed his hand on the doorknob and the door swung open.

This room was not empty.

It was a big room, a very big room. The floor underfoot was covered by rotting leaf litter. The walls were plastered, and he was able to see the shadowy outlines of faded frescoes. Vines curled riotously across the beams in the roof space, and climbing roses drooped from flexible stems. There were several trestle tables overladen with seed trays, pots and garden tools. In the air hovered the sweet stench of decay. Several narrow windows, obscured by foliage, lined the walls. A gaseous green light filtered through the dirty panes.

Something swept past his elbow. A black shadow. The crow had returned. It descended on something in the far corner of the room and perched itself on top of two humplike objects covered by what looked like sacking. From where Gabriel stood, he couldn't see what they were. The light wasn't strong enough.

Hesitantly he walked forward. Something told him that he did not want to go any closer, would not want to see what was underneath the sacking. He took another step forward. A sense of foreboding hammered at his brain. No, no.

He put out his hand to remove the hemplike cloth and the crow screeched. It flapped its wings in agitation. No, no.

The wail was now deafening. His fingers gripped the cloth and it started to slide off the objects, caught for a moment. With a determined gesture he ripped the entire length of it clean off.

Minnaloushe's body was covered with flowers. Big, white, star-shaped flowers the likes of which he had never seen before. They were growing from inside of her body; the thick stems were sprouting from deep within her flesh, pushing vigorously up through the skin. The flowers gleamed with health and vitality, every petal perfectly formed. Her eyes starry white chambers, her mouth hemorrhaging snowy blooms. Her hair shot through with tender shoots of green.

Next to her was Robert. Red flowers for him, not white. Red as the fiery petals on the humpback tree shading the swimming pool at Monk House. And suddenly Gabriel knew where Morrighan had buried the boy.

He staggered back.

Gabriel . . .

His name uttered like a sigh. Like the wind blowing through leaves. The sound made his palms go clammy. It came from behind him.

The sigh solidified into a whisper. *Ga-bri-el.* A soft, drawn-out whisper—three syllables.

"*Ga-bri-el . . .*"

And the air was heavy with the scent of musk and frangipani.

She was dressed exactly the same as when he had encountered her in his first ride. A long dress made of velvet, black but not black, the luscious fabric shot through with emerald thread so that when she moved, the folds of her dress gleamed with light. The sleeves were tight fitting as was the bodice, the dark color accentuating the pallor of her skin. The neckline was delicately pleated and very low cut, and he could fully see the tattoo of the *Monas* on the soft swell of her breast. From her neck dangled the pendant with the letter *M*.

But her true black hair was uncovered, the hood of the cloak turned down. She was not wearing the mask. And why should she? They knew each other now. Oh, yes, they knew each other. No need for subterfuge. No need for hide-and-seek any longer.

Ga-bri-el . . . She lifted her hand. Beckoned.

He looked away from her and down at the blooming bodies at his feet. Robert bleeding fiery petals. Minnaloushe's skin looking like alabaster: transparent but shot through with shadows. Underneath the fine pallor lay patches of decay, but still the flowers blossomed with heedless vigor. A bizarre marriage of fecundity and death. A grotesque image conjured up by Morrighan's mind to keep her sister alive in her memory.

He stretched out his hand tentatively, mesmerized by the sheen of the white petals.

Don't do that.

He looked back at Morrighan. Her blue eyes glowed. Her crimson mouth was fire.

Leave her. Come with me.

Bitch! He was suddenly suffused with fury. Murdering bitch! He lunged at her. She sidestepped—a slight movement. He was punching at air.

A glimmer of amusement came through from her. And he supposed it was ridiculous. He could pick up that sharp-edged trowel from the table and push it into her body and nothing would happen. In this universe created by her mind he was impotent. It was only inside the portal that he'd be able to wreak destruction and turn this palace of the memory to ruin.

That is, if he survived.

A feeling of futility swept over him. Maybe he should simply stay here. Stay with Minnaloushe. He was never going to be able to escape this labyrinth anyway.

Come. Impatient now.

No.

Come.

He shrank back.

Something nudged at his feet. He looked down.

The entire floor was covered by rats. A heaving, seething mass of squealing, shuddering bodies, evil eyes, whiskers, teeth sharp as razors. His shoes were covered with rats; the rodents were jostling against his ankles.

He looked up. Morrighan had disappeared. She had left him alone with his nightmare.

This is not real, he told himself despairingly. This is just a memory image. Just something conjured up by Morrighan's mind. Not real. But the next moment one of the rats fell down on him from one of the trusses in the ceiling space. He could feel the plump weight of the rodent as it slapped onto his shoulder, the claws scrabbling and then hooking into his skin. The next moment the animal had sunk its yellow teeth into his neck. The pain was intense. He tugged the rat off his neck and threw it away from him, shuddering with revulsion. He stumbled toward the door, kicking at the fat bodies crowding his feet. The door. Escape.

He fell out of the room and slammed the door behind him.

She was waiting for him outside. *Come*.

He followed.

* * *

In the bed inside the loft apartment Frankie moved restlessly, her head shifting on the pillow from side to side. Vaguely she realized that her heartbeat had sped up enormously. She was suspended in a twilight world where her mind was interfacing with that of the man who was lying beside her, now oblivious to her presence. The link was tenuous; she was receiving only fragments of images and emotions. And a few moments ago, she had received a burst of emotion so violent that the link had almost severed completely, the turbulent static of his thoughts just about wiping the scan clean.

It was better now. She was picking up the pattern again. A corridor silvered by moonlight. Quick steps. The shadow of a woman sliding sinuously along a curving wall . . .

CHAPTER FORTY-TWO

He was following her shadow. She moved quickly, always staying a few steps ahead of him. Once or twice he had lost sight of her completely as they sped down a long, winding corridor, but each time her shadow had stretched behind her, a dark shape on the moon-stained wall, lengthening and contracting, showing the way.

They were now once more traveling through a populated section of the memory palace, the unfinished building site of Minnaloushe's imagination swallowed up somewhere far behind them.

The rooms through which they traveled at present were all filled with mystical objects. A man with the head of a baboon stared at him dispassionately. A white horse neighed madly and tossed its blood-soaked mane. In one room his astonished eyes saw that he was walking on water. Deep down below him were millions of drowned books, some closed, some twirling slowly with pages spread open in fanlike beauty.

He knew that these were talismanic images—magical images—but he had no comprehension of what information they represented. He was walking through these halls of knowledge without any understanding. It was simply a disturbing, alien world.

And he was lost. He had no idea how many doors she had opened, how many rooms they had traversed. He had lost track of the number of images they had encountered. He didn't care. He would never be able to remember the way back. All he was interested in now was reaching the portal. And he had no doubt that was where she was leading him.

He kept his eyes on her moving form. She had a lovely way of carrying herself, every step graceful but hinting at the power and strength gathered in the fine muscles. Her hair was upswept, allowing him to see the slender stalk of her neck. Her profile was pure. She was a beautiful creature.

And she was a warrior. Strong. Sleek. On guard. Ready to go into battle. *Mhor Rioghain.* Great Queen of war and death. He was no match for her. Even Minnaloushe had miscalculated her sister's ruthlessness.

Why had Morrighan in the end decided to kill Minnaloushe? An accident, she had said. Not planned. Only Morrighan knew if this were true. Morrighan had needed Minnaloushe to help her build the palace. But maybe jealousy and paranoia had come together in one devastating moment of lethal rage.

Two warriors. Minnaloushe's mind had been the subtler, Morrighan's the more ferocious. Minnaloushe had delighted in practicing mental judo, using her adversary's strength against her. Morrighan's mind cut like a katana. A few well-placed sword strokes demolishing the whole with ruthless precision. No ambiguity.

And in the end ruthlessness had prevailed. Or had it? If he could reach the portal and release Minnaloushe's spell, she might well be the final victor.

He was aware of a hum in the air. He had heard this sound before. He knew what it signaled. A tremor ran through his spine.

In front of him, Morrighan had stopped. She placed her palm against an uneven stone set into the smoothness of the wall.

The wall slid to one side.

The vast room was as he remembered it. As he had dreamt it.

The portal. It had haunted his sleep for so long. Now that he had reached it he felt strangely calm.

Her link with Gabriel was fragile. At times Frankie would see clearly and the emotions she picked up from him would be true, but then the scan would break up and she'd see only fragments, incoherent images. But as he entered the portal, her first impression was as detailed as an etching: a vast space with slowly revolving stone walls densely encrusted with mysterious sigils and fantastic signs. She had never been inside this space before, but she recognized it immediately. Gabriel had talked about it so often.

All these symbols, she knew, could be combined and recombined into infinite patterns of code. This was the heart of the memory palace; the power station driving the entire structure. Above the massive circular walls the domelike ceiling floated insubstantially, bathed in light.

And then there were the thirty doors. They formed a semicircle and looked innocuous. But behind one of those doors lay pain and insanity. Open it and an information overload would burst through your brain like water breaking through the wall of a dam.

For a brief moment she remembered the aneurysm nestling inside the soft tissue of Gabriel's brain, a grenade waiting to explode.

She sensed the awe, the fear now starting to coat Gabriel's thoughts. It seeped into her own consciousness like ink absorbed by blotting paper. But part of her mind was cool, an outsider looking in. And she was concerned: Where was Morrighan? She wanted Gabriel to find Morrighan, but his focus had slipped away from the woman. He was fully absorbed by the idea of the portal itself. And with the horror lurking behind one of those doors.

Gabriel was looking upward at the ceiling high above him. He turned on his heel. The illuminated dome spun with him. It made Frankie dizzy.

The scan was breaking up again. One moment the spinning ceiling, then a distorted glimpse of the phantasmagorical symbols on one of the walls rushing past her uncomprehending eyes like an animated frieze.

Where was Morrighan?

What secrets did this chamber hold? What magic?

Gabriel looked up, and the dome of the ceiling above his head was filled with celestial light.

You had your chance to understand. You did not take it.

He whipped around. He had forgotten about Morrighan. She was standing barely a foot away. Her signature was suddenly overpowering. Musk. Frangipani. Curiosity. Intense excitement. Powerful chemicals rushing through her brain, sparking a reaction inside his own mind as well.

Death's fingerprint is in our DNA. It sets our fate. The grave is journey's end for all of us. But the memory palace—oh, Gabriel. The memory palace transforms the journey from drudgery to ecstasy. Once you've tasted the rush of the memory palace, the ordinary life is a withered flower.

A part of him realized that she desperately wanted him to comprehend the magnificence of her creation.

He gestured at the gigantic stone walls with their enigmatic symbols. "Was this worth killing for?"

Is becoming a magician not worth everything?

She placed her hand on his shoulder and drew even closer. He could feel the heat from her body. A small, shameful part of his mind was reacting to her physical closeness. Her thigh brushing his. The soft swell of her breasts. The pale skin accentuated by the bruise of the *Monas*: a rough kiss made visible. The urge to touch his fingers to that highly erotic bruise was overwhelming.

"No." He tried to move away from her. "Minnaloushe—"

Minnaloushe? As if the name were a foreign word and she was inquiring as to its meaning. She tightened her grip on his shoulder. *Minnaloushe was faint of heart. But you and I are the same: we crave the thrill. We ache for it.*

We crave the thrill. She understood him well. For him too, risk had always been the ultimate turn-on. And risk had its rewards. In his own life risk had usually paid off. But if he miscalculated this time . . .

He looked into her blue eyes and knew he was looking death in the face. She was lethal.

Behind her shoulder he could see the doors lined up. One of those doors was the entrance to Pandora's box. If it opened, he would probably not survive the onslaught.

He pushed the thought aside. Time to act.

Deliberately he placed one hand against her breast. Her skin was as soft as he had imagined it would be. He placed his other hand behind her head and drew her face to his. His fingers moved inside her hair, loosening it so that it fell to her shoulders in a dusky cloud. As he touched his lips to hers, her eyes remained open, locked with his. Blue pools fringed by inky lashes. They told him nothing.

He tightened his grip in her hair. "You are insane."

I know. A ripple of amusement from her. *Exciting, isn't it?*

Pain shot through his lip. She had bitten him. He tasted blood.

He pressed his fingers against her breast with such force, he knew he was hurting the tender flesh. But her mouth softened and he could feel her tongue moving gently. Her breath was sweet. *Gabriel.* She whispered his name like an incantation. *Gabriel.*

An incantation. A spell. But he had his own spell. It was time to set it free.

He placed one hand against the small of her back and the other around her shoulders and drew her to him even more firmly. She did not resist. For the first time her eyes closed, shuttered by a languorous sweep of lashes.

Her body so soft, so slack, but a rippling coming from deep within her. A slow smile crossed her face.

He struggled to focus. Concentrate, Gabriel. It is time to remember. Remember . . .

When I entered the House of Blood and Air
I saw the dusky portal
I saw the princes of the dark dwelling

The fragments of text floated through his mind. Minnaloushe's magic code.

I saw men of arms
buried in black graves
and my name is . . .

Morrighan's eyes flew open and he felt her mind snap back in alarm. *NO!*

He tightened his grip on her shoulders. "What is your name, Morrighan?"

She was shaking her head back and forth.

"Say it!"

Twenty-two. The word left her lips in a moan. *My name is twenty-two.*

> *You breathe your name*
> *In my ashen ear*
> *And pen secrets on my soul*
> *I am the whore and the saint*
> *I am the wife and the virgin*
> *And my name is . . .*

She lifted her hand and her nails raked fire across his cheek. Without hesitation he slapped her across the face and slammed her body against the wall. The breath left her lips in a painful gasp.

"Say it!"

He had never seen such hate in anyone's eyes. She was trying to fight the compulsion; he could see the muscles in her throat contracting. But the words left her mouth as if of their own volition.

Seven. My name is seven.

Almost finished. Only a few more lines . . .

> *Like the speckled wolf*
> *I will travel by your side*
> *Like the charcoal crow*
> *I will wing the soil*

She was weeping and her crying was silent and fierce. Snail smears glistened on her cheeks. She collapsed in his arms, dead-weight, and as he let her go, she sank to her knees. Her head was bowed, the black hair parted, and he glimpsed the nape of her neck, vulnerable. Reaching down, he cupped his hand under her chin, twisting her face around. She looked at him with drowned eyes.

Please, Gabriel. Don't do this. It's not too late. You can still take my hand and we can travel together. Forget about . . . her . . . You used to love me too. Don't you remember?

She stared at him with those blue eyes, and images of their summer together spooled through his memory. Morrighan, her lovely mouth aglow, smiling at him as they dance at Minnaloushe's birthday. Morrighan sitting in the peacock armchair, her eyes closed as she listens to the notes of a violin. Morrighan working in the garden. Her dress is bunched up above her knees; there are dark patches of sweat under her arms and her thin blouse is clinging to her breasts. She is humming underneath her breath. She is happy.

But then another image. Morrighan standing in a window, framed like an object on display, her eyes dispassionate. Behind her shoulder the curve of a staircase . . .

He stepped back from the woman at his feet. As the last lines of Minnaloushe's spell slotted into his memory, Morrighan's lips pulled away from her teeth. Pink tongue glistening. Eyes like space. Her hair black seaweed.

Speak not, I
Dead are my lips, my cut lips
But my name, my whole perfect name is . . .

Her lips moved painfully:
My name is Eldaah.

It was over. He closed his eyes briefly.

The next moment she screamed. It felt like a steel needle lobbed into his brain. One of the doors flew open. An avalanche of information rushed through the opening with a sickening roar. It swept him off his feet as though he were a matchstick in the path of a hurricane.

He had become a fleck of dust in a storm of blinding movement and was being propelled forward with such unimaginable force—with such speed—that the objects he encountered along the way dissolved into a demented visual landscape: chaotic, dissonant, like a reel of film edited by a mind no longer sane.

Images beautiful and profane stared at him from the chaos. A figure, its spine encircled by the sinuous form of a snake, flashed briefly past him, followed by a boy dressed in flowing robes, a book to his chest, one finger against his lips as if admonishing Gabriel to silence. A child, its chest ripped open, was cradling its pulsing heart in its own two hands. Gabriel stretched out his hands toward the child, but the next moment it had disappeared and he was teetering on the edge of a precipice, and far down below him was an entire city submerged under ice, and he could hear the voices of angels screaming. Birds fell from the air with crushed beaks and torn wings.

Control the input! Keep it clean! His defenses were crumbling. His eyeballs were straining inside his head. His body was disintegrating under the impact of the sensory overload. And still it continued, the images pouring into his mind, his skull shuddering with noise and turbulence. And among the madness and confusion the crow—grown immensely large—flying past him in a mighty rush of air.

And now he was inside a vast, many-tiered chamber spiraling downward into blackness. One moment he was looking down into this labyrinth and the next he was falling, falling down the wide vertical shaft, getting closer and closer to the blackness beneath him. Doors—millions of doors—spinning past the edge of his vision. His mind struggling for a fingerhold, scrabbling for something with which to anchor his sanity. Frankie. He could sense her anxious probing, but it was so faint, so faint, like fingers tapping against glass. Oh, God, he couldn't hang on any longer. He couldn't process—

Sudden quiet. The silence of infinite spaces.

Then he heard her voice.

Gabriel. The word a desolate moan.

I am lost . . . A whisper traveling down the long corridors, bouncing off the steep walls, echo upon echo. *Lost . . . Lost . . . Lost . . .*

Gabriel . . . Don't leave me here . . .

CHAPTER FORTY-THREE

The smell was the first thing he registered. Disinfectant. And then the green dusk of a hospital room. He was also aware of a gentle clicking sound against the windowpane. Rain?

He was hooked up to monitors. There were tubes stuck in his arm. He touched his hand to his forehead, and his fingers recognized the gauzy feel of a bandage.

Slowly his eyes traveled around the room. A Formica nightstand. A matching dresser. A chair with a crumpled blanket, tossed to one side as though someone had vacated the chair only recently. There was a paper cup on the nightstand.

He saw all of this without any sense of curiosity. For a while he simply lay there listening to the rain tapping against the window. He closed his eyes.

When he woke up again, the room was bright with light. On the seat of the chair next to the bed, the blanket was neatly folded.

The light hurt his eyes and he closed them again quickly.

"Gabriel."

He turned his head on the pillow—wincing at the pain skewering through his neck—and peered through slitted eyes at the figure standing on the other side of the bed.

"Gabriel. Look at me." Frankie brought her face closer to his. "Hey, you." She was smiling.

"What . . ." His voice was a croak. Behind Frankie's shoulder, a nurse in a navy blue uniform poked her head around the door for a few seconds before disappearing again.

He tried again. "Am I OK?"

She was still smiling. "You will be. Are you thirsty? Do you want some water?"

"How long have I been here?"

"Five days. Three days in intensive care. You've been drifting in and out a number of times."

"I don't remember."

"Well, you've been mostly out of it. Are you in pain? Shall I call the nurse?"

"No." He moved his shoulders awkwardly against the propped-up pillows. Now that he was actually able to focus on his surroundings, he didn't want to be drugged up. He wanted to know what had happened.

As if anticipating his next question, Frankie said, "Dr. Dibbles will be here soon to explain everything to you. It was a close call. The brain aneurysm ruptured and they had to operate. But you'll be OK."

"Good to know." His thoughts were cotton wool. He tried to concentrate on Frankie's smiling face. "What about you, Frankie? Are you OK?"

"I'm one hundred percent. Although I did come out of that ride with one hell of a migraine, I'll tell you that. But I'm all right now."

"No bad dreams, huh?"

"No dreams whatsoever. I can't even recall the ride at all, to tell the truth. I have no memory of it. Nothing, not even fragments. It's as though the slate was wiped clean. Weird." She hesitated. "And you? Do you remember anything?"

An image flickered through his mind. A dizzying replication of doors and winding corridors. A woman's voice whispering, the sound fragmenting into a kaleidoscope of echoes: *Don't leave me here . . .*

He felt suddenly very tired. "I remember."

"She's here, you know."

"What?" He stiffened and his stomach knotted involuntarily.

Frankie nodded. "Four doors down."

"Why?"

"She's in a coma. But they don't know why." Frankie watched him steadily. "There was no physical trauma to the brain. No brain swelling or brain bleeding. Not like with you. She's simply . . . unconscious."

"How did she get here? Did you—"

"Not on your life." Frankie's voice was emphatic. "I wasn't even aware she was in the hospital. Apparently the cleaning lady discovered her unconscious and called for an ambulance."

"How do you know all this?"

"By chance. Morrighan has a cousin who came to visit. We met at the coffee machine and she and I made friends."

Frankie smoothed the hair from his forehead. "But don't worry about any of this stuff right now, sweetheart. You should rest."

"I suppose so." His voice sounded exhausted even to his own ears.

Frankie leaned over and kissed him lightly on the cheek. "Go back to sleep. We can talk about it later."

He placed his hand on her wrist, holding her back. "Frankie . . . thank you."

"Oh," she smiled again. "You're welcome."

"No. I mean it. I owe you everything." Tears came to his eyes. "When that door flew open, I started falling . . . falling into darkness. And that's when I felt your mind reaching out to mine, hooking on. You saved me."

"Shh. Go to sleep."

He closed his eyes obediently. Frankie's voice came as though from far away. "Everything is going to be fine now. It's all over."

That evening he went for a walk. He was hooked up to an intravenous drip on wheels, and he had to drag the entire contraption with him. The wheels made an unpleasant squeaking sound on the linoleum.

He shuffled down the corridor using baby steps and feeling like an old man. He was not in pain, but he was so weak. The idea that his muscles would regain their former strength seemed almost inconceivable.

It was late. The evening meal was long finished and the last visitors had left. The wide corridor down which he was moving was empty. He could hear the sound of a television set coming from one of the rooms behind him, but most of the rooms leading off the passage were darkened.

Four rooms down, Frankie had said. He stopped just inside the doorway.

The room was only dimly lit, but there was enough light for him to see. Her face was pale in the gloom. Her hands rested flaccidly next to her body. She did not look sick. If it weren't for the wires and machines you would have thought her asleep.

Hesitantly he moved closer to the bed. She was very still. He could hardly see the movement of her breast as she breathed. Her eyes did not roll inside the lids. Her fingers did not twitch.

Was her mind still as well? That beautiful, corrupted mind?

She had approached life as though it were a blood sport. She had been a warrior. Now she was a sleeping princess. But no prince would be coming to her rescue.

Don't leave me here . . .

Her desperate plea would haunt him for the rest of his days.

Where was she now? Was she walking through endless passageways? Was she desperately searching for a clue, a sign, something that might make her remember the order of places and the order of things? The knowledge of it was a shadow on his heart. It was diabolical. To search for order and find only confusion. To know the horror of being lost forever.

They had joined in a battle of the minds, the two of them, but he felt no victory. He felt only loss and a profound sorrow.

"Morrighan," he whispered.

The lovely face remained completely blank.

"Forgive me."

CHAPTER FORTY-FOUR

He remained in the hospital for another twelve days, and he did not make the journey to Morrighan's room again.

Not until the day he checked out.

Frankie was at his side, her arm hooked through his, his overnight bag in her other hand. He took a last look at the hospital bed in which he had spent so many hours. He would not miss it.

It was visiting hour, and the corridors were filled with people looking either anxious or relieved. As they walked down the wide passage, he was deliberately keeping his eyes straight in front of him, not looking left or right. But from the edge of his vision, he knew they were approaching the door that led to Morrighan's room.

He stopped. "I must go in."

Frankie was reluctant. "That's not a good idea."

"It's something I have to do." He pulled on her arm.

As they entered the room, a plump woman dressed in a mustard-colored tweed suit got up from the chair next to the bed.

She nodded at Frankie. "Hi, Frankie."

"Hi, Lisa." Frankie spoke gently. "How are you doing?"

"All right." The woman smiled, but the smile did not dispel the resigned sadness from her face. "Is this your friend?" She looked at Gabriel.

"Yes. He's being discharged today, I'm happy to say."

"That's great news. I'm Lisa Duval, by the way. Morrighan's cousin."

"Pleased to meet you." They shook hands briefly. Her palm was moist. She had not inherited the beauty gene so blazingly obvious in her two cousins. But her eyes were kind.

He had been avoiding looking at the bed, but now his eyes drifted toward the figure lying there. His breath stalled.

Morrighan no longer looked like a sleeping princess. In some indefinable way she had aged. Her skin looked chalky and grayed. The black hair was pushed back in a no-nonsense fashion behind her ears. The hair seemed lank.

"How is she doing?" Frankie was actually whispering.

"Not good."

"Maybe she'll get better." Frankie sounded awkward.

"No." Lisa Duval shook her head. "Morrighan scored very low on the Glasgow Coma Scale."

"The Glasgow Coma Scale?"

"It is a standardized system used to identify the degree of brain impairment." There was a parrotlike quality to Lisa's response. She had obviously been talking to the men in white coats. "Morrighan's total score out of fifteen was very low."

"So the doctors—"

"The doctors don't know anything." There was a quiet vehemence in Lisa Duval's voice. "They still don't understand what happened to her. There's no physical reason for her coma. It's a mystery." She dabbed angrily at her eyes. "Excuse me. I think I need to go to the bathroom. But very nice meeting you." She held out her hand to Gabriel again. "And good luck."

He shook her hand numbly.

After she had left the room, it was quiet between him and Frankie. They didn't look at each other.

The hospital sheets were folded neatly cross Morrighan's stomach. Her arms were by her sides. Her hands were large—out of proportion to the rest of her body. He had never noticed that about her before. The nails seemed tinged with blue. Large green veins stared from the skin.

"We did this to her. Minnaloushe and I."

"You had no choice."

"There's always a choice. You said so yourself."

"Morrighan brought it on herself, Gabriel. You have to put this behind you now."

"I have to do one more thing."

Frankie looked at him questioningly.

"Do you think Monk House is empty?"

Her voice was wary. "I suppose so. Why?"

"I need to get in there."

"What!"

"I need to download *The Promethean Key*."

"I thought you had a copy. The one you showed Professor Stallworthy."

"That copy is imperfect, remember. I never managed to download the code for the portal. I need the whole thing."

"Why?" Frankie's eyebrows were high against her forehead.

"I'm just interested." He realized how evasive he sounded.

There was a long silence. "You're lying." Frankie's voice sounded utterly disbelieving. "You want to become a memory artist yourself. That's what this is about."

"Don't be absurd." But Gabriel was unable to meet her eyes.

"Gabriel. Talk to me. What's going on with you?"

He searched for an explanation. "You remember I told you about that guy in the creepy magic shop? The one who gave me the amulet?"

Frankie nodded.

"Well, he told me that one can become addicted to madness. Develop a taste for it. He said once you start walking down that road there is no turning back. You start craving the rush. At the time I had no idea what he was talking about." He paused. "I do now."

He looked into Frankie's eyes and he saw the incomprehension. How to explain to her that ever since the last ride, he had felt an insatiable hunger to experience the rush of the memory palace again? How to explain that ever since he had woken up from the operation, life seemed unbearably stale? It felt as though his senses were dulled.

Colors were not as bright. Sounds not as resonant. A layer of dust coating every object.

Frankie seemed almost relieved at his stumbling explanation. "It's only the aftermath of your surgery, Gabriel. Of course things will look flat and miserable to you after what you've been through. You're tired. Give it time. You'll bounce back."

He shook his head. The malaise he was suffering from went much deeper. The ride had been frightening—the most frightening experience of his life—but it had marked him. The world around him now seemed deeply pedestrian. Utterly banal.

As he looked at Morrighan's still figure, he had a vivid memory of her standing inside the portal, vital and glowing, describing to him the magnificence of her creation. Taste of it, she had said, and ordinary life can never again satisfy you. And she had smiled, triumphant.

Only now did he know what she meant. And for the first time he understood—truly understood—the restless hunger that had driven Robert Whittington to join Minnaloushe and Morrighan in their quest for transformation. He had caught the sickness as well. It burned steadily in his blood, and he knew he would never be free from it. He wanted to be a solar magician. He had become a searcher himself.

"I thought I had beaten her."

"You have."

"No. She has infected me." He clenched his hands into fists. "I need to get *The Key*."

"Gabriel, leave it alone." Frankie's eyes were scared.

"I need it, Frankie. Unless I get *The Key* . . ." He stopped. He felt suddenly cold at the idea that he might never feel the rush again. Life would be a desert.

He *had* to get *The Key*.

It was within reach. He knew Morrighan's true name: the password to the portal. If he could fit password and portal together, he could feed his hunger. It would be Minnaloushe's gift to him.

His eyes rested once more on the motionless figure. He felt such guilt. But his hunger was stronger.

He looked back at Frankie. "Monk House will be empty. I'll slip in and download *The Key* from the computer. No one will know."

He took a deep breath. "And then I'll be free."

CHAPTER FORTY-FIVE

No one will know.

The woman in the hospital bed heard the words. She was in a coma but her inner eye was still alive. It was damaged—but it was picking up input from the brick-and-mortar world around her like a broken antenna. Voices, movement, flashes of color. Brief bursts of information from the real world before she'd sink back once more into the torment of her own mind.

She was in hell.

She was trapped, searching obsessively for a key, a room, the right door—some way to escape the nightmare in which she had become marooned. If she could rediscover the order of places and things, she would wake up. She knew this with every cell in her body. But she had lost her compass. Minnaloushe and Gabriel had made sure of that.

But she still had her inner eye. Minnaloushe had not been able to take that away from her. It was broken, yes, a faulty aerial of the mind, but at times it allowed her a brief escape from the memory palace before she tumbled back into hell, searching, searching.

She had a sense of voices close to her and of bodies standing next to her bed. Her damaged brain realized it was a woman. And a man. *Gabriel.*

Her mind shrieked. The shock clamped her inner eye shut and she almost lost the connection. She was slipping back into the memory palace. Rooms, corridors, doors. Endless doors. *Three doors to the left, cross the drawbridge . . .*

No! Stop! Concentrate!

I'll slip in and download The Key *from the computer. No one will know.*

Fury gripped her. She had offered the prize to him and he had refused it.

Refused *her*.

How to stop him?

He now had the password. If he put the password and the portal together—

Two doors down, one up. Second door from the right . . .

No, no. Oh, God. She felt total despair. Concentrate, Morrighan. Focus. She tried to calm the hurricane inside her mind.

Gabriel and the woman were leaving. She sensed them moving away. Their voices were growing fainter. Then they were gone.

He was probably on his way to Monk House right now.

Stop him!

If she could stop him from downloading *The Key*, *she* would have the final victory. Without *The Key*, Gabriel would be condemned to a life of aimless searching. He would never feel achievement again. Only hunger.

How to stop him downloading *The Key*?

How?

She still had her inner eye, but maimed as it was, she would not be able to scan him or get into his mind. He was too strong.

But maybe she could use it another way.

And then it came to her. The solution slipped into her mind like the breath of a ghost.

Her inner eye had always been her own private gift, something Minnaloushe could never fully understand. And her skills had evolved. No longer were her powers confined to the inner world of the skull. Objects in the real world could be manipulated as well. Minnaloushe had not really comprehended how much the memory palace had allowed her remote viewing powers to grow. Which meant that when Minnaloushe created the spell, she had left her sister's RV skills out of the equation.

Her viewing powers were no magic bullet. She knew that. For her, there was no escape: the memory palace would always pull her back into its orbit. She would forever tumble back into the labyrinth of endless staircases and chaotic passages and doors. But maybe, just maybe, she could muster all her strength and focus long enough to allow her inner eye to travel briefly.

Maybe for a brief moment . . . just until she had time to do what she had to do . . .

The woman in the hospital bed was completely still. Her breathing was quiet. But her inner eye was roaming. She was going home.

CHAPTER FORTY-SIX

The windows of the redbrick house were shut tight and the air inside held the odor of neglect. Dust had accumulated on the surfaces.

The house was empty but traces of its occupation were still visible. The velvet cushion on the seat of the big peacock chair held the imprint of a body. A book was facedown on the coffee table. Next to it was a mug half-filled with cold coffee. On the rim of the mug was a kiss left there by the pressure of a woman's lips. A black coat drooped spread-eagled over the back of another chair, its sleeves dangling down the sides like tired arms. The faintest of fragrances clung to the wool.

But the overwhelming smell in the room was of decaying flowers. The stems of roses rotting in stagnant water. Potted plants dying in cracked soil. Even the fleshy petals of the orchids were wrinkling and turning brown. Not enough time had passed to drain them of all their juices and so the smell hovering over the blighted plants was strong and dank. On the shelf above the worktable was a glass box, and inside it the desiccated body of a dead spider.

The workbench held two computers. Here too the dust had settled, a film of particles clinging to the crystal screens. The computers were switched off. Their faces were blank.

A sudden click. As if touched by a ghostly hand, one of the screens lit up. At the same time, deep within the computer's brain a built-in virus started running. The virus had been created many years before by the owners of this machine—a back door in case something went wrong. A precaution they never thought they'd need. They had crafted the lethal code well but they had never seriously considered they might ever have to pull such a deadly trigger. Because, if set in motion, the virus would destroy the work of a lifetime and lay to waste a magical universe.

As if still powered by the same hand, the pages in the document started to scroll down the screen and as they scrolled by, they disappeared—the contents of these pages erased from the memory and from the hard drive of the mechanical host. Forever out of reach of any thief.

Signs, sigils, sacred numbers. Graceful drawings and plans: divine architecture. Enigmatic spells and incantations. Lines of magicized code. An enchanted palace of the memory scrolling implacably—irrevocably—into forgetfulness.

Seven miles away in one of the private rooms in Wing C, Nurse Kendall was bathing the limp limbs of a patient.

The poor woman. Nurse Kendall rubbed the moist washcloth along her charge's finely muscled arm. She was obviously an athlete, but very soon the honed musculature of her body would start wasting away.

Nurse Kendall placed the unresponsive arm back on the bed. Gently she pushed the black hair away from the patient's forehead and touched the washcloth to her face. What a terrible fate. A fate worse than death if you asked her. The consultants were very negative about this one. No fairy-tale awakening was likely to happen here.

Such a lovely face. But as with the body, the beauty would fade quickly now. Although, this morning the patient looked strangely radiant. Her expression was almost one of satisfaction—as though she had pulled off a great achievement. And for one moment, Nurse Kendall even thought the black-haired woman might have smiled.

EPILOGUE

"I am about to seek a great Perhaps."
—François Rabelais's dying words

"Excuse me? Is that you?"

As the words left her mouth she blushed fiercely, already regretting the impulse that had made her speak to him.

The man sitting on the park bench a few paces away from her looked up, and then glanced over his shoulder. When he realized she was indeed talking to him, he looked at her carefully and lifted an inquiring eyebrow.

Again she blushed, cursing her fair skin. She had always found it difficult to talk to good-looking guys and this man was attractive. Never mind the white in his hair. As her mum was fond of saying: Some guys will always put the fizz in your lemonade, no matter what.

Taking a deep breath, she pointed at the book in his hand. "That's you, isn't it?"

He turned the book around to look at the photograph on the back cover and smiled. "I'm afraid so."

"So you're a writer."

"Among other things."

"I was going to be a writer, you know." As she spoke she suddenly remembered the streak of yellow staining the shoulder of her blouse. She had wondered whether she should change her top before coming to the park. Now she wished she had.

He gestured to the empty space beside him. "Won't you join me?"

"Thank you." She sat down on the very edge of the bench. "I just need to keep an eye on Pippa." She pointed to the sandpit where Pippa was squatting on her fat little legs.

He moved over more fully to his side. "Is that your little girl?"

"Yes. And I have a baby at home. It threw up all over me this morning." What on earth made her say something so stupid, she thought despairingly. Everything about this man was elegant and here she was talking about baby spit.

But he did not seem disgusted. He was looking at her intently. He had really nice eyes even though she was now able to see the deep lines at their corners.

She looked back at the book in his hand. "So what is it about?"

He hesitated. "It's a story. About a traveler . . . searching for his true name."

"Oh, I get it. Like he has amnesia?"

"In a way."

"How did it happen?"

"He was cursed."

She looked at him dubiously. "Can I have a look?"

"Please."

The book was open in the middle and she started to read aloud, stumbling a little over some of the words.

One of the crueler jokes of creation is being burdened with brains capable of conceptualizing a state of higher consciousness we have little hope of ever achieving. But we can strive, walking with hands outstretched like a blind man trying to orient himself in an alien place. And sometimes our clumsy fingers graze the mind of God.

She was disappointed. "This doesn't sound like a thriller. Or a love story."

"Oh, but it is. It is both."

"Does it have a happy ending?"

"Let's say . . . the right ending."

"I like happy endings." She shrugged, embarrassed. "I know that's silly. Most people in the real world are not happy so why should people in books be happy, right? But when I write my book, it will end nicely." She suddenly noticed that Pippa was scooping globs of sand into her mouth. "Pippa! Stop that!"

Glancing back at him, she said self-consciously, "Kids. They wear you out. But you probably know all about that."

"No. I never had children."

She wondered why not. No ring on his finger—although that did not mean anything, of course.

She sighed. "I wouldn't give up my little ones for all the money in the world. But I keep thinking there must be something else besides, you know? Something more. Stupid of me, isn't it?"

His lips twitched. "If no one wanted more, evolution would stop in its tracks."

For a while there was silence between them. She watched him from the corner of her eye. He was very lean. His skin was dark as though he spent a lot of time in strong sun. Did he travel?

"Does he break it?"

He looked surprised. "Break what?"

"The curse. You said your hero lost his name because he was cursed."

"Well, that's the twist. He realizes it wasn't a curse to begin with."

She frowned. "How's that?"

"At the start of the book he thinks he is cursed. But by the end he knows it is better to have seen fleetingly than not to have seen at all. It is better to go through life in pain but awake . . . than anesthetized and unaware."

She wished she could come up with something clever to say. Something that would interest him, show him that she understood what he was saying. Suddenly she felt tired. Glancing at her watch, she stood up. "Look at the time, will you? I have to go feed Tommy."

She held out her hand a little awkwardly. "It was really nice meeting you."

"And you." He took her hand in his and for just a moment she had the strangest feeling that a current was flowing from his fingertips into hers. But it was over so quickly, she knew she must have imagined it.

He stepped back. "Good-bye. I hope you get to write that book of yours."

"Yeah, I will do one day." She picked up Pippa and settled her on her hip.

As she started walking, she suddenly stopped and looked back at him over her shoulder. "I still don't see how it's a love story, you know."

He watched the two figures—mother and daughter—become smaller and smaller until they disappeared through the far gate and he could no longer see them.

The book was still lying on the bench where the girl had left it. He picked it up and placed it in his shoulder bag.

The shadows on the ground had lengthened and the hint of a chill was in the air. As he shrugged into his jacket, he felt the outline of his wallet through the folds of fabric. Taking out the leather case, he opened it. Inside was a ten-pound bill and a passport-sized photograph. The face captured by the camera was youthful but the colors in the photograph had faded in the many years since he took it.

Gently he brushed his thumb across the surface of the picture. They had both been young then. But even in those days she had had a maturity beyond her years and had shown signs of the quiet courage that was such an integral part of her being. It had never deserted her, not even during her final battle with the illness that took her from him two years ago.

Love is the greatest healer, she had told him once. And she was right. Through the years she had walked by his side, her love a balm for his incessant yearning.

The hunger. It drove him to travel obsessively in fierce pursuit of the mystery he had once glimpsed so briefly. The door had been closed in his face but if he kept knocking, maybe—just maybe—it might open again.

His travels and studies had stretched his mental horizons; rewarded him in ways he could not have imagined. Sometimes he was able to look at the world around him with such clarity it made him weep. But there were other times when he felt as though he walked without a skin. The years of searching would scratch dry in his throat, like dust. And always, always the hungry shadow waxing and waning within him.

Frankie had accepted his restlessness; had coped with his despair on the days when the shadow took over. Not uncomplainingly—she was no saint, after all—but steadfastly.

Theirs had not been a grand passion—no delirium, no fevered brows—rather a thing of quiet beauty. As the years passed he discovered that trust, gratitude, and a love more serene spin their own kind of magic. Most people feel alone, even when together. He and Frankie never did. They had known each other in full.

Not a grand passion. But a love story?

He pushed his hands into the pockets of his jacket and started walking. The light was beginning to fail now, and on the horizon he could see the evening star.

Oh yes, most certainly a love story.

The End

NOTE

I was inspired to bless my characters with the gift of remote viewing after reading about a top secret program of the United States government called Project STARGATE. Before being closed down in the nineties, STARGATE received federal funding and its director, Dale Graff, trained and used remote viewers to gather intelligence information and to search for high-profile objects and people. Notable successes included tracking down a missing Soviet plane and assisting the Drug Enforcement Administration (DEA). These adventures are chronicled in Mr. Graff's books *River Dreams* and *Tracks in the Psychic Wilderness*. I have to confess that the remote viewers in *Season of the Witch* are especially gifted—even more so than the talented viewers who belonged to STARGATE—and that the phrase "slamming the ride" is completely my own.

The Art of Memory is the other big theme in my book. It is a highly esoteric subject, and I had to simplify many of the issues involved in order to meet the demands of a work of fiction. For those readers who would like to acquaint themselves in greater depth with the fascinating but rigorous world of Giordano Bruno, Ramon Lull and Giulio Camillo, I strongly recommend Dame Frances Yates's definitive work on the topic.

I used Benjamin Woolley's book *The Queen's Conjurer* as the source of my information on John Dee and am indebted to Erik Davis for his writings on gnosticism and information culture. Over the years I have read more books on enlightenment than I can recall, but Mark Hedsel's *The Zelator* remains one of the best.

In her spell, Minnaloushe makes use of fragments from the Mandaean gnostic text called *The World of Darkness*; Psalms 14 and 25, Thanksgiving Psalms from the Dead Sea Scrolls; the gnostic tract titled *The Thunder, Perfect Mind* and a Manichaean text written in

Old Turkish called *Salvation of the Soul.* However, as this is her own, unique spell, she has adapted these fragments according to an idiosyncratic interpretation and knowledgeable readers will therefore notice significant changes from the original texts in word and concept. The numerology she uses is Pythagorean numerology.

The name Eldaah means "Knowledge of God." In Genesis 25:4, there is mention of Eldaah, son of Mídian, of Abraham with Ketúrah.

Any readers who are interested in a behind-the-scenes peek at how I came to write *Season of the Witch,* please visit my Web site: www.natashamostert.com.

ACKNOWLEDGMENTS

Season of the Witch was a joy to write—and an adventure. Many thanks to everyone who was there with me, slamming the ride.

I am indebted to the entire team at Penguin Dutton. In particular, I am privileged to work with my editor, Julie Doughty. Julie, thanks for insisting that I deepen the emotional heart of the book.

And then there's Jonny! Innovative, tireless and totally hands-on, Jonny Geller is the kind of agent authors dream of having in their corner. I am also immeasurably grateful to Deborah Schneider for all the hard work she did on my behalf and for believing in this book right from the start.

To my wonderful friends and first readers—Catherine Gull, Diane Hofmeyr, Sonja Lewis and Niki Muller—thank you all. Your feedback is treasured. A special thank-you to Gaynor Rupert, whose meticulous eye was invaluable as always, and who saved me from embarrassment more than once. Fellow scribe Ian Watson is a Jedi, and I am grateful for his support and advice.

Thanks to my brother Frans, for reading through the manuscript in one sitting and for catching a fatal flaw in the book, which might have escaped us all. Thanks to my brother Stefan, who always reminds me to think visually. Thank you to kickboxing champ Carlos Andrade for keeping this desk-bound author healthy and for not allowing me to take myself too seriously.

Hantie Prins, my mother, is an imaginer and a constant source of inspiration. She walked this journey with me.

Frederick, my brilliant, compassionate husband, is my lifeline. If not for him, I would never have the courage to turn dreams into words.

ABOUT THE AUTHOR

Natasha Mostert is also the author of *The Midnight Side, The Other Side of Silence* and *Windwalker*. Educated in South Africa and at Columbia University in New York, Mostert holds graduate degrees in Lexicography and Applied Linguistics and has worked as an academic and a freelance journalist. You can see more at her Web site: www.natashamostert.com. She lives in London.

Please read on for an excerpt
of Natasha Mostert's next novel. . . .

Rosalia came into his life during his gap year. He had just turned seventeen, and hiking on his own through Europe felt like a great adventure. All around him was beauty: soaring cathedrals, museums like jewel boxes, ethereal frescoes, heroic sculpture. He was happy. It was a year in which time was suspended and reality kept at bay.

But after ten months he was running out of money. Soon he would have to return to England and decide what he wanted to do with the rest of his life. He had no idea what this decision would be, and the knowledge that such a defining moment awaited him made him feel emotionally exhausted.

Palermo was to be the last stop on his journey. He arrived late in the afternoon but still in time to visit the city's most famous tourist attraction.

He drew his tongue over his dry lips; he was thirsty. On his way to the catacombs, he had become lost. He did not speak Italian and had difficulty following the broken English of the shop owners he asked for directions. It all felt slightly nightmarish as he walked through Palermo's alleyways, his legs becoming ever more tired and heavy. He looked straight up at the far sky above him; it was a glazed, parched blue. There was no relief from the heat, even though the tall houses on either side almost touched one another and threw deep shadows.

In here it was cooler and very quiet. The tourist buses had all left. Even the hooded Capuchin monk who had taken his donation with listless fingers had disappeared. He was on his own: all alone with eight thousand mummies.

The most surprising thing was that the bodies did not smell— there was no odor except for dust. He wondered if they had ever smelled. Maybe when they were first placed inside their strainers and left to dry, there would have been a stench of rotting flesh. Even the porous lime scale would not have been able to damp down completely the fruity smell of human ooze. But after an eight-month stay in darkness, these corpses would have been taken from their cells, washed with vinegar and lime, and exposed to open air—fresh as a housewife's laundry.

He looked down at the guidebook in his hands: *In 1599, Capuchin monks discovered a way to preserve the dead, and Sicilians from all walks of life flocked to be buried here in the Catacombe dei Cappucini. The deceased often specified the clothes in which they wished to enter the afterlife, and many stipulated that their garments were to be changed over time.*

His eyes traveled up the twenty-foot walls until it reached the vaulted ceiling. The mummies lined the walls in rows: a shriveled library of dead people. Monks, lawyers, shopkeepers, matrons, and maids. Virgins with steel bands encircling their heads to indicate their untouched state. All were dressed, and many were standing, some with hands folded across their stomachs and a jolly slant to their heads. Others screamed silently with open mouths. Many had lost ears, or were missing jaws and hands. Others had defied the passage of time with more success: the caramel flesh truly mummified and the eyes still cradled within dusty sockets. There were even mummies with ropes around their necks, but another glance at the guidebook told him that these were not the corpses of criminals but the remains of pious men. The ropes were not nooses, but symbols of penance worn by the monks during their lifetimes and carried with them into death.

Death. As he walked slowly down the long death-choked corridors, he wondered at the ambiguity of this word. When did death take place? Did death come when the brain stopped? His father, a physician, had told him that the brain sometimes continued its electric dance for up to ten minutes after the heart had ceased to supply it with blood. The "master switch" was what his father called the brain. The conductor. The commander in chief.

But he remembered his grandmother's death. His father had given permission for her organs to be harvested, and she was to become what was known as a "beating heart cadaver." On the day she was pronounced no longer alive, he remembered leaning kiss-close and marveling at the color of her skin. Her brain had flatlined, but she was hooked up to a respirator and her heart was beating. Inside her liver was a pulse. Her hands were warm, and she would bleed if she were cut. This was his grandmother. They told him she was dead, but she looked alive.

The practice of mummification was outlawed in 1881. But in 1920 an exception was made for three-year-old Rosalia Lombardo, nicknamed "Sleeping Beauty." Her father, stricken with grief, begged a certain Dr. Salofia to keep his daughter "alive forever." Remarkably, Dr. Salofia managed to defeat the process of decay. Rosalia is a marvel and looks like a pretty sleeping doll who might awaken at any moment. Dr. Salofia's secret died with him: no one knows the method he used to preserve the little girl.

She was lying in a glass coffin in the chapel, and her face was innocence itself: the nose pert, the mouth sweet, the cheeks infant plump. Her ears were tiny shells, and long lashes feathered her closed eyelids. The soft pink bow on top of her head made her look vulnerable, as did the wispy tendrils of hair tumbling over her forehead.

He stared at her, not quite believing how perfect she was.

How could her father have borne it to leave her here? Why preserve a three-year-old child and leave her to sleep under the gazes of a thousand leering scarecrows?

A beam of late-afternoon sunlight fell through the tiny leaded window and made it look as though a sheen of sweat was on her brow. And in that instant he suddenly had a clear understanding of how his future must look. Life-defining moments sometimes happened serendipitously. In that one moment—in that most unlikely of places—the course of his life was set.

Rosalia was not about preserving the dead. Rosalia was about making a wish. A wish to stop time—a wish, in fact, for eternal life.

Keep her alive forever. A father's desperate plea. And clever, busy Dr. Solafia with his chemicals and fluids and overreaching genius had gone to work. But he was not a healer—he was a preserver. He had succeeded in keeping intact a perfect shell, but in the end, that was all she was: a shell. The brain dead. The heart dead.

Maybe the master switch was neither the brain nor the heart. Maybe the answer to life lay elsewhere. . . .

When he arrived back in England, he enrolled in university to study medicine. His father was convinced he had played the deciding role in helping his son decide on a profession, but that was not the truth. It was not his father who had been the key, but a little girl with a pink bow in her hair.

And now, every night before closing his eyes, he would think of darkness coming to the chapel of the *Catacombe dei Cappucini* and tiny Rosalia sleeping in her glass case, a thousand mummified bodies pressed close around her like an army of the dead. And it would remind him that the strongest wish of all was to live. To live forever.